The Shadow Hour

KATE RIORDAN

Culture NL Ltd SC043891 Motherwell Library Hamilton Road, Motherwell MOT	
7 778834 04	
Askews & Holts	04-Mar-2016
AF G	£7.99

PENGUIN BOOKS

PENGUIN BOOKS

UK | USA | Canada | Ireland | Australia
India | New Zealand | South Africa

Penguin Books is part of the Penguin Random House group of companies
whose addresses can be found at global.penguinrandomhouse.com.

First published 2016

001

Text copyright © Kate Riordan, 2016

The moral right of the author has been asserted

Set in 12.5/14.75pt Garamond MT Std
Typeset by Palimpsest Book Production Limited,
Falkirk, Stirlingshire
Printed in Great Britain by Clays Ltd, St Ives plc

A CIP catalogue record for this book is available from the British Library

B FORMAT ISBN: 978–1–405–91744–5
TPB ISBN: 978–0–718–17929–8

www.greenpenguin.co.uk

MIX
Paper from
responsible sources
FSC® C018179

Penguin Random House is committed to a
sustainable future for our business, our readers
and our planet. This book is made from Forest
Stewardship Council® certified paper.

To my husband, with love

'All governesses have a tale of woe.' Mr Rochester,

Jane Eyre

Prologue

So much can change in a single moment. Imagine a green English field: pretty enough, but so unremarkable that it doesn't even have a name. There's a spire in the distance, a pale cluster of sheep grazing in the shade of a chestnut tree and a farmer's boy sitting on a stile, smoking. He turns his face up to the spring sunshine and closes his eyes as he exhales. That's when he hears it: a low, thrumming vibration in the earth beneath him, coupled with a ringing in the air that's almost too high-pitched to hear. He opens his eyes and looks down the slope of the field to where he knows the railway siding is, hidden behind the hedgerow.

Afterwards, he finds it hard to describe what happened next. People ask him, of course – policemen, his mother, even a newspaperman who slips him a whole packet of Player's. What he does manage to tell them, haltingly, seems entirely inadequate. He just can't put into words the great calamity of it. He can't explain how one minute he was sitting there in the peace and quiet, minding his own business, and the next everything seemed to happen all at once – noise, smell, blinding light, and an unseen force so powerful that it knocked him clean off the stile. The closest he gets to the truth of it is what he says to his mother that evening when he lets her tuck him into bed as he

1

hasn't since he was little. 'It was like Heaven and then it was like Hell,' he says simply.

He dreams that night of what he saw, after the light and the bang so loud he didn't hear it but *received* it, a breath-stopping thump in the middle of his chest. There was hardly any sound when he got himself up, either; only the ringing he couldn't shake out of his head. He tottered down the field to the gap in the hedgerow, dimly aware that the sun had gone and that the dark was caused not by falling dusk but by rising smoke. He steadied himself against the fence and peered through the hot, swirling air.

A dark hulk of metal lay on its side, halfway up the opposite bank. Dotted here and there were small fires, glowing out of the blackness, like will-o'-the-wisps on a lonely night. Further up the line a couple of carriages were twisted out of all shape and reason, as though they'd been no sturdier than bales of straw on wheels. Beyond that, other carriages were still on the tracks, some leaning drunkenly, others right side up. From these he could see shapes emerging and it took him a moment to realize they were people. He was stunned by this: that anyone else in the world could still be alive.

He looked back at the ruined carriages and, as the dense air began to lift and lighten, he found he could absorb more detail. The glitter of smashed glass. A cardboard suitcase spilling its contents, like a disembowelled animal. A splayed book, streaked with ash, pages fluttering. A woman's round-toed shoe, mercifully without a foot still in it. And then a glimpse of white so clean and pure that he couldn't believe he hadn't noticed it immediately. There was something moving in it, or above it, and he began to climb the fence to go to it, compelled by some instinct deep within him.

But when he'd clambered over and looked again for that flash of brightness, he saw a figure approaching, as dark as a raven, in a long coat and hat. He watched as the man bent and gently gathered the white thing up, holding it aloft for a moment before tucking it carefully inside his coat. The boy understood then what it was. It was a miracle. A miracle flung from the wreckage of a ruined and smouldering railway carriage, somehow unsullied, somehow unscathed.

It's not always as simple as beginnings, middles and ends. Not all stories should be regarded as a straight line, with the past at a distance and the present close at hand. Some, like this one, are formed like a circle, with something terrible and secret at the core, and everything else radiating out, ripples from a raindrop on water.

One

Grace, 1922

It was a small, unobtrusive advertisement in a Cheltenham periodical that took me to Fenix House in 1922. The *Looker-On* was issued weekly, and my grandmother had been getting it delivered to our house in Bristol for as long as I could remember. The few lines that would alter the course of my life lurked near the bottom of a page full of other advertisements, sandwiched between a request for a lady's companion who would be willing to exercise a small dog, and a vacancy for a plain cook with impeccable references and clean habits. I know it by heart still.

'GOVERNESS', it stated at the top, in large, black-inked capitals.

> YOUNG LADY *sought for seven-year-old boy who cannot attend school. General lessons required with possibility of light nursing duties. Competitive terms include room with picturesque view. References essential. D. Pembridge, Fenix House, Nr. Cheltenham.*

'Do you understand?' my grandmother said. She had laid the periodical in front of me, the corner of the page carefully folded down to mark the place.

I saw that she was trembling with her discovery. Her grey eyes shone, and for a moment I could see exactly

4

how she must have looked when she was young; when she was my own age.

'I think so,' I said cautiously, because I wasn't sure I did. 'It's them. The Pembridge family. But isn't it a strange coincidence that they're advertising for a governess? It's just what they must have done all those years ago, when you went there.'

'Oh, but it's not a coincidence,' she said. 'This is what we've been waiting for.'

'We?' My voice sounded light, amused, but unease was creeping through me. 'What have I to do with it?'

'Why, everything, my love. Why do you think I have been telling you about Fenix House all these years?'

'I thought they were just stories. I thought you wanted to tell me about when you were young.'

'Well, I did, in part. But there was a point to it, too. It was *preparation*. Preparation for when you would go there yourself.'

My grandmother had always been an accomplished teller of tales. My childhood was a silver thread hung with the pearls of them. Even after I'd left childhood behind, they lived on agelessly in my mind, easily as vivid as anything that actually happened to me in those early years. So much so that, looking back, it was sometimes hard to see where the joins were: where the hardwood of my own memories met my grandmother's more pliable recollections.

All my favourite stories in her repertoire were about Fenix House. She had been there in 1878, governess to the daughters of the house, and I felt I knew the terrain of that single summer as well as the lines and folds of my own upturned hand. I believed I could have walked blindfolded through the place, surefooted as I explored its rooms by touch and sound alone. The hallway tiles of cream, umber and Wedgwood blue hard under the soles of my shoes, the curving banister smooth under my fingertips, softened by years of polishing. A child's cry ringing out from the nursery above, and the porcelain rattle of a servant's tray below.

My grandmother was Harriet Jenner then, and when she told me how she had admired the view out of her bedroom window at Fenix House each morning, I believed I saw with her the gold and green Gloucestershire landscape that tilted this way and that as it undulated away into invisibility.

I suppose, at the time, I preferred Harriet's past to my own present. I was a newly made orphan when I first heard about Fenix House and its inhabitants, so perhaps a part of me drew comfort from hearing about a time when my parents were as safe as I could imagine them, snug in their unborn-ness, which I imagined as a cocoon suspended in the dark, hidden in the shadows beyond the stars.

They were killed on the railways, between London and Bristol on the famous line built by Isambard Kingdom Brunel. The spring of 1910 turned out to be unusually lucrative for the newspapermen. First, Halley's Comet had dazzled and humbled with its fiery silence as it blazed across the skies, its tail of deadly cyanide generating a hundred apocalyptic headlines. Then, as if that wasn't news enough, Europe's uncle and *bon viveur*-in-chief, Edward VII, had died, presumably of a life well lived. No one knew it then, of course, but his funeral on the twentieth of May was the last of its kind, a spectacular turning-out of rank and royalty that numbered no less than nine crowned heads. Gathered from all corners of the continent for one final occasion, most of them would soon be scattered for good: variously deposed, exiled or murdered.

But other, smaller, lives were lost that spring, and names that should have remained in safe obscurity were instead immortalized in smudged ink on flimsy paper. The day after the King's funeral, my parents were among them. Death, such a remote spectre when it had been decked out in royal splendour, or borne on the tail of ancient rock, had now come for my mother and father. Along with nineteen others, a series of small misjudgements and mistakes had propelled them out of this world and into the fleeting infamy of the late editions.

Back in the parlour, twelve years on from those momentous few months, I read the advertisement again, though the words were already imprinted on my mind. I'm not sure I'd yet fully absorbed what my grandmother had said about my going to Fenix House.

'Of course, you should be able to get a few excellent references,' she was saying thoughtfully. 'Thank goodness we didn't wait any longer for you to start teaching.'

'References?' I interrupted, my voice sharp. 'References for what?'

But even as I spoke, I began to understand. Not only the years of stories, but my grandmother's sudden insistence when I reached the age of twenty that I take on a handful of young pupils, to whom I would teach the rudiments of art, arithmetic and literature. An old cliché had come to me when she first mooted the idea: *I am following in her footsteps.* I'd liked the continuity of that notion and, even more, I'd liked the idea that she was finally viewing me as a grown-up, who might be allowed to forge some connections and independence of her own.

Now, all my pride in those two years of tutoring folded in on itself, a façade as flimsy as a theatrical stage flat. The small girls I'd taught had played alongside me in nothing more than a dress rehearsal. My grandmother had meant for me to go to Fenix House as a governess all along, precisely as she herself had done half a century earlier. Though for what ends, I could not guess.

Two

Three weeks later, the governess-nurse position having been secured for me via letter, I found myself at Temple Meads station, preparing to leave Bristol behind. The place was thrumming with activity. Engines flared and then roared as they were stoked. Whistles shrieked and were answered by sudden evacuations of hissing steam. The low burble of conversation ran on underneath those more violent sounds, except for the occasional self-conscious shout of greeting or goodbye. Impervious to the din were the red-brick walls, which rose to meet the curving roof of wrought iron and smut-clouded glass.

Everyone but I, or so it seemed, thought Brunel's station quite an ordinary place to be. While they hurried to and fro, I stood and drank it in with all the absorption and wonderment of a child. Of course, I hadn't been a child for some time: I was now twenty-two, the same age as the century. But though I'd often felt as if my childhood had halted abruptly on the day of the railway accident, there, in the confusion of the crowded terminus, I felt more unworldly than I had in years.

I took one last look around before I boarded my train, quite as if I might never set foot in the city again. Noticing my hesitation, a porter sprang forward and handed me up into the carriage, though I would have liked to linger a moment more. My voice when I thanked him was hoarse;

my mouth dry from sudden nerves – not only because I was leaving behind everything I had ever known, but because I had not been permitted to travel on the railways since 1910.

When my grandmother and I had embarked on one of our rare day-trips in the intervening years – to the coast at Weston-super-Mare and, once, to Bath – we had, at her insistence, gone by charabanc. For me to take a train, alone, on such an important day, felt like the sort of temptation Fate would be unable to resist. That my grandmother had shown no such anxiety reassured me only a little.

'But I've told you, you're meant to go to Fenix House,' she'd repeated blithely when, a week earlier, I'd expressed my consternation after she'd produced a railway ticket for me. 'I didn't like to take the chance before, not for just any old day out, but if you're on your way to Fenix House, nothing will happen to you. Trust me, Grace, it's meant to be. I've seen it.'

Despite my grandmother's persuasive conviction that I should go, the fluttery feeling in my stomach persisted as we pulled clear of the city. During the last weeks, I had convinced myself that leaving home was exactly what someone of twenty-two should be doing – that if I remained much longer within the comforting confines of home then I would never leave at all. Now, though, the train carrying me further and further from the familiar, I wondered if I had made a terrible mistake. Even as the rhythmic movement of the carriage rocked my fellow passengers to sleep, I felt doubt unfurl inside me and begin to spread. This left me with no appetite for the sandwiches my grandmother had made me that morning but I ate them anyway, homesick and already remorseful for being cold to her when we had said our goodbyes.

I had just forced down the last mouthful when the train began to slow for the last time. Gloucester, with its limestone cathedral rising like a ship out of the surrounding floodplain, was already behind us. The next stop was surely mine: Cheltenham Spa.

No one was meeting me; I was to take a bus or, if I preferred, a taxi. Either way I would be reimbursed, or so said the letter my grandmother had folded inside my travelling case that morning. I quickly decided on the latter, wishing to be on my own during the last part of the journey.

Visiting a place that has lived so long in your mind is a peculiar experience – like entering a recurring dream only to find it not quite the same after all; the familiar slightly skewed. So, while the bends of the hill came where I expected them and the road tipped upwards as dramatically as I knew it would, the trees that crowded in on the left, obscuring the limestone crags I knew must lurk behind them, were more menacing than I'd been given to expect.

The gates when we reached them from the short, steep drive were in a state of disrepair. One had come off its hinges, the rusting iron wedged into the gravel at an angle. The other was ajar by six inches and moving in the wind. A great thicket of azaleas just beyond seemed to be gaining on them with the stealth of an army moving silently through the dawn but, when I looked more carefully, I saw that the heart of the shrub was dead – a dark, hollow void whose end I couldn't see. I hadn't expected this and it made the nerves in my stomach flutter again.

The driver wouldn't go any further and I didn't bother

arguing with him once I'd got out and seen the scratches made by the drive's straggling bushes on the polished paintwork of his doors; I was anxious that he would demand compensation.

He went round to unlash my trunk, allowing it to land heavily on the muddy ground that, on closer inspection, had once been laid with stone in a neat herringbone pattern. Now it was ruined, by time or neglect or a combination of both: every other stone was cracked or loosened and undermined by weeds. There were some tense minutes as he attempted to turn the cab around, the wheels slipping on wet mud and stone worn smooth, but eventually he made the road again and I was alone.

The wind, which was much fiercer on the hill than it had been down in the town, whipped around me in a fury, pulling at my new grey cloche and sending the trees into a frenzy of creaking movement. Every time a new gust flung itself at the open gates, which I had approached but was now reluctant to go through, it let out a moan that was unnervingly human.

Hesitantly, I put out a hand to grip one of the old iron bars and felt the unbending frigidity of it through my glove. I realized I was probably standing on the very spot my grandmother had, almost fifty years before.

Until then, Fenix House had been a setting in a story: suspended in time until my grandmother and I chose to revisit it. Only now did I truly understand that the real house had been there all along, decaying and deteriorating, like any building offered up to time and nature.

From my position at the gates, much of the garden was hidden by the colossal azaleas. All I could see of it were the laurels and firs that towered over everything, dwarfing even the house. The laurels shook their branches, leaves shivering, and the tops of the firs swayed, and though I knew it was only the wind moving them, they felt to me like expressions of wrath, directed at those who had allowed the once-resplendent garden to fall into ruin.

The carriage sweep, of which I could see a portion, was also a sorry sight. The gravel was thin and patchy, showing the earth beneath, like a balding carpet; weeds and grass had taken hold in patches. No doubt it had once been flat and smoothly raked; now it was even more pitted than the remnants of the brick drive I was standing on.

And beyond it lay the house – the house about which I had heard so much; a house I had hoped would be a familiar friend in peculiar circumstances. In truth, even before I had noticed the laurels and the firs, and the appalling condition of the carriage sweep, I had looked through the bars at Fenix House and then glanced quickly away, as one averts their gaze from a stranger with a damaged face. Initially too cowardly to face it squarely, I now forced myself to absorb it.

It wasn't quite ruined, of course. The roof was still on and the window glass intact. None of the walls had given up and simply fallen down, just as none of the chimneys had plummeted through the roof's slates one stormy night. But what had happened was almost worse. Caught in the act of decline, somewhere between faded elegance and utter decrepitude, you could still see – and therefore mourn – glimpses of the charm and idiosyncratic beauty it had once possessed. In some places the stone had darkened in sooty streaks; in others, where the guttering had been allowed to fracture and leak, it had been stained by trails of rust- and moss-coloured damp. The stone balustrade that rose to the front door had lost one of its roundels, which still lay where it had fallen and rolled, like a guillotined head. The six steps leading up were cracked and chipped, those gashes of newly exposed stone seeming pale and vulnerable.

But something else was wrong, too. It wasn't just the condition of the house: it was the scale of it. Elements of it were familiar – the gables, the corner turrets, the curious blend of architectural styles – it was just that . . . well, I'd thought it would be larger. I'd expected a pile built by titled old money, rather than a house that was certainly large but not on the grand scale I'd envisaged. It looked like a residence for an affluent Victorian industrialist and his family, which is exactly what it had been, so why had I anticipated more? My grandmother had once said, '*Every-one* knew of Fenix House.' I hadn't invented that, I was sure. And yet my taxi driver had never heard of the place, asking me to repeat the address twice. Still, he was as young as I – the house may have begun its slide into obscurity before either of us was born. Besides, perhaps everything that seemed imposing and impressive to a child looks shrunken when glimpsed through adult eyes.

I studied the house again and the version I'd carried for so long in my head faded, like a photograph hung in a sunny room. I might have managed a hollow laugh if something akin to respect for the dead hadn't stopped me. Shaking off the air of mingled diminishment and disorientation, I straightened my hat, smoothed down my coat and, leaving my heavy trunk to the mercy of the deserted drive, passed through the gap in the gates.

Three

Approaching the house, I saw some scant signs of habitation. A wooden crate, which had been left on the top step next to the front door, was cleaner and newer than anything around it and was possibly a recent delivery, perhaps of food. And although the windows were rimed and bleary with dust, curtains had been pulled across some. As I glanced at one, a downstairs room in the octagonal tower closest to me, I thought I saw the fabric twitch. Someone inside was watching me.

Perhaps I was made clumsy by the thought of them witnessing my progress across the carriage sweep or perhaps I was just unlucky, and wearing a new pair of heeled shoes on an unpredictable surface, but I caught my foot and went crashing forwards. Ignoring the stinging pains in my knees, I scrambled to my feet, horribly humiliated that the Pembridges' first impression would be of a foolish girl sprawled in the dirt, and annoyed that I'd ruined a new pair of stockings. On standing I realized I had also turned my ankle so could only limp up the steps to the door, wincing as I went.

The bell, when I pressed it, made no sound, though I tried it twice, leaning with my ear to the door the second time. I went to knock but stopped. The thick oak was likely to absorb any sound I was capable of making, while the panels of sagging stained glass in the door's upper half looked liable to fall out and shatter if I so much as tapped on them. If someone had been watching me, they would surely have come by now. Cheered by the thought that my tumble might have gone unobserved after all, I reached for the brass doorknob and tried it. The handle was not only easy to turn, doing so soundlessly, but the door was unlocked. I pushed against it and stepped gingerly inside.

I was expecting tiles – hard encaustic tiles laid out in a pattern of geometric stars – but my footfalls were muffled by something softer: rugs or mats, I couldn't be sure which because the light was so dim. The only source of it came through the stained glass of the door, which I had closed quietly behind me, reaching weakly into the hall to wash it with patches of murky colour, jaundiced yellow and dusty pink.

It was just as I was thinking that there had been some mistake or trickery, that there was no D. Pembridge or anyone else living at Fenix House now, that the advertisement for a governess had been part of some elaborate game of my grandmother's, when an insistent ringing sounded somewhere deep in the otherwise silent house. I stepped backwards in fright, putting all my weight on my tender ankle, the pain of it making me suck in my breath.

The noise went on without pause so it was a few more seconds before I realized I could hear another sound, far less strident but much closer. I looked up and there, illuminated by a pool of soft light, were neat rows of carefully strung copper wire, some of them traceable back towards the gloom of upstairs while others branched off to rooms whose doors were closed. As I watched, one of the upstairs wires repeatedly vibrated and I saw in my mind the housemaid Agnes, who'd been there in my grandmother's day, raise her head and curse as the mistress's bell trilled. But this wasn't in my imagination and it wasn't the opening of one of my grandmother's tales. There, in that moment, someone somewhere in the house, which I had begun to suspect was abandoned, was ringing for a servant.

Just as the quiet descended again, leaving nothing but a jangling echo reverberating through the air, there was a scraping sound followed by a crash, like smashing glass. It seemed to come from below my feet. Sure enough, and after a stunned silence lasting a full half-minute, I heard heavy, uneven steps mounting a staircase that must have run down on the other side of a baize-covered door almost hidden in the wall.

Glancing over my shoulder, I tried to calculate whether I had time to fling the front door back, limp across the gravel and pull the shrieking gates shut behind me. *And what then?* said a voice in my head. *Drag your trunk down the hill until you reach Cheltenham?* I stayed where I was, despite the misgivings that swelled in me, bracing myself as the steps got louder and the baize door was finally shoved open.

From behind it came a woman in her sixties, who swung one hip as if the joint was locked in place, giving her an unfortunate rocking gait. She was wearing a dark dress with a grubby white collar and around her neck was a key on a string. Her hair looked in desperate need of a wash. Frazzled strands straggled down her face, and the rest of it was scraped back severely into a thin bun on top of her head. The few hanks that hadn't yet turned grey were the same vivid orange as the streams of rust that had been allowed to stain the stonework outside.

She stopped dead when she saw me standing there. 'And who might you be?'

'Miss Fairford,' I managed.

She betrayed no sign of recognizing my name or understanding that she should offer hers. 'Was it you ringing that bell or one of them up there?' she said instead, managing to convey her contempt for 'them' with a sharp nod in the direction of the stairs that ascended upwards into the dark. I wondered, with a twinge of something that was part apprehension but also part excitement, exactly who she was referring to.

'Oh, no, it wasn't me,' I said hurriedly. 'I have just this minute arrived. I did try the doorbell but no one came and so I –'

'There's always one or other of 'em ringing them bells,' she muttered, as though I hadn't spoken. 'They don't give me a minute's peace.'

I became aware of a slightly unpleasant odour seeping into the hall and realized it was probably coming from the woman in front of me. Noticing the smell seemed to make it stronger and, though I tried to breathe through my mouth rather than my nose, I thought I could detect not just grease and sweat but something more acrid. Looking into her eyes, I saw that they were not quite focused: was that chemical alcohol? It would account for her lack of shock at finding me standing in the hallway.

As though she knew what I was thinking, she turned belligerent. 'Who did you say you were again? You've a look of someone, though I can't think who now – I've got a headache that would fell a horse. And hold on a minute, how do I know you aren't just here to steal something?

Letting yourself in like that! I must say, you've got a nerve.'

By way of reply, I rummaged in my handbag and brought out the letter, which I held out to her. She half snatched it from me and pretended to read it, her eyes not moving to scan its lines. Her sight probably wasn't good enough to decipher it in the dim light. Either that, or she couldn't read at all and was ashamed to let on.

'It's a letter of engagement,' I said politely, tentatively. 'I am the new governess. My grandmo— I mean, I wrote to Mr Pembridge with my arrival date. Which is today.'

'Oh, did you now? Well, I'm the housekeeper. Mrs Peck to you. It does ring a bell now – like everything else in my life, eh? Bells ringing every which way I turn. What did you say your name was again?'

'Miss Fairford. Grace Fairford.' I plucked the letter out of her hand before she could tuck it into the bodice of her filthy dress. I knew I sounded prim but I had assumed Fenix House's housekeeper would be someone closer to the Mrs Rakes who had ruled over the servants in my grandmother's day.

As if once more she could hear my thoughts, her mood altered again, her face taking on an expression of vast self-pity. 'I'm afraid you're not seeing the best of me today, Miss Fairford,' she said, with an extravagant sniff. 'I've been out of sorts these past few days and it don't help that I get no let-up from them,' she rolled her eyes heaven-ward, 'and never mind whether I'm bad with it or not. I've got a funny hip, you see, and it's murder in the damp weather. It aches that much I don't get a wink of sleep. In truth, I haven't slept a night through this century, that's how rotten it is.'

'I'm sorry to hear that, Mrs Peck. I expect the house's position on the hill makes it very exposed to the weather.'

She nodded. 'Dreadful exposed. We get the easterlies coming through here on a straight line from Siberia. It don't matter how many rags I stuff in them windows, the wind still finds a crack and in it comes, wi' no mercy. Chills me to the bone, it does. Goes right through me.'

I nodded, though I wasn't sure how the house, its eastern face entirely protected by the steep rock that rose up behind it, might ever feel the frigid breath of a wind from the Russian steppes.

'Well, you'll soon see for yourself what a lonely, god-forsaken spot you've come to,' Mrs Peck continued more cheerfully. 'Where are you from anyway?' Her tone was almost friendly now that she thought she had found a sympathetic ear.

'Clifton in Bristol,' I said. 'I've lived there all my life.'

Mrs Peck sighed. 'Ah, now, Bristol's a place that would suit me nicely. A great big city like that, with theatres and shops on your doorstep, and pleasure boats and what-have-you to take a trip on. I reckon I'd be a new person down there, instead of which I'm stuck up here, on top of this hill. I'll have been here fifty years this November. Half a century, and much more than half my life, I'll be bound. If you can believe it, I was a girl of twelve when I first came. Green as grass, I was, thinking I was bettering myself, that I could go from here to one of the grander houses down in Cheltenham, in Montpellier or Lansdown, or even to a house in London eventually, with another year or two's experience under my belt. And yet here I still am.'

I struggled to concentrate as she catalogued missed opportunities and the injustices that had been heaped upon her over the years, the most recent of which was her employer's refusal to buy a vacuum cleaner. Instead my mind had halted at the number of years she had said she'd been at Fenix House and was now trying to subtract it from 1922. As subtly as I could, I checked the decades off on my fingers. 'But if you've been here so long,' I interrupted, 'then you must have known –'

I stopped. I'd remembered what my grandmother had said to me that morning. That I was old enough to make my own way in the world on my own merits. That I needn't mention she had been there before me because I shouldn't feel as though I was in her shadow. For once in the last few weeks I had agreed with her. I would do this on my own.

'Known who?' Mrs Peck demanded, annoyed I'd cut her off in full flow.

'Oh, no one. I just meant to say that you must have known the family – and the house – for such a long time,' I stammered. 'You must have been a kitchen maid when you first came, I suppose. Or . . . or were you in the scullery to begin with?'

She was immediately indignant, as I had hoped she would be, my slip forgotten. 'I certainly was not in the scullery! Well, not all the time, anyway. Some of my duties were upstairs. I was second housemaid, I'll have you know.'

Mrs Peck was Agnes. Of course she was – I couldn't believe I hadn't immediately made the connection between her quick temper and once-fiery hair. I didn't know whether to laugh or run from the place. Just as Fenix House had stood there rotting, so had Agnes. While my grandmother had married and given birth to my mother, made a new life for herself in Bristol and then brought me up, Agnes had been there all the time, answering the same bells with the same bad grace, her life trundling along the same narrow, predictable tracks.

I must have been staring at her oddly because she tucked the string with the key inside her clothes, shot me a suspicious look, then clumped off towards the stairs, swinging her hip and theatrically drawing in her breath with each laboured step.

'You go in the parlour a minute,' she called. 'I'll be down when I've seen to His Nibs. It's bound to have been him ringing. Nine times out of ten it is.'

I wanted to ask who His Nibs was but she had turned and was already pulling herself up the stairs, one puffy red hand over the other.

Four

After Agnes had disappeared upstairs, I went to the parlour door. As I twisted the handle, I forgot to brace myself for the inevitable dishevelment. As my grandmother had told it, this had once been the prettiest room in the house, flooded with light and perfectly proportioned. Unlike most of the other downstairs rooms, it had also managed to escape Mrs Pembridge's fondness for swathes of heavy fabric and light-sapping wallpapers. Fine, faded Turkish rugs in shades of rose and gold had covered the floor and the walls had been papered with a subtle stripe the colour of palest butter. Two sofas, a wing-backed chair and various occasional tables had been thoughtfully placed for intimate conversation or contemplation through the French windows. Here, said my grandmother, light damask curtains had been held back by satin bows, perfectly framing both the delicate wrought iron of the veranda and, beyond it, the glorious, sweeping views of the valley far below.

Now the view was all that remained of its former loveliness. The wallpaper had darkened with soot and age and in the dampest corners was peeling, as though it wanted to quit such a sadly diminished room. The curtains were limp and watermarked, the rugs made colourless by ancient seams of unswept dust. Piles of yellowing old newspapers dated back to the war years.

It was as I'd bent over to study the full horror of a pair of revolting old slippers that I heard the front door open and slam so hard that the stained glass rattled alarmingly. Before I'd had time to compose myself, a tall man with black hair and a fierce expression strode in through the open parlour door.

'Who the devil are you?' he exclaimed. 'And why are you in my house?'

Perhaps it was the poor welcome I had already received from Agnes, or the weeks of uncertainty, or the knowledge that I had been sent here, to this pitifully ravaged house, for reasons still opaque to me, but I felt suddenly so cross that I had to take a deep breath before I spoke. Even so, my voice shook.

'My name is Miss Fairford. I am here to fulfil the post of governess. I presume you yourself appointed me, sir.'

To my astonishment, he laughed: a great rusty bark that seemed to surprise him as much as it had me. 'Oh, yes, of course,' he said, his face so transformed by amusement that I felt myself immediately disarmed. 'I had entirely forgotten you.'

'Well, if you have changed your mind,' I said, 'then I can of course return to Clifton.' The possibility of escape set off a sharp pang of yearning deep inside me.

He grimaced, his mouth twisting, and it struck me that he might be suppressing another smile. 'No, unfortunately for you, Miss Fairford, I have not changed my mind. Have you changed yours, perhaps? Is Fenix House not quite what you were expecting?'

'No,' I heard myself saying, some wretched stubbornness in me winning out. 'I have not changed my mind.'

24

'Good. My son needs a woman in his life. A woman other than Agnes, that is.'

'But surely . . . I mean, isn't there . . .?'

'His mother's dead,' came the blunt reply.

'Oh, I'm sorry.' A deep blush stained my cheeks.

'Look here, I haven't properly introduced myself,' he said gruffly, after an awkward silence. 'Very remiss of me, though one can't really be blamed for becoming rusty at social nicety when one lives in this place. My name is David Pembridge.'

He stuck his large hand out towards me. His nails were clean and trimmed and there was a gold signet ring on the little finger. His grip when he took my hand was gentler than I expected.

'Grace Fairford,' I said quietly, still chastened by my thoughtlessness.

'Well, Miss Fairford, now that we are introduced, perhaps you'll follow me.' He set off for the stairs. 'You can meet the boy now, if he isn't asleep. Then, when you've unpacked, you'll take dinner with us, I hope. It'll make a pleasant change to look at a woman's face over the soup and, besides, I don't bother with the class and position nonsense that went on here in the past, not if I can help it. The war has put paid to so much of that and, in my opinion, not before time.

'It's like the Black Hole of Calcutta up here,' he called, over his shoulder. 'Watch your step, won't you?' As he disappeared into the gloom, I hurried after him, arriving at the upper landing to the sound of tearing fabric. Light flooded the upper hallway from a large window missing half its glass. What was left in the frame was jagged and lethal.

'I really must have that seen to,' he muttered under his breath. 'Can't leave it like that. Asking for it.'

Even as he spoke I could see he was distracted, that other thoughts were already pulling his concentration away from the death-trap window. I had no idea which Pembridges actually lived here now, beyond the boy I had been engaged to teach and look after, but David Pembridge's strange behaviour – intense one moment and distracted the next – went a good deal of the way to explaining the state of the house. The fate of the broken window offered a clear illustration of what had caused, and continued to worsen, Fenix House's decline. Something needed mending but was left and eventually subsumed into the list of other things already left to rot or fall apart. Perhaps he had simply given up after his wife died, her loss making the upkeep of the house seem irrelevant or pointless. I wondered if he had broken the window himself, putting his fist through it after drinking too much whisky out of one of the smeared tumblers I'd seen in the parlour.

'Are you coming?' He broke abruptly into my thoughts. I looked up to see that he had started down a passage branching off from the landing. 'Watch this runner now,' he called back. 'There's a ruck in it. Another damn thing that needs seeing to.' He turned and gave me a wry look. 'This is why I never usually let anyone new into the house. I start seeing the place through their eyes and realize how appalling it is.'

I could hardly demur without lying outright so I followed without a word. The carpet runner underfoot was not just rucked but frayed and grubby. I couldn't see any evidence that Agnes – or Mrs Peck, as she would have it –

did any work at all. Though the old wallpaper, this time the colour of dried blood, wasn't peeling up here, it was still wrecked beyond repair. I stopped and bent to look at the damage properly.

Something, or someone, had slashed a long, horizontal gouge in it, about two feet up from the skirting-board. As it progressed along the landing it wavered and almost petered out, then began again, the blade or whatever had done the damage jabbing deep into the plaster with renewed force.

I looked up to see that Mr Pembridge had opened the door at the end of the passage and was peering into the black void of the room beyond it. I hurried to catch him up, deciding that there would be better times to ask him what on earth had happened to the wall.

'Lucas?' I heard him call softly. 'Are you awake?'

He ventured further into the room and pushed the door almost closed behind him, leaving me stranded on the wrong side, straining to hear any sounds that might be issuing from within. At first there was nothing but a rustling that might have been someone shifting around in bed. Then there was such a long period of silence that I stopped trying to listen and let my mind drift. Caught off-guard by a thin but piercing wail, I jolted in fright.

'No!' came a child's high, plaintive cry. 'I won't!' The voice might have been muffled with sleep and thick with cold but it was also determined.

'Come now, another day is almost gone.' I just caught David Pembridge's gentle murmur. 'And, besides, your new governess is here to meet you.'

There was a creaking of floorboards, presumably as he

moved to the window, because it was followed by a dragging sound that must have been heavy curtains being pulled back to admit some daylight. As I watched the narrow section of visible wall through the crack in the door, black nothingness faded to grey and finally settled on a pale, washed-out blue.

At this sudden invasion of light, an outraged roar went up and something heavy – metal or thick china, perhaps – was dashed to the floor, where it bounced off something softer with a dull chink. An instant later, Mr Pembridge flung back the door and barged into me, almost knocking me off my feet. His hands went out instinctively to catch me, which meant pulling me towards him. For a moment our faces came disconcertingly close.

'I completely forgot you were there,' he said.

'Is he – is Lucas quite well?' I said tremulously, the words loud in the cramped corridor. We were still too close to one another and I found myself shaking him off and backing away until I met the wall.

'You can't meet him today, after all,' he said. 'He's not fit to be seen by anyone.' His voice rose to a shout, and I knew he meant for the boy to hear him. He was angry, that much was clear, but his face was also twisted by something more complicated.

He pulled the bedroom door shut without going back to close the curtains and paid no heed to the cry that went up as he strode down the passage to the stairs, leaving me to scurry after him. It was a pitiful sound because it was a child's voice, but there was also raw fury in it – and in that, he sounded many years older than seven.

After the aborted attempt to meet my new charge, I felt

as though things were growing stranger by the minute, and that soon I would descend utterly into the weird realm of dreams. That impression was only heightened when Agnes reluctantly agreed to take me to the room that was to be mine.

'I'll bring your trunk in later. No harm will come to it for the time being,' she said, as we climbed the first flight of stairs.

'It's rather heavy, I'm afraid,' I said vaguely – it had just occurred to me that I might be put in the same room my grandmother had once occupied, a lovely one, apparently. 'I thought there'd be someone . . . a boy or a –'

'And now you know there's only me,' cut in Agnes, grimly. 'I've had to lift the dead weight of a man before now so I'm sure I'll manage a lady's trunk right enough.'

I had heard much about the room my grandmother had been given during her tenure. It had apparently been large and rather luxuriously appointed for the position of governess, taking up a whole corner of the house. As such, it had offered two aspects – one to the south and the other, more spectacularly, to the west. There had been a thick carpet of rose pink and a cream marble fireplace, and the brass bed was wide enough for my grandmother, who was a tiny five feet tall without her shoes, to sleep horizontally, had she chosen to. It had been also on the first floor with the family's bedrooms, which was a privileged place for any employee to be. I could picture it so clearly that, when Agnes continued up the second flight, I couldn't help but let out a disappointed 'Oh!'

She looked back at me. 'What've you stopped for? You're up here.'

So I would be in a different room, after all. I supposed it was to be expected that things might have changed in the interim. It was just that I had found the idea of staying in her room rather comforting.

My room on the attic floor was small and spartan – the single tiny window placed so high up between the sloping eaves that I would have to stand on tiptoe to see out of it.

'Not much to your liking, then?' said Agnes, when she caught sight of my face.

'It will do, thank you. It's just that I . . .'

'This room has always been good enough for the governesses of Fenix House, I'll have you know.'

I looked at her sharply. 'Really? Always?'

She gave a curt nod, then clumped off down the uncarpeted passageway. It was decades since my grandmother had been there; perhaps Agnes was mistaken, or had just wanted to put me in my place. Perhaps the answer was in the room with me. I dropped to my knees and peered under the single bed. It was something my grandmother had mentioned once, in passing, years before, and it had stuck with me, not only because I couldn't imagine her doing such a thing but because, as a child, it had shocked me a little.

It was too dark to see anything down there so I took hold of one of the bed legs, which were on castors, and pulled. With an unoiled squeal, the whole thing shifted enough for me to see the skirting-board. Years of dust lined its grooves and, as I swept the first runnel clean with my finger, I saw them. The marks my grandmother had once made. They were the spiky gashes of a schoolboy vandal and as unlike her meticulous copperplate as the act of inscribing them had been to her normal character. She hadn't told me why, but I presumed she'd done it for the reasons anyone marks a place they have been and are unlikely to return to – for posterity and, more precisely, to anchor oneself in a particular place and time. *HJ*. I pressed into the letters hard with my fingertip, whether out of yearning or lingering resentment, I wasn't sure.

Leaning back on my heels, I brushed the dust from my hands, wondering what was tiny flakes and fibres of paint, varnish and cotton, and what might have been infinitesimal remnants of my grandmother, left behind in 1878. It was clear, after all, that this had been her room, whatever she had told me about carpets and marble. A long strand of hair had caught on my skirt, a thread of spun gold against the dark grey wool, and I picked it off, twisting it so tightly round my finger that the tip turned white. I knew, somehow, though the colours were so similar, that it wasn't mine but hers, caught on some long-expired breeze and blown under the bed, lurking just out of reach of all the brooms and cloths that had come after, waiting patiently for me to discover it. I couldn't understand why she had lied about her room, but decided to put it down to a combination of storytelling licence and pride. She had always been so proud.

Once Agnes had brought up my trunk, I tried to make a start on my unpacking but it wasn't long before I thought I'd better go down for dinner. I had just shut my door behind me when I thought I heard a noise behind the door at the other end of the attic floor – the side that faced the hillside and never really got any light. It wasn't Agnes: I would have heard her heavy, uneven tread as she struggled back up. And there were no other servants; Mr Pembridge and Agnes had both said so. I didn't know if any other Pembridges were still living but, even if they were, I didn't see why they would be in the attic.

There was another noise then, and because I was listening properly that time, I thought it sounded more specifically like a rustle or shuffle, perhaps of feet moving into a new position. Going closer to the door, I became aware of other background noises, what might have been the creaking of old floorboards as someone moved slowly around, a soft whirring that went up and down slightly in pitch and then, once, a low, muffled peep. I had the urge to duck down and look through the keyhole but thought instead of what I would say if I was caught standing there, like a prurient chambermaid from an old penny dreadful. Feeling rather foolish, I hurried down the stairs.

Despite what David Pembridge had said about joining 'us' for the evening meal, I had expected to find him alone in the dining room. I could hear Agnes in the depths of the house, apparently clashing pan lids in a renewed burst of indignation, and my mysterious charge was presumably still in bed. But there were two people sitting at the enormous mahogany table with curved ends – my employer and an older man with a full head of curly salt-and-pepper hair, which stuck out in curious clumps and had clearly not been brushed for some time. He was quite short, and very thin under his patched jacket of tweed, which had been buttoned up wrongly, its breast pocket stuffed with assorted pencils, a brass rule, a magnifying glass, a leaking fountain pen and a neatly peeled twig.

As I closed the door softly behind me, this second man

leaped to his feet and, in his haste to come over and greet me, knocked over his chair. Pembridge rolled his eyes but said nothing, merely getting up to right it.

'Thank you, David,' cried the stranger, who barely came up to my employer's shoulder. 'I am a clumsy ass of the first order, my dear,' he said to me, as he approached, hands outstretched, fingers feeling for mine. 'I'm afraid you'll have to get used to it. My eyesight is very bad and I'm notorious for losing my spectacles. It's a good day if I don't break anything – you need only ask Agnes if you want confirmation of that. She would be more than willing to describe my numerous mishaps, I'm sure.'

As he fumbled for my hand, I saw that his deep brown eyes were slightly unfocused. He blinked slowly into my face, rather as a newborn creature would, then moved his gaze upwards, turning me slightly and craning to see my hair.

'I am Miss Fairford,' I said quickly, emphasizing the name, suddenly and rather irrationally fearful he would notice the colour of my hair, the distinctive warm shade so like my grandmother's had once been. He was just about old enough to have been there in her day. I looked at him again: the contents of his top pocket, the eager smile. Could he possibly be Bertie, the young son of the household in 1878? I couldn't think who else he might be. Bertie had been so very fond of my grandmother. He had aged, of course, yet his hands in mine felt as small and warm as a child's.

'Ah, yes, that's right. Miss Fairford,' he said delightedly. 'And fair not only in name, from what I can make out.'

'Which, as we have established, is not a great deal,' remarked Pembridge, from his place at the table.

33

I wasn't sure whether he meant to insult me or the older man's eyesight but I felt the heat rise in my cheeks all the same, and was grateful the room was, like so much of that house, badly lit, in this case by a single pendant light that hung above us, illuminating only the ceiling rose.

'This is my uncle,' continued Pembridge, in carefully bored tones, as he reached for a bottle of wine and began to brush off the dust that had gathered at its neck. 'Bertie Pembridge.' He said the first name rather contemptuously, perhaps disapproving of the childish diminutive for an ageing man.

At this confirmation, I did my best to keep my expression politely blank but it was no easy feat. Like Agnes before him, here was a second relic from another era made flesh and blood but, as with Agnes, flesh and blood ravaged and thinned by time: every year writ in pouched and scored skin and in fast-failing eyes and trick hips. I suddenly felt so disorientated that I thought I would faint. Indeed, standing there in the dining room on my first evening at Fenix House, I don't think I would have felt much more disturbed if, instead of grasping eagerly at my hands with his, Bertie had moved towards me – his body leached of colour, his edges flickering and wavering – then stepped right through me.

Instead, he squeezed my fingers harder. 'Now, Miss Fairford, I have a proposition for you,' he said, his voice thrilling with excitement.

Swallowing nervously, I nodded. 'Yes?'

He beamed. 'After dinner, if there's still enough light, I wish to show you the garden.'

It was Bertie who had introduced my grandmother to

Fenix House's splendid garden, many years earlier. The coincidence made her seem very close in that decrepit dining room and I wondered if, back in Clifton, she was thinking of me.

It was late summer after the railway accident when she first began to tell me about her time with the Pembridges. She hadn't been there very long: not even half a year had passed before she left to marry my grandfather. All my favourite stories of that time were about the three Pembridge children, of course. She had always looked happy when she spoke of them, though I'd begun to sense something darker beneath her reminiscence in more recent years: an undefined shadow my child's eyes had missed.

'Do you know?' she would often say, after she had finished a story. 'I can remember those days like they happened a year ago, not more than thirty. It's as though they get clearer, sharper, even as the years keep turning.'

In fact, our minds hold no master-key of memory. What we are really remembering when we dredge up something from the past is what we recalled the last time we thought of it. And so on and so on: a little more reality lost and a little more imagination creeping in until, a dozen recollections down the line, we would stake our lives on the fact that we chose a red dress that day, not the blue we actually wore. And, perhaps, that a time in our lives was easy and content when the truth was much more complicated.

Five

Harriet, 1878

The geographical location of Fenix House was not what Harriet Jenner had been given to expect from her correspondence with the Governess Institution of Rodney Road, Cheltenham. Indeed, though she could not recall the precise words of the letter, which now languished at the bottom of her battered valise, she felt sure that winter gardens, pleasure lakes and pump rooms had all been listed as close at hand. In fact, the hansom cab she had taken from the station had, to her growing dismay, clipped purposefully past the elegant crescents and squares of the town's heart and onward through an outlying and less salubrious district until – with much creaking and horse-whipping – it had begun to ascend a steep hill.

Close to the point where the road began to level out, curve around the hill and leave civilization behind altogether, the driver finally brought the horses to a standstill. After checking with him through the flap in the roof that there was no other house of the same name in the town, Harriet clambered down and watched with resignation as he turned the horses round to begin the descent.

When the cab was finally out of sight, she surveyed the scene briefly, though she was too jaded after the journey from London to give the splendid panorama more than a cursory look. She turned back to the lane that the driver had pointed to, which twisted up and away from the hill road. A stone plaque set into the dry-stone wall on one side confirmed that Fenix House lay further on, as yet out of sight. Taking up her valise, a vestige of more affluent times for the Jenners, she began to pick her way wearily upwards.

It wasn't until she reached the ornamental iron gates that she caught her first glimpse of Fenix House, and with it came the strangest sensation. Just as she stood looking at the house, so it seemed to stare right back at her, the surrounding trees whispering and jostling for their own view of the interloper. With an impatient shake of her head, she dismissed this as an ill-timed and unhelpful manifestation of her strange talent for presentiment. She referred privately to these fractured visions of the future, which were often garbled and misleading, as 'the glimmers'.

Fenix House was bigger than she had envisaged – further proof that the glimmers rarely proved trustworthy enough to be entirely relied upon. Its pale stones were arranged in a hotchpotch of styles, from Dutch to Elizabethan, as though a group of dissenting architects had been given the run of it. In short, it was a curious sort of place: Gothic but charming; lonely yet distinguished; eccentric but impressive. Although Harriet wasn't quite sure what to make of it, she knew already that she liked it very well.

As she closed the gate behind her, with a clang, a tall, spare figure in a dark gown appeared from an unseen side door. Without any appearance of hurry, she crossed the gravel swiftly and almost silently, as though, perhaps, she hovered an inch above the ground. Up close she was strikingly raw-boned and fleshless, her prominent nose and dark, close-set eyes initially giving her a hawk-like appearance. The top of Harriet's head barely reached the woman's broad shoulders.

'Good afternoon. You must be Miss Jenner.'

It was not a question but Harriet, who knew she was inclined to chatter when she was nervous, forced herself only to nod.

The woman, as statuesque as one of the towering conifers, radiated a stillness and calm that immediately disarmed Harriet. Her racing heart slowed even as the older woman studied her with eyes that, she saw now, were both serious and kind.

'My name is Mrs Rakes,' she said. It suited her sharp angles but not, thought Harriet, her temperament. She had heard dreadful stories of country housekeepers, who terrorized servants and governesses alike, and was glad that Mrs Rakes seemed such a mild example of the species.

'I'm sure you are tired after your long journey,' she continued, 'so I will take you up to your room before you are introduced to the rest of the staff and, of course, your charges. The mistress, Mrs Pembridge, may want to see you, or she may not. She has not come down today.'

Harriet followed Mrs Rakes up the steps and into a spacious hall laid with tiles in wonderful star-shaped patterns of red, cream and blue. They gleamed as though they'd been polished only minutes before. Two different wallpapers, both of the latest style, had been hung above and below the dado rail, though little could be seen of the stripe on the upper portion because the wall was so densely covered with framed pictures, which extended right the way up the stairs. Jaunty hunting scenes jostled for space with oils of naval battles and a sepia family photograph, while half a dozen wavering watercolours had clearly only merited inclusion because someone in the house had painted them. Aside from these there were half a dozen potted plants in rude health, standing sentry on carved stands, and a complicated umbrella and hat receptacle made of oak, which gave off the pleasant aroma of beeswax. Someone, in a room above, was playing a slightly tortured scale on a violin.

Absorbing this ambience of comfortable wealth as she followed Mrs Rakes up the stairs, Harriet did not at first notice the thin figure standing at the top. Strands of her flyaway hair were lit from behind by the setting sun, giving her an appearance that would have been unearthly if it were not for the dingy cap they escaped from. The effect was of a halo, but when Harriet drew level with the girl, there was nothing angelic about her expression. Her hands, which were clutching a blacking box and broom, were well on their way to being ruined, the knuckles chapped and split and nearly as livid as the sunset behind her.

'Agnes, this is Miss Jenner, the new governess,' said Mrs Rakes. She turned to Harriet. 'Agnes is our kitchen ... well, I should say that she's our second housemaid.'

Harriet smiled gamely at the girl, who stared back insolently.

'Agnes, go down and fetch Miss Jenner some hot water,' said Mrs Rakes, peremptorily. 'No dawdling, please.'

The governess's bedroom was up another floor and, though the eaves sloped down steeply, they weren't low enough to be of any concern to someone of Harriet's small stature. A threadbare rug on the bare boards was clearly a remnant from a grander room downstairs but the bowl and jug on the washstand were unchipped and decorated with pretty blue flowers. The iron bedstead was narrow but, again, Harriet's diminutive size would come to her rescue. A fire had already been laid in the grate, ready to light, and the room was well dusted and aired. Standing on tiptoe at the window, she saw that her view was of the valley to the west and thought she might, in time, come to appreciate the carpet of green and gold that rolled away into the distance.

When Mrs Rakes had left her alone, she unlaced her boots and lay back on the bed. Even as she listened out for the dour Agnes's tread on the stair, she let her mind drift briefly back to London, and the life she had lived there. Things would be very different for her here, at Fenix House. She had been brought up as a lady but she would never be one now, and while she was certainly a good deal higher than someone like Agnes, she had to remember that her position in relation to the housekeeper was rather more ambiguous.

The Governess Institution had learned a little of Harriet's background – her father's loss of fortune some years before and his eventual death two months previously from a malignant tumour in the stomach – but she wondered how much of it had been related to her new employers. Not much, she hoped: the very last thing she wanted from these strangers in their big, rambling house on a Gloucestershire hill was pity. Though she and her father had never warranted a housekeeper, there had once been a maid like Agnes and a governess for Harriet, too.

Going once more to the tiny window, her breath clouding the glass, she marvelled at how swiftly things could disappear, with so little left to show they had ever been.

Six

Mrs Pembridge, as anticipated, was not well enough to receive the new governess. In fact, she had sent down instructions that she was not to be disturbed by anyone for the rest of the evening. Even so, the bell for her bedroom rang three times in the quarter-hour when Harriet was being shown the kitchen, larder, pantry and scullery, and introduced to the rest of the small staff.

The cook was as tiny in height as Harriet but as fat as one might expect a country cook to be, and would have been well able to fit three or four of the governess inside her capacious apron. She gave Harriet an appraising look, without even the ghost of a smile.

'Cook is Mrs Rollright,' said Mrs Rakes, as she led Harriet out of the kitchen and down a narrow passage. 'Perhaps, like mine, it is a rather appropriate name.'

Harriet turned to her to see if she was mistaken but, no, there was definitely a flicker of mirth in the housekeeper's eyes and playing around her mouth. She smiled back, glad of an ally in a strange place. She certainly didn't think she could count either Agnes or the redoubtable Mrs Rollright as such, not yet.

Mrs Rakes led her into a small servants' parlour, where a lanky young man with freckles and knobbled wrist bones, Agnes, and two other girls, as dark-haired and rosy-cheeked as gypsies, were variously mending or drinking tea.

'Now, everyone, this is Miss Jenner,' said Mrs Rakes, her quiet but commanding voice causing them all to look up. 'She is to be governess to Miss Helen and Miss Victoria. You've already met Agnes, Miss Jenner. Our coachman – also footman on occasion – is John here, and these two sisters are Mary and Ann. Mary is the elder and she is our first housemaid. Ann has joined us recently to be scullery maid. The gardener and his boy you will meet soon. The boy, Ned, lives at home, and Dilger has a cottage further up the hill from the Cucumber House. He prefers his own company.'

Just then the little brass bell to Mrs Pembridge's bedroom trilled for the third time.

'Perhaps I'll send word up with John that *I* do not wish to be disturbed by *her* for the rest of the evening,' muttered Agnes, as she got to her feet.

'Off you go, Agnes, and mend your manners,' said Mrs Rakes. 'Give her a drop of the tonic that came this morning and I imagine she'll be off to sleep directly.'

After the girl had gone, the housekeeper led Harriet back towards the stairs.

'You mustn't mind Agnes's proud ways. She's a decent girl at heart. The mistress has given her notions above her station by calling her a housemaid when she's nothing more than a tweeny, but she likes people to think there are two maids above stairs in her house, so what are we to do?

'Now, if you don't mind waiting a little longer for your own supper – which you will eat after the other servants with Mrs Rollright and me, unless you object . . .' she paused until Harriet realized she was supposed to shake her head '. . . I thought you would like to meet your charges before they are put to bed.'

The nursery took up a corner of the house directly below Harriet's room in the eaves and, though it wasn't likely to be a chilly evening, a fire had been lit in the large grate. The two Pembridge girls had been drawn to it like cats. The elder was lying on the hearthrug, deep in a book. The other, sitting with her back to her sister, had stripped her doll to her petticoats and was about to feed a tiny satin dress to the flames.

'Put that down, Victoria!' exclaimed Mrs Rakes. 'Will you burn all your things to a cinder? Where is the fire-guard? Helen, why are you not watching your sister?'

The younger girl, whose cherubic blue eyes, pink cheeks and white-blonde curls were evidently belied by her character, wrinkled her tiny nose and threw the scrap of fabric to the rug. 'Who are you?' she said rudely.

'I am Miss Jenner,' Harriet replied, with as much cheer as she could muster. 'I am to be your governess. How do you do, Victoria?'

'The Queen and I have the same name, you know,' the little girl said archly.

Harriet raised an eyebrow and turned instead to the other child, who had looked up from her book with eyes darker than her sister's. She was altogether plainer, Harriet observed, which perhaps accounted for her more biddable appearance.

'You must be Helen,' she said to her gently. 'What are you reading?'

'*Off on a Comet*,' the little girl replied shyly, holding the book aloft. 'It's by a Frenchman.'

'Ah, yes, Mr Verne,' said Harriet. 'I haven't yet read that one, but I enjoyed *A Journey to the Centre of the Earth* very much. Perhaps I might borrow it when you have finished?'

Helen smiled tentatively. 'I would let you, but you must ask my papa as it's his book. He lets me borrow them if I'm careful.'

Harriet sighed. 'Just as I used to borrow from mine. Now, let me see if I have this quite in order: you, Helen, are nine years old, and Victoria is six. Is that correct?'

Helen nodded but Victoria was too engaged in pulling her doll's arm from its socket to answer.

'Victoria, Miss Jenner is speaking to you,' said Mrs Rakes.

'I'm not six, I'm three,' she replied, the words deliberately unformed.

'She's not!' her sister said hotly. 'Mama always babies her and thinks it amusing when she speaks like that, but she's seven in October.' She turned to Victoria and gave her a small shove. 'If you're three then you must be the biggest, fattest three-year-old in all England!'

'Helen, you will not speak to your little sister in that coarse way, as you have been told many times,' said the housekeeper, reprovingly, as she stood back from fixing the fireguard into position. 'Both girls can be difficult in their own ways,' she said, in an undertone to Harriet. 'As you will see. But the mistress thinks it is Helen who needs the firmer hand.'

Harriet thought the reverse was true, but held her tongue. She suspected that Helen lashed out because she was not her mother's favourite and knew it. Plain but clever, she seemed open to the point of transparency, while Victoria was very pretty and not without guile.

'Agnes will put the girls to bed each night but you will

be responsible for them during the day. You will have breakfast and the midday meal with them, too. I presume that is satisfactory.'

They were back on the stairs, which were now lit warmly by pools of gaslight, the ranks of pictures concealed by blank reflections of polished glass.

'They have very different characters, I think, Helen and Victoria,' ventured Harriet.

'You wouldn't know they were sisters at all,' agreed Mrs Rakes.

'There's a boy too, isn't there? I forget his name.'

'Robert, like his father, though we call him Bertie. He's eleven. He's usually to be found in the gardens or the woods beyond – no doubt that's where he is now, poking under a rock or in a bird's nest. He goes to school in the town.'

'And is his father at home?'

'No, he won't be back until tomorrow. He works for the railways and is kept away quite frequently. When I say he works for them, he is newly made principal assistant to the locomotive and carriage superintendent for the Great Western Railway.' She looked wryly at Harriet. 'He also owns a minor railway with a group of other gentlemen. I'm sure the mistress would prefer he owned it outright but what he has pays for all of us here, and it paid for this house, too.'

After her supper with Mrs Rakes and Mrs Rollright, Harriet excused herself, saying she needed to unpack her things and prepare the next day's lessons. Really she craved her own company, and the privacy to cry – just as she had done every evening since her father's death. She allowed herself this daily indulgence for only a few minutes, mindful that without a strict limit the tears might never stop. With no memories of her mother, she was determined not to forget her father's face, as well as his familiar smell of tobacco and warm wool, and the sounds he made quite unconsciously – the clearing of his throat, the sigh of relief when he sat down, the rumble of his voice as he murmured an old song on the way up to bed. Remembering him – and their house and the London streets of which she had known every cobble, brick and tile – was far more painful than forcing herself to forget, but without them she was quite alone in the world, and that was more painful still.

Seven

The next morning Harriet woke early, then washed and dressed quickly. The temperature had dropped overnight but there wasn't time to light a fire and wait for it to warm the room. Once she was neat in her dark dress, her bright golden hair gathered decorously at the back of her head, she peeped out of the high window. A fresh wind was ruffling the fronds of the enormous conifers, and dark clouds were scudding across the sky from the west. When she put her fingers to the window frame, she could feel the day's chill breath.

In the nursery on the floor below, she discovered a slightly undersized boy with the same brown hair and hazel eyes as Helen. Wearing a miniature military outfit and a grave expression, he had seated himself opposite his sisters. Next to him was an empty place, presumably meant for Harriet. Agnes, not a whit less sulky-mouthed for her night's sleep, was doling out eggs with a clatter.

'Don't like eggs,' said Victoria.

'Yes, you do,' returned Agnes and Helen in unison.

The boy, who was surely Bertie, had jumped to his feet on Harriet's arrival and now put out his hand to shake hers. She wondered momentarily if he was going to bow and was slightly disappointed when he didn't.

'How do you do, Miss Jenner?' he said solemnly. 'I hope you won't object to sitting next to me.'

Harriet's mouth twitched. 'I should be honoured,' she said. 'Is it Bertie I have the pleasure of meeting?'

The boy reddened. 'Oh, I didn't even say, did I? What a dolt I am. In truth, I would prefer to be called by my full name, Robert, like my father. I am quite grown out of "Bertie", though no one else can remember not to call me it. I think, perhaps, as I'm new to you, then it might be just as easy for you to remember "Robert" as "Bertie". Do you think so?'

'Well, I can certainly try, if it would not cause too much confusion,' said Harriet, ignoring the singsong chant of 'Bertie! Bertie!' that Victoria had gleefully taken up. In fact, he suited 'Bertie' perfectly and she knew she would never be able to call him anything else.

When the meal was finished, Bertie asked if he could show Harriet the garden before he left for school. 'There isn't time to see everything very thoroughly, so I will pick the very best parts to show you now, to whip your appetite, and then we will go round again more carefully when I return from school this afternoon. Is that agreeable, Miss Jenner?'

'I think *whetting* my appetite this morning is an excellent idea, and I'm sure it will save Mrs Rakes a job.'

On realizing his mistake, the boy frowned and looked to see if she laughed at him. Seeing that she didn't, he brightened again. 'Very good, let us commence our tour, then,' he said and, with that, pulled back the nursery door with a flourish.

The garden, given that it had required cultivation on the slope of a steep hill, was ingeniously laid out over many different levels, giving it an air of those resorts found cascading down towards the Mediterranean Sea. They began on the side of the house that faced the valley, where Harriet stopped a moment to sniff the air that was so much sweeter than London's.

'Do you like it, Miss Jenner?' said Bertie, his face tense with hope.

'Oh, yes,' she breathed. 'It's wonderful.'

The pristine lawn swept down towards the road and coach house in layers that reminded Harriet of a flounced skirt, one edged with curving flowerbeds instead of lace. On the highest of these, accessed from the house by French windows, was a croquet lawn. She had never played the game and Bertie quickly extracted a promise that she would let him teach her.

Ascending the hill on the other side of the house, beyond the carriage sweep, the garden became more intriguing and private. In truth, it was not so much one garden as half a dozen, some separated by brick walls that bellied out in places, while others were divided by sections of dark and neatly clipped yew. A maze of box was not yet fully established but, Harriet noted, had already grown a good deal taller than the trying Victoria. They didn't go any deeper in than the first corridor of dense, rule-straight foliage, Bertie beckoning her on, but she felt the air change nevertheless, turning cool and still. Looking about her, she wondered how tall it would be in fifty years' time, and how much more hushed and secret.

Further up the garden, reached by a smaller branch of the curving path they had begun on, a rockery was crammed with delicate alpines and, above it, a curious tree that Bertie told her was a monkey puzzle. 'After a great deal of thought, I've decided it's my favourite of all the trees,' he remarked gravely, before taking her higher, towards a series of low-lying outbuildings and glass-houses.

'Mrs Rakes mentioned a cucumber house last night,' she said to Bertie, who had turned to survey the view down towards the house with pride. 'Is there really a whole glasshouse devoted to cucumbers?'

He shook his head, with the weariness of a much older man. 'Goodness, no. We couldn't possibly eat enough of 'em. Mama calls it that because she once went to a very grand house where they had different buildings for every-thing – oranges, mushrooms, orchids and all sorts of exotic things.'

'So the Cucumber House is to the garden, then, what the second housemaid is to the house?' she queried inno-cently.

He thought for a while, then burst out laughing. 'Oh, I see! That's really a capital joke, Miss Jenner. I shall always picture Agnes as a cucumber now.' Well pleased with that, he took Harriet's hand and led her back to the path that wove upwards through the garden's many mysterious compartments.

'What time must you leave for school, Bert— Robert?' Harriet reminded the boy gently.

'Oh, I have seven or possibly eight minutes yet.'

'And do you like your school?'

His brow furrowed as he thought about it, and Harriet wondered if his opinion had ever been sought before. 'On the whole, I like it well enough. At my school some fellows are on the classical side and some on the military. Can you guess which I am, Miss Jenner?'

She pretended to think, though his uniform made it clear enough. 'You look a brave sort of boy, so I guess . . . the military side. Am I right?'

He smiled uncertainly, a blush creeping up the back of his neck. 'Yes, quite right. I will probably go into the army one day, like my uncle Jago. Mama thinks I ought to. She says it's much more heroic than working on the railways. My uncle is in India, you know, and Mama misses him dreadfully.

'Now, we have time for one more thing and this is the best of all,' he announced. 'I am not even allowed to go there by myself.'

They passed a potting shed and a scrubby strip of earth, which Bertie informed her was for the growing of potatoes, and entered a part of the garden apparently allowed to run wilder. Above them, spindly birch trees grew in profusion, their limbs still quite bare for the season. The only sounds came from the crows that huddled high in the narrow branches, like splotches of ink, and the soft swish of Harriet's long skirts through the dew-soaked grass.

She was about to ask if it was much further when Bertie stopped and pointed triumphantly. Peering hard, she could see nothing more remarkable than a large hillock of soil and moss among the trees.

'Look very hard, Miss Jenner. Can you see the bricks?'

He was right: it wasn't just mud – she could see the cross-hatchings of mortar.

'It's an ice-house,' said the boy, triumphantly. 'Have you been in one before?'

'Never.'

They reached the front of the strange building. A low, broad door was set into the brick, its handle – more like a lever – made of dull brass. Bertie ran to it and, with some effort, wrenched it down and pulled back the door. Once it began to swing, its weight added to the momentum and nearly knocked him over.

Even from her distance of a few feet, Harriet felt the cold hit her, like a frigid wave. Fascinated, she stepped over nettles and fallen twigs to reach the doorway.

'Careful!' cried Bertie, from behind her. 'It drops away quite steeply.'

As her eyes began to adjust, she saw that he had not exaggerated. The floor of the ice-house was at least six feet lower than the ground outside it. Just to the left of the doorway, a ladder was attached to the wall by half-rusted nails.

'As you see, it's empty now,' he continued, 'but we are due to have a great block of ice delivered next month, in time for summer. They lower it in and cover it with straw and it lasts for months if we keep the door shut tight. I'm going to ask my father if he'll let me chip some off for Mrs Rollright one day. She won't go anywhere near it, says it makes her blood run cold – which I thought quite a stupid thing to say because that is precisely what it's meant to do – and John says he has enough to do with the horses without clambering around down there with a pick just so that Mama can have a sorbet. Of course, if it's desperately hot, like it was two summers ago, then we keep the meat and fish here too. Don't you think it's marvellous, Miss Jenner?'

'I do, though not so marvellous that I would like to find myself trapped inside.'

Bertie nodded sagely. 'That's true enough. My father and I once calculated that the air would likely run out in a day, two at most.'

Harriet shuddered. She hadn't liked enclosed spaces since she'd hidden in a linen cupboard during a childhood game of hide and seek. The door had stuck fast and, though there had been no shortage of air, there had been something horribly suffocating about the starched stacks of teetering cotton and the brush of hanging articles against her head in the pitch dark.

With the ice-house door carefully closed again, she was glad to be clear of the trees and back under the weak sun, which was just starting to warm the winding path down to the house. Bertie, realizing the lateness of the hour, ran ahead to the brougham that was waiting for him on the carriage sweep. Before climbing up, he turned and gave her a salute, which she, her mind still up the hill in the cold, clammy depths of the ice-house, almost returned.

Eight

When she got back to the house from the garden, Mrs Rakes was waiting for her. 'The mistress will see you now,' she said, and Harriet thought she could detect sympathy in the housekeeper's voice.

Mrs Pembridge's rooms were in the opposite corner of the house to the nursery and occupied one of its two octagonal towers. Harriet was shown into what appeared to be a lavishly appointed sitting room, though it was difficult to be sure: the curtains remained closed against the day and the gas lamps had been turned down as low as they would go, pitching her out of early morning into evening. Through an open doorway she could see a bedroom no less opulently equipped, a gargantuan brass bed strewn with silk pillows. In the sitting room's grate a heaped fire threw out heat as well as the odd spark, which threatened to set light to the swags of emerald green velvet that covered the mantel.

So dimly lit was the room and so numerous were the chairs, footstools, rugs, ornaments, picture frames, glass scent bottles, discarded clothes, scattered copies of the *Illustrated London News* and assorted frills festooning every item of furniture that Harriet didn't at first notice the room's occupant.

'So, you are the governess,' came a languid voice from one shadowy corner. Harriet peered harder and saw the mistress of the house stretched out on a chaise longue that matched the wallpaper, which might have been dark green. She appeared to be clad in a pale, slippery garment consisting almost entirely of ribbons.

'Good morning, Mrs Pembridge. I am Miss Jenner.'

A pale hand fluttered in the gloom and Harriet realized she was being directed to sit down on a hard chair close to the stifling heat of the fire. She hoped she wouldn't faint and tip headlong into it.

'Is it the flames reflected in your hair or is it red?' said Mrs Pembridge. 'I do hope it's not red. Staff with red hair always have the most dreadful tempers. You need look no further than Agnes for confirmation of that.'

'I think it's closer to gold than red,' replied Harriet, cautiously, though it was difficult not to bridle at such a personal remark. 'Or perhaps bronze.'

She saw the slash of a raised eyebrow.

'Bronze indeed! How old are you, Miss . . . Miss . . .?'

'Jenner. I am twenty-one, Mrs Pembridge.'

'A dangerous age. You are passably pretty, are you not? No, pretty is not the word for it. I am pretty. You are rather small, of course, and much too thin, but I think you might be called striking.'

Harriet flushed and was briefly glad of the fire, which had already made her cheeks hot. 'You are kind to say so.'

'Well, the firelight is very flattering, of course. Now, Miss Jenner, I hope you are a modest sort of woman. I cannot allow callers at this house. By callers, I refer, of course, to followers. *Men*, Miss Jenner. I have lost two maids and a housekeeper to marriage in the last few years. My lesson is learned in that regard.'

Harriet forced herself to smile. 'I do not know a soul in this part of the country except those under your roof, Mrs Pembridge.'

'Excellent. There is very little temptation to be found in either John or Dilger, and Ned is but a boy, so that is a weight off my mind. You have met my daughters?'

Harriet nodded. 'Yes, indeed. I was introduced to them when I arrived yesterday. I met your son this morning. He showed me the garden.'

'Bertie? Oh, Lord, did he drag you up to the ice-house? He is quite tediously fixated upon it.'

'Yes, he did, and I found it fascinating.'

'Did you now?'

'He also showed me what I believe is known as the Cucumber House. It was quite the grand tour.'

'I see.' The eyebrow was raised again.

'He wishes to show me the rest later, when he returns from school.'

'That's as may be,' said the mistress, testily, 'but don't forget you are here for the instruction of my daughters. You will find Vicky an easy pupil, quick-witted and a sunny, contented soul, just like her mama. Helen, though, is quite a different proposition. She was contrary from the moment she was born, had unending bouts of colic until she was two and flatly refused to utter a word until she was three. I was convinced she was an imbecile but she was simply stubborn. Her father adores her but her sheer obstinacy endears her to no one else. If the agony of that particular confinement wasn't seared into my memory, I would believe her a changeling.'

'She seems to be fond of reading,' Harriet tried, rather shocked by the mistress's lack of discretion.

'Oh, reading! There is something singularly unattractive about a woman reading a book, I always think. Hunched and squinting in a corner while everyone else is being sociable and amusing. And, of course, it ruins the posture and the eyesight. I hope you will make it your first priority to broaden Helen's appeal. She can scarcely play a note on the violin I had her father purchase at no little expense, and her drawing is rudimentary at best. I don't know if you happened to see some of my little paintings in the hallway, Miss . . .?'

'Jenner. And, yes, I did see some very . . . subtle water-colours framed on the stairs, though I assumed them to be the work of a professional artist.'

Mrs Pembridge tittered delightedly, the sound reminiscent of teaspoons rattling against china. 'Oh, no, my dear. They are by my own hand. Subtle, you say?'

Harriet took this sudden upturn in spirits as an opportunity to scrutinize the woman opposite her more closely, shifting slightly to the side so the light from the fire fell on the mistress's face. What she saw when her eyes adjusted made her rear back in her chair, her hand involuntarily going to her mouth. Mrs Pembridge, still smiling to herself, had returned to picking at the contents of her breakfast tray and didn't notice. Harriet, heart juddering, thanked God for the closed curtains.

Could it really be her? If it was, she hadn't seen her for more than ten years; a woman barely out of girlhood on her way to her wedding. She thought about little Bertie, the eldest of the Pembridge progeny, who was eleven. It was possible, if she'd got with child as soon as she was married.

Harriet studied her again, peering as boldly as she dared through the thick, swirling heat of the room. The pale hair, singed to frizz at the ends by the irons that curled it into tight ringlets; the blue eyes and pouting lips, so accurately replicated in her younger daughter; the plump figure and thick, creamy skin – it might very well be the same woman, a decade older. Then, as if to seal the matter, Bertie's words chimed in her head: *I will probably go into the army one day, like my uncle Jago*. With a brother called Jago and so resembling the girl she had last seen in a crowded London street, it must be her: Louisa Dauncey.

At that moment she – Mrs Pembridge, as she was now – claimed to be worn out, having risen incautiously early, and instructed Harriet to ring for Mary to collect her tray so that she might return to bed. The new governess, to her profound relief, was dismissed.

On the staircase, she almost collided with Mrs Rakes.

'Miss Jenner, you are very pale. What is the matter?'

Harriet looked blindly at the housekeeper, her thoughts held fast by a cold bright day in 1866.

'I – I am well,' she stammered eventually. 'It is only that I – Mrs Rakes, what is Mrs Pembridge's name?' She couldn't keep the words from rushing out of her.

The housekeeper frowned in confusion. 'The mistress's name? Why, I can't think why you would want to know such a thing unless . . . Do you think you know her? Is that why you have gone so white?'

'No . . . I mean, I'm not sure.'

Mrs Rakes studied her, clearly perplexed, but then seemed to relent, as if she understood the gravity of the question, if not the governess's trembling hands and wide, staring eyes. 'Before she was married, she was a Miss Louisa Dauncey. She came here from London.'

'Yes,' said Harriet, almost inaudibly. 'Yes.'

'So you do know her?' The housekeeper's voice was gentle.

After a pause, Harriet shook her head. 'No. I thought I did, for a moment, but I was mistaken.' The words came out woodenly and she didn't think they would be believed. 'Will you excuse me, Mrs Rakes? It was so hot in that room. I must go outside and get some air.'

Hastening down the stairs, she could feel the housekeeper's puzzled gaze on her but nothing would have entreated her to stay and explain, let alone admit that, while the mistress evidently did not recognize Harriet, Harriet remembered the woman who had once been Louisa Dauncey very well indeed.

Nine

Grace

Twilight's delicate blanket cloaked Fenix House quickly that first evening, the day's colour leaking away in the time the three of us took to eat a quiet dinner. It was a reminder that summer had waned; the nights lengthening as autumn stole in. Inside the dining room, our pudding bowls lay abandoned, the contents only half eaten. It was one of Agnes's staples, apparently: a lumpen yet runny trifle that made up in sherry for what it lacked in fruit. I soon gave up, forcing in one more mouthful before gratefully laying down my spoon. As soon as I did, Bertie got to his feet, eager to take me outside and introduce me to the garden.

'It's too dark to go out now,' said David Pembridge. I thought I could detect a note of satisfaction in his sardonic tone. 'You'll only brain yourselves on the old rockery.'

Bertie hurried to the window and peered out despondently. 'You are right, of course. I can see nothing but my own rather disappointing reflection.'

'Perhaps you can show it to me tomorrow,' I said brightly, as the pendant light above us began to flicker violently.

'Damn this house!' cried my new employer, slamming his wine glass down on the cloth so hard that I feared for the fragile stem. 'I had that wiring checked not two weeks ago.'

'I always think of it as Mama,' said Bertie, mournfully, his eyes scanning the cracked and tobacco-stained plaster of the ceiling.

'What in God's name do you mean by that?' said Pembridge, irritably.

Bertie waved one hand about nervously. The other fumbled for his glass. 'Oh, you know. The lights, the noises.'

'Noises?'

'Oh dear, I must be being obtuse again. The creaks in the night. The footsteps on the stairs when we're all in bed. The bells ringing from rooms that have been empty for years.'

'My dear Uncle, are you trying to tell us that you believe the noises of a decrepit old house such as this one – the natural sounds old wood makes as it expands and contracts – are some sort of . . . manifestation of my grandmother?' He laughed grimly and shook his head.

Bertie looked dejected. 'It's just my fancy, of course. I'm not such a rational being as you, David. It's simply that Mama's character was so very powerful. I cannot believe there is nothing left of her.'

Tutting, his nephew reached for the bottle of wine, splashing a ruby inch or two into my glass before upending the rest into his own. Then he reached under his chair for a newspaper and began to read intently, as though signalling his unwillingness to engage in any more ridiculous conversation. He glanced up, perhaps feeling my gaze on him, and I quickly turned to Bertie. 'What was she like, your mama?' I blurted. I genuinely wanted to know. My grandmother had said so little about either Mr or Mrs Pembridge. I hadn't noticed their absence in the narrative as a child – much more interested as I was in the children, and the rather exaggerated characters of the servants. It was only now I was at Fenix House that I realized how scarcely I knew the erstwhile master and mistress. I presumed both of them were dead now.

'Well, if anyone was going to haunt this old pile, I suppose it would be her,' said Pembridge, from the depths of his newspaper. 'I was only a boy when she died but I remember her with a special sort of clarity.'

I was just wondering where he slotted into the family tree – whether he was Helen's or Victoria's or some later sibling's son – when the pendant light stuttered again, making all of us look up. With a popping sound, half of the bulbs went dark.

'Perhaps you're on to something after all, Uncle.'

Even in the dim light, Bertie looked distinctly nervous. 'Of course, I simply adored Mama,' he said shakily, as if she was listening from a point somewhere above his head. 'She was an exquisite thing when we were young, with golden curls and eyes the colour of . . . cornflowers. Or delphiniums, perhaps.'

'I remember them as paler, colder than that,' said Pembridge.

Bertie put his head to one side and sighed. 'You may be right. She was, as I have said, quite a character. No one who met her ever forgot her. She always had to have the latest styles – dresses, shoes, even furniture and wallpaper. When she was very ill, at the end, she still insisted she had her bedroom entirely redecorated. It perked her up immensely when it was finished but she was already so weak that it couldn't revive her entirely.' He smiled sadly into his glass. 'Of course, she didn't think much of me.'

63

'Oh, I'm sure that's not true,' I said reflexively.

'No, really, my dear. You're kind to say otherwise but I wasn't the son she would have liked to have. He would have been strapping and brave, more like her brother. I was never brave. I didn't have her golden hair either. Vicky got all the Dauncey looks.

'I was supposed to follow my uncle into the army. But I wouldn't have been cut out for it, and fortunately I was too old for the Great War. I expect I would have been a dreadful liability if I'd been conscripted. Uncle Jago was stationed in India when I was a boy. To hear him, you'd think he'd quelled half a dozen mutinies on his own. Who knows? Perhaps he had. I'm sure Mama thought him capable of it.' He glanced upwards again. 'He would visit us here when he came home on leave, though of course that was never often enough for Mama. She was at her happiest when he was here.'

'It was the only time she was happy at all, or so I was told,' said Pembridge. He stood and fetched another dusty wine bottle from a sideboard.

'Oh, now, I don't know about that,' said Bertie, frowning and holding out his glass. 'She was uncommonly close to her brother, though – that certainly is true. I remember one visit in particular. I must have been eleven or twelve because that was the summer Miss Jenner was with us –' He broke off, gazing myopically into the middle distance.

I went completely still. *She was really here*, I thought, with an absurd kind of amazement. Of course, intellectually, I had known that – and her initials in the skirting-board were undeniable proof on their own. Somehow, though, it was in that moment that the past – *her* past – actually became real for me.

I looked at Bertie, who was still distracted by memories of his now-distant childhood, and then across at his nephew. Pembridge's expression as he turned his glass round, deep shadows gathering beneath the angular planes of his face, was utterly inscrutable.

'Yes, I think it was that summer,' said Bertie, quietly, almost to himself. 'I suppose it was the last time.'

I was about to ask what he meant when Agnes barged through the door. 'You not like your trifle, then?' she threw out, on catching sight of our bowls.

'It wasn't one of your finest,' said Pembridge, levelly.

'Ever the charmer,' she said, under her breath, as she clattered crockery on to a tray.

'I suppose a pot of coffee is out of the question?' he said, as if he hadn't heard.

'There's only the dregs left. I'll order more tomorrow. And some light bulbs while I'm at it. They never seem to last two minutes in here.'

Bertie looked pointedly at Pembridge, who refused to acknowledge him.

Agnes eventually stumped off and peace settled upon the room again. I wanted to ask about my grandmother – about Miss Jenner – but thought I stood a better chance when Bertie and I were alone. I could bring the subject up when we walked around the garden, perhaps. I was reluctant to say anything that might give me away in front of my employer, who seemed at once entirely self-absorbed and as sharp as a blade. Perhaps it was silly of me to keep the connection to myself, especially when Bertie obviously remembered my grandmother so fondly, but I found I wanted to stand alone for once – for the Pembridges to judge me for myself and not as a pale imitation of her; a mere shadow. There was something deeply liberating and novel about this idea.

'Mr Pembridge,' I began, keen to keep the conversation in the present, 'I wonder if I might ask you a few questions about my work here.'

He fixed me with a penetrating stare. His eyes were so dark in the gloom that I couldn't distinguish between the irises and the pupils. I looked down in order to have the courage to keep talking.

'The advertisement mentioned the need for a governess *and* nurse. "Light nursing duties", I believe it said precisely. As was explained in my letter, I am rather more experienced in teaching. I suppose I wondered . . . Well, what is the nature of your son's illness?' I swallowed and made myself look up.

'The *nature*?' he said, as though it was a filthy word.

I nodded, determined not to stammer out anything else until he'd answered what was surely a reasonable question.

'I think it's best that you see for yourself tomorrow,' he said eventually. 'It's not a simple thing. It's not as though he's tubercular or has lost the use of his legs, or something of that kind.'

Bertie winced at the blunt words.

'I see,' I said. 'And do you think he will be well enough to see me tomorrow? He didn't seem particularly willing today, if I may say so.' I swallowed audibly.

'Look here, I'll make sure he sees you soon. There will be no problem with that. He was off-colour today, I'll admit, but aren't we all sometimes? God knows I am.'

I lowered my gaze again to the rather dingy tablecloth,

feeling as though I'd been put in my place unfairly. I hoped he wouldn't say anything else. I had a horrible feeling I might cry if he did. A combination of his chilly bearing and the dark press of night all around us had brought on a sudden and acute wave of homesickness. I felt all my brave, bright thoughts of independence go out, one by one, just like the bulbs above us.

It soon became clear that he wasn't going to say anything more about his son, or anything else. Bertie, too, seemed rather downcast after his initial enthusiasm about the garden. I made my excuses and left them there in silence as soon as I politely could. *This is an unhappy house*, I thought, as I went up the stairs. It wasn't just the poor condition of the place. Misery, loneliness and regret seemed to leach out of every badly papered corner, lifting tiles and staining plaster as they bedded in over the years.

When I reached the attic floor, the noises I'd heard earlier seemed rather more sinister now it was so thoroughly dark, and I found myself wondering, with a creeping sense of unease, whether anyone could be up there. I hadn't attempted to ask about the rest of the family at dinner – if there was any.

I regretted that now. I'd found Lucas's outraged, disembodied cries unnerving enough. To think there might be another person in the house I hadn't yet laid eyes on, whom I had perhaps only heard, was positively chilling. As for Bertie's mama, I didn't dare think about any lingering incarnation of her, surrounded as I was by the dark of that peculiar house – a dark that seemed blacker and thicker than any I had experienced before.

Ten

In my room, I took off my shoes and got into the narrow bed without undressing. The nearness of my grandmother's initials was less of a comfort than I'd hoped: in a strange way they made her feel even further away. Arranging the pillow so it cushioned my back from the iron bedstead, I pulled the blankets up to my chin and looked around the little room that had once been hers. Perhaps it was there, in that narrow bed, that she had first had an inkling that someone would follow her to Fenix House – not my mother, but someone who would come later: me. *It's meant to be*, she had said so implacably when she had found David Pembridge's advertisement. *I've seen it.*

That my grandmother had the sight – or a sixth sense, or a knack for clairvoyance – was never particularly astonishing to me. Nothing is, if it's all you've ever known. She called those disordered pieces of the future 'the glimmers', and until my parents died, they meant little more to me than other mysterious-sounding ailments that seemed to come with age, such as our next-door neighbour's thickened heart and the butcher's wife's nerves.

The glimmers had rarely come often or reliably enough to prove useful, and on the day my parents were killed, they hadn't saved the lives of two people she loved. The events of that cloudless spring day in 1910 had only reinforced her belief that whatever it was she possessed was as much a curse as a gift. After all, what could be crueller than a premonition that arrived before the news was brought but too late to send a warning?

She was downstairs in the parlour when she felt them go that day. She never used the word 'pass', which was what other people said the dead did.

'No, Grace, it's something quicker and stronger and . . . brighter than just "passing",' she had explained to me, a few days later, when I had come to understand that my parents would not be returning to the house the four of us had lived in together all my life, and that from now on my grandmother and I would be there by ourselves. 'When the soul is released, it goes as fast as a silver bullet fired from a gun. There's a great tearing upwards into the blue.'

Her description made me think of Halley's Comet, which I had so recently watched with my parents from the suspension bridge that Brunel had somehow contrived to throw across Bristol's deep gorge, from Clifton to Leigh Wood, and which I could see from my bedroom window. Children who are beloved believe themselves to be at the heart of everything but there, on the bridge, held aloft in the air by that great iron necklace, I had felt as tiny and insignificant as I really was – a speck of matter between two great nothings, one falling away to the muddy bottom of the River Avon and the other reaching up darkly towards the flickering comet, itself only a little less distant than the stars.

'So a soul,' I said gravely, feeling it was important to find a documented comparison, 'is like Halley's Comet. Is that what you mean, Grandmother?'

She paused and frowned and then, decided, nodded

once. 'A comet, yes. That's an excellent way of thinking about it. They haven't merely *passed*. The comet has taken your mother and father off on a great journey into infinite space.'

'Does that mean they'll come back in 1986?' I said hopefully, though the date predicted for the comet's return, which my father had read to me from his newspaper, sounded as strange and remote to me as 1066 or 1488.

Rarely one to falter in the face of logic, I saw her do so then and, for half a moment, her grey eyes glowed with the falsehood she had just told. She never let me see that again, that tell-tale glint of a lie.

On the morning that changed so much, she was sitting at the small writing desk stationed in the brightest corner of the parlour. My father had his own study and my mother, by her own admission a restless soul, never cared to sit at a desk, so this was my grandmother's private nook, where she could always be found after breakfast, reading the Cheltenham periodical that was delivered in preference to my father's copy of *The Times*.

When she sensed what had happened, or was shortly about to, I was two floors above her, leaning out of my bedroom window and into the sun. I had long been forbidden to do this for fear I would fall out and be smashed on the cobbles below so I had closed my door, which meant I didn't hear her cry out.

With the benefit of hindsight, I have wondered if that was the first time I ever experienced some version of the glimmers myself. You see, while the moment when my grandmother sat me down and told me about the accident became as murky as the Avon's silted waters, as veiled as

Leigh Wood's whitebeams wrapped in a winter fog, I could always remember the one when I became an orphan with absolute and uncanny precision.

It was, as I have said, a cloudless day. After a listless week of drizzle and buffeting winds, that morning's sky of cerulean blue seemed all the more glorious by comparison. Glorious but also fitting, it seemed to me – for this was the day my age would finally be written in double figures, a milestone of maturity I considered significant and had therefore approached with great solemnity.

After a special breakfast of Cook's kedgeree, which my grandmother and I loved, I left her to her paper and went back upstairs. My presents were to come later, once my parents had returned from an expedition to London for my father's work as a port and sherry merchant.

When I reached my room after breakfast on that momentous day, I closed the door carefully behind me. Lemon sunshine flooded the window and I realized that they would have boarded their train at Paddington and were probably speeding through placid green fields towards me. I could see them as if I was peeping in at the carriage window: my mother's gaze on the gentle landscape, my father shaking out his newspaper, and stowed in the luggage racks above them, I hoped, a package or two meant for me.

A church bell began to peal, strident in the soft air, and drew me to the window. I counted the chimes aloud with reverence, knowing that it must be ten o'clock: ten o'clock in the year of 1910 on my tenth birthday. The symmetry seemed significant and perfect. Looking up, high above the glinting chains of the suspension bridge, I could see a trio of peregrine falcons gliding nonchalantly on the warm currents of air that rose out of the deep gorge. Dizzily far below them I could imagine – for the river was set too deep between the rock for me to glimpse it – a boat peeling back the sluggish, cocoa-brown waters of the Avon. The scene before me, though deeply familiar, was tinted pink and gold that day – or perhaps my memory has embellished and fixed so vividly in my mind the last morning of my old life.

At precisely the same time I was at my window, a signalman in his box on the Great Western Railway, some forty-five miles to the east, was drifting into a light, dreaming sleep. An hour earlier he had asked to be relieved from his shift after a long night up with the youngest of his five children, who had contracted the scarlet fever. There was a fellow who was willing to stay on and work Albert Reed's shift for him: he knew of his troubles at home because the two played amateur cricket together in the summer months and were on good terms. His offer was refused.

Before he'd fallen asleep, Reed had moved a slow goods train to the down line, in order to let the Cornish Riviera Express pass unimpeded on its way to London. This was quite an ordinary thing to do, especially when the sidings were already occupied, in this case by another goods train and some rolling stock. There would have been plenty of time to return the goods train, which was pulling eight trucks of coal, to the up side of the tracks and send it on its way.

Reed heard the Cornish train clatter by but, after that, remembered nothing until he jolted awake to find the goods train still waiting on the down line. He glanced at the clock, and then at his timetable, the closely typed numbers dancing in front of his tired eyes. Just as he grabbed for the lever that would have moved the goods train out of the way, he heard the sounds that would never leave him, not for the rest of his days. First, the frantic whistle of the goods train as its driver realized what was bearing down on them, then the futile screeching of brakes from the express. Finally the impact itself, which made the signalbox shake and flung Reed to the floor.

While I, at my window, felt nothing but a heightened pleasure in simply being alive, terrible images were racing through my grandmother's mind: twisted metal, smouldering wood and torn bodies. The only redemptive element in the vision was a miraculous flash of unscathed white amid everything that was blackened and charred, but there was no detail so she couldn't work out what this might be. All of that swept through her, even as I closed my eyes against the blissful spring sunshine.

In the months afterwards, I found my mind straying often to a clock I had first seen on a walk with my father through the tangle of streets at Bristol's noisy heart. Prominent in the pale stone façade of the Corn Exchange, it was merely handsome on first glance. A closer look revealed something strange. Unlike the clocks I was familiar with – my father's silver pocket watch and the grandfather clock that lived in the hallway, the brass bob of its pendulum hidden behind a fairy-sized door – this clock had two minute hands: one black like the hour hand and the other a ghostly shadow hand of red.

It was a Saturday afternoon and my father and I happened to be passing the Exchange as the hour struck. I glanced up and then, puzzled, again.

'Papa, why is there a third hand on that clock?'

He followed my gaze, then smiled down at me. 'Ah, now, the red hand marks Bristol Time,' he said, as though time belonging to one place or another was the most reasonable thing in the world. 'As for the black hand, well, that's the time in London – or what is properly called Greenwich Mean Time. Do you see that the black hand is always marching ahead of our time by ten minutes? We are a little slower-paced in the west, perhaps.' He laughed at that and again when he caught sight of my baffled face.

He went on to explain that the railways had insisted time become the single, definitive fact I had always assumed it to be. As we stood there, looking up at the clock amid the bustle of an ordinary Saturday afternoon, time had been standardized for nearly seventy years by the Great Western Railway on which my father regularly travelled to London. The city of Bristol had stubbornly clung to its ten-minute lag until 1852 but that was now a distant memory, the red hand nothing but a relic of a lost era – an era before time, and distance, had been contracted by steam-powered iron.

'Do you know what Dickens said about Railway Time?' my father said, as we crossed Broad Street and turned into Wine Street. I knew who Dickens was: my mother had read *Great Expectations* to me a chapter at a time. 'He said: "Now there is even Railway Time observed in clocks, as if the sun itself had given in." He preferred the old way of doing things, you see.'

I thought I did, and even more so after my parents died on the railway that had made Bristol Time obsolete. I pictured the red hand of the clock most nights before I slept, my eyes on the dimly glowing square of my curtained window, lit from behind by streetlamps and the moon. Another ten minutes might have made all the difference, I thought, in the near-dark, my fingers worrying at the satin-edged square of muslin I could no longer sleep without. If the signalman had fallen asleep ten minutes later; if my parents' train had been delayed by ten minutes; if the goods train had set off ten minutes after the appointed time – just one of those small calibrations would have been enough to change their course and, with it, mine. More abstractly, I believed that if my mother and father had remained on Bristol Time, they would have been saved.

That was my first inkling of how treacherous time could be, but also how elastic – stretching out a lifetime or as brief as a snap of the fingers; the speed of a comet's light to reach the eyes or the long years before they will glimpse it again. The plodding tick of the grandfather clock in the hall no longer meant anything to me. It was much later that this revelation resonated: when I realized that, just as ten minutes ago could also be now, so could the events of half a century before sidle up from behind to loom large, suddenly as pressing as today's.

Eleven

The next morning I was informed that I would not meet Lucas that day either. Despite Pembridge's assurances the previous evening, he thought it would be best if I waited a little longer: Lucas had apparently woken with a sore throat.

This suspended me in a strange limbo: I was employed to do a job of work but kept from it. By late morning, having done nothing but write a not very informative letter to my grandmother, I was bored. I wandered into the dining room to find the newspaper Pembridge had been reading over dinner. It didn't make for a cheery diversion – thirty-nine men had been buried underground after a pit explosion in Cumberland and Lloyd George's ailing coalition seemed to be hanging on by a thread – and I soon gave it up. Sitting in the silent dining room, watching the dust motes turn, my left foot going to sleep under the right, I felt less like a much-needed member of staff and more like a forgotten house-guest at the sort of peculiarly English country pile that featured in P. G. Wodehouse's stories.

I decided to find some company, but Pembridge I hadn't seen since he'd informed me that Lucas wasn't up to meeting me, and I didn't quite dare visit Agnes's domain below-stairs. That left Bertie, who, when I found him, declared that he would be my host until I could take up my duties.

'It will be my great pleasure to show you the extent of the place,' he said happily, as he led me out through the parlour's French windows, whose paint was peeling off in strips. He was wearing a pair of round wire spectacles, though I thought the lenses must need replacing with stronger ones, so evident was his need to peer at close quarters and polish them every few minutes with a creased handkerchief, as though his blurred outlook was the fault of smeared glass, and not his own failing sight.

Though it was beginning to feel humid, the early September sun was hidden behind a blank expanse of thick white cloud through which I could see no chink of blue. It was headache weather, the cloud growing brighter and more blinding every minute. Under it, Bertie and I were like players trapped under limelight, the heating stage beneath us the brown, untended grass of a once-magnificent garden. It was a shame for him: everything, even a sorry old house, is lent a degree of charm, if not beauty, by the sun's flattering, gilded touch. That day's harsh light had turned the world dreary and depressed.

'Of course, it's not quite what it was,' he said apologetically, though I didn't think he knew the extent of its decline. The pristine lawn had probably been the first thing to go, I thought, its rolled emerald stripes undone in weeks. The hedges, too, had gone quite literally to seed – the dark yew infiltrated by weeds, its once carefully contrived mushroom caps now misshapen and bulbous. Even the little eye-catcher secreted at the top of the bare rockery was spoiled, covered entirely by a screen of wisteria so outlandish and sprawling that it had proved its own undoing, the weight of the upper branches causing them to collapse on to the lower. Some of it lay in a withering heap, faded petals as dry as dust; other clumps were already dead at the root, as grey and brittle as old bones.

'I'm afraid the azaleas by the drive have rather had it, too,' explained Bertie. 'You probably saw them on your way in. They're not easily missed. The firs are in rude health, though. The monkey puzzle, too. I always adored that tree.' He gestured triumphantly upwards and we both craned our necks to see the top of the exotic giant.

'What about the ice-house?' I said, without thinking. I had done it again – been so struck by the way in which the past suddenly veered close that I had almost given myself away. Fortunately, it wouldn't have occurred to Bertie in a thousand years that I was hiding any secrets.

'How clever you are to guess,' he said. 'We *do* have an ice-house. Not that it's been used in half a century. I don't go up so far any more. The ground is much too uneven for a blind old duffer like me. But I suppose I can take you there, if you would really like to see it. I must tell you that we can't look inside. It's locked up now, has been for years and years. Lord knows where the key is.'

'Oh, no, we needn't go,' I said quickly. I told myself I was refusing for the sake of Bertie's eyesight; in fact, I suddenly didn't relish the idea of him leading me up there, the thought of it making me oddly uneasy.

'I say,' he said, after a moment's thought, 'shall we go and look at the maze instead?'

If you hadn't known it was a maze, you might have assumed it was an enormous bank of hedge separating two sections of garden, like the yew. Inside, however, perhaps due to lack of sunlight, it was not as overgrown as I had expected. Although paths once laid with gravel were now carpeted with thick springy moss and considerably narrower than my grandmother had described, they were still passable. At the top, where the sun had been able to do its work, the foliage grew wild and unchecked. In many places it met in the middle, forming a series of almost enclosed passages in every shade of green, from the chartreuse of the backlit leaves overhead to the soft forest green of the moss-sown ground.

Bertie turned to check that I was still behind him, his face rather ghoulish in the strange, close air. It smelt musty as we worked our way into the maze's depths, like a damp old cellar.

'It's so deuced dark in here,' said Bertie, rather shakily. 'I haven't come this far in ages.'

'You do know the way out, I suppose?' I said lightly.

He laughed nervously. 'What is it they say – keep the wall on your right shoulder? I never understood that. Surely the walls are on both sides in a maze. Otherwise it's just a hedge.'

I didn't really mind that we were, for the time being, trapped in the puzzle. It was a relief to be out from under the hard white sky, the green light inside the maze as restful as the cool waters of a woodland brook.

'You mentioned a Miss Jenner last night,' I said, after a time. I was walking ahead of Bertie and it took me a moment to realize that he'd stopped. I looked back at him. 'Are you all right? Do you need to rest?' We had passed a stone seat a minute earlier, tucked into a cleft in the thick foliage.

He smiled sadly. 'No, no. It was just what you said about

Miss Jenner. To hear that name is an experience I'd almost forgotten. It went with my boyhood. When you said it then, the whole came back as a picture far more vivid than anything I will ever see again. Not just her but the house as it was, and all the people who were here then. They are gone now, most of them, and yet they remain so deeply familiar that, if you could only commit to paper the pictures in your mind – and, of course, I have no such ability – you might render them with total accuracy, down to the last freckle, the last eyelash.'

He looked up at me, his eyes slightly unfocused. 'I think I will have a little rest, if you don't mind terribly. Can you remember where that seat was?'

We found it easily enough. Both of us sat down, the seat's narrow dimensions forcing us closer than virtual strangers would choose to be. Not that he felt like a stranger. He smelt of pencil shavings and soap and unwashed hair, which I suspected had little altered since the summer he had met Miss Jenner.

'I liked her immediately,' he said, after a while. 'She was a tiny thing, at least a head shorter than you, and had large grey eyes. Grave eyes, was how I thought of them. What colour are yours?' He peered at me and I fought the urge to look away because mine were grey like hers. 'Are they green?'

I nodded. He had forgotten that everything had a green tinge inside the maze. I hoped it dulled my hair, too, like an old penny.

'She wasn't governess to me, of course,' he continued, 'only to my sisters. How envious I was of them! I couldn't wait to return from school and see her.'

'Why did you like her so much?'

'She was kind to me, and patient. My father was always kind in a distracted sort of way but I think he only really had eyes for Helen. She was clever, bookish like him. Victoria, of course, was the apple of Mama's eye, and very amusing. I – well, I was just sort of there. My own fault, of course. Nothing much about me.'

'I wouldn't say that at all.'

He turned to me and smiled. 'Ah, you are kind, just as Miss Jenner was. Lucas is fortunate to have you to take care of him. It's true, though, you see. I was the only son and heir and I even mucked that up. Never married – could never imagine marrying, really. I always understood romantic love as something pure and quiet, done from a distance.'

'Like a knight of old.'

'Yes. Although a knight without any of the terrifying quests and dragon-slaying. A knight who stayed at home, in his garden.'

'Did you love Miss Jenner a little?'

'Oh, yes. She was wonderful. After she left, things were different. Perhaps it was coincidence or I am recalling it wrongly but, to my mind, it all somewhat . . . dimmed after that. My father seemed to be at home more, and that was an improvement, but Mama . . . Well, I suppose there must have been some unhappiness before. She had always had her little moods and obsessions, of course, but they passed soon enough, like sudden spells of bad weather. Not after that summer, though – after that she hardly left her rooms. Of course, that was to do with my uncle, too, there's no denying that . . . Anyway, for me, the pure, uncomplicated happiness you can only feel as a child went with Miss Jenner.

'It was around this time of the year when she left.

Everything overblown and dying on the stem, the summer retreating. I've never liked autumn since. The colours that everyone raves about – the leaves turning on the trees and all that – all they do is remind me of her hair. She never said goodbye, you know. I cried about that, in secret. My father was upset, too, not that he would have admitted as much to me, of course.'

I frowned. 'Your father was upset about what?'

'About not being able to say goodbye to her. I think he was away when it happened, and by the time he got back, she had gone. It was me who told him and he went quite still. It struck me because he looked precisely as I felt.'

Bertie's hands were tightly clasped in his lap. He released them and let out a long sigh. 'What a lot of time has gone by and yet it's all so sharp, so fresh.'

I didn't press him any further. Instead, I helped him gently to his feet and, after a couple of turns, we found our way out of the maze quite easily, perhaps because we weren't trying to. After its sepulchral light, we had to shade our eyes against the harsh glare of the day. Walking back towards the house, I was glad of the silence between us. My mind was going over what Bertie had said about my grandmother's leaving, and how her own account of the same events seemed off-kilter again.

I glanced at him but he was lost to his memories. How was it that she'd neglected to say goodbye to someone she had apparently been so fond of? As she had told it to me, her departure had been quite the event – the entire household gathered on the drive to wave her and my grandfather off to their new life together. What Bertie had told me sounded altogether more muted.

As for her employer's reaction to her departure, I wasn't sure what to make of it. But, then, she hadn't been there long – only a single summer, really – so perhaps he was put out that he would have to advertise for a governess again. That seemed reasonable enough and yet it didn't quite convince me as an explanation. Perhaps in my next letter I would ask her.

The Fenix House stories had never been a single tale that progressed in linear fashion. Instead my grandmother had hopped back and forth in time, alighting upon bright little vignettes, like a magpie lured from the sky by the glint of tin – all of them chosen, or so I thought, for my entertainment.

Since my own arrival at the house that had loomed so large in childhood, I was beginning to see that the world I'd thought I'd known so intimately was not as complete as I'd believed it. The absence of Mr Pembridge and the mistress – as well as the army-officer uncle – seemed a little odd. Though perhaps it was understandable: any little girl would have been more interested in hearing about the children of the household and, besides, my grandmother wouldn't have wanted to keep reminding me that I was now lacking my own mother and father. But then there was the house, which was not quite what I'd expected – sad and diminished as it was – and the curious fib about the pink and cream bedroom.

The gap between reality and what had been so alive in my head yawned a little more. I suppose I was still feeling a bit homesick and disorientated, and therefore inclined to be a touch dramatic, but I felt those alterations and adjustments as a loss, even a strange sort of grief.

Twelve

Harriet

Sitting on the top step outside Fenix House's front door, Harriet attempted to compose herself. When her breathing had finally slowed, she allowed her mind's eye another glimpse of the girlish Louisa in her pretty bonnet, her face turning to the brother beside her in the carriage. She could recall little about the younger brother, Jago, beyond his fair hair, which was somewhat darker than his sister's and closer to the colour of honey. More than that, she hardly knew. She had been too busy watching Louisa. That the girl, now a grown woman, might be in the same house as Harriet was almost too much to comprehend.

She stared at the view before her: the curve of the carriage sweep, like a stretch of shingle beach, the sea a profusion of blue phlox. A dense thicket of azaleas separated the drive from the terraced garden, promising a spectacular show soon. Beyond and above them, further up the hillside, there were parcels of flawless lawn, glimpses of garden buildings freshly painted in green and white and, distantly, the pale brushstrokes of the silver birches that hid the ice-house. If she had chosen to look even higher, she would have been able to make out, where trees and shrubbery were finally exhausted, the jutting and jagged facets of limestone cliffs.

In fact, she was blind to it all, trying to recall if there had been any sign, any glimmer of the coincidence that had been about to bludgeon her. Perhaps there had been, she reflected. It was just that her memory of Louisa Dauncey was so well-worn that she would likely have missed any premonition. She had thought of that cream and blonde girl with the china-blue eyes so many times that she needed only a flash of the whole to dredge it up again with all its original intensity of feeling. The carriage, the tumult of the street around her, even Jago – all had narrowed and dimmed over the years until the only thing she saw clearly was Louisa's face. It was then that the fury would gather in her, and it was not spitting red and fiery but dull violet and pewter, like fresh bruises or the Thames in a storm. It made her narrow frame shake.

Although the sun was attempting to burn off the band of cloud that had wrapped itself around the hill, the wind had grown even colder since her tour of the garden with young Bertie. Its dank fingers brushed the back of her neck and chilled her bones until she was roused from her thoughts. She stood and shook out her sober skirts, stamping her small feet to get the blood running into them again. If she didn't go in soon, Mrs Rakes would come looking for her and demand further explanation. Harriet had seen the questions in the housekeeper's eyes and wasn't yet ready to answer them.

As she turned the brass knob and closed the front door softly behind her, an image of her father came into her mind so vividly that it felt like a blow. The last of her anger leaked away and she found she had to press her fingers to her eyes so that a sudden welling of tears did not overflow them.

In the memory, she and her father were in Devon, where they had gone to stay for a few weeks in early summer. They were on their way to visit a clifftop ruin and he was sitting in the carriage next to her, laughing heartily at something she had said. The tableau resembled that of Louisa and her brother, except that in this instance she had been a participant, not an unseen observer seething with anger and resentment on the road below.

Though bodily she stood in the silent hallway of Fenix House, she was in her mind entirely ignorant of it. Instead she saw an overarching Devon sky of periwinkle blue and, beneath it, hedgerows of hawthorn, with cow parsley and red campion. They grew in such profusion and were so tall that she hadn't been able to see over them to the sea, which she had been able to smell. The scent was silvery fish and dark blue and salt to her, but her father had told her it was ozone. That holiday had been the last they had taken before everything changed – the last before Harriet had felt something as dense and as poisonous as lead enter her soul whenever she thought of Louisa. From that moment on, as far as Harriet was concerned, Louisa was to blame for everything.

Twelve years after she'd seen Louisa in that carriage, Harriet's resentment hadn't dissipated, only wormed its way deeper within her. Now, finding herself within the walls of Fenix House, she felt it stir again. It was one thing to understand that no one for many miles knew much about her, or cared to, quite another to realize that someone did know her, but could not remember her because she did not signify and never had. It was a bleak thought and might have undone her, had another realization not pierced her more sharply than the first, like a pin through the soft pad of a fingertip.

It was unnerving that the glimmers had neglected to warn her about this momentous reunion, but no matter: it was sign enough that she had stumbled upon Louisa Dauncey at all. Encountering the same woman after so many years, not a face glimpsed in the street or in a better seat at the theatre, but lying dishevelled in her own rooms, surely marked a change in Harriet's fortunes. What else could such an unsettling coincidence mean? That was when the word lit up in her mind, the letters an arrangement of thorns. Revenge. Surely that was what had brought her to Fenix House. What form it might take was still murky and undefined but she was confident: something would make itself known to her.

This conviction galvanized and fortified Harriet as nothing had since her father's death. Catching sight of herself in a mirror as she made her way to the nursery, she saw that her grey eyes glittered with secret purpose. She allowed herself a smile and was pleased at the effect against the backdrop of rich wallpaper and dark wood. Her teeth glowed palely and two spots of warm colour stained her cheeks as if she'd just pinched them.

On entering the stifling nursery, she found Helen and Victoria lolling lethargically on the hearthrug once more, the latter idly poking at a doll's eyes with what looked like a miniature dagger, the blade flashing in the firelight. Looking about her, and taking in the sticky remains of breakfast on the table, dolls' clothes, Helen's discarded violin and two half-made beds, Harriet felt again the new purposefulness rushing through her veins. She bent and took the little knife from Victoria, retrieved its decorated sheath from the floor, and stowed them in the pocket of her skirt. Before the little girl could protest, she clapped her hands. 'This room will not do for lessons,' she exclaimed. 'We will have to find you another or you will not learn a thing.'

Neither girl seemed able to muster a reply. She left the room and descended the two flights of stairs to the servants' quarters. In the parlour, Mrs Rakes looked up from a bound ledger in which she was entering a column of tiny, meticulous figures in black ink.

'Are you feeling better now, Miss Jenner?'

'Oh, yes, I am quite recovered, thank you,' Harriet heard herself say, in clear, determined tones. She hurried on, keen that Mrs Rakes shouldn't raise the subject of the mistress again. 'But the nursery will not do, I'm afraid – not for lessons.'

'Oh?' Mrs Rakes put down her pen.

'I wondered if there was a spare bedroom or some other little-used room downstairs we might move to.'

The housekeeper seemed puzzled rather than outraged. 'The nursery is quite a large room. There is a table and –'

'It is not the size of the room but that it is where the girls sleep and eat and have their leisure. They are up there now, half asleep in front of the fire. There is no fresh air within, and little natural light as the window faces the hill. Unfortunately, it is not conducive to learning.' She came to an abrupt halt.

'I see,' said Mrs Rakes. 'Well, I suppose the morning room might do. It is never used as it was intended. The mistress is usually indisposed until noon and prefers her own rooms, as you have already seen for yourself.'

'It sounds ideal. I will supervise the rearrangement of the furniture, of course. I presume there is already a desk there for writing letters. That will do for me but the girls will –'

'Miss Jenner, I think you forget yourself.' She smiled kindly to soften the reprimand. 'Now, before we run away with ourselves, I must tell you that I cannot possibly allow rooms to be moved about without speaking first to the mistress and possibly Mr Pembridge too.'

Harriet coloured, though the reminder of her place had been gentle enough. She tried again, more deferentially this time, though it didn't come naturally to her. 'Might you give your permission, Mrs Rakes, as housekeeper? The mistress has returned to bed and Mr Pembridge, as I understood it, will not return until later. I should hate to waste a whole day . . .' She tailed off.

By the time the long-case clock in the hall had roused itself to strike two, Helen and Victoria were quietly occupied in the morning room: Helen writing an account of a trip to Gloucester Cathedral so Harriet could determine her grasp of spelling and grammar, and Victoria drawing a picture of her greatest desire, which was not a doll or a dress but a large, savage dog. As the room was south-facing (the sheer wall of rock to the east precluding true morning sun anywhere in the house), a great deal of light now poured in through the window behind the desk Harriet was now sitting at.

She felt satisfied with the results of her efforts as she observed the two heads bent over their books – one fair, one dark, the sun bestowing a halo on each. The bitterness that had risen in her like acid was temporarily quelled and channelled. Her conviction that she now understood her purpose at Fenix House was fortifying. For too long she had felt herself to be wearing a heavy, dun-coloured cloak, which was not only her grief but a self-pity that didn't suit her natural propensity to high spirits and optimism. It was a great relief to shrug it off and know herself once again. She would no longer be a pathetic, friendless creature but her father's avenging angel.

Helen's head snapping up brought Harriet back to the morning room and her official role as governess. Victoria, whose concentration for the previous ten minutes was unprecedented and therefore unsettling to her, was glad of the interruption.

'What is it, Helen?' said Harriet.

'I thought I heard the gate. Papa is coming back this afternoon.' She cocked her head to listen again.

When the front door was opened, then carefully closed, Harriet didn't have the heart to keep Helen from rushing to the door and calling into the hall, her small sister on her heels. Harriet followed and was just in time to see a large bear of a man emerge from the shadows. His thatch of thick hair and hazel eyes recalled Helen's, the skin around the latter creased as though he smiled often, which in fact he did. Mary, who had arrived at the door too late to intercept her master, heaved up the large bag that had been left there and made for the stairs.

'Thank you, Mary, and it is Miss Jenner, is it not?' Mr Pembridge said, as he moved forward, his voice rich and sonorous. He followed his daughters back into the sun-streaked morning room and stopped when he saw how it had changed. He seemed to fill the room, which suddenly appeared smaller. 'Good Lord, you've only been here five minutes and already the house is turned upside-down.'

Harriet's nerve briefly deserted her. 'Well, of course it can all be put back. It's just that I thought your daughters would benefit –'

'No, I like it!' he interrupted. 'My wife never uses it and it's a pretty room. Why shouldn't my daughters have use of it?'

Helen, who had attached herself to him, smiled up at him as he stroked her hair, smoothing down the wayward tendrils that had escaped her plait.

'And what do you think of this pair, then?' he said, as he held out his free hand to Victoria, who pranced over to embrace him about the legs, her tiny elbow finding its way into Helen's side. 'One the image of her mother and the other just like me.' Helen beamed at the last.

'They seem very nice girls,' said Harriet, carefully.

'Is that all? Come, Miss Jenner. They are a little more interesting than nice, I hope.'

'I prefer not to judge anyone I meet so quickly, sir,' she said. 'You will have to ask me again in a week.'

Fortunately he laughed at her pert remark, which had slipped out before she could stop it. 'Very good. I'm glad to have you with us, Miss Jenner.'

'Thank you, sir.' It occurred to Harriet that she would only come up to his watch pocket, were she to stand so close to him. As she was thinking this, he looked into her eyes with an intensity that momentarily convinced her he could read her mind. Colouring, she glanced down, flustered, and pretended renewed interest in the girls who were still hanging off him.

Helen was gazing upwards, a beatific smile making her lovelier than Harriet would have thought possible, but Victoria was watching her new governess with a disconcerting expression. Harriet knew the little girl had noticed the blood rising in her governess's cheeks. Mr Pembridge saved her by disentangling himself and walking over to the window. She could see russet embers in his hair and neat beard as they were caught by the sun. He moved in a very careful way, she thought, as though he felt he should compensate for his size. The way he walked and turned and ran his huge hand along the windowsill – all of it was executed with a surprising grace and deliberation.

'Where was your previous situation?' he said over his shoulder. 'I seem to remember something about London.'

Harriet wondered if her inexperience would count against her and if she therefore dared lie. But his face was so kind and open that she did not want to. She did, however, wish that Victoria was not there to hear her answer. As if he had read her thoughts again, he turned to Helen.

'My love, take your sister and go downstairs. Tell Mrs Rollright I am quite famished and have been thinking about eating a slice of her game pie since we passed Stroud.'

Helen, loath to leave her beloved father, glanced at the bell pull, which might have summoned Agnes or Mary, but then, with only a small sigh, she grasped Victoria's hand and dragged her out.

When she was sure they had gone, Harriet cleared her throat. 'In answer to your question, Mr Pembridge, this is in fact my first situation as a governess. But I was well taught myself, first by my own governess and, later, by my father.'

He nodded and she knew he had gleaned something of her reduced circumstances. 'And your father now?' He let the question hang.

'Dead, sir.' She said it baldly because it was quicker and cleaner, like a slammed door wrenching out an agonizing tooth. Again, he seemed to understand her implicitly: that she was not being callous, that her manner served to hide what was the very opposite, and he nodded gravely.

'Do you have any other family?' His voice was gentle.

She shook her head. 'None who are close. My mother died giving birth to me and I was her first. There are a couple of elderly cousins on my father's side and I have been staying with them these last months. They were very kind to me but we hardly knew each other. I couldn't impose on them any longer. I knew I must make my own way and that is why I am here.'

'You must be very brave, Miss Jenner. I have a large family – not just those you have met in this house but a sprawling collection of aunts and nephews and second cousins, and I can't imagine how it would be not to have them. How it would feel to wake each morning and know yourself to be alone in the world.'

Harriet looked down at her little boots and made herself count the buttons the leather laces were tightly looped through, up and down. It would be terrible if she wept in front of him. Her silence made him realize what he had said.

'Forgive me, I am putting this badly. What I am trying to say so inelegantly is that you are not alone now. You are here at Fenix House with us. I like to think we are not servants and masters here so much as a large family. Of course, Mrs Pembridge finds me rather eccentric in thinking such a thing.' He chuckled.

Harriet, for whom another wave of tears threatened after hearing his kind words, could manage only a weak smile in return. 'Thank you. It is very good of you to say so. I have always thought of governesses as being somewhere in between, neither fish nor fowl. Higher than the servants, perhaps, but lower than the family. My own governess, Miss Harrison, whom I remember quite fondly, was nevertheless a remote sort of person. Perhaps I understand better now why she was like that.'

'Well, I hope you will not be remote with us. Helen, I think, has warmed to you already. She is a child who opens like a flower when shown some interest and affection.'

'That was plain to see just now, when you came in.'

'She and her mother are not so easy with each other as she and I are. If she was to get some approbation from another woman – from yourself – I think she would come on very well. Victoria, on the other hand, has quite a different temperament.'

Harriet glanced up and saw that a smile was playing about his mouth, as though he was trying to hold back his amusement. 'Yes,' she said, forgetting herself once more. 'Despite her tender years, she is probably less in need than her sister of my – or anyone's – approbation.'

To her relief, he only laughed. 'Indeed. Vicky is well named. She is Fenix House's own little empress and never mind that she is only six.'

A soft knock at the door made Harriet realize how long they had been talking, alone, in the peaceful, light-steeped room. It was Mary with a tray. Helen was behind her, craning to check that her father hadn't vanished again. Victoria had presumably made good her escape from any further lessons.

'Will you take it in here, sir, or would you prefer the study?' said Mary.

'The study, if you please. I must not keep Miss Jenner another moment. Helen, where is your sister? Run and find her and tell her the school day is not yet over.'

Before he went from the room, he paused. Mary had gone ahead to the study and they were alone again. He seemed for the first time to be at a loss for words and instead looked thoroughly at her for a long moment. Harriet, her mind made blank by this scrutiny, stared back. Eventually he seemed to rouse himself and left without another word or even a smile.

After he'd closed the door behind him, with such care that she barely heard the mechanism click, Harriet took a deep breath and turned back to her desk to await her charges. As she did so, she caught sight of herself in the mirror above the mantel. To her dismay, her hair had worked itself loose from its pins, and was in the process of unwinding down her back. In the sunlight it gleamed as though polished, rosy sparks among the gold. Her heart thumping with embarrassment that not only Mr Pembridge had seen her in such disarray but Mary too, she twisted and pinned it so tightly that it hurt her scalp.

'Oh, what does it matter?' she muttered, to reassure herself. 'It was only my hair come down.'

She stopped and met her eyes in the glass again. To someone who could not read her thoughts, they were without guile. She tried to push the notion away but, having admitted it, she could not now banish it.

She saw him again at the door, looking back at her before he left. Had she imagined it? No, she did not think she had. He had been . . . yes, distracted. She told herself its cause had likely been something else: he had remembered a task he must do, perhaps; he was tired from his journey; he was thinking that he had not yet gone up to greet his wife. But she did not believe it was any of those things, not really. What had distracted him was her.

Thirteen

Bertie returned from school about an hour after Harriet had released Helen and Victoria from their first day of lessons in the converted morning room. She had remained there by herself, reading a couple of chapters of a new novel and thinking again about what had passed between herself and Robert Pembridge. In truth, she had found it difficult to concentrate on her book, and had needed to read each page twice, her thoughts persistently drifting back to her employer. In the end, she gave up and was just passing the front door on her way to the stairs when Bertie burst through it, his cap askew and his cheeks pink.

'Oh, Miss Jenner!' he cried, his cheeks reddening with pleasure. 'This afternoon I had a horrible feeling that I had imagined you. I grew so convinced of it that I couldn't cogitate my Latin verbs and Sir threatened to birch me.'

'Fear not,' Harriet said, with a smile. 'I don't appear to have vanished into thin air yet.'

He shook his head in wonder. 'I can't tell you what a relief it is.' That settled, he peered over towards the coat-stand. 'Is my father back?'

'Yes, a couple of hours ago. I believe he is in his study.'

The boy started to leave her, then hesitated, a frown of indecision creasing his narrow brow.

'Why don't you go and look in on him now and then

you can show me the rest of the garden, as we discussed this morning?' she said soothingly.

His face cleared. 'Oh, you remember! Yes, I'll go to him immediately. I'll meet you back here in three minutes' time. Is that acceptable?'

She put on a grave expression. 'I think it will have to be four minutes. I must go and change my shoes.'

He nodded thoughtfully and consulted the long-case clock. 'Yes, I think that might make it closer to four. Then, let us say adee . . . adoo . . .'

'Adieu?'

'Yes! Let us say . . . that, until thirty-seven minutes past the hour.'

He waited for her nod of assent, then trotted off in the direction of the study, whistling as he went.

After the conclusion of the second part of the garden tour, at least half of which was spent in the maze, a horticultural puzzle Bertie admitted he simply couldn't solve, Harriet sent him up to the nursery and took herself downstairs to the servants' quarters. She hoped to catch Mrs Rakes alone so she could see whether the housekeeper would make any comment about her possible acquaintance with the mistress in London. If she did, Harriet was hoping to pass it off as a case of mistaken identity.

Once that was done, she thought it would probably be time to supervise the children's supper in the nursery. After that she would be released from her duties. Although she had accomplished much in a single day, which still gave her some lingering satisfaction, she couldn't help thinking of her own room and solitude with longing. She had come to understand since her father's death that loneliness was not just the preserve of those by themselves. It could be felt even more keenly in the company of others – especially if those others were elderly cousins, or socially above you, or below you, or small children.

Mrs Rakes was in the kitchen with Mrs Rollright, who broke off talking when Harriet appeared at the door. 'Miss Jenner.' She nodded, and Harriet wondered whether she had said it to warn the housekeeper of her presence.

Before she had had a chance to read the two women's faces, Agnes bustled in carrying a tray piled with dirty plates and cups. She looked so altered that Harriet couldn't help but stare at her.

'I didn't recognize you then, Agnes, with that smile on your face,' remarked Mrs Rollright, who had also noted the change in the maid's countenance. 'If you've found another crown down the back of the mistress's chaise, you'd better hand it over to Mrs Rakes.'

'It's not that,' said Agnes, scornfully, her smile briefly slipping. 'Her brother's coming. Captain Dauncey. *Jago*. He's due in three weeks. She's just had a letter from him.'

Mrs Rollright sighed profoundly. 'And he'll be wanting all his usual favourites, I suppose. That man eats enough for four and none of it the cheap stuff. Do you remember he ate an entire Charlotte Russe the last time he graced us with his presence? No wonder he's running to fat, these days, and him a soldiering man, too. Them Indians could mutiny all they fancied with the likes of him in charge. He wouldn't be able to catch 'em.'

Agnes gave her a pointed look as she went through to the scullery.

'Oh, I know I can't talk,' said the cook, her hands smoothing her apron over the mound of her stomach. 'But I don't pretend to be no army officer either.'

'The mistress hasn't mentioned anything to me about Captain Dauncey coming,' said Mrs Rakes, with a frown.

'Well, how could she?' said Agnes, through the propped-open doorway of the scullery, where she had begun scouring an enormous pile of copper pans. 'I said – she's only just had the letter. His ship's docked at Southampton but he says he's going to London on some business or other first.'

'The mistress is delighted, no doubt,' said Mrs Roll-right. 'The only time she smiles is when he's here. Well, I shall have to begin a list of what we'll need. I won't be caught unawares – not like last time. Pigeons in jelly he wanted at the drop of a hat one day. Oh, and a syrup sponge to follow, if you please. I ask you!'

While this was going on, Harriet had been battling to keep her face expressionless. She had seen Mrs Rakes's eyes flick over her when Agnes mentioned the Dauncey name, but she had managed not to so much as blink. Inside, though, her mind was busy. Another of them was coming to Fenix House.

She went back upstairs without a word to Mrs Rakes and, not wishing to be intercepted by one of the children just yet, slipped out of the parlour's French windows and into the garden again. There were plenty of nooks in which she could hide herself and, thanks to Bertie's thorough tour, she now knew where they were.

After considering the miniature eye-catcher just above the rockery, she made instead for the maze, judging it the least likely place she would be disturbed. There was a small stone bench about halfway in and, finding it easily enough, she sat down to think about what she had just learned.

She had not expected Jago Dauncey to come. There was no reason why he wouldn't, she saw now, but the vast oceans and tracts of foreign soil between Gloucestershire and India had seemed enough to preclude the possibility. She knew his arrival would put a different complexion on matters; she just couldn't guess how. Her fixation – almost a monomania – was with Louisa. Josiah, their father, she had thought might be dead by now and, indeed, Bertie had confirmed this only half an hour before, when he had mentioned in passing his London grandfather and used the past tense. *Good*, Harriet had thought, little knowing that she would soon be hearing of the brother's imminent arrival.

In a literal sense, Jago was nothing more to her than a gleam of fair hair crowning a large head as it turned away in a carriage, and an already-strapping silhouette, framed in the lit window of a red-brick house on a freezing night. The object of her hatred was Louisa, but he was still a Dauncey, and that hardly endeared him to Harriet. Even so, she couldn't understand why Agnes's announcement had made her blood run cold.

Perhaps it was simply a matter of numbers. She had pitted herself against a single foe – a foe she had hated for years because she had so carelessly, frivolously, altered the Jenner fortunes – but now there would be two. It was more than that, though. When Agnes had said Jago would be there in just a few weeks, she had experienced the strange sensations that generally heralded a glimmer: a clamping and fizzing at her temples, and a crawling, creeping feeling up her legs. She closed her eyes and pressed her fingers into the sockets until she saw fireworks of orange and scarlet. Oddly, she thought she heard them, too: a series of explosions.

A picture flashed across her mind, so fast that she couldn't latch on to it. All she was left with was the feeling it evoked. It wasn't simply pain or anger, although both emotions were part of the whole. She closed her eyes again but saw nothing except the frozen ground under her ten-year-old feet in the garden of the Daunceys' Hampstead house. She finally comprehended the emotion she was trying to identify, the answer tumbling into her mind as clearly as if it had been written out in the Daunceys' frost-silvered grass that day. It was shame.

There, in the silken and shadowy air of the maze, she realized how cold she had grown. The chill of the stone seat had penetrated her skirts, and her fingers when she flexed them felt stiff. In her hurry to find the way out, she took a wrong turn and experienced the momentary panic of the lost, the maze's green walls rising up on either side of her, identical and indifferent to her confusion. Then, quite suddenly, she saw the way out and rushed towards it, grateful to be back in the mild spring sunshine.

Fourteen

One evening, a couple of weeks later, after the children had gone to sleep, Harriet shifted uncomfortably on the bed where she had perched herself. A thin bolster was doing a paltry job of cushioning her back from the wall she rested against. In her lap was a pile of mending the mistress had expressly asked Mrs Rakes to give her – all of it clothing that belonged to the careless Victoria, who had somehow managed to wrench off lace trimmings, pull down hems and wear holes in new woollen stockings. Harriet hadn't yet begun on it and it was already past eight. Letting her head fall back against the wall, she closed her eyes. The cool smoothness of the limewashed plaster was surprisingly soothing, clearing the headache that had descended during a noisy suppertime in the nursery.

She had risen at seven that morning, just as she had done every morning since arriving at Fenix House, and not a single minute since had been her own. During the long hours of the day, when she was either teaching, supervising meals or averting quarrels, she thought of her small room in the eaves as a sanctuary to which she could hardly wait to retreat. What she always forgot when she looked at the clock and calculated how many hours she had yet to wade through was that time alone with her thoughts brought its own troubles.

Instead of enjoying the quietude of the neat room she

had pictured all day – the glow of a single candle, a benign moon peeping in at the window, herself peacefully reading – she was usually too overcome by her own anxious thoughts to do much more than undress, pull the blanket over herself and hope that sleep came quickly. For it was when she was by herself at night that the fears that always lurked in the corners of her mind crept out of the shadows to dance, large and lurid.

Despite Mr Pembridge's kind words that first day in the morning room, Harriet knew that she was alone, truly and profoundly alone, in the world. It was this cold certainty that waited for her in her room each evening. Though her grief for her father seemed fathomless, it was also poignant, a blanket she could draw around herself and be briefly lost in. The past, however pale and insubstantial mere memory rendered it, was a place of comfort compared to the future, which promised nothing but unending days of the same. And beyond that, when old age encroached and she could no longer work . . . Well, Harriet could not think that far ahead and hope to keep her sanity.

The mending still untouched, she did what she had lately taken to doing whenever fear threatened to undo her. She played again in her mind that scene in the morning room. Not the kindness he'd shown her, though that was comforting, but the crackle of something like recognition between them. There had been no pity or charity in it, and it had made her feel more like her old self than anything had in a long time.

Frustratingly, she had barely glimpsed him since, which she knew was not just unlucky circumstance but evidence that he had not sought her out. His interest had certainly been lit that day, but the oxygen of further meetings was never generated and she was worried that those first tentative flames had been snuffed out. Some nights, when the household slumbered, he seemed so remote that it was a shock to remember his person lay somewhere in the house below her. The previous night she had even held her breath to see if she could detect his, deep and regular, and probably quite untroubled by dreams of her. Of course, that had been nothing but foolish fancy: she could hear nothing of the kind, only the scratch and rustle of mice in the walls and, from somewhere in the black depths of the woods behind the house, the melancholy hooting of an owl.

She wondered now whether she dared give up the mending and simply go to bed, but then a smart little rap sounded on the door. It was surely Mary: only her light step on the bare boards would have gone undetected. As she opened it to see she was right, Harriet's heart began to thud. She knew instinctively that this wouldn't be some trifling message from Mrs Rakes.

'Mr Pembridge asks if he might see you in his study, miss,' the girl said. 'But only if you weren't otherwise occupied, he said.'

'Oh, no. I mean, there is the mending, of course, but I . . .' She forced herself to stop talking and took a breath. 'Thank you, Mary. I will go down directly.'

She had passed his study many times, and never without wondering what it was like inside. Along with his bedroom, which, as far as she could ascertain, he never shared with the mistress, it was the only part of the house that was presumably his alone, with none of the mistress's influence and taste inflicted upon it. She had no reason to pass his bedroom, tucked down its own narrow passage on the first floor, but she had to walk past the study daily on her way to the morning room.

As she knocked on the door, she wished she'd taken the time to check her reflection in the glass, not that she could do much to improve her severe dress or the decorous way her position forced her to wear her hair. She put her fingers to her cheeks to pinch some colour into them and found them already hot to the touch.

Instead of calling out for her to come in, as she'd expected, he answered the door himself, his face no more than a foot or two from hers.

'Miss Jenner,' he said. 'I hoped you would come.'

She blinked, unsure what to say. Of course she would come: he, her employer, had summoned her.

'Come in, come in,' he said, his eyes darting around the hall before he stepped back to let her pass. She felt the lightest touch on her shoulder as she did so, which made her cheeks burn even hotter.

He gestured for her to sit down opposite his enormous carved desk. She hadn't thought of it on the stairs but now she was gripped with fear that she had been found at fault. Perhaps it was the tiny dagger; perhaps they thought she'd stolen it. Her mind churned through what she would do, where she might go, if she was dismissed.

'Have I done something wrong, sir?' she said anxiously.

'Oh dear, no. Not at all,' he said. 'I'm sorry you might have thought that. Quite the opposite, in fact.'

She looked down at her lap, too proud to show him how she relieved she was.

'It's just that I've been meaning to speak to you ever since I saw you,' he continued. 'Saw you with Bertie, I mean.'

'We were not in the garden long,' she began, unable to let go of the notion that she was in trouble, and also remembering what the mistress had said. 'I know my responsibilities are not with him but with your daughters.'

'No, no, that is not what I meant. He came to see me and said he was about to show you the rest of the garden. I believe you'd already gone out that morning.'

'We didn't have time to see everything then.'

'He said how kind you'd been, how interested you seemed in what he had told you. His face was alive with pleasure at the thought of going back to you, and then I watched you both, from here. You talked so easily together, and he was so animated. He's a sensitive, solitary boy – almost unworldly – and I think he finds school difficult at times. He would prefer to be outside, and by himself, so it was a pleasure to see him enjoying another's company like that, and so naturally, too.

'I wanted to thank you for that, Miss Jenner, and I'm sorry it's taken me so long to do so. I have been distracted by my work with the GWR. There has been a great deal going on – a dispute between the patternmakers and the draughtsmen, the details of which I won't bore you with.'

Harriet didn't know what to say. The warmth in her cheeks had spread through her whole body at the thought of him watching her unobserved from his window.

Perhaps he gleaned something of this because he hurried on, his own colour deepening: 'I also wanted to say that I have had excellent reports of you from Mrs Rakes regarding my daughters – and from them, too, in fact.'

'From Victoria?' she asked, in genuine wonderment.

He leaned back in his chair and laughed. 'Yes, even from her. She was not as effusive as Helen in her praise, of course, but I know Vicky and she grudgingly approves of her new governess.'

'Well, I confess you have surprised me, Mr Pembridge. I hardly know what to say, though I am glad that you – and your children – approve.'

'Oh, we do,' he said, and gave her another of the intense looks he had imparted on her first day. It had the effect of pinning her to the back of her seat. 'Is there anything you need?' he said, after a pause in which Harriet had swallowed nervously.

'Need?' she echoed faintly. She would berate herself for sounding so idiotic later, though her employer didn't seem to mind. She had the curious feeling she could do and say little wrong in his eyes.

'Yes. Are you warm enough in the attic? Do you have sufficient … paper and books? Helen mentioned you borrowing one of mine, and of course you are welcome to borrow anything.' He gestured at the full shelves around them. 'Anything, Miss Jenner, truly.'

Harriet swallowed again. 'My room does very well, thank you. But … well, I would be glad to borrow a book, if you really don't mind. When I don't have mending to do, I like to read a chapter or two before bed but I didn't bring many books with me and –'

'Mending? Why are you mending? You are a governess, not a nursemaid.'

Harriet bit her lip. She didn't want to cause trouble. 'Oh, it's not much, just a few of Victoria's things . . . I don't mind.'

'I do, though. You should not be straining your eyes darning after a day in the schoolroom. I will talk to Mrs Rakes about this.'

'Oh dear, but I . . .'

He smiled. 'Mrs Rakes likes you quite as much as everyone else. There will be no resentment. Though, of course, if there ever is, from anyone, you must come to me.'

She nodded her thanks. 'Will that be all, sir?' She didn't want to go but, incapable as she seemed of intelligent conversation, she thought it would be better if she left him.

He sighed and stood. 'Yes, that was all. You may go now, Miss Jenner.'

'Thank you for what you said before,' she said falteringly. 'I am very grateful for it. And for the offer of the books.'

'And I for you,' she thought he said, but so softly that she couldn't be sure. She wondered if she dared ask him to repeat himself but he'd turned to one of the shelves.

'Try this one,' he said, pushing a slim volume into her hands. 'If you don't like it, feel free to come in here and exchange it for another.'

She didn't have time to look at its title because he was already holding open the door for her. As she ascended the stairs, she listened for the click of it closing but it never came. She was fairly certain that he was watching her go, just as he had watched her in the garden.

She waited until she'd reached the safety of her little

room before she looked at the book's title. She was hoping its selection might show some thoughtfulness: the Verne novel, perhaps, to show he'd remembered what Helen had no doubt told him. In fact, his choice was much more arresting. She opened it and turned to the flyleaf, unconvinced that the name on the spine wasn't deceiving her. But no, there it was again: *Jane Eyre*. Of all the books in that study, he'd chosen Charlotte Brontë's story about a friendless governess who marries her employer.

Heart thudding once more, she tried to turn the first page but realized it wasn't cut. None of them were. It was a new copy. Unless it had sat unread on his shelves, he had bought it for her. There was, of course, a chance that he didn't know what it was about, or perhaps only that it featured a governess, like her, but she didn't believe this, somehow. It was a message, and for that night, at least, she would not think about the differences between her Mr Pembridge and Jane's Mr Rochester – chief of which was that the former had a wife who, far from being locked in the attic, was very much the matriarch of the house.

Fifteen

Grace

On my second full day at Fenix House, I woke up on the wrong side of the bed. I still hadn't unpacked properly, and the truth was that I had long been accustomed to my grandmother doing everything for me. That was rather shameful and knowing it made me even crosser. I felt worse when I discovered that my new dark blue gabardine suit, the skirt of which was shorter than any I'd had before and came down only to my calves, was horribly creased. My grandmother had pressed it carefully before packing it and I should have hung it up immediately. I sat down on the bed, clutching it to me, and cried far harder than any amount of crumpled clothes warranted. I'd just blown my nose and taken a shaky breath when I noticed that she'd embroidered a cluster of tiny silver stars surrounding an ornate 'G' on the lapel of the jacket, and that reduced me to sobs again.

I presumed I was to continue taking my meals with the family in the dining room, so when my face was present-able again I went down to see if there was any breakfast to be had. Pembridge was hunting for something when I got there and didn't immediately see me come in. The table was littered with newspaper and crumbs but there was a solitary piece of cold toast left in the rack.

'Good morning,' I said, too softly. He didn't hear me but continued lifting up piles of papers and damp-spotted books that had been strewn across every available surface. It was a dreadful mess in the unforgiving early light.

I cleared my throat and tried again.

This time he jumped and spun round, face pale. 'Good grief, you scared the life out of me.'

To my annoyance, I couldn't meet his eye. 'I'm sorry, I did try twice, but you were so busy looking for something that I –'

'My uncle's damn spectacles. The man loses them a dozen times a day.' His complexion had regained its colour to such a degree that I wondered if he was embarrassed that I'd startled him. 'Perhaps if I refused to look for them every half-hour for him, he would take better care of them.'

I saw that he was also embarrassed because he'd been caught in an act of kindness towards his uncle. Instantly I felt less afraid of him. Perhaps all that barely contained wrath was bluster.

'Do help yourself to some breakfast,' he said. 'What there is of it. I'm afraid the days of silver tureens piled with scrambled egg and kippers are rather behind us. Shall I call Agnes?'

'Oh, no,' I said, keen not to make a fuss. 'Some toast will do nicely, thank you.'

I spread butter on the last slice, even though I hated cold toast. Biting into it and chewing made an awful din and I wished I was alone. Pembridge didn't seem to notice, though, too busy frowning at something in the middle distance.

'I – er – hope you had a decent night's sleep?' he finally said.

I hurried to swallow my mouthful and inhaled a crumb. To my mortification, I began to cough and splutter.

Pembridge poured a cup of stewed tea and pushed it towards me. I drank it in one gulp, though it was as stone-cold as the toast.

'I thought you were going to expire on me,' he said drily, when I'd recovered. 'I was wondering what on earth I'd tell your people.'

'Person,' I croaked.

'I beg your pardon?'

'I don't have people, only a person. My grandmother.'

He blinked. 'Oh, I see. And are you . . . fond of her?'

I smiled, despite my embarrassment. He had no small-talk at all. 'Yes, of course. She brought me up after my parents died.'

He nodded and then, apparently at a loss for anything else to say, went back to searching for Bertie's spectacles. A minute or so later, he strode out of the room without another word. It was only as I sat there in the silent dining room, trying to decide whether he had no manners or was simply awkward, that I realized he hadn't mentioned Lucas. I had a half-hearted look for him when I'd finished my paltry breakfast, even venturing down to the kitchen to ask Agnes, but there was no sign of him. Bertie, too, was conspicuous by his absence; Agnes said she'd seen him head off to the woods at the crack of dawn with his butterfly net and logbook.

I supposed I had the morning to myself again. Not wishing to return to my room, I wandered through the rather musty-smelling hall, pausing to wipe the dust from a couple of the pictures that hung there from sagging wires. One was a family portrait photograph typical of the Victorian era, with its exotic studio backdrop, potted aspidistra and soberly dressed subjects. Like the better parts of the house, they looked oddly like the people I had imagined from my grandmother's stories, from Helen's serious expression to Victoria's cherubic ringlets. Bertie had hardly changed. Mrs Pembridge was an older version of her youngest child, just as I'd pictured her, though I hadn't expected the petulant curl to her lip. Mr Pembridge's arm, which was draped around his wife's waist, looked wooden, as though the contact hadn't been a spontaneous gesture but a suggestion by the photographer.

I could have studied them all day but I drifted on, trying to guess what lay behind each of the closed doors. If I hadn't thought myself alone, I don't think it would have occurred to me to try one, but I did, and found myself choosing between the two doors at either side of the parlour.

The morning's sunshine had been replaced by a lowering sky that was leaking rain, like a dirty sponge. Bleary patches of coloured light that had filtered through the front door's stained glass now disappeared altogether. As the sound of the downpour strengthened into a solid hiss, the house seemed not only to darken but press in around me. A loud drip began to fall somewhere, as regular and insistent as a music room's metronome. I held my breath, and realized I was listening for the notes of a violin scale to ring out. It was that eerie notion that had me grasping the handle nearest to me. I suppose I wanted to make a noise of my own in the anticipatory quiet.

I knew there was a library of sorts somewhere close to the parlour and hoped I'd got the right door. It had served as a study in my grandmother's day. Perhaps I could go in and borrow a book; there wasn't much else I could do until the rain stopped or Pembridge returned and took me to meet my charge.

The room was dust-sheeted and almost entirely dark, with heavy curtains pulled closed to keep out the light. I had thought the rest of the house quiet until I stepped inside. It felt as though not a single particle of the air had been disturbed in decades and my intrusion had got the room's attention. My skin was already prickling when, faintly, I heard one of the servants' bells ring before it was cut off abruptly, as though a hand had reached up high on the wall in the servants' quarters to muffle it. My eyes now accustomed to the gloom, I could make out next to the fireplace the brass bell pull that would still be connected to the system. I had the strange feeling then that if I kept looking at it, it would begin to turn. Backing out of the room hurriedly, I closed the door with a bang.

Thankfully, the next door I tried was the right one: the large desk was dust-sheeted but the bookshelves that lined the room had been left uncovered. It didn't feel as unused as the last room but neither had it occurred to anyone, including Agnes, to venture inside with a feather duster for some time. I knew, even before I plucked a slim volume off one of the shelves at random, that every book in there would be seamed with dust and rippling with damp, and I was right.

Putting it back, unable to muster the inclination even to flick to the first chapter, I wandered over to the high windows, predictably smeared with dust. Rubbing a spot clear with my hand, I peered out. All trace of the morning's Indian summer had fled, the heavy skies now apparently resigned to autumn proper. A listless despondency curled around me. I'd always preferred the light and long evenings of the warmer months.

I looked again at the rows upon rows of old books, and didn't think I could rouse myself to find a single one I wanted to read. Frustrated, I had just decided I would go upstairs and write to my grandmother, saying I didn't much like it at Fenix House and would it be too defeatist if I came home, when I saw the picture in the shadows of the room's darkest corner. All my boredom and antagonism fell away. I knew instantly it must be of Mrs Pembridge. Not the mistress of my grandmother's time, but the late wife of David, mother to Lucas.

The portrait must have been six feet tall, presumably life-sized, and enclosed in an old-fashioned, rather fussy gilt frame. Like everything else, it was rimed in dust. Despite that, the woman in the painting looked somehow pure. Tall and lean, she was dressed in a crisp, high-necked white blouse and a skirt the same dark brown as her hair, which was pulled back off her face more severely than I ever wore mine. On her little finger, next to her wedding band, she wore a small opal ring, milky-blue with fiery sparks at the heart of it, rendered in the portrait by the finest brushstrokes of red and yellow. I went closer, drawn to her because she reminded me of someone I knew, and that was when I noticed the plate set into the gilt at the bottom of the frame: Francesca Pembridge, 1890–1918. I had been right.

Now that I was so close to her, she seemed to tower over me. Unlike those portraits beloved of ghost tales, where the subject's gaze seems to follow you about, it was impossible to catch Francesca's eye. Wherever I stood in relation to her, she looked over me, or somehow through me, like someone at a party watching the crowd over the shoulder of a crashing bore.

I looked at her for a long time, trying to establish precisely the sort of person she might have been. Her height and slightly narrow features might have made her haughty but I didn't think that was it. The word that eventually came to me was remote. Her smile was vague, her almost-black eyes trained on something in the distance; she seemed hardly aware that she was being painted.

It struck me then whom she looked like. I hadn't grasped it immediately because I had never seen him look anything other than irascible or confounded in the short time I'd known him. She reminded me of David Pembridge. It wasn't her features that were like his – grudgingly, I thought he was probably the more attractive of the pair – it was her colouring: like him her eyes were dark, her hair shone like polished wood and her skin would have looked sallow in winter but browned quickly under the sun. And they were both tall, of course – if the portrait was a true likeness, she must have been only a couple of inches shorter than him – and he was easily six feet. My eye strayed again to the neat letters and numbers on the small plate at the bottom of the picture. She had died in 1918, four years earlier, the same year the war ended.

It can be quite endearing when couples resemble each other, when it's a process that happens over decades of marriage, as though the years of intimacy – doing the same things, living in the same rooms, breathing the same air – gradually manifest themselves in physical similarities. There is another type, though: people who naturally prefer those like themselves out of self-regard, whose wives or husbands act as a mirror image. Pembridge struck me as just the sort of man to choose a wife who could pass as his sister.

I realized in the same moment that she was apparently everything I was not – tall, dark, aloof and mysterious – and felt oddly rattled. Then I remembered she was dead, and had probably died knowing she was leaving behind her small son, and felt guilt prick me in the empty study. Abandoning all pretence at borrowing a book, I hurried to the door without looking back, afraid I would finally meet her gaze and find it full of reproach.

I was just pulling the door shut behind me when Pembridge strode round the corner. He was intent on his own thoughts, eyes cast down to the grubby floor, and only noticed me when, in barging past, he brushed me with his arm. If I hadn't already shrunk towards the study door, he would probably have knocked me flying.

'Oh, it's you,' he said gruffly, his eyes coming back into focus. He passed his hand over his face, then seemed to see me properly. 'You've been in the study.'

'Yes, I –'

'No one goes in there now.'

'So it seems. It's very dusty. I'm sorry if I wasn't supposed to go in. It's just that I didn't have anything to do and –'

'I told you yesterday, my son simply wasn't up to meeting a stranger.'

With some effort, I tried a placating smile. 'It wasn't a criticism, just a statement of fact. I was looking for a book to read. I'm sorry if that room is out of bounds.'

'I didn't say it was, did I?'

He was much more contrary and argumentative than he had been earlier, and it was difficult not to make some equally irritable retort, employee or not. Instead, I couldn't help but let out a sharp little sigh, and looked down at my feet in case I was tempted to roll my eyes. When I glanced back up he was still staring at me intently. Determined not to keep looking away, like a simpering girl, I forced myself to hold his gaze, though my cheeks burned.

'So, did you find a book?' he said eventually, with a shrug so jerky it completely undermined the gesture.

That emboldened me and I held out my empty hands. 'Apparently not.'

He twisted his mouth into that peculiar smile of his. 'Nothing to your taste in there, I suppose. So what will you do now?'

'Well, perhaps Lucas and I might be introduced. Or is it still too soon?'

He hesitated, then sighed. 'Look, there are some matters I must deal with today, but I will take you to see him tomorrow. Will that do?'

I nodded. He still hadn't dropped his gaze.

Neither of us said anything for a long moment and I felt so awkward that I started to gabble. 'If the rain has stopped, I could amuse myself by going for a walk,' I began, my voice artificially bright. 'Perhaps you can recommend a pleasant one through the woods. I would ask your uncle but I haven't seen him all day and . . .' I came to a halt.

He raised a dark eyebrow. 'I wouldn't have had you down as a lover of the outdoors.'

'Oh? And what would you have had me down as?' It came out with more of an edge than I intended.

He shrugged again. 'Well, more of an indoors type, obviously. You know the kind of woman I mean: wanting a fire lit in June, not going out if it looks remotely damp. Happier curled up with one of those novels other women write – and you wouldn't have found any of those in the study, I'm afraid. Or other feminine interests: embroidery and ribbons and that sort of thing.'

'Goodness, I had no idea "ribbons" was a pursuit.' I knew I sounded rude but I was too irritated by his arrogance to care.

He smiled wryly. 'Women have made hobbies of less.'

'Surely you're forgetting those men who make a lifetime's work of collecting something very specific that's of no use to anyone.'

He moved fractionally closer to me and I realized, to my increased annoyance, that he was enjoying himself. 'Like my uncle and his butterfly spotting, you mean?'

'Oh, no. I meant . . . Well, I would never be rude about your uncle. He's such a dear man.' I couldn't meet Pembridge's eye any longer and dropped my gaze. 'Anyway, I can assure you I'm not remotely interested in ribbons.'

'Perhaps not. Well, there is a pleasant walk if, as it seems, I've misjudged you and you're not afraid of a spot of rain. It goes through the woods and past the quarry pool if you keep on for long enough. It's rather pretty up there.'

I took that as an olive branch and was so foolishly pleased about it that I didn't immediately absorb what he'd said. My grandmother had never mentioned any quarry pool, only the ruins and the Devil's Chimney that teetered over them. 'A quarry pool?' I said, rather late and much too sharply.

'We call it the Blue,' he said, in a soft tone that made him sound like a different person. 'You'll see why if you go there. My son christened it when he was tiny.'

I thought the 'we' probably didn't refer only to himself and Lucas, and felt the presence of the portrait in the room behind me as though it were a living creature.

'Before you go,' he called up the stairs as I began to climb them.

'Yes?'

He held out a letter. 'This came for you. From your *person*, I presume.'

'My person?'

'Your grandmother.'

Sixteen

In the event, I didn't go to look for the Blue that afternoon. The rain showed no sign of letting up and, determined as I was to prove Pembridge wrong about me and women in general, only a fool would have gone out in it. In fact, I realized with a reluctant twinge of amusement, going out in a heavy downpour was precisely the sort of thing a heroine in one of the romances he had referred to so disparagingly would do – a silly girl who would then have to be rescued and carried back dripping, head lolling prettily, before being tucked up in front of a roaring fire. Besides, I didn't have the boots for it and my outdoor shoes – intended for sedate walks on pavements or dry grass – would have been next to useless on the steep paths that led up into the dark woods, the summer-dry earth probably already turning to thick mud. Instead, I returned to my room and thought about the portrait.

She had died at the end of the war that Pembridge was the right age to have served in, though he didn't use any military rank now. Was the date significant? It seemed so, not least because Lucas must have lost his mother while his father was still away, or when he had only just returned. No wonder the boy seemed so troubled.

The war that would change so much for so many was remote to me. It had barely been allowed to encroach on my closeted existence in Clifton. My grandmother had made sure of that. I only realized afterwards what an achievement this was: one tiny woman, a miniature King Canute, who was almost able to hold back the tide of the Great War.

There were moments when it trickled in, of course – especially when one of her 'sad ladies' visited and I was banished to my room while she combed her mind for glimmers of the woman's soldier son, reported missing in the Flanders mud. Other than that, the war was mostly reduced to what I could glean from the relentlessly cheerful periodical posted to her each week from Cheltenham – the one that had eventually brought me to Fenix House. The war was like a difficult book I wouldn't have chosen to read, with too much complicated detail, no clear narrative arc, and only the bravery of the men and the grave, beautiful names – Mons, Neuve Chapelle and the tolling bell of the Somme – to love about it.

I was almost exactly eighteen and a half on Armistice Day. In terms of experience, and though my inner life was rich and full, I might as well have been thirteen or fourteen. I thought again about Lucas, who was only seven but who probably knew more about the consequences of war than I did. My mind drifted back to his father. He had no visible injuries but I had gleaned enough from the newspapers to understand that that meant little. Sometimes the damage to the mind was far more insidious. To have lost a wife so soon after didn't bear thinking about. I resolved that I would try to be less prickly with him when he took me to see Lucas, however awkward he made our exchanges, and despite my suspicion that he considered me rather silly.

My eye fell on the letter from my grandmother. Part of me wanted to rip it open and feel closer to home, but another didn't want to read it at all. I was worried it would set off my homesickness again, certainly, but there was something else in my reluctance. I traced my finger over the tiny, perfectly formed handwriting I would have known anywhere. She had practically exiled me, or so I felt in my more vulnerable moments, and now here she was already, asking to be let back in.

Of course I opened it in the end.

Dearest Grace,

It was all I could do not to sit down and write to you the minute you were out of my sight. In the event, I could wait only a few hours because already it is not the same without you. No, let me begin again, for I am not saying what I really feel. It is so hard not to retreat into meaningless platitudes in a letter.

Truly, I find myself lost without you, my darling granddaughter. The house is a silent tomb with only myself in it, the funereal mood only briefly lifting earlier when Mrs Spratt came in and began clattering about. Her noise will be a comfort to me now, and I think I will even come to welcome her smashing my ornaments as she does, just for the distraction and fuss of it.

I didn't tell you this morning but I dreamed of Fenix House last night. At least, I think I was dreaming, I passed such a disturbed night that I could hardly tell whether I was awake or not. Perhaps it was a glimmer — only your letters will confirm that. The place was not at all as I recall it. It seemed reduced: a ramshackle place, dilapidated and neglected, the garden overgrown and choked with weeds. It took me a moment on waking to realize that it wasn't real.

Do you forgive me now, Grace, now that you are there? Did I do the right thing in encouraging you to strike out on your own, even though you are all I have remaining in the world? Perhaps it is too early for you to tell but I feel sure you will think so eventually.

Write to me as often as you can, my darling. No detail is too
small for me. I want to know everything about how it is there for you
— not just the outline but the detail inside it. The particular colour
the house turns when the setting sun creeps down it. The sharp scent
of the fir trees where the garden meets the wood. The soft slap of
shoes on the kitchen's flags. How Bertie gulps when he tells a long
story and thinks you're growing bored. How Agnes pushes back her
hair with the front of her wrist, as though her hands are perpetually
covered with flour. All of it. How many years have passed since I
was there, and yet how a part of me yearns for it still.

Your loving grandmother,
Harriet

I sighed and let the single sheet of paper drift to the floor by
my bed. It had told me virtually nothing of home when that
was all I wanted to hear: the comforting, everyday minutiae
of her forays to Whiteladies Road or across the Downs. It
was a melancholy letter – not the cheery note about new
adventures I'd expected – and I wondered if being alone
with her thoughts so much would prove bad for her spirits.

Turning on my side, I peered at it from above. To anyone
other than me, it would have been extremely disconcerting
to hear that she had dreamed of Fenix House's true state,
and that she knew without being told that Bertie and Agnes
were still in residence, but it hardly shocked me. I had grown
up with her uncanny gift. What I found odd was something
subtler: how she'd signed off – not just as 'grandmother' but
as 'Harriet'. It would be 'Miss Jenner, governess' next.

All through that evening, and after I had gone upstairs to
bed, the rain continued to fall. An insistent dripping, just

like I'd heard in the hall, started up shortly after midnight – I know the time because I noticed my little travel clock when, admittedly unnerved by the sound, I switched on the lamp by the bed. I poked around but couldn't find any evidence of a leak, and was just about to get back under the covers when the deluge grew in intensity, as if someone had turned up a dial. I went over to the window and reached up to pull back the curtains so I could watch it. A sheet of water blocked my usual view of the valley – it must have been gushing off the steeply pitched roof above me, unhindered by any working guttering. It was as if I lived not in a house but a cave behind a waterfall. I stood watching it for a time, then went back to bed to try again to sleep – the hiss and beating of the rain as lulling as it was dramatic. I had the vague thought that I would wake up to find Fenix House had broken free of its foundations and was sailing down the steep hill to drift on the plain of the valley below.

The rain didn't cease until half past two the next morning, the sudden absence of sound waking me again. This time, I felt as alert as if I'd had a full night's rest. I hadn't closed the curtains properly, and now that water was no longer cascading off the roof, a bar of cold moonlight lay across my feet.

I listened to the abrupt absence of rushing water. The drip was back, lingering, hesitant. Every few seconds a drop fell and landed on something hollow. After a time, it began to slow, and it was when the gaps had stretched out to last nearly a minute, and I was finally growing sleepy, that I heard it.

At first it was just a sound that inveigled its way into my thoughts and disturbed their rhythm. Then it must have come louder because it shook me out of the beginning of a dream. Fully awake again, I pushed myself up on my elbows and listened. Just as a drop fell, it came again, a noise that was higher and sharper than the other but otherwise unidentifiable.

I tiptoed to my door and opened it quietly. The house was utterly silent. I could detect no sound from the room at the other end of the floor, and Agnes, who slept in what had once been the servants' sitting room and who, according to Bertie, snored like billy-o, was three floors down and out of earshot. I waited, my feet cold on the dusty boards and the flesh of my hip hurting where it pressed against the door-frame.

Just as I thought it wouldn't, it came again. A high, keening wail in the distance. It rose in pitch, then fell away, quite the most desolate sound I had ever heard. Every hair on my body rose and prickled and I fought the urge to shut the door, return to my bed and pull the covers over my head.

Instead, I crept along the hall and down the stairs, only pausing when the cry came again, this time freezing me to the spot because it was so much clearer. Going towards it went against all my instincts: I had never been very brave at night and, as a child, had often asked my grandmother if I could sleep with a nightlight burning in my room. Perhaps because I had already been asleep, and was in a place not quite familiar to me, I acted as if I was in a dream, when we do all sorts of foolish and dangerous things we would never consider in sober daylight.

That is not to say I wasn't frightened: my heart was juddering and thumping with every step, especially when I reached the narrow passage that led only to the boy's room. By the moon's unearthly glow, a little of which filtered in through the broken window, I could just make out the dark slashes along the wall, like the scars left by the claws of a savage animal. There, in the near-dark, my body tensed for the next cry.

When I got to the door I didn't knock but went straight in before I could lose my nerve entirely and dash back up the stairs. An alertness in the room, matching my own, like a current that reverberated through the stale air, told me he had heard me come in.

'Lucas,' I half whispered. 'Lucas, can you hear me?'

There was no answer but an angry rustle of bedclothes. I crept closer until I was standing over the black hulk of the bed. His curtains were much heavier than mine and barely any light penetrated their thick weave. Still, as I stood there, I began to make out something pale in the centre of the bed's dark mass that might have been a nightshirt. Trembling, I put a hand towards it, intending, I suppose, to offer some human comfort to one who had evidently been in distress or had a nightmare.

Before I could make contact with a small shoulder or arm, I was slapped away with surprising force. I stumbled back, gripping my hand, which was stinging where it had been hit, and – more from fear than indignation – wrenched back the curtain nearest to me. Heavy, it shifted along the pole only a few inches, but gave enough light for me to see him.

He was half sitting up, his body twisted round where he had moved to bat me away. His skin had a pallor that was only a shade darker than the milky cotton of his nightshirt – a chalky grey that spoke of many months out of the sunlight. His hair and his eyes, in stark contrast, were as dark as his parents', his eyes turned into inky voids by the gloom. They were unsettling enough, but it was his expression that chilled me. Despite the poor light, I could see that his features were screwed up in cold, blank fury, the large eyes narrowed, his teeth bared, like something feral cornered in its lair.

Though it took everything I had not to turn and flee, I made myself approach him again. It occurred to me that he was trapped between the waking world and sleep, and that he wasn't angry with me, only in some kind of dream that was potent enough to make him move and cry out and generally appear to be conscious. I knew, somehow, that someone in that state shouldn't be woken, only protected from any danger and comforted once they came to. Moving slowly, I pushed a water glass back from the very edge of the table next to the bed, and untangled the sheet from where it had wrapped around his foot.

He had curled in a ball now, and his breathing was steadier. I pulled up the straightened sheet and retrieved the blanket from the floor. His hand, when it had hit mine away, had been ice-cold. I left the curtain as it was, thinking that a little morning light, when it broke through, would do him good. After watching him for a few minutes, to check that he was settled, I gently touched his thin little shoulder in goodbye. 'I shall see you again soon,' I whispered, before closing the door behind me.

In the narrow passage, I took the stairs up to the attic floor two at a time, hoping I wouldn't wake anyone with the thudding of my feet on the uncarpeted wood. I had been looking down in case I missed my step, so when I glanced up and saw another pair of feet on the topmost stair, I put my hand to my mouth to stifle a scream of pure fright, my hand gripping the banister so that I didn't rear backwards and fall.

Wrapped in an old checked dressing-gown was an elderly man. His beard desperately needed combing, as did his hair, which stood out as a snowy halo of pale flames, licking against the darkness of the attic. Though he was bent and hollowed with age, his chest concave and his shoulders hunched, you could see from his bones that he'd once been quite a large man: someone who had been a presence in any room he walked into. Despite the state of him now, there was still some dignity in his bearing.

'Who's there?' he cried, looking about him wildly. His voice was feeble, unsure, and I understood in a rush of comprehension that he couldn't see me — that his eyes were not as good as mine in the dark. For an absurd moment, the name Dilger entered my head. Had the reticent gardener been kept on for his service to the family, a faithful, now infirm old retainer given bed and board in the attic? But then I thought of Bertie's poor eyesight and wondered whether it was a family trait. Could this person be . . .?

Before I'd even formed the thought, the old man called out again, his voice even more tremulous. He sounded close to tears and his words, mumbled and blurred as they were, apparently confirmed what I had only just that second begun to suspect.

'Is it you? Have you come back, my little Helen?'

Of course I should have stepped forward then to introduce myself as the new governess, like any normal person of compassion and sense. But this man was surely old Mr Pembridge, someone I'd assumed dead in the ground and, many years before, my grandmother's employer. The eeriness of the scene left me unable to speak, let alone take him gently by the arm and lead him back to his room. I watched, frozen, my legs shaking, as he shuffled closer to the top of the stairs, his apparently sightless eyes blinking, his trembling hands reaching blindly for someone who had not been a little girl for decades and was certainly not within the walls of Fenix House now.

Even as I was living this moment, I was distanced from it by its Gothic horror. It was as though I had stepped into the pages of the sort of Victorian novel popular when my grandmother was a young woman, except that the shameful secret in the attic here was not a madwoman but a confused old man.

What finally roused me to action was the fear that he was about to step forward and tumble down the stairs, probably taking me with him, as well as badly hurting himself. I rushed to the top, intending to take him back to bed, but just at that moment he stopped and shuffled backwards, apparently having given up all hope of finding anyone, his shrunken shoulders sagging even further, an unsteady hand going to his face in a gesture of defeat or grief, I wasn't sure. Eventually he moved slowly back towards his room. It was as black as a crypt in there; I could make out nothing behind him before he softly shut the door.

Seventeen

Harriet

In the final days leading up to Captain Dauncey's arrival, a multitude of deliveries kept Agnes running back and forth to the service entrance, which was tucked down a short flight of stairs beyond the front door. Among the meat, fish, oysters, candied fruit, cases of wine and myriad other goods that were arriving in preparation for his visit, there was the consignment of ice that Bertie had told her would arrive in time for summer.

'For me, the ice arriving is truly the beginning of the season,' the boy said dreamily, as he watched the men unload a great straw-covered block and set off on the arduous journey up through the garden towards the icehouse. Unable to look on passively, he left Harriet on the lawn and ran around the men, proceeding to direct them minutely, and crying out when they seemed likely to stray from the winding path.

It wasn't just Bertie's ice that signalled the change of season. The wind that had needled at Harriet through the window on her first morning had been replaced by a caressing breeze. An overnight downpour had turned the garden lush and verdant. Dilger's boy, Ned, was kept busy scything and rolling the springy, lustrous grass, which seemed to grow an inch a day; he had to be persuaded into the kitchen to have his calluses dressed by Mrs Rakes, and sat there, blushing under the scrutiny of Helen, who greatly admired him.

The mistress, generally a stranger to the morning, was up and dressed before ten on some days, and was even seen outside in the garden on one occasion, armed with a white parasol and apparently inspecting the progress of Dilger's beds: the legions of larkspurs that, from a distance, were a haze of lilac, magenta and violet; the cornflowers, whose colour brought to mind the cool depths of faraway seas; the extravagant, immoderate beauty of deep pink peonies and pale yellow roses. The mistress's particular favourite was not one of these English country blooms but a type of lily lately ordered from the nursery at the bottom of the hill. It was the colour of a fresh bruise, with waxy petals that reminded Harriet unpleasantly of lolling tongues.

'You'd think Mr Disraeli was paying a visit, or perhaps even the Queen,' Mrs Rollright was heard to mutter between devising menus, ticking off lists of goods from suppliers, and directing John in stowing an enormous side of salted bacon in the larder. The footman-cum-coachman had already polished the family's entire collection of silver. In the upstairs rooms, Mary went about with a bowl of vinegar, rubbing down every stick of furniture until it gleamed, while Agnes took all the rugs up to the scrubby grass next to the vegetable gardens and beat them with unusual vigour, coughing as clouds of dust and smuts rose to darken the air above her, like a plague of blackfly.

Such was the level of industry among the servants that Harriet offered to lend a hand. Mrs Rakes shook her head, a slightly scandalized expression on her face, but Mrs Rollright, who had been listening to the exchange, was somewhat friendlier after this, or so Harriet thought.

As for the lessons in the morning room, Helen increasingly shone, while Victoria determinedly resisted learning, displaying all the concentration of an indolent kitten. This eventually resulted in a particularly vocal clash of wills one morning, after Harriet had decided to stop accommodating the little girl's skittish moods and instructed her sharply to sit still in her seat for a whole hour, writing out her alphabet until there was visible improvement. To Harriet's frustration, the letters had not become more legible with the repetition. Instead, Victoria demonstrated her fury at being made to stay inside, when the sun was out and the sky as blue as her eyes, by making her letters so large that her exercise book could not contain them. Undeterred by this, she continued writing on to the desk, the India ink – she was using a pen she had pilfered from her sister – bleeding darkly into the grain.

Harriet noticed this rather late, having been distracted by Helen, who was quizzing her about the ancient Egyptians, with whom she had lately grown obsessed. It was only when she straightened up from bending over Helen's work that she saw what the younger sister was doing.

'Victoria!' she cried. 'Stop that immediately. Put that pen down!'

The little girl blinked prettily in a display of uncomprehending innocence, but couldn't help the corners of her mouth turning up in a smirk. Pushing the nib of the pen into the rough surface of the wood had ruined it, and caused ink to spatter not just over her hands and cuffs but up the front of her snowy-white pinafore. 'But I was try-ing my best, I was,' she insisted, as she rubbed her face with inky hands, speaking in the baby voice that always drove her sister into instantaneous fury.

'What a dreadful mess you've made of the desk and yourself!' Helen cried, in anguish, Queen Nefertiti forgot-ten. 'You've broken that nib, too, and it was mine, given to me by Papa. You know you're only allowed a pencil. You did it on purpose, you – you horrid, wicked little girl!' She burst into tears of pure frustration.

Harriet approached Victoria and crouched. 'Victoria, go up to the nursery, please,' she said, as sorrowfully as she could. 'I will follow you in a few minutes. I suggest you sit very quietly, without touching anything or making a sound, until I get there and then we will talk about what has happened. Go on now.' To her astonishment, Victoria looked as if she might burst into tears. Perhaps Mr Pem-bridge had not just been flattering her; perhaps she had earned the little girl's favour.

Unfortunately, she must have met her mother on the stairs because the latter soon swept into the morning room, a vision in silk the colour of blackberries. As well as this gown, which was rather startlingly inappropriate for a Tuesday morning at home, she wore an expression of both outrage and satisfaction. Harriet supposed she had been waiting some weeks for an opportunity to upbraid her newest employee.

'Miss Jenner, I have just found my daughter looking most mournful on the stair. She says you have sent her to the nursery.'

'That's correct, Mrs Pembridge.'

'She is quite distraught.'

Harriet's scepticism must have shown in her face because the mistress lost her temper and began almost to shout. 'Furthermore, her pinafore – new only last month – is beyond repair. Her face and hands are also stained with ink. I hope you can explain, Miss Jenner.'

'I was teaching her to write the alphabet. Unfortunately she is late to learn it, compared to other children of the same age, and this makes her frustrated. That is understandable. What I cannot condone in the schoolroom is wilful damage, not just to her dress and her sister's pen but to the furniture.' She gestured at the ink blots that had seeped into the grain of the desk's pale wood and spoiled it. 'That is why I dismissed her, but . . .'

The mistress hadn't taken her eyes off Harriet and now spoke over her. 'Are you insinuating, Miss Jenner, that my daughter is stupid? That she has not been adequately educated before your arrival?'

Harriet felt hot in her high-necked dress. 'You misunderstand me. I said – or insinuated – nothing of the sort.'

'I hope not,' said the mistress, coldly. 'For that would demonstrate both arrogance and insolence on your part. Do not forget, Miss Jenner, that we are paying you to teach our daughters, not banish them to the nursery.'

'What is going on in here?' Mr Pembridge was standing in the doorway, looking from his wife to Harriet. 'I could hear the commotion from my study.'

'Nothing of importance, Robert,' said the mistress. 'You may return to your work. I am dealing with it.'

She turned back to Harriet and opened her mouth to

resume but Mr Pembridge lingered in the doorway. 'My dear,' he said carefully, 'I do think that Miss Jenner might be allowed to continue her methods without interference from us. I believe there's already been an improvement . . .'

The mistress's face had darkened almost to the colour of her dress as he spoke and Helen, otherwise forgotten at her desk, let out a small whimper.

'As you seem to know best, I will take my leave,' the mistress snapped, in a dangerous undertone, before stalking from the room. They all felt, as well as heard, her door slam upstairs.

Mr Pembridge looked beseechingly at Harriet. 'I rather fear I have made matters worse,' he said.

Harriet glanced pointedly at Helen so that he didn't say any more. She wished she could thank him for his intervention but it was impossible in front of his daughter. 'Not at all, Mr Pembridge. It was nothing, really, and I will fetch Victoria back now. I'm sure John will help us get this ink off the desk. I'm sorry if we disturbed you.'

She passed out of the door, careful not to brush against him, and started up the stairs.

'Have you begun on the book yet?' he called after her, his voice artificially light.

She stopped and turned back. 'Yes, I have, thank you. It was a . . . good choice. A thoughtful one.'

'So you like it?' His face, level with her button boots, was boyish with hope. She suddenly realized how much Bertie resembled him.

'I like it very much.'

'I thought of it straight away, when you came to us.'

'Which book did you lend Miss Jenner, Papa?' Helen had come to the morning-room door. 'Was it *Off on a Comet*?'

'Not that one, no,' he said, and bent to kiss the top of her head. 'Another one, about a governess like her.'

Harriet smiled before hurrying on up the stairs, half happy and half fearful of what he might say next.

Eighteen

In the next days, Harriet thought constantly of Robert Pembridge. Whenever she heard his voice or his step in some other part of the house, she had to resist the urge to pat her hair into place and to pinch some colour into her cheeks. Not that they needed it: the mere thought of him striding into whichever room she was in and looking so intently at her again was enough to heat them.

There was no excuse she could manufacture to leave her charges in the morning room so she might, apparently accidentally, meet him in the hallway; too often she heard him close the front door behind him and crunch across the gravel to the waiting carriage, the clang of the gates a minute later confirming that he had gone again to his work on the railways. Then Helen and she would sigh, Harriet inwardly.

Each night, when she had reluctantly put down *Jane Eyre* and blown out her candle, she explored her feelings for him. Perhaps it is because I am so friendless, she thought, that I have latched on to the first person – the first over the age of eleven – who has shown me any interest. But in her heart she knew there was more to it.

Now, in the quieter moments of her days in the morning room, she hardly ever pictured a young Louisa Dauncey in her mind's eye – the toss of her pale curls, her satisfaction that people on the street were looking at her.

Instead, she saw the husband and, just as she had imagined him asleep on the floor below hers at night, by day she thought of his warm eyes and smiling mouth, his large hands and careful manner. She imagined innocent scenarios in which she met him on the stairs or as she passed the door of his study, and dismissed others that could not possibly take place: a knock at her attic door one evening because he wanted to talk to her alone among her own things, or a summons to accompany him on a journey in the brougham. Even daydreams had to be grounded in plausibility: anything else was cheating, she felt, which stripped it of any pleasure.

It was ironic, then, that when they next found themselves together in the same place at the same time it was under circumstances that Harriet would never have invented. It was the last day before Captain Dauncey was due and, despite the loveliness of the day – a warm, delicate breeze issuing fragrant puffs of air, clear skies and a golden hue bestowed upon everything – the garden was empty. Naturally the servants were hard at work inside the house, intent on their final preparations, the mistress was resting and Bertie was at school. Tired of Victoria's fidgeting, and wishing to feel the sun on her skin, Harriet suggested that they abandon their books. 'It is too lovely a day to stay inside,' she announced. 'We shall go for a walk.'

Victoria cheered and flung down her pencil immediately. Helen looked up blearily from the atlas she had been poring over.

'Come, Helen,' said Harriet. 'The Sahara will keep. The sun is shining here today and we must make the most of it.'

'But it's only eleven o'clock.'

'What if we turn our walk into a botany lesson?' she suggested, ignoring Victoria, who was rolling her eyes.

Helen relented. 'Very well,' she said gravely. 'And I suppose we could count it as geology, too.'

It had been acknowledged by everyone in the household that the garden, always at its best during early summer, was particularly beautiful that year. Accompanied by Ned, who was even more reticent than Dilger, they toured it thoroughly, Harriet teasing each plant's name out of him by using all the charm she could muster.

'Doesn't he know any other words?' said Victoria, after twenty minutes. The boy reddened and Helen turned on her sister.

'Stop being horrid!' she said in a furious whisper. 'Ned and Dilger are very clever indeed to have made it so pretty. Not everyone wishes to hear silly chatter like yours all the time.'

Victoria poked out her tongue but didn't say another word. Out of the corner of her eye, Harriet saw Helen smile at Ned, whose blushes were renewed.

After half an hour, Harriet paused on the upper lawn, wondering what they might do next.

'Let's go to the ruins,' said Victoria.

Helen tutted. 'You *would* think of them.'

'What ruins?' said Harriet.

'There are some falling-down buildings up the hill, just beyond our land,' said Helen. 'There used to be a quarry there but the men have moved to another part of the hill now. It was too dangerous, you see, because it's so steep and the trees grow so close.'

'A man died,' said Victoria, with glee.

'He fell,' explained Helen, earnestly. 'There's a tall column of rock they call the Devil's Chimney. He was dared to climb it, even though it's not safe, and he did but then –'

'He fell off and smashed his head,' finished Victoria.

'Well, that sounds like a delightful place to visit,' said Harriet, drily.

'I don't like the ruins, they make me shiver, but the woods are quite pretty,' said Helen. 'It's shady under the trees.'

Harriet considered. It was hot on the patch of grass where they stood, the high sun beating down on their uncovered heads. Looking up, she saw that there wasn't a single cloud, only a domed ceiling daubed in a single shade of deep blue. Down towards the valley, where the hills eventually flattened into the grey line of the western horizon, the patchwork of green and gold pastureland was not blurred by the usual haze but sharply delineated by neat stitches of dark green hedgerow.

'Perhaps we ought not to be out in the midday sun,' she said. 'The shade would be better. Especially since we forgot to bring our hats. And I suppose the exercise will be good for us.'

Victoria clapped her hands. 'I can lead the way, Miss Jenner. I know it as well as Helen.'

The path was reached not by heading towards the icehouse but by passing through the iron gates. Instead of turning left and walking downhill to the road, Victoria turned right. Here, the going quickly became steep and muddy. It also narrowed to the extent that they had to brush carefully past nettles and push aside bobbing heads of cow parsley. Someone – perhaps Dilger or more likely Ned – had, here and there, plugged the earth with red bricks, so that it was easier to gain a foothold. Breathing heavily and wishing her corset was looser, Harriet was about to announce that the walk must be abandoned when the path took them round a sharp corner, at which point it widened and levelled off.

Soon they were entirely under the canopy of trees, with all fragments of blue sky screened off and only the bright, lime-coloured translucence of the leaves to indicate the brilliance of the sun beyond. There, bathed ethereally in the eerie green light, the air was deliciously cool. Even the contrary Victoria seemed soothed by it, as well as the fluting song of a blackbird high above.

Eventually, Victoria pointed to where the trees up ahead parted, and Harriet glimpsed bare rock on the far side of a deep, hollow clearing. Whether by time or quarryman, the cliff face had been sheared off brutally, revealing a dozen shades of cream, grey and gold. These long vertical gouges were interrupted by horizontal crevices at intervals of six or seven feet, like the vertebrae of an enormous, crushed spine.

Shielding their eyes from the sudden glare, they walked down into what might have been a pretty glade, had it not been for what were surely Victoria's ruins. Their disrepair made them look much more ancient than they must have been: most of the rough-hewn walls that were still intact stood no more than a couple of feet high. Boulders too large to have been part of the buildings were scattered around and inside the shells of them, and had presumably broken off from the sheer rock face above.

Though Helen remained timidly at Harriet's side, Victoria had run off and was now clambering on all fours up a bank to reach the most complete of the dwellings, if that was indeed what they had been.

'Be careful, Victoria,' Harriet called, and was startled to hear the last syllables echo around the clearing: '*Or-ia, or-ia!*'

Helen visibly shuddered. 'I've never liked it here, Miss Jenner.' She pulled up her sleeve and proffered her bare arm, where Harriet could see the gooseflesh rising. 'They say a party of young ladies came here once, to picnic. There were twenty of them, as well as three schoolmistresses. The carriages that had brought them were told to wait on the hill road but when no one had returned by twilight, a couple of the drivers went to search. There was no sign of them, not even a ribbon or a shoe. None of them was ever seen again.'

'I don't believe a word of it,' said Harriet, briskly. 'Every lonely place has a macabre story attached to it and I'm sure I've heard something like that one before.' Despite her jolly tone, she felt her own flesh prickle and rubbed at her arms.

'That's the Devil's Chimney!' shouted Victoria from her rock. Her pale curls, lit by the sun, glowed white, like flames of phosphorus.

Harriet thought for a moment about the mistress's face if she had to tell her that Victoria had fallen and broken her neck, and shuddered as Helen had. Knowing that no reprimand would bring the child down to safety until she was ready, Harriet turned instead in the direction she was pointing. It was undoubtedly a sinister thing: an impossibly tall and narrow column that looked as though a mere whisper of wind would bring it toppling down. It wasn't a single finger of rock but a great stack of separate stones haphazardly assembled by a particularly dull-witted giant, who had chosen almost the summit for one of the largest blocks, where it teetered dangerously.

'A man climbed up there?' Harriet asked in disbelief.

Helen nodded mournfully.

'The top is where the devil comes out,' Victoria informed them. Her words ricocheted about, the cradle of rubble and earth acting as a rudimentary amphitheatre. Harriet imagined she could see the top of the column shifting slightly. 'That man didn't really fall. The devil came up out of Hell and pushed him. Agnes told me that when he hit the ground, his head exploded into pieces like a ripe – Helen, what's that big fruit called?'

'A melon,' said Helen, bleakly.

'Victoria!' cried Harriet, coming to her senses. 'That's quite enough. You are the least ladylike girl I have ever known. Get down from there this instant.'

'You should listen to your governess,' a deep voice boomed, just behind her. 'She's very wise.'

Helen screamed and clutched at Harriet's sleeve, who only just managed not to cry out herself.

'Papa!' yelled Victoria. 'Helen and Miss Jenner thought you were the devil come to take them up the chimney and throw them off.'

Harriet whirled round and there he was: the man who had taken up residence in her thoughts was standing but five feet away. He must have left his jacket behind because he wore only shirtsleeves. He was carrying a walking stick that, clearly, he didn't need. Helen, squeaking with joy, rushed into him and clamped her arms about his waist.

'Miss Jenner, I beg your pardon if I frightened you,' he said. 'This place throws the voice so that you don't know which direction it comes from.'

'I wasn't frightened,' she said, then looked down at her trembling hands and smiled ruefully. 'Well, perhaps a little. But I would not have been so easily startled had your daughters not been telling me such lurid tales.'

'But it's true about the quarryman, isn't it, Papa?' said Helen.

'I'm afraid so. Other men had been injured before that – loose rocks falling on them and so forth – but it was the death that finally took them to another part of the hill. The men said they would strike rather than work in such a dangerous place.'

'And it's true, isn't it, Papa, that it was the men who smashed some of the buildings down?' said Helen, her eyes wide and solemn as she looked up at him.

'Well, yes, but you mustn't worry about that. It's long past. Now, go and see if you can climb as high as your sister.'

Helen went off with a determined expression.

'I really ought to make Victoria come down,' Harriet said. 'It doesn't look safe.'

He smiled. 'You must let children run about and, occasionally, hurt themselves. They don't learn otherwise and become either foolhardy or fearful when they're older.'

They watched Helen clamber up the rocks, her teeth gritted. Victoria watched her from above, arms folded, a pitying look on her pretty face.

'Helen will always best her sister in the schoolroom. Out here, where Vicky is so much bolder, she can't help feeling triumphant.'

'That's a generous way to view it,' said Harriet.

He laughed, not even slightly affronted. 'You are still unsure about my younger daughter, then?'

Harriet began to protest but he held up his hand. 'No, no, you are entitled to your opinion. Just because a person is a child, it does not make them easy to love. In fact children, who, unlike their elders, tend to say precisely what they are thinking, are often very unlikeable indeed. But you must wait a little longer before you make your final judgement. Vicky grows on one. She is what you might call an acquired taste. She can be selfish and, no doubt, she will be vain in a few years' time, but she is brave and full of life. She can also be very amusing.'

Harriet found herself rather envious of her charge, then inwardly cursed herself. How absurd to be jealous of a six-year-old.

Mr Pembridge broke into her thoughts. 'I haven't seen you for a few days, Miss Jenner. How are you, and how are you finding life at Fenix House generally? You have been with us for some weeks now.'

She tucked a loose strand of hair behind her ear, surreptitiously checking that the rest had not come down again. 'I am quite settled in now, sir, thank you.'

'Forgive me, but I don't wish to be called "sir" at home. Though I suppose it wouldn't do for you to call me Robert, despite that being my name.'

'I – well, perhaps I might call you Mr Pembridge then?' She had already been doing so in her head. In fact, occasionally she had thought of him privately by his forename.

He grunted. 'Not much better, is it? As long as you leave off "sir" – it makes me feel at least eighty-four. I shan't, of course, presume to address you by your first name. Harriet, isn't it?'

She nodded. It felt curiously intimate to hear him say it.

'It suits you. Do you know, you have the most . . .' He stopped and scuffed at the loose earth underfoot with the toe of his stout boot. It was a curiously boyish thing to do and it emboldened her.

'You cannot stop there, Mr Pembridge.' She was astounded by her daring.

He smiled. 'Very well. I was going to remark on your hair. It's the most extraordinary colour. My wife said that it's almost ginger but I see now that it's gold. Or perhaps bronze.'

'My father always said there were too many colours in it to count them,' she said quietly. In her self-consciousness her hand fluttered around her head again, though there were no more loose strands to tuck away.

'Let's walk on, shall we?' he said, after a time. 'Come, girls! Or Miss Jenner and I will leave you behind.'

There were paths at every turn, some sloping steeply upwards while others fell away, over lumpen tree roots and drifts of bone-dry leaves from the previous autumn, into deep craters in the forest floor. They walked on quietly, Helen and Victoria some way back, their companionable squabbling reduced to a vague chatter no more intrusive than that of the birds that trilled and flapped in the branches above them. She felt easier with him outside than she did in the house.

'So, Captain Dauncey will be here tomorrow,' she said. 'A great many preparations have been made for his visit.'

'Not that he'll notice, of course.'

'No?'

He seemed to consider before he spoke. 'My wife's brother is a charming man when he wishes to be. They were very close as children and remain so to this day, as you will see for yourself. She finds it very difficult knowing he is so far away. She would prefer he lived here.'

'He is stationed out in India, I believe? Bertie told me.'

'Yes, that's right. He enjoys the life there, I gather. It suits him. He's a very . . . gregarious man. It always proves rather too quiet for him here. He promises my wife he'll stay for weeks but then suddenly finds he must leave early. Deaf to Louisa's protestations, he returns to London for the rest of his leave.'

Harriet took a little breath. 'And where does he stay while he is there? I mean that . . .' Her mind was suddenly full of the red-brick house in Hampstead she remembered from that fateful childhood visit. Was it Jago's now?

Robert glanced sideways at her. 'Both my wife's parents are dead. The mother when the children were very young. The paterfamilias, Josiah, quite a formidable character, went a few years ago. He could hardly move around by then, of course. Terrible gout. Not that it stopped him eating and drinking as he always had. His son rather takes after him in that way.'

'That would explain Mrs Rollright's many lists,' she said, trying to banish the memories that always made her feel so diminished and so angry. She didn't want to spoil that magical walk.

'And what about you, Miss Jenner?' Mr Pembridge said.

'What about me?'

'Just how you are really finding it, I suppose. I would hate you to be polite.'

'No,' she said truthfully. 'I am much happier here than I was.'

He beamed with pleasure. 'I'm so glad. I also wanted to tell you that I've thought a great deal about what you said that first day, in relation to Vicky and Helen – about not judging people too quickly. You can tell I've taken it to heart, just as you did when I asked you to give Vicky a little longer before you washed your hands of her entirely.'

Harriet laughed and nodded for him to go on.

'Well, I wanted to say that I have been attempting to apply this theory at my work. Unfortunately I seem to be of a different disposition from you. I see the man and, while I still hardly know him, I believe I can see his essence. After that, my judgement seems only to grow more clouded and confused, infected by sympathy for the man's situation, amused by some tale or other he tells me, or taken in by the quality of his work. I'm sure your method is much sounder.'

Harriet thought hard. She had spoken as she had only to conceal her initial dislike for his youngest child – a child she could see herself warming to, who was making a genuine effort at her lessons now.

'Perhaps what I should have said, sir . . .'

He looked at her pointedly.

'Well, then, *Mr Pembridge*. What I should have said is

that I would try not to judge *a child* too quickly. Their character is not formed and they have not yet learned to rein in their less . . . appealing qualities.'

He smiled. 'But old goats like me can be instantly appraised?'

She was about to object politely but the soft green air was having a curious effect on her, putting her at ease as she hadn't been for many months – even before her arrival at Fenix House, in the tiny, stifling and trinket-crammed home of her father's cousins, where she had lived in constant fear that she would turn and knock some knick-knack from its perch. 'Oh, almost instantly,' she said archly. 'Certainly within the first couple of minutes.'

He laughed. 'And what, then, did you make of your employer in the morning room, in those crucial first minutes?'

'Well, I suppose I thought him to be a good father of affable temper, whose only fault was his own desire for the approval of his employees.'

He smiled briefly, then looked serious. Harriet wondered if she had gone too far.

'I don't know that I see that as a fault,' he said.

'No, it isn't, of course. I only meant that –'

'Please, I am not offended. Not in the least. I realize of course, not being completely devoid of humour, that you were poking fun, albeit gently. But it made me think of my other employees, those outside the house.'

'I presume you mean the men who work on the railway, rather than Dilger and Ned.'

'Yes, indeed. It's interesting what you said – oddly perceptive, even if it was accidental. I have been told more than a few times that I am too easy on the men, that it does them no good when I try to come down to their level.'

'But you don't believe this?'

'No. Are they not as human as you or I? Do they not have children as I do, and fears in their minds when they wake in the middle of the night?'

'Well, I can certainly vouch for the fact that I am much the same person now as I was before circumstances dictated that I must earn my living.' She smiled sadly up at him. One of the things that had frightened her most about her reduced station had been the way people treated her once she had no money. The worst had been those who knew she had been comfortable before: viewing her as a salutary reminder of how far bad luck could also drag them down, and therefore handling her as if she might be contagious. On the rain-soaked day of her father's funeral, her wrap heavy with moisture and her flimsy shoes letting in the dark wet clay that sucked underfoot, Harriet remembered how some of the mourners' nostrils had twitched when they offered her their murmured condolences, as though her fall from grace had imbued her with an unpleasant odour.

Back in the woods, Victoria was complaining that her feet ached from such a long walk and, too soon, they turned back the way they had come. By now, Helen had slipped her hand into her father's and was walking between him and Harriet. Though she had been enjoying her first lengthy conversation with Mr Pembridge, Harriet was grateful for the little girl's presence, which had shaken her out of the unhappy memories their talk had churned up.

She was even gladder when Helen insisted on describing exactly why she liked Miss Jenner as much as she did, ticking off each admirable quality on her fingers.

When they began the steep descent to the house, Victoria, who had been lagging behind, swiping at the undergrowth with a stick, overtook them and cantered down it at some speed. 'Aren't I the bravest girl you ever knew, Papa?' she called back over her shoulder and half tripped over a rock in doing so.

'Hah!' cried Helen, who had let go of her father's hand and stumbled on ahead to catch her sister.

Mr Pembridge turned to Harriet and offered his arm. 'We are not quite as nimble as them, I think.'

She took it and felt quite breathless, telling herself that was merely the work of the sun, under whose glare they had now returned. The acrid, soporific smell of the vegetation that pressed in on them seemed headier than it had before. Soon it was too narrow to walk abreast but he seemed reluctant to let her go, instead taking her hand – which was bare in the heat – and stepping ahead of her, turning back to ensure she had her footing. She realized that some weed or other, equipped with furred and sticky leaves, had thoroughly adhered itself to Mr Pembridge's trousers and her own dress, and laughed. By now they were approaching the gate, which stood ajar where the girls had raced through.

'Ah, so here is my husband, and with him – fancy! – the little governess.' The voice, light and hard, cut through the still, syrupy air. The mistress stood on the other side of the gate. Even from where she was, Harriet could smell her scent, so different from the natural smells of the garden – the warming earth, the freshly cut grass and the now-blazing azaleas. It was exotic and heavy, capable, it occurred to Harriet, as she blushed and swatted at the clinging leaves, of giving one an almost immediate headache.

'My dear, how lovely you are against the flowers,' said Mr Pembridge, nervously.

She gave him a stony look, then turned to Harriet. 'Miss Jenner, I do hope you possess a second gown. That one will have to be cleaned and brushed.'

Harriet's cheeks darkened again. The mistress was wearing canary yellow. Two hours earlier, when Harriet had stood back to let her sweep past on the stairs, she had been wearing something quite different. No doubt there would be other changes of dress before the day was out.

'My daughters have just rampaged past me and into the house like a pair of savages,' she continued. 'I trust you have planned something quieter for the remainder of the day.'

'I thought it would be beneficial for them to take some exercise in such lovely weather, Mrs Pembridge.'

'Oh, I'm sure. Did you also think it beneficial for my husband?' She laughed, though it came out as a rather alarming shriek. Her eyes were icy blue against the hot pinks and purples of the azaleas that framed her.

'I met their little party by chance,' said Mr Pembridge, sounding strained. 'You know how I like to walk on the hill.'

'I had no idea you were even returned from Swindon,' said the mistress, dismissively. 'You must have gone straight out for your walk without a word to anyone.'

'Well, as Miss Jenner rightly said, it is such beautiful weather. I did not wish to disturb you, my dear. You have been so busy with preparations for your brother's visit.'

At the mention of the captain, she looked mollified and held open the gate to usher her husband through. 'Well, you shall come in now, and let me show you what I have done with his bedroom. I have been directing John to move things about for the last hour. You would not think it the same room.' She clasped his hand in hers and gave him a glittering smile, her creamy curls catching the sun as Victoria's had among the ruins.

As they moved off towards the house, he glanced back at Harriet, an apology in his brown eyes. The mistress waited a few seconds more, knowing intuitively that Harriet continued to watch from the wrong side of the gates. When the woman finally turned, to fix her with a cold stare, Harriet understood immediately that it was a silent warning.

Nineteen

Grace

I woke with a start the next morning, half convinced that the night's peculiar events had been a dream. I'd overslept, and when I got to the dining room, breakfast had been cleared away. Pembridge was in there alone, his papers and books spread out over the cloth, heedless of crumbs and stains. I was about to apologize for rising so late when he waved for me to sit down opposite him.

'Sit down, please, Miss Fairford. You have waited patiently to begin your duties and I am grateful for that. However, before I take you to meet Lucas, there are some things you should know first. Things I . . . well, things I didn't think I could possibly explain in a letter.'

I swallowed nervously as I took the seat that had already become mine at dinnertime. If Lucas was to remember that I'd come into his room, I didn't know what I would say. I knew I should admit to my nocturnal wanderings there and then, but I lacked the nerve. Something about Pembridge's intensity warned me off mentioning Lucas's cry, let alone the spectre of old Robert Pembridge on the stairs. The latter's presence had nothing to do with my duties at Fenix House.

Pembridge seemed to consider what he wished to say for a long time before he spoke. What beams of sunlight could reach round to that side of the house came blearily in through arched windows that rose nearly to the ceiling. They were Gothic and fussy, with plenty of nooks and flourishes in which grime could gather. From my angle, every fingerprint and careless swipe of Agnes's feather duster was caught and illuminated, every dust mote gilded. In contrast, Pembridge was a shadowy bulk in his chair, as dark as the half-dozen dead flies that lined the windowsill.

'My son has what is euphemistically termed a delicate constitution,' he began, in a low tone. 'Most of his life he has heard himself described that way. Words like "delicate", "fragile" and "weak". I sometimes wonder if they have made him accept things too easily but it's too late to change that now. Of course, he's been worse since his mother died, particularly at night.'

At the last words, he seemed both furious and agonized. I kept silent, suspecting that any murmurs of sympathy would make him despise me.

'If I am entirely truthful, I would say things are not just worse since my wife died but have been getting progressively worse with each passing month. It's rather a vicious circle, you see. I keep him in because of how he is, which makes him frustrated and angry and more likely to be ill. That in turn makes him all the more furious. And so it continues. He's barely been outside this summer. One doctor we had refused to see him after a few weeks. He was a quack anyway – none of his tonics made the slightest difference to Lucas's moods.'

He lit a cigarette and pulled on it hard. The smoke formed a dingy wreath that encircled him. 'He's almost eight now but his reading and writing are of the standard of a younger boy. When I've tried to improve things he grows quite agitated. And then the nights . . . He seems to have stopped sleepwalking, thankfully, but he still has what they call sleep paralysis. He cries out and appears conscious when he isn't, caught somehow between dreaming and waking. Miss Fairford, I feel I should have said at least a little more before I engaged you. I see that now. There have been some episodes of . . . violence, though not for many months now.'

The word made my stomach turn. I thought of him slapping my hand away.

'Lucas is a good boy at heart,' Pembridge continued. 'It's his illness that makes him so unhappy, and the lack of good sleep doesn't help. He has seizures because of the former, you see. They used to come every few days but now his medicine stops most of them. Unfortunately, there are side effects. It's a case of deciding which is the lesser of two evils.' He sighed and stubbed out his cigarette, his fingers going to his temples to massage them. 'We've never been able to get the dosage right. Too much and he's virtually catatonic, any less and he's quite wild. If he doesn't take them at all – he went through a stage of hiding his medicine and we didn't know until the seizures came back with a vengeance – he's quite like his old self. Or, rather, the self I see glimmers of occasionally, how he would be if he'd been allowed to grow up a normal boy.'

I nodded, the word 'glimmer' jarring. 'And you say his illness worsened when he lost his mother?'

'He didn't lose her,' Pembridge replied, as he reached for his cigarettes again. 'She hasn't rolled under the table or gone down behind the skirting. She's dead.'

I dropped my eyes in embarrassment. I heard him fumbling with his lighter, then jumped when he threw the packet at the hearth.

'Christ, listen to me,' he said. 'The boy's temper is probably inherited, nothing to do with the bloody epilepsy. Look, I apologize, I'm not used to talking of it. The thing is, I was away in France until he was four. He hardly knew me so his entire world was his mother. I'd barely been discharged when she died so he lost her and got me instead – some silent, miserable chap he scarcely recognized. No wonder he was disturbed.'

I thought of the pinched white face I'd seen in the darkened bedroom. 'Disturbed' seemed about right. The next thought I had chilled me. 'I heard something thrown when you went into his room the other day,' I said cautiously. 'And those marks, on the wallpaper outside it.'

Pembridge let out another sigh. He looked exhausted. 'I don't know where he got the knife. It was a penknife of mine, in fact. I used to carry it about – perhaps I dropped it in his room. Perhaps he stole it. We were out in the garden that day so none of us heard him hacking at the wall. It was my aunt's daughter, Essie, who stopped him doing anything worse. She was quite fearless, by the sound of it – went straight up to him and confiscated it.'

His aunt? I briefly wondered whether it might be Helen or Victoria, but was too distracted by thoughts of Lucas to pursue it then.

'Did he smash the window, too?' I said, the possibility suddenly occurring to me. Forewarned was forearmed, I thought, with no small amount of trepidation. I was beginning to dread the task ahead. In comparison to what now awaited me upstairs, the last days of purposelessness were taking on a rosy-hued glow.

'Yes, that was him, but it wasn't deliberate. I believe he was asleep, and it's possible he was when he damaged the wall, too. Apparently he was lucky he didn't hit an artery. He put his bare fist right through the glass.'

'You said in the advertisement that you required a governess as much as a nurse. In fact, the emphasis was rather more on the former, I would say.' I spoke quietly but I felt deceived. It was no exaggeration to say I'd been brought there under false pretences. 'Do you think I can help Lucas? You see, I would like to very much, but I'm not a trained nurse.'

'I know that. The wording of the advertisement was not intended to be misleading. I think it was a rare burst of optimism on my part, actually. I'm convinced that a woman will bring Lucas back to us. Some affection and attention, some female care. He's so much better when Essie is here but she's too young to do more – my aunt wouldn't hear of it anyway. My point is that I believe, in time, you will be able to teach him.'

'But first I must nurse him, reach him.'

He spread his hands. 'If you are willing to.'

Beneath the temper and the impatience he seemed rather desperate and I had a fleeting urge to take his hand across the table. In that moment, I would probably have agreed for his sake alone, but I also felt desperately sorry for the little boy upstairs, even if he had rather frightened me in the night. Before I could change my mind, I nodded. 'I can't promise a miracle, Mr Pembridge, but I will do my best. For Lucas.' I blushed at the last – not that it would even have occurred to Pembridge in his distracted state that I would have done it for him.

Watching him rub his eyes, I wondered when he had last had a good sleep himself, never mind his son. He hadn't mentioned anything about his war years and I wondered again if he'd come through unscathed. Who knew what played on his mind? Even if the war hadn't affected him too badly, the death of his wife immediately after must have done. In a place such as Fenix House had become, I could imagine dark thoughts swiftly unravelling a man. I realized there were four generations inside its walls: four generations of unhappy males, eking out a paltry existence together.

'Thank you,' he said, in the end. 'I'm grateful to you. The thought of trying to find someone else now . . . Yours was the only response, you know.'

I didn't like the thought of that, as though all the other prospective governesses had read something sinister into the small, square advertisement and dismissed the position out of hand. It was too late to dwell on that now, though. I was there, not they.

As we reached the first-floor landing, I thought I heard a shuffling noise from above. Robert Pembridge alone in his room, I supposed. I glanced at Pembridge but he gave no sign that he had heard. The old man had called out for Helen in the night and I wondered whether she was Pembridge's mother or the aunt he'd just mentioned.

Although he had been easier to talk to that morning than he had been since I'd met him, I still had to steel myself to ask. We'd just started down the passage that led to Lucas's room, the rather sinister gouges in the wall just visible in the gloom.

'Mr Pembridge?'

He looked back at me, the shadows around his black eyes even deeper in such bad light.

'You mentioned an aunt. The one with the daughter, Essie. Can I ask her name?'

He frowned, presumably unable to work out the answer's relevance to me. 'Aunt V? Well, it's Victoria, though I never call her by it. Why do you ask?'

It simply wasn't the right time to mention his grandfather, or ask why the old man had been so upset about Helen in the night – Helen who must be Pembridge's mother.

'I just didn't want to confuse anyone,' I said dismissively, and gestured towards Lucas's closed door. Besides, those other Pembridges were slipping from my mind already. I was thinking again about the boy I was about to be put in charge of. 'Disturbed', his father had said. The word seemed to slink around inside my head, like something cold and dark and sinuous.

Twenty

Lucas's bedroom smelt sour, of old milk and unwashed sheets. I hadn't noticed it in the night, probably out of fear. When Pembridge pulled back the curtains and bright sunlight streamed into the room I saw I was right: the bedclothes were tangled and grubby, and a half-eaten bowl of porridge lay abandoned on the floor. I didn't think Agnes had delivered it that morning: a thick, beige rind had formed around the top. The rest of the room was no less chaotic. Toys scattered the floor, pencils had been upended on the desk while drawing paper had been scrawled on, screwed up or ripped into pieces. A long cable snaked around the floor and disappeared mysteriously under the bed. With a wrench, because I had so treasured my childhood books, I spotted a splayed volume of illustrated fairy tales with some of the pages yanked out of the spine.

As for the boy, he was curled into himself and facing the wall. His white nightshirt was as dingy in the unforgiving sunlight as the sheets. When Pembridge said his name, he feigned sleep, though it was obvious he was awake from how stiff he was, and from the way his eyelids flickered. With a pained glance at me, Pembridge reached out to touch his son's bony shoulder.

'Come now, Lucas. Don't be foolish. You must meet Miss Fairford or she will go away and then we'll be back where we started.'

When there was no answer, he forcibly turned the boy so he was on his back, propped up slightly against the headboard. Pinned there so he couldn't roll over again, Lucas turned his head to the wall instead, his eyes squeezed shut and his small face rigid with what might have been fear or fury, perhaps both.

'Hello, Lucas,' I said gently. 'My name is Grace Fairford. You can call me Grace, if you like.'

He pressed his lips together as though to stop himself accidentally replying.

'We don't have to do anything very difficult at first,' I continued. 'To begin with, I thought you might like to hear some of the stories my grandmother used to tell me. They're quite good ones.'

The boy's expression didn't change. Pembridge let out a grunt of exasperation and gave him a slight shake. 'Answer her, then, for God's sake. And open your eyes. She'll think you're a wolf-child, not able to speak at all.'

In response, Lucas went limp like a ragdoll, one arm dangling off the bed.

Pembridge let him go, stalked to the other end of the room and slammed a cupboard door that had been left hanging open. I flinched as the whole room seemed to shudder. Lucas didn't even blink.

'Mr Pembridge, why don't you leave Lucas and me to get to know each other?' I said, as firmly as I could. I didn't like the thought of a little boy being so inured to his father's explosive temper.

To his credit, Pembridge seemed shamed by his outburst, stroking the wood of the cupboard he'd just treated so violently. 'Yes,' he said quietly. 'I think that would be best. I'll go.' Without meeting my eye, he left, closing the door with a careful click.

I turned to the child who was now in my charge. He still hadn't moved. Slowly and deliberately, so I didn't startle him, I moved towards the bed and sat on the end.

'I expect you're quite tired of being cooped up in here,' I said.

He didn't move a muscle.

'I know what it's like being stuck at home all the time, without friends of your own age. It was just like that for me too.'

He still hadn't moved but something about his eyes and his breathing convinced me he was listening, that he was now quite alert.

'My parents died when I was a bit older than you, and after that it was just my grandmother and me. She did her best and we were very close but it wasn't the same. I suppose I wasn't a normal sort of girl after that.'

He bit his lip and I wondered again if he was trying to stop himself talking.

'This is the first time I've really been out in the world. It must seem very humdrum here to you, but it's rather exotic for me. Perhaps you will introduce me to it properly and we will become friends, Lucas. I should like that. I've barely had any friends and I'm twenty-two years old. It's a bit sad, really, isn't it?'

'Didn't you go to school?'

I did my best not to show surprise at the sound of his voice, or the question, which he flung out at me like an insult. 'No, I didn't. I wanted to but my grandmother kept me at home and taught me my lessons there. I was only thinking this morning about how I used to watch the local girls walking past on their way to school in their boater hats and envy them dreadfully. I always minded it most in the autumn, the beginning of a new school year, when it's all crisp and cool after the long summer.'

'They wouldn't like me at school anyway.' He was looking at me now, fixing me with eyes as dark and smouldering with frustration as his father's.

'What makes you think that?' I laced my fingers together so I wouldn't be tempted to stroke and tidy his hair, which stuck up in greasy tufts.

'Because I'm always ill and such a dreadful weakling, of course.'

'Well, it's hardly your fault if you're ill, and as for being a weakling, you look quite wiry to me. Small but strong.' I wasn't just flattering him: when he'd hit my hand away in the night – a night he seemed not to remember, thankfully – it had hurt.

He considered this and then, as if remembering something, sat up and looked over the side of the bed to the floor. When he saw the cable that looped around the dirty porridge bowl his eyes flicked nervously up at me. 'I saw that when I came in,' I said. 'What is it?'

'I can't tell you. I promised I wouldn't. Do you think my father saw it?'

'I think he was too worried about you to notice.'

'He was not! He hates me. He only liked my mother.'

This time I couldn't help it: I reached out to him. He shook me off, frowning. I sat quietly for a minute or so, resisting the urge to tell him he was wrong. He would rightly feel he knew better than I, a virtual stranger.

'So are you going to tell me what this cable is?' I said eventually. 'I'm desperate to know. I'm good with secrets. I won't tell anyone, cross my heart.'

'And hope to die?'

'Oh, yes, and do stick a needle in my eye if I break my word.' I smiled at him and thought his mouth twitched.

'I oughtn't to say but as you've promised . . . It's a crystal set, you see. A wireless. I listen to it when I'm bored, which is quite often. That big wire is for the headphones but there's another wire that makes it work called the "cat's whisker". It's a jolly good set. My great-uncle gave me it, and bought the licence for it, too. It cost ten shillings, you know.'

'Bertie, you mean?'

'Well, I don't have any others,' he said scornfully, as he delved under the bed.

I helped him drag out the small wooden case of the crystal set, both of us lifting it together on to the small table by the bed. After tussling with indecision for a moment, Lucas solemnly handed me the headphones.

'Oh, but I've never used one,' I said. 'You'll have to show me.'

He feigned exasperation with a roll of his eyes but I could see how enthusiastic he was, his fingers trembling as he turned the dial. His other hand clamped on to the headphones, which were too large for his small head, and his face became intent as he listened for sounds. 'There!' he cried, pulling off the headphones and shoving them towards me. 'Can you hear it?'

It was very faint and crackly but I could hear something, a series of distant noises, which eventually formed into music as I picked up their thread. Though I suppose I had been humouring him, concentrating on drawing him out, I felt unexpectedly thrilled. Here was the outside world, miraculously breaching Fenix House's lonely and crumbling fortifications. 'Yes, yes, I can. And wait, someone has started to sing!'

Lucas's eyes shone. 'I expect it's Dame Nellie Melba. I heard her last week, doing her trill.'

I handed him back the headphones with a happy sigh. 'Oh, I can't tell you how much I would have loved a set like this when I was a girl.'

Seeing that my enthusiasm was genuine, he gave me a small smile.

We spent another hour or so together, turning the dial when we lost the signal, which I learned was stronger on the hill than it would have been in the valley. When Lucas began to look exhausted, unused as he was to so much excitement or company, I told him I would let him rest, returning at midday with something good to eat.

He frowned with displeasure that the game was over and I held my breath, wondering if he would bat me away in a fury. But then he seemed to realize how sleepy he was and merely lay down. I pushed the window open to get some fresh air circulating, tidied up the worst of the mess, and pulled the blanket straight around him, careful not to touch him.

I nearly cried out when I slipped silently out the door. Pembridge had just reached the other side of it. At least, I hoped he had.

'You haven't been there long, have you?' I blurted. He'd given me such a fright.

'Hush, he'll hear you,' he said, with a smile. He took my elbow and steered me swiftly down the landing.

'But have you?' I said, when we got to the top of the stairs. I was rather flustered by the physical contact, as well as embarrassed that he might have been listening to me chattering on.

'You're being very brusque with your employer, you know,' he said. I peered at him more closely: he seemed almost cheerful. 'I was only there for a few minutes. I just wanted to check you were getting on all right,' he went on. 'My son's temper is not very predictable, as I have explained. It looks like I was right, though, eh?'

'About what?'

'About you. Women are much better with children than men. I think he's taken to you almost as much as he did to Essie. It's not easy being right so often, I must say.'

I smiled before I could stop myself. 'Well, what about your uncle? He's a man and yet he's obviously made an effort with Lucas.' I stopped, remembering my promise.

Pembridge looked thoughtful. 'What? Giving him the wireless, you mean? Yes, I had no idea the old devil had smuggled it in. I must say, it was kind of him. I'd never have thought of it. I'll thank him later.'

He turned to appraise me again and I found myself taking a small step backwards. It wasn't that he was standing too close but the way his eyes bored into me made me feel as though he was.

'So, Miss Fairford, do you think you might do some good here?'

'Well, it's rather early to say, but I hope so. Lucas is a bright boy and I liked him very much.'

Pembridge positively beamed, his face so entirely transformed that I simply stared at him. 'Yes,' he said wryly. 'I have been known to smile, every couple of years or so.'

'I shall see if I can make you smile as often as weekly, then, now that I'm here,' I said, but colour flooded my cheeks as soon as the words were out. The gentle sarcasm I'd intended had made me sound fast, and not a little sweet on him.

To my relief, he let it pass. 'There's another letter come for you. It's down there, by the door. A nice fat one by the feel of it. Will it be from your grandmother again?'

'I suppose so,' I stammered, still mortified that he might think me flirtatious. 'I'll go and read it in my room now, Mr Pembridge, if I may. While Lucas is sleeping.'

'Yes, of course, take your time,' he said, and when I glanced up, I could tell he wasn't laughing at me. Oddly, he looked quite as awkward as I felt.

Twenty-one

Perhaps it was having spent time with Lucas, but my thoughts when I got back to my room were full of my own childhood. My grandmother's stories of Fenix House had done a good job of filling the void left by my parents after they died. In fact, they had done more than this, encroaching upon my own, first-hand, memories of the years before the accident until they began to shrink and dim, eventually reduced to a few dislocated scenes and sensory memories.

These precious fragments I allowed myself to bring out only occasionally, during moments of particular poignancy. I was terribly afraid I would use up their potency, or eventually distort them, like a teddy bear flattened and faded by too much love. I guarded them as fiercely as a museum curator, keeping them under glass in a specially darkened room of my mind.

They weren't much, I suppose. The alternately rough and silky texture of an embroidered skirt my mother liked, peacock blue. My father's spread hands on the dinner-table while he talked, fingernails square, like small spades, and trimmed almost to the quick. There were others that were more amorphous: the sensation of carrying something fragile but heavy across a slippery floor; of being woken in the night and taken to see something important behind my parents' bedroom door.

I understood very early that my grandmother didn't like me dwelling on these things.

'What are you thinking about?' she would say, her intuition unerring whenever I was sad. When I admitted I was missing my parents she would hold out her arms and, when I had been gathered in close, begin a story. I felt my mind filling with her words, my scant little memories shoved further towards the back; like padding a hollow stomach with soft food. She was good at that.

Sitting in the weak light admitted by the attic room's small window, knowing that I was without her for the first time in twelve years, I felt some of my resentment at being sent away dissolve. I suddenly wished desperately that she was there with me. No one at Fenix House really knew me; no one understood me as she did. A ripple of fear went through me at the thought that no one else probably ever would: she had set the bar too high in that regard.

'I'll write to you often,' she had said, when she saw me off to Temple Meads. 'Promise you'll write back.' I had let her embrace me but felt too confused and hurt that she was letting me go so easily to do much more than stand limply in her arms. When I had looked back at her through the oval window glass of the motor taxi, she had seemed tiny and frail. Old, even.

I knew I would cry if I didn't distract myself so I reached for her letter, which lay unopened on the washstand.

'Dearest Grace,' it began. 'Thank you, my darling, for your letter, which I read with great interest.' I paused. Was she teasing me because I hadn't said anything much at all? I couldn't tell at a remove – I needed to see her face, to hear the tone of her voice to know. I continued reading, wondering if she would provide me with the sort of banal anecdotes from home that I wanted to hear. I should have known that my grandmother was anything but banal.

The first morning after you left, I found myself going from room to empty room. It's what people do when someone they love has died so suddenly that they cannot yet accept it. In truth – and I can tell you now you're a woman – I had the same urge after your parents were taken from us. I didn't for your sake, Grace, the little girl left behind, who was already so confused and bereft. Now I am entirely alone here, however, I feel as though the place has doubled in size. I drift about and ask myself, Have the rooms always echoed so? Have the ceilings always been so high? I must say, it feels entirely wrong that, of the family who once lived here together, it is I, the oldest, who is the only one remaining.

Yesterday, to stop myself wandering aimlessly through the silent, spotless house, I sat down in my customary corner of the parlour. I gazed out of the window and watched the wind hurl the rain first one way, then the other. It spattered the glass, and it seemed to me that each drop was a tiny protest at your leaving. You took the last of the summer when you went, my darling, and serves me right, too. As I sat there, I asked myself whether I should have persuaded you to go.

Then, at first to distract myself, then because I understood that I needed to do it, I started writing down my story. I've never kept a diary, and suddenly it struck me why. It was because it would make it all so permanent, so certain. There would be no shrinking from the truth in its entirety. And you see, darling Grace, I have not told you everything of what happened to me in the time before I was your grandmother. I thought my past was mine alone, to shape as I pleased, but now that you are at Fenix House at my instigation, I see that is no longer the case.

I want to do it properly, so I must start at the very beginning. How the words have flowed out of me since I began! It has been like a river that, once it has started to flood, cannot be staunched. The next few pages are what I have written so far. They are for you, Grace. Write again soon, my darling.

Your loving grandmother,
Harriet

On a fresh sheet of paper, without heading or preamble, she had begun her story.

In the very same year my father took me to be christened at St George the Martyr in Holborn, a house was being built a hundred miles away, in the far north-west corner of the Cotswolds. The place chosen for its construction wasn't a convenient or easy one, not that this would have been likely to deter the indefatigable Victorian spirit. Perhaps it even acted as encouragement, for it was completed in a mere seven months: a pale grey house of ten bedrooms built high on the hill its stones had been quarried from. They called it Fenix House, for the mythical bird who rose from the ashes. I couldn't know then, tiny as I was, that one day I would have to rise from my own bed of ashes.

It had been intended that the house's lofty position, above the valley in which the spa town of Cheltenham nestled, would bestow upon it a commanding appearance. In fact, its isolation gave it a wistful, solitary aspect. It was more than that, though, and for those who believe such fancies can be applied to the inanimate, Fenix House had about it a patiently expectant air — as though its stones and timbers, its trees and lawns, its potting shed and the red-brick ice-house hidden among the birch trees all knew that something would unfold there, but were content to stand sentry on the hill, waiting to see who might come and what might be. When I arrived in the early summer of 1878 – no longer a babe in arms but a young woman of twenty-one – that wait came to an end.

I sighed. I could feel myself being drawn in, but for an account that purported to be the unvarnished truth, it opened very much like a story. I couldn't help but feel intrigued, though: for all those tales of her governess years, I had never heard much about *her*. It was all event and detail, I saw now – descriptions and names and conversations. She had kept her inner thoughts and feelings to herself. Until now, perhaps. I read on.

Let us go back again now, because the beginning of the story – a story that would shape not only my destiny but yours too, Grace – took place a decade earlier, in London. I was a little girl of ten at the time, living in a world that had to make do without wirelesses, aspirin and light bulbs that burned for more than a few hours. If you had seen me then, a skinny scrap of a thing with only my bright hair to catch the eye among the surge and swell of all London's life, your gaze wouldn't have lingered for long. It would have been easy to dismiss me as another casualty of the city where people too often forgot that fortunes could be lost as well as made. And, you see, Grace, my father had just lost his or, rather, had had it lost for him. The difference in my case was the glimmers, the strange gift I might otherwise never have discovered.

During the period leading up to his ruin, my poor father had grown increasingly distracted and morose, questioning his own judgement and worth as a man of business. He found it difficult to rise each morning and take himself to the auction house he owned, and which had provided our comfortable living all my life. Its profits had been falling slowly for some months and now, from neglect caused by worry, had begun to tumble a little faster.

One sultry night, which he said reminded him of the hot summer of 'fifty-eight, when the Great Stink had risen off the Thames and he had wanted to cover my tiny nose and mouth so I wouldn't breathe the foul air, he lay wakeful in damp sheets. He was just wondering whether he would ever get to sleep when he heard a tentative knock on the door. It was me, face pale and eyes huge, dark with shadows.

'What is it, my love?' He knelt and held his arms out to me. I was trembling, my nightdress wet through with sweat. 'Was it a dream?'

Held in his embrace, face pressed into his shoulder, I shook my head. 'What, then?' He prised me gently away, but I couldn't meet his eye.

'It was like a dream,' I said eventually, so quietly that he had to turn his good ear to me to catch the words. 'But I was awake, I know I was.'

After much coaxing, I told him that I knew – I simply knew – that something bad was going to happen. There was going to be a fire, I said. As I lay in my bed, I'd heard the roar of it as it consumed dry wood and paper; I'd seen its orange glow against the dark sky, where dense smoke had blotted out the moon; it had curled into my nostrils and made me cough.

He carried me to the window and lifted me up so I could lean out. 'Can you smell it now?' he said.

I took a great lungful of the turbid London air and regretfully shook my head. 'But I wouldn't, Father,' I said. 'Not yet.'

He took me back to bed, humming an old lullaby that I would usually have told him I was too old for, and stayed until my eyelids fluttered and closed.

The next morning he set off early for the auction house, moved by the closeness he'd felt to his daughter in the night – and found the place burned to the ground. He had been careless in attending to correspondence in recent months, and it transpired that the insurance policy he had taken out against fire years before had expired. Having lost most of his savings already, and with his business now in ruins, he was left almost bankrupt.

In the months following the disaster, Cook, the maid-of-all-work and my own governess were dismissed with regret and excellent references because there was no longer enough money to pay them. It was around this time that I began to slip out of the house to wander the streets. My fading father, who spent most of his days shut in his study with his head in his hands, knew nothing of this and would never have allowed it if he had. I felt compelled to escape the quiet house occasionally: to hear people shouting and laughing and living; to watch the women on the market stalls, their cheeks mottled and their lips cracked from the wind, children of my own age selling meat pies, cheap cigars and posies of violets.

All of London continued even as my father despaired over another demand from a creditor, but its indifference was oddly comforting: proof not only that life went on but that there was an endless supply of it, just beyond the front door. Perhaps it was what I had now privately taken to calling the glimmers, or perhaps it was a natural resilience inherited from the dead mother I had never known, but when I was out there in the heave and shove of it, I knew I would be all right. Though my father never spoke of it, I sometimes wondered if the fear etched in his face when he looked at me was entirely due to our uncertain future. I, on the other hand, wasn't frightened that I had known about the fire, only saddened that it had happened at all.

One day I went a different way from usual, away from the stench

and bustle of the market and river to where the streets were some-
what cleaner and quieter. There was a steady stream of carriages
passing by – the reason I noticed one in particular was because two
old ladies ahead of me stopped and pointed. It was an open carriage
carrying a girl I had seen once before, at the beginning of my father's
troubles. She must have been eighteen by then and it was clear that
she was on her way to her wedding.

As her carriage rolled past, and her cold eyes passed over me
without a flicker of recognition, I felt something hard and unrelent-
ing enter my soul. As far as I was concerned, that girl was to blame
for everything. It was on her whim that my father had invested in a
scheme that would ultimately fail, and it was she who had refused
us admittance to her father's house when we went there to beg. As
far as I was concerned, she might as well have lit a match and
thrown it into that tinder-dry auction house herself.

That was where it ended. I turned over the loose leaves to
make sure I hadn't missed anything but I'd heard enough
of my grandmother's stories over the years to know that
she told them in tantalizing instalments. 'Always leave
them wondering what happened next,' she would say,
before tucking the bedclothes around me and putting out
the light.

What was peculiar was that I had never heard any of this
before – not the auction-house fire that had evidently occa-
sioned her first glimmer, or anything of her father's
downfall. As many children would, I had found comfort in
the repetition of her cache of Fenix House stories, to the
degree that I would chastise her if any of the details altered,
or were told in the wrong order. But this was all new to me.
I had never asked how she came to be a governess, which

was rather incurious of me – I suppose I had known it for so long that it had become unequivocal fact. It had never occurred to me that behind her need for paid employment lay a tale of financial ruin, as well as a deeply ingrained hatred for the mysterious girl with the cold eyes – the girl my grandmother blamed for all of it.

Intrigued as I was by this earlier version of my grandmother, who had previously arrived fully formed in my imagination at the age I had now reached myself, I couldn't think why she was telling me now about those formative years. My concern was – and she'd hinted as much at the start of the letter – that she was now spending too much time alone with her thoughts. The idea of her being lonely made me feel so guilty that I reached for pen and paper to write back to her immediately. It wasn't just guilt, of course. I also wanted to know more.

Twenty-two

Harriet

The morning of Captain Dauncey's long-awaited arrival was overcast and rather unpleasantly humid, driving the mistress into a frenzy of despair. Harriet discovered this on her way to the morning room, when she heard the woman's raised voice behind her closed door and stopped to listen.

'It's as if *He* has done it to spite me!' she cried, quite audible through the thick oak. Harriet wondered if Robert was in there with her and felt a stab of jealousy.

'Jago so hates it grey and nondescript,' continued Mrs Pembridge, unhappily. 'He always says it depresses the spirits more than anything else when you're in the country. Of course, it would be a different matter if we lived in town.' The last was said with venom.

'My dear, the carriage is at your disposal all day. If you wish to take your brother into Cheltenham, then John will drive you.'

So it *was* Robert. Harriet was immediately more alert, just at the sound of his voice.

'You know very well it's not the same as walking from my own house in the middle of everything, escorted down the Promenade by my dear brother, where everyone might see us and stop to speak.'

'But you have told me many times how you detest walking any distance,' replied Robert, reasonably.

The mistress snorted in derision. 'Oh, how you relish any opportunity to misunderstand me! I said I hate walking here on the hill, up into that horrible, lonely wood, where the only soul I'm likely to meet is a filthy quarryman. A genteel turn around Montpellier Gardens in one's new hat, and on the arm of a man in uniform, is a different thing altogether, as well you know.'

At this juncture, Harriet slipped away silently, anxious that the mistress was about to quit the room in a temper and find her governess eavesdropping outside the door. Heart fluttering in her chest as she went downstairs to find Helen and Victoria, Harriet reflected that the household's hysterical atmosphere had begun to infect her.

In fact, the mistress needn't have worried about the weather: by the time Captain Dauncey arrived – four hours later than the mistress had been given to expect – the sun was peeping through the last few lingering clouds, casting flattering shadows on the smooth lawns and perfectly trimmed hedges, and softening the rawer angles of the house. Lessons had been cancelled for Helen and Victoria, though Bertie had been sent to school as usual. In the event, Harriet might easily have managed a few hours' tuition, for the captain had missed not one, nor two, but three trains from London. He also had missed the presence of John atop the Pembridge carriage, which had been waiting outside the station for him from mid-morning. The honoured guest eventually arrived at the bottom of the drive in a hired cab just after three.

The mistress had only briefly left the window that

afforded the best view of the gates when Captain Dauncey came through them. Harriet, who was in the downstairs hallway, was the only person on that side of the house and therefore the only person to hear his arrival: heavy footsteps crunching across the gravel and the creak of the front door as it swung open. Unsure whether to shut herself in the morning room or run upstairs, her indecision meant that she was still fixed to the spot when the bulk of the captain stepped inside the house. His hair was lighter than she remembered, no doubt bleached by the fierce Indian sun, and his complexion much darker for the same reason, the back of his neck and hands scorched a deep brick-red.

Apparently unaware of Harriet's presence, he called loudly to no one in particular, 'What's this? No one here to greet the returning hero?'

Turning to throw his hat down on the nearest surface, he finally caught sight of her hovering nervously in the shadows. His eyes, which were the exact chilly blue of his sister's but slightly more protuberant, took her in with a long, sweeping stare that made her blush.

'Well, look what we have here,' he said, with a broad smile. 'I'm certain I've never had the pleasure, Miss . . . ?'

'Jenner,' she said, her voice steadier than she felt. Just like her face, the name didn't light any spark of a memory in those blue eyes. 'I am governess to your nieces.'

'Ah, a governess. That would explain the rather severe dress.' He smiled again. 'I must say, Miss Jenner, if I may be so bold, they don't often come like you.'

'No?' said Harriet. 'And how do they generally come?'

'Oh dear, I've offended you. I meant it as a compliment. It's just that most of the governesses I have come across are rather plain.' He tossed her another of his disarming, blue-eyed smiles. Harriet suspected he doled them out quite freely in the company of women.

He had just opened his mouth to say something else when the mistress uttered a scream from the landing above and launched herself down the staircase, like a child on Christmas morning.

'Jago, is it you at last? I didn't hear the carriage. I thought you were killed or worse. I thought – I thought you would never come at all!'

Reaching the last stair, she shrieked again and ran at her brother who, to her evident delight, took hold of her strenuously whittled waist to swing her round. On her second turn, she spied Harriet and immediately stiffened, her eyes narrowing. The captain placed her back on her feet and she turned her face up to him, expression beseeching.

'I hope you haven't been standing here talking to the governess when I have been upstairs, not even knowing you had arrived.' She stood on tiptoe so that her prettily pouted lips were just a couple of inches from his.

He placed his hands on her waist again. 'Come now, Lulu. I've thought of nothing but seeing you for days. For weeks! I arrived but half a minute before you knew of it.'

She reached up to stroke his cheek, her face wreathed in smiles again. 'Good. I want you all to myself this afternoon. Robert has his work, Bertie is at school and the girls can see you later. I kept them off their lessons but I've changed my mind. It shall be just the two of us.' She turned to Harriet. 'Miss Jenner, find them something quiet to do for the rest of the afternoon.' All warmth had drained from her voice. 'My brother and I wish not to be disturbed.'

With that, she made for the stairs, pulling him after her, her soft white hands plucking at his. 'Now, come straight up here with me and see your new room,' she trilled. 'It's quite transformed. Then we will have tea in my little sitting room, like we always do when you are here. How burned your dear face is – I would hardly have recognized you. Oh, everything will be well now that you're back, darling Jago.'

As she chattered on, Harriet remained where she was, unable to tear her gaze away from the pair of Dauncey siblings, whom she had once thought never to see again. As she stood there gaping, Jago risked a glance over his shoulder. Gratified that he had caught her watching him, he gave her yet another of his rather dazzling smiles. Oddly, it made the blood in her veins run briefly cool, just as it had when she had first learned he was coming to Fenix House.

'Was that him?' whispered an excited voice behind her. It was Agnes, whose face was a picture of combined exhilaration and longing. 'Oh, Lord, these last days have dragged so that I thought today would never come. I didn't even hear him arrive and I've been listening out for that carriage on the drive for hours. How did he look, Miss Jenner?' she asked, in a surprisingly courteous, pleading tone.

'I think he must have missed John and come by cab. As for his appearance, I would say he looked rather sunburned,' she said, more crisply than she'd meant to. 'And very large.'

Agnes was indignant. 'Well, he's a proper man, in't he? You wouldn't catch the likes of him in an office, doing nothing but moving around piles of paper.'

At that moment, a bell rang insistently downstairs.

'That'll be him and the mistress wanting something!' Agnes cried. She shoved open the baize door that led to the servants' stairs with her hip. 'I'll go, Mary,' she shouted down. 'You said I might, remember?' After smoothing her apron and pinching her cheeks, she took a deep, shuddering breath. 'Please God that he remembers me,' she murmured, as she started up the stairs.

The silly girl is in love with him, Harriet thought. If she was to be entirely objective, she could see the physical appeal of a man like Jago. The sheer size of him alone would attract many women: the large, capable-looking hands; the long, sturdy legs; the broad shoulders and chest that did a good job of hiding the beginnings of a paunch. Then there was the ruddy skin that contrasted so well with his blue eyes, and the pale gold hair that curled better than his sister's ever would.

There was something else about him, too: something more difficult to define. A smooth yet watchful knowing-ness was the closest Harriet could get to it with words. He was a man who enjoyed women, to a degree and in particular contexts, and he knew they generally liked him. Harriet remembered him as a rather clumsy boy, but the oafishness had gone, replaced by something infinitely more assured. Many women, even his own sister, would find themselves fluttering and simpering in the presence of a man like Captain Dauncey.

Harriet, though, was not going to be one of them.

Instead, she found herself slightly repelled, as though he was a dish so rich that only a small helping would bring on a bout of nausea. Behind her eyes, she felt the leaden beginnings of a clamping headache. Her legs, too, felt restless and strange, almost as if the blood moved too fast in them.

Twenty-three

She didn't see much of Captain Dauncey in the coming days. As good as her word, the mistress kept him very close, only allowing him out of her rooms for brief walks to secluded corners of the garden or for meals. The children were granted brief audiences with their uncle, for which they were cleaned and brushed much more thoroughly than usual, then hastily dispatched before they could bore or irritate him.

To her relief, Harriet heard Captain Dauncey more than she saw him. When he and the mistress were in her sitting room, which was directly above the morning room, it was possible to discern the low, rumbling tones of his voice through the ceiling, frequently followed by shrieks of high-pitched laughter from his sister.

As for Mr Pembridge – who, in the privacy of her thoughts, she now called Robert all the time – she saw more of him than she had dared hope possible. Busy as she was with her duties, she could say with all honesty that this wasn't her doing: if there was any contrivance, it must have been on his part. Not that these frequent but short meetings were particularly satisfactory to either of them. Every time they happened to find themselves in the same part of the house, someone would reliably come upon them before they had exchanged a word. Usually it was Helen or Victoria, or one of the maids passing by with buckets or trays, and even, once, to their mutual embarrassment, a dangerously slopping chamber-pot.

On another occasion, when they had stopped outside Robert's study to greet each other after he'd returned from a visit to London, Captain Dauncey had happened to stroll around the corner and, apparently oblivious to any awkwardness, asked if he might join them. Harriet and Robert had looked at each other helplessly – longingly – while the captain swiftly steered the conversation towards himself.

Despite Harriet's instinctive distrust of the mistress's brother, it was hard to deny the positive change his presence initially wrought over the household. The cloud of the mistress's dissatisfaction, which generally hung over them as a grey pall, had evaporated within a few hours of his arrival. This, despite the extra work created by a guest such as he, did much to put the servants at their ease. In Agnes, his presence brought about a startling transformation, turning her instantly from sour-faced to soulful.

'She looked almost comely just now when I caught her mooning over the potato peelings,' said Mrs Rollright, with a wondering shake of her head. 'She's scrubbed herself from head to foot, too, and our Agnes is normally no friend to the carbolic soap.'

The weather was apparently in collusion with this altered mood. Day after day dawned not just bright and clear but unusually warm – even the breeze that never normally abated so high on the hill turned to a hot, sultry breath. Dilger and Ned were kept busy until twilight, not only weeding and pruning but quenching the garden's inexhaustible thirst. One afternoon, just after midday, it began to rain without preamble – a sudden, savage deluge flung down from an angry cloud that had appeared from nowhere. It seemed to pause directly over the house even as the sky over the valley to the west remained a benign blue.

'It's like the monsoon!' the captain cried from the lawn to his sister, who watched from her bedroom above. He had run outside on hearing the downpour gather strength, and was now joined by Victoria and a more hesitant Helen. Victoria began dancing around with her arms outstretched to the heavens, like a thing possessed, while the mistress leaned out of her window, laughing at the spectacle. A floor below, in the parlour, Harriet had gone to watch silently from the French windows. By now, the rain had darkened the captain's golden hair to the colour of toffee, the long ends of it dripping down his neck and soaking the collar of his shirt. 'Come out here, Lulu,' he coaxed, his head tipped back. 'It's wonderful. Just like India.'

'Darling, I couldn't possibly do such a thing. My hair will get wet and I'll catch my death.'

'Nonsense! It's warmer than a bath out here.'

Harriet opened one of the French windows and put her head round it. The humid air rising from the rapidly saturating lawn engulfed her, like a warm wave. She would have loved to step out into the rain but the captain's heavy presence, as well as the mistress watching from above, stopped her. 'Victoria, Helen, come in at once,' she said, knowing she sounded like a killjoy. 'You'll be soaked to the bone.'

At the sound of her voice, the captain swung round.

His eyes lit up when he saw it was her, and she felt her every nerve jangle in response.

'Well, if it isn't Miss Jenner come to join us. You're not afraid of a bit of damp like my sister, are you?'

'I would rather remain inside, thank you,' she said primly.

He sauntered over to where she was standing, pulling at his shirt, which was, by now, plastered to his skin. 'You don't like me much, do you, little governess?' he said, too softly for anyone else to hear.

All of Harriet's articulacy abandoned her. 'I – I don't know – I don't know how you have reached that conclusion, Captain.'

He shook the rain off his hair, like an enormous dog. 'I'm not offended, little Miss Jenner. It's merely something I have observed about women. Most of them enjoy my company but the few who don't can't abide me. There doesn't seem to be anything in between, I'm afraid. I rather like that, though – anything but indifference, eh?'

He was by now so close that she could see each droplet of moisture suspended in his fair eyebrows. She could smell him, too, and he gave off a very different scent from Robert Pembridge, whose mingled aroma of pipe smoke and lime cologne brought to her mind a vague idea of a gentlemen's club in summer: fans stirring the heavy air, like oars rippling a river, a cool wash that made the leaves of potted palms shiver in its wake. The captain's smell was earthier and much more foreign, spicy even, as if he'd brought to Fenix House not a vestige of his British Army garrison, but the chaotic Indian streets beyond it.

She was about to make a flustered reply when the

190

mistress appeared behind her in the parlour, her tread as silent as a stalking cat's. 'Fetch my daughters inside for their luncheon,' she said shortly to Harriet, though her eyes were already seeking out her brother's. 'Well, here I am,' she said to him, summoning a coquettish smile. 'You have persuaded me out, you brute.' She held out her hand for him to take it and stepped delicately on to the brilliantly green and steaming lawn.

The captain stole a last glance at Harriet, just as he had done before, but she stubbornly refused to acknowledge it, looking instead towards her charges and attempting again to call them inside. This turned out to be futile: even Helen had by now got a taste for the invigorating rain after nearly two weeks of drought.

Agnes, no doubt drawn to wherever the captain happened to be, had also joined the fray, daringly removing her cap and letting the downpour pull her frizzy, rust-red hair loose from its pins. With her face turned up to the full sky, hair soaking into smooth auburn runnels over her shoulders, Harriet understood why she had once overheard Mrs Rollright say that the girl could look comely when she had a mind to. The mistress obviously thought so too, and it wasn't long before Agnes was sent back to where she belonged with a single withering look.

Although she was the most outwardly changed, it wasn't just Agnes who was altered by the arrival of the captain. Everyone had taken on a new sheen and luminosity in the altered atmosphere of the house, the sensuous weather curling around them all, like ribbons of slippery silk. Even Mrs Rollright had ceased to be a plump parcel of ill humour wrapped in a shapeless old sack of a dress.

Her skin, Harriet noticed for the first time, was quite remarkable: as poreless and dewy as a girl's.

As for Harriet, even her fatigue at the end of each long day couldn't stop her thinking of Robert each night before she slept, the high-riding moon bright on the floorboards. Kicking off the blanket and fanning herself with the sheet in the close air of the attic room, she hoped he might be doing the same. In truth, she thought he probably was: the meaningful glances he sent her way were surely proof enough.

That night, sleep wouldn't come at all, particularly once she'd noticed how thirsty she was. She had used the water in her jug to wash after undressing for bed, pressing a cloth to her neck and breast and feeling the water heat immediately against her hot skin. Once she had thought of the dark kitchens at the bottom of the house, where she could turn on the tap in the scullery and wait for the water to run clear and cold in her cupped hands, she knew she would get no rest until she went down. It was too warm to bother with a shawl so she crept down the stairs in her nightgown, her heart nearly stopping when she caught sight of herself in the hall mirror, a floating apparition of gauzy white.

On the worn steps to the servants' quarters, she thought she heard a noise and stopped to listen. Only Agnes slept in that part of the house, on a pallet pulled out each night in the servants' sitting room. Mrs Rakes and Mrs Rollright occupied rooms on the same floor as Harriet, either side of the tiny box room Mary and Ann shared, while John slept in the coach-house loft, above the horses. The sound came again: a rhythmic creaking and the odd gasp. Suddenly comprehending, Harriet clapped a hand over her mouth to stop a bubble of hysteria escaping.

It was difficult to tell precisely where the noises were coming from. She stood paralysed, torn between darting back up the stairs before she was detected and slaking her thirst at the tap. Her parched throat won and, besides, she thought whoever they were, they would probably be in the servants' sitting room.

She was wrong. They were in the kitchen, two bodies crammed up against each other in the darkest corner. Even so, the moonlight was bright enough to illuminate Agnes's face, her fuzz of unpinned hair casting a wild shadow on the distempered wall behind her. Her eyes were not closed but fixed on the man who faced her, who was pushing her hard up against the scrubbed dresser where Mrs Rollright kept her scales and the new-fangled knife-cleaning machine she scorned to use. To Harriet's shock, the man was not one of the staff, as she would have expected, but Captain Dauncey.

She stepped back into the corridor, out of sight. Her cheeks burned as she listened, and she wished she could stop up her ears. Better still, she wished she had never left her room. Once she had gathered herself, she started back up the stairs as stealthily as she could, though she was unable to stop herself running up the last few and letting the baize door swing freely after her with a creak.

Her face was still hot when she got into bed and pulled the sheet up to her chin. A flurry of emotions was sweeping through her, so fast and disordered that she struggled to identify them. Chiefly, she was unaccountably furious. Was that for Agnes's sake – Agnes, who was scarcely a woman yet, whose feelings for the captain were certainly genuine but surely unrequited? A little, perhaps, but she was mostly angry for herself. So did that mean . . . No, surely she could not be jealous. She didn't even like Jago Dauncey, and not only because of his last name but for his character. He was so insufferably vain and arrogant, swaggering around the house like the worst kind of swell, as though the place belonged to him and not his gentle brother-in-law.

But more than she disliked him, she felt intimidated by him: his gaze, once stripped of its patina of charm, was more predatory than that of any man she had ever known. Indeed, it was as if he could see right inside her when he fixed her with those slightly popping eyes of coldly blazing blue. Perhaps, then, she was simply jealous of the act itself, her loneliness making a small, shameful part of her crave something of the raw, animal intimacy she had just witnessed. For a guilty moment, she tried to picture the scene with two different players: herself, with Robert pressed into her. But, try as she might, she couldn't make it work in her mind until she allowed the captain to take her employer's place. Turning over with a cry of frustration to face the wall, she pulled the pillow over her head and tried to empty her mind of all thoughts, especially those involving Jago Dauncey.

Twenty-four

The following Sunday dawned bright and butter-yellow but this soon gave way to a cold, persistent rain that shared nothing in common with the sultry, monsoon-like deluge of the previous week. It began to fall just as morning service ended in the church at the bottom of the hill. Thanks to the addition of the large captain, there wasn't enough room inside the brougham for all of the family and Robert swiftly volunteered to walk back with the servants, making Harriet's heart lift. The mistress opened her mouth to protest but when the captain whispered something in her ear she seemed to forget her husband, instead bestowing an intimate smile on her brother.

The walk to Fenix House was longer by road than it was along an old country route that would take them over a stile and up through a steep pasture.

'Shall we try the country way?' Robert suggested. 'I believe the rain is only going to get harder.' He smiled encouragingly at his female servants. 'The sheep have cropped the grass pretty close so I don't think our feet shall get too wet.'

Though neither intended it to happen, at least not in front of the others, he and Harriet quickly pulled ahead of the party, who were deferentially keeping pace with a crimson-faced Mrs Rollright. The going was reasonably hard but not as steep as the path that led up to the woods and the Devil's Chimney, and Harriet found the sensation of the cool rain on her face much more inspiring and life-affirming than the sermon they had just endured.

In truth, she had not so much endured as ignored the vicar's indistinct monotone, which was nigh-on impossible to attend to in the still, dust-thickened air of the church. Poor Bertie must have shared her low opinion: about half an hour in, he had gone to sleep, clipping his chin on the back of a pew as he slid dramatically to the stone floor. This had created a protracted and enlivening diversion, which included a large quantity of blood issuing from his bitten tongue, the mistress being caught in a dead faint by her brother and both Victoria and Agnes being scolded for laughing – all of which was much appreciated by the less devout members of the congregation.

'And what were your thoughts on this morning's sermon, Miss Jenner?' ventured Robert, after they had been walking in companionable silence for a while. Some way behind, the sounds of Mrs Rollright's laboured breathing could just be heard.

Harriet racked her brains but for the life of her could remember nothing of what the Reverend Samuel Boyd had said. She saw again Victoria's and Agnes's shoulders shaking with laughter and hid her own smile. 'Well,' she said eventually, 'I thought it was very . . . informative.'

He gave her a quizzical look. 'Yes, I suppose so. In truth, I don't think I absorbed half of it. That church is like an ice-house usually, but today I could hardly stay awake. No wonder Bertie dropped off.'

'Yes, and quite literally, too. I hope he's all right. Though . . .' she hesitated and then risked it, believing he would take it in good humour '. . . it was a welcome distraction, I couldn't help but think.'

Robert didn't bother to conceal his amusement. 'I don't think he was the only one brought back to attentiveness by that tumble. As for the sermon, I believe the overarching theme was the sin of envy. Coveting one's neighbour's wife or – or servant, I suppose.'

Harriet turned to study his face but there was no ulterior meaning that she could detect. She cast around for something to say in response. 'I realize that envy must be a sin, and a deadly one at that, but I also think it one of the most natural in a human being.'

Though she had only been trying to make conversation, the red-brick Hampstead house materialized before her with unnerving clarity: the careless, taken-for-granted wealth spoken of by every well-pointed brick wall and fresh-painted window frame, not that she would have identified such trappings as a child, only taken in the whole. Then, she had simply been cold and frightened by something far worse than the creatures she had once thought prowled in the dark recess under her bed. She had looked at the Dauncey house, warm and rich.

Now she was a lowly governess, she viewed that memory rather differently. She understood that the golden light she had seen pouring through the windows was so pure because a housemaid had got up in the thin light of dawn to clean them, vinegar stinging in the cracks of her hands. Perhaps if she had looked higher than the red bricks to the slate roof, she would have seen a dimmer light glowing in an attic room, like her own at Fenix House, where another friendless governess kept her meagre possessions; another governess who would have had to tolerate Louisa Dauncey, this time as uninterested pupil.

Either view, child or adult, boiled down to envy, she supposed. Envy in the past that Louisa had never known money troubles, and envy now that she had such a husband as Robert. There was a second sin Harriet knew she habitually committed, too: the sin of pride was so potent in her that she couldn't resign herself to a reduced station in life. Even as she felt a belated sympathy for servants like Mary or Agnes, who toiled up and down the stairs with back-breaking bed-warmers, it terrified her to think that she was as close to them now as she was to the mistress, unhappily suspended in an earthbound purgatory.

She came back to the rain-shrouded field with a jolt, though Robert seemed not to have noticed her absence.

'Perhaps you're right,' he said thoughtfully, as they paused to rest, turning to face the view that was opening up at their backs. They had left Mrs Rakes, Mrs Rollright, Agnes and Mary some way behind. 'If it's not envy we feel, it's discontent. It's certainly difficult to remember all that's good, sometimes, and instead fixate only upon what's . . . less pleasing.'

'And what can be less pleasing to you?' she asked, before she could stop herself. *What more could you possibly want in your charmed life?* she managed not to add. The bitterness of her childhood memories had temporarily turned her against even Robert.

'You think me ungrateful,' he said gently. 'I try not to be. I have my children, a large, commodious house, servants who run and fetch for me, and my work – work that, unlike so many men, I generally enjoy.'

'And your wife,' she broke in. Something about where they were, beyond Fenix House's boundaries, as they had been on the walk in the woods, made her bold. 'You have a wife I'm certain many men would covet.'

She saw him look sideways at her but kept her eyes resolutely forward, focusing instead on the rainclouds that hung in ragged festoons above them, like a series of curtains about to drop in a tired old theatre.

'Perhaps they would,' he muttered. 'No doubt she looks the part of an enviable wife. And yet . . .'

He turned to her as a warning growl of thunder in the west caused the approaching Agnes to shriek. Harriet knew he would need little encouragement to open his heart to her. She could see it in his hazel eyes, which seemed as full of sadness as the clouds above them brimmed with rain. More than anything, she wanted to go to him and comfort him, but she could not. Though he stood but a foot away from her, it was impossible. Instead, reluctance dragging in her every atom, she moved not towards him but forwards, her arms out to commiserate with the dripping servants, calling shakily, 'Oh, but aren't we all wet through!'

She was still trembling when she climbed the final flight of stairs to the attic floor, and it was not just because she was soaking, or even because of the nature of her conversation with Robert. After their exchange had been so awkwardly curtailed – the rest of the walk back to the house taken up with prattle about the weather with the servants – she had then had the misfortune of meeting Captain Dauncey on the first-floor landing. Taking in the long, dripping tendrils of her disordered hair and the dark patches of moisture on her dress, he had simply stood and smiled at her, both of them in the full knowledge that he was blocking her path.

When he had finally stood aside, she'd known that he continued to watch her as she hurried away. He was, no doubt, noting with amusement her embarrassment, which she knew must be humiliatingly evident in her clenched hands and stiff shoulders, the latter of which had risen with tension until they were almost up around her ears.

Though she had never thought to before, she turned the lock in her bedroom door, though she took care to do it silently, for what reason she wasn't sure. So as not to offend him? No, she didn't care a fig for that. It was because she didn't want him to know that she was sometimes afraid of him. She understood instinctively that betraying fear to someone like Captain Dauncey wouldn't invite his pity: it would make her more vulnerable to a predator who had scented blood. Sinking on to her bed, not caring for the moment that she would dampen the bedclothes, she allowed herself to think of Robert.

Despite their circumstances, she felt safe with him – safer than she had felt since her father had died. If she was in Louisa's position, well, she would be the most contented woman in England. That the mistress seemed to have no idea how lucky she was only added to Harriet's vast contempt for her. Unlike the captain – who would admire someone like Harriet only for her hair, her figure and how much she might accommodate him – Robert was a kindred spirit, someone, she believed, who would peer into her very soul if he was allowed to.

As she shifted position on the bed, her gaze was caught by the gleam of the little dagger she had confiscated from Victoria on her first morning at Fenix House. She had overheard the mistress complaining to Mary about its disappearance and, in doing so, learned that it had been a token from her brother, who had brought it back for her from India. A miniature dagger, with a curved blade and a scabbard studded with tiny garnets, Harriet presumed it was used for trimming ribbons and cutting threads, not that either was an occupation with which the mistress generally bothered. Harriet had been using it to cut the pages of *Jane Eyre*.

She knew she should have given it back, but something had stopped her. Whenever she touched it, it gave off its own peculiar heat, like a nugget of metal glowing deep beneath the earth's crust. She reached for it now and a flaring nerve, like a drip of iced water, ran down her left temple. The same thing had happened when she'd first thought about returning it and, in truth, she'd known then that she wouldn't. It didn't feel like stealing, somehow – and not only because it belonged to someone she despised. It was more that she felt she should have it, that it was destined to be hers. It fitted in somewhere, though more than that, she didn't know.

A noise made her shove the little dagger under her pillow. A note was being pushed under her door. For a terrible second, she thought it was from the captain – that he had been inspired to send a message after encountering her on the landing below. Though she couldn't hear his heavy step, she waited a full minute before she went and picked it up. Seeing her name written not in a man's hand but Bertie's (she knew his rather shaky copperplate from his schoolbooks), relief coursed through her.

On closer inspection, she realized it was not just a sheet of paper but an ingeniously folded package, painstakingly contrived. There was something light inside, which, despite Harriet's care, fell to the floor as she opened it. Assuming it to be a dead leaf, she turned her attention to the many times folded note that accompanied it.

Dear Miss Jenner,

Here is a small token of my esteam. I hope you will like it. It is a small copper, which is quiet a common species of butterfly in the woods here, but even though it is not a very rare or unusual type, I thought of you when I saw it. I do not mean that you are common, just that you are quiet small and most particlary copper – at least your hair is sometimes, when the fire is shinning on it. That is why I thought of you, because this species is called the Small Copper (Lycaena phylaeas).

Do not fear – I did not kill it for you. It was already dead when I saw it under the sorrel bush near the big beech. I cannot yet call myself a true lepido butterfly collector because I don't like to pin them, only to see them fly about. Sometimes I catch one in my net just to see its markings better, but I always let it go again.

This is a very long note for such a small present. I'm sorry if it is not a very good thing to get – or if you are afraid of dead things, as Mama would be, but I wanted you to see the colours.

From your humble servant (sadly not pupil),
Robert Pembridge (the boy, not the father)

As gently as she could, she knelt and scooped up the gossamer-light creature, fearful it would turn to dust in her hands. She avoided looking at its furry body, determined that she, unlike the mistress, would not mind touching something dead. Turning it over revealed its glorious markings in many different shades – not just copper but russet, primrose and ochre. She didn't know it then but it was an old butterfly, its colouring faded to something subtle and soft, more like her own rosy-gold hair than Agnes's fiery strands. Looking about for somewhere safe to keep it, she settled on a corner at the back of the washstand that never got wet and was also well away from any draughts. As she placed it there, its colour rich against the plain wood, she found herself smiling. Sweet Bertie and his gift had rinsed Captain Dauncey's grubby insinuations clean away.

Twenty-five

Grace

Once Lucas and I had been introduced, my days at Fenix House fell into an easy rhythm. Between us, we had brought his bedroom into some sort of order, and I had braved Agnes's domain so that he would have some nicer, more tempting food and be fattened up a little. I had even persuaded her to prepare him some approximation of a peach Melba, in honour of Dame Nellie and his wireless passion, though she grumbled at having to plunder her precious hoard of tinned fruit.

As for my nights in the attic, I slept soundly, having grown accustomed to the noises that occasionally emanated from behind Robert Pembridge's door. I hadn't yet summoned up the courage to ask his grandson why the old man spent his days there, or what he did. It wasn't for lack of curiosity: I simply didn't think it was any of my business. I was there to care for Lucas, nothing more. Of course, for all my honourable intentions, I might have asked Bertie, but a spell of dry, mild weather kept him outside in his beloved woods during the day.

One Saturday morning I happened upon him in the parlour. I was looking for Pembridge's discarded newspaper, which contained an announcement that the King was going to speak on the wireless for the first time in a few weeks – something I knew Lucas would want to cut out and keep. I was so intent on my hunt through the close-printed pages that I didn't even hear Bertie come in.

'What do you think, Miss Fairford?' he said hopefully. 'You may be brutally honest. I can bear it.' He had gone to stand in front of the foxed overmantel mirror, frowning at his rather cloudy reflection.

'Oh, you gave me a start,' I said. 'I'm sorry, but what do I think about what?'

He looked crestfallen, though he made a valiant attempt to cover it. 'Oh dear, have my careful ministrations made as little difference as that?' He turned to the speckled glass once again. 'Yes, of course, you're right. I'm a fool to think otherwise. In truth, I'm a lost cause.'

I studied him anew, desperate not to hurt his feelings, and finally identified some evidence of sprucing up: his hair combed and somehow, at least on one side, flattened; his top pocket emptied of its usual detritus and now sporting a leaf-green handkerchief; his squashed brown boots exchanged for a pair of polished brogues.

'Wait a minute, I do see a difference,' I said, in a rush. 'I can't have been looking properly before. You've got new shoes and your hair is . . .'

'Combed!' he cried, instantly delighted. 'Yes, you're absolutely right. What a brick you are for noticing. Our eagle-eyed Miss Fairford has detected a change in old Bertie, however fleeting.'

'Are you . . . going out?'

He laughed, a short peal of surprised amusement. 'Out? Goodness, no. Out is the woods, and as far as the Blue, if I need a good walk. Where I go, "out" does not require any spit and polish. No, my dear, we are expecting visitors – one of whom is even sharper-eyed than you. I can't do much about the clutter in here – I wouldn't know where to begin – but I like to show willing in terms of my personal appearance.'

For a moment I thought he might be referring to his father. It was Saturday: might that not be a good day for a family gathering? A family dinner, even. I thought I could discern, now that I thought about it, a damp and rather sour smell on the air that was surely boiling cabbage.

'My sister Victoria and her daughter,' said Bertie, with as much apprehension as fondness. 'She is finally returned from her latest adventures. It has been so very quiet without her visits. Of course, she'll be very busy now she's back – she's always busy, always terribly in demand.' He shook his head in wonderment. 'Before they went this time, she had been put in charge of a chapter of the Freedom League in Cheltenham, as well as some sort of soup kitchen for destitute soldiers. So many of them were in desperate straits, she said, with scarcely more than their service medals to their name. There was also something she was doing about the question of . . .' He reddened. 'Oh dear, it's rather delicate.'

I looked at him questioningly.

'*Birth control*,' he mouthed, with a fastidious grimace. 'But it's the suffrage question that's always got her most exercised – it's dreadfully close to her heart. She was in the WSPU back in their day, you know . . . I'm fairly sure that was the final straw with her husband, actually. He was convinced she would disgrace him by getting herself arrested for smashing windows on the Promenade. What's your take on all that women's business, Miss Fairford? Are you a . . . well, an agitator of some sort? I'm rather more a status quo man myself, I'm afraid. No backbone, you see.'

'So they haven't arrived yet?'

I whirled round. Pembridge stood in the doorway, his expression veering between cantankerous and amused. 'Lucas says he won't be coming down because his egg this morning was too runny,' he added. 'We shall see about that.'

'Oh, he'll be down in a flash when he hears Essie's voice,' said Bertie, from the mirror, where he was still poking at his hair.

Pembridge raised an eyebrow when he saw this. 'I don't think your hair will be my aunt's first priority after months abroad.'

'You would be surprised, David. She has been gone so long this time that you have forgotten her gimlet eye,' replied Bertie.

'In case you're wondering, Miss Fairford, my aunt Victoria and her daughter, Essie, will be here shortly. They've been travelling since the beginning of the summer – my aunt has a passion for gallivanting that we can only hope Essie shares, since she has to go too.'

Just as I felt excitement stir inside me, a much stranger sensation prickled at my temples: cold, like melting ice droplets. I blinked a couple of times and they retreated.

'You don't need to be here, of course,' Pembridge continued. 'It's Saturday and I'm sure you're entitled to a day off by now. I'm afraid the buses are rather infrequent on the hill but, as you like walking, you might enjoy a stroll into Cheltenham. It's half an hour's brisk walk, perhaps forty minutes, to Montpellier. Leckhampton and South-town are nearer, more or less at the bottom of the hill, but not as genteel. I prefer them but you may not.'

I looked at him in confusion. 'Do you want me to leave?'

His pained expression was that of the perpetually mis-understood. 'It is your day to do as you please. Stay or go. It is of no consequence to me. I only meant that you need not wait for my aunt's arrival out of any sense of duty or . . . *politeness.*' He uttered the last word with contempt and I couldn't tell – as I often couldn't with him – whether the contempt was directed at me or the concept.

'I have limited interest in shops and cafés,' I said, as air-ily as I could. In fact, and to my annoyance, I felt quite stung. I had assumed I would be introduced to the guests as a full member of the household, which I suppose was another example of my naivety.

Pembridge raised a sceptical eyebrow.

'Not all women care for shopping,' I went on. 'I shall go for a country walk instead. To see this Blue you men-tioned, perhaps. It's much drier today.'

We all turned to look out of the French windows. Though there had been no more rain since my unnerving encounter in the night, the sky was pregnant with new clouds. A slanted, bluish darkening over the Malverns was almost certainly a heavy shower already in progress. It would likely head our way.

'Well, if that's what you wish to do . . .' He paused, then seemed to relent. 'Why don't you ask Agnes to show you the boot room? There are dozens of pairs of old wellingtons in there – something is bound to fit you. Take a mackintosh too – I don't like the look of that sky.'

'Thank you,' I said awkwardly. He had an unerring knack for making me feel self-conscious. I turned to Bertie. 'I hope you enjoy your reunion with your sister.'

'We shall be beaten about the head with her political opinions, I'm sure,' said Pembridge, in such a jocular tone that both Bertie and I stared at him. 'As well as given a blow-by-blow account of her travels, of course. Believe me, Miss Fairford, when I say it will be a lucky escape for you.'

He stood looking at me in his queer, intense way, and I realized that he was trying to make up to me for virtually ejecting me from the house. What a strange creature he is, I thought, oddly pleased.

'She is rather forthright, Miss Fairford,' said Bertie. 'You have to keep your wits about you.'

Emboldened by Pembridge's efforts, and certain that I was otherwise going to miss another of my grandmother's memories summoned from the past into vivid life, I thought it might be a good moment to ask about Helen. Perhaps she was abroad, as her sister had been, and that was why her father missed her so. My grandmother had told me how fond she was as a child of maps and atlases.

'Well,' I said to Bertie, 'I'm sure I would be very interested to hear her opinions, particularly on the women's question. And her adventures abroad I would love to hear of, too. I've been virtually nowhere. Is your other sister also away overseas?'

Bertie turned ashen. His brown eyes, magnified behind their spectacles, began, alarmingly, to fill with tears. It was Pembridge who rescued me. 'Sadly not, Miss Fairford.'

His voice was almost as gentle as it had been when he'd gone in to Lucas that first time. 'My mother died some years ago, though you weren't to know.'

Unhappy that I had upset Bertie, and probably Pembridge too, I couldn't leave Fenix House quickly enough, however intrigued I was about Victoria. Pushing away thoughts of the young, serious Helen I had been told about and who was now sadly gone, evidently before her time, I dashed downstairs and dragged Agnes, tutting, to the boot room. I insisted that the first pair of wellingtons I tried on were the perfect fit, though in fact they were far too big. Rolling her eyes, she handed me two pairs of thick woollen socks to pad them out.

'Where are you off to in such a hurry, then?' She stood with her hands on her hips as I wrenched on the last sock. She was cleaner and tidier than I'd yet seen her; presumably because of Victoria's return.

'I thought I'd go for a walk in the woods. It's my day off.'

Agnes snorted. 'Day off! Chance would be a fine thing for some of us.'

'You must have time off. There are laws about it, aren't there?'

'Oh, they'd give me a day and another half-day too, if I wanted it. It's what I'd do that's the trouble. I've no one to see and nowhere to go. So I reckon I may as well just stop here.'

I studied her face. She sniffed sadly and gazed wistfully into space. She was doing it for sympathy, of course, but there was truth in what she said. Her world had narrowed to the size of Fenix House's acreage long ago. 'Why don't you come with me?' I said. The words were out before I'd thought what it would be like to spend a significant amount of time alone with Agnes.

'Me, come with you, for a walk?' she asked incredulously.

'Why not? It's ages till lunch – it's only just gone ten. Are you needed to serve at the visit?'

'Not till later. She likes to get her own cup of tea, says I don't make it right.'

'What about the food?'

'Meat's in. Cabbage and sprouts is on. I suppose I could spare an hour or so.'

She was pretending reluctance but I knew that underneath she was flattered. Now that I had relinquished the opportunity, I couldn't think of anything I wanted to do more than go for a solitary walk. The pleased blush staining Agnes's cheeks cheered me, though.

After ten minutes of fussing – changing clothes, informing Pembridge as to where she was going (probably daring him to forbid her when, of course, he would never have given her the satisfaction) then setting out a tea-tray for Victoria – I was holding back the stubborn gate for both of us to squeeze through.

Twenty-six

We didn't talk on the steep path into the woods. The way had been so narrowed by stinging nettles, bindweed and the trailing white wisps of old man's beard that we were forced to walk in single file. I was worried that the going would be too much for Agnes and led at a slow pace. In fact, limp aside, she was either kept fit by all the stairs she climbed in the house or determined not to show me otherwise. She stayed on my heels the whole way, her breathing not much harder than mine. When the path finally flattened and took us under the canopy of trees, we stopped for a rest.

'It's been a while since I did that,' she said, one hand kneading her bad hip. 'I tell you, it's a sight easier without stays. I never bother with them, these days. Much to Mrs Granger's approval, o' course.'

'Mrs Granger?'

'She who's coming today. Miss Victoria, as she were.'

It was almost impossible to imagine Victoria as anything but a trying six-year-old. I realized with a jolt that she'd be at least fifty now.

Agnes gave me a sideways glance. 'Well, officially she's Mrs Granger.' She looked around and dropped her voice, though the chances of anyone eavesdropping in the quiet woods were virtually non-existent. 'They don't spend more time together than they have to – haven't for ten, eleven years now. He's got a family house, out Tetbury way. Great big coffin of a place it is, freezing, even in high summer. She don't like it, never did, really, so she makes sure she's off on her travels whenever she can manage it, that girl of hers going along too. I tell you what, though, and talking of coffins: the mistress must be turning in hers to think of her little Vicky as good as divorced.'

'So, she wasn't alive when they began to lead separate lives?'

'Oh, no, the mistress has been gone twenty years. More, I should think. I never was much good at my sums.'

'What did she die of?'

'She was always ailing, that one. If it wasn't one thing, it was another. Her chest was weak and it was the consumption that got her in the end. She used to go to the seaside a couple of times a year and that always put the colour in her cheeks, but then she'd come back and start failing again. She reckoned it was the damp on the hill side of the house. Or the air in general. She always insisted the windows were kept shut, whatever the season. Really, she'd have rather been in the town. Cheltenham's always been known for its cures – not just the water but the mild air down there, in the valley. The mistress never liked being stuck up here, away from it all. It was one of the few things she and I saw eye to eye about.'

We lapsed into silence. The trees over us were still thick with dusty leaves, though they were beginning to drop. There was no sun beyond the canopy, only clouds, and if I hadn't known the time, I would have guessed the end of the day was approaching fast.

'Shall we walk to the ruins, go and see the Devil's Chimney?' I said suddenly. My grandmother had told me about that strange place, how her first sight of it had been pointed out by Victoria, who was probably in the kitchen at Fenix House now, measuring tea leaves for the pot.

Agnes stopped and looked at me warily. 'You been talking to Mr Bertie?'

I nodded as convincingly as I could and, after another searching look, she seemed to accept this.

'He's often confused about the past,' she went on, 'though not as bad as . . . Well, he's stuck in it half the time, I should say. He must have been when he said that to you, any road. The Devil's Chimney's long gone, and so have the ruins.'

'Gone?'

'Come on. You'll see what I mean when we get there.'

It took us another ten minutes and, as with the journey up the hill from the station, the path felt jarringly familiar at times. I wondered what my grandmother was doing in that instant, to the south in Bristol. Hearing about Helen had made me miss her again. I knew she would be missing me, too, but I at least had a new place and new people to distract me, even if I felt I half knew them already. She was in the same place and alone.

'I bet you're thinking about home, aren't you?' Agnes said, breaking into my thoughts.

To my embarrassment, her unexpected perception nearly undid me, and I had to gather myself before I answered, in case I burst into tears. The sudden pang of homesickness had crept up on me as stealthily as it had in the dining room on my first evening.

'Don't upset yourself now,' she said awkwardly, patting my shoulder. 'It's understandable. Every governess and maid we've had has been the same. Even I shed a tear when I first arrived, and I couldn't wait to leave home behind. Seven brothers and sisters, a ma who don't like you, and a pa what drinks too much will do that to you.' She stopped and uttered a short, bitter laugh. 'I suppose this is home now, for me. I'd have liked my own place one day, however humble, but I suppose it wasn't to be.'

I dabbed at my eyes with my handkerchief as we set off again. Apart from our feet rustling fallen leaves and snapping twigs, the woods were oddly silent. I could see now why Agnes had dropped her voice earlier: it was almost as if the trees were listening.

'I must be the latest in a long line of governesses,' I said softly. High above us in the canopy, the topmost leaves shivered in a breeze that couldn't be felt deep in the heart of the woods. At a crossroads of five different paths that suddenly chimed in my memory, I turned right for the ruins before Agnes signalled for me to do so. She didn't seem to notice.

'We haven't needed a governess for years,' she said. 'But there was a flurry of them when Bertie's sisters were young – he went to school, you see. He's probably told you about that. Well, after the third left because of Victoria's shenanigans, their father relented and let them go to the Ladies' College. No doubt that's where Madam got her ideas about emancipation and suffering and what-have-you. Personally, I don't know what good the vote would do me, if I had it. What have them men in London got to do with me?'

'Did they all leave because of Victoria?' I said.

'Not the first, not directly, anyway. She was a tougher nut to crack than those what followed.'

I felt my scalp prickle. 'What was her name?'

'Jenner,' said Agnes, without hesitation. 'Harriet Jenner. She had spirit, that one. I liked her more than the rest of 'em put together – she were braver than she looked. You should have heard her and the mistress that last day, before she went. Me and Mary were listening in the stairwell, eyes like saucers.'

I frowned, wondering what she meant. I might've asked but at that moment we came to what should have been the clearing my grandmother had described so vividly: the land scooped out like a bowl, the ruined dwellings at the bottom of it and the tall stack of rock that was the Devil's Chimney teetering on high. It was so changed that I would never have thought it the same place. Victoria's beloved ruins of almost half a century before had been transformed into what Lucas had so aptly christened the Blue.

It had a savage sort of beauty. Although I supposed it was man-made, just as the former ruins had been, I felt as though Agnes and I were the first to discover it. After the muted, earthy tones of the woods, the colour of the Blue was astonishing. In fact, Lucas's name for it hardly did justice to the expanse of opaque milky turquoise before me. It was so exotic in that setting, a glacial beacon against the mild and pleasant English landscape, that it looked alien, other-worldly.

'It steals your breath away, don't it?' muttered Agnes, at my side. 'You forget until you see it again.'

I tried to superimpose my image of the former ruins upon the unmoving waters before me but I was too dazzled by the incredible colour to manage it. Against the threatening sky above us, which was darkening even as

Agnes and I stood there, the pool glowed ever more vibrantly. I think we were both half hypnotized by it.

'Is it deep?'

'Not as deep as it looks. You'd think it carried on, down and down, till it reached the centre of the earth. But it don't. It's maybe ten, fifteen feet at the deepest part. That's enough to get into trouble, though, and it's not just the depth – it's what's in it. You wouldn't want to take down too many mouthfuls, however pretty it might look. It's full of poisons, they say, metals and rock dust and dead things. All kinds of muck.'

We stood quietly for a minute. 'And what about the Devil's Chimney?'

'The top stone came off, didn't it? We all knew it would one day. Then they pulled the rest down when they flooded the valley. It's all down there somewhere, under the water. You can't see much – the water's too cloudy – but there's boys what swim in it on hot days. You can't keep 'em away by telling 'em it's dangerous. You know how boys are – a danger sign to them is a red rag to a bull – but it's said that the fallen stones have made strange shapes. That it's almost like one o' them drowned villages, like they have in those valleys flooded to make reservoirs.

'It's not just the stones from the Chimney – there were buildings here once, too. They were for the quarrymen. One poor soul fell off the top of the Chimney one day . . . fell or jumped, no one was sure. How Miss Vicky used to harp on about that! Anyway, these days, the boys dare each other to swim through where the doors and windows used to be set into the cottages that had been put up for men like him. It's not easy when you can't see and you're holding your breath. Every few years one of them drowns. And if they're not drowning themselves, they're shattering their bones jumping off there.'

She pointed upwards. Behind the far side of the Blue, the cliff face rose tall and impassive, in dozens of shades of grey, ochre and sand. About thirty feet above the surface of the water there was a narrow, eroded ledge. You could see from the skidding trail of loose stones how the local boys scrambled down to it from the grassy clifftop, where I could just make out a roll of trampled-down barbed wire.

'There's a wooden sign up there, warning folks off,' said Agnes. 'I can't see it so they must have kicked it down again. It's put back up but a day or two later it's down again. Once it was thrown off altogether and found floating in the Blue.'

I saw it then, as clearly as if I had spied inside Agnes's mind. A white square with DANGER in bold red capitals floating in a sea of brilliant blue. A nerve at my temple flared, but it was cold again, like a drip of ice water. It rolled from my hairline down to my cheekbone. I put my fingers to it even though I knew nothing would be there.

'This place has always brought something out in folk,' said Agnes, a strange smile lighting her face, smoothing the lines away.

The air had turned colder while she'd been talking and I didn't think we'd beat the rain home. The pool, the looming rock and the dense trees behind us seemed to be waiting for it to begin, an anticipatory hum circling around us, just below my hearing. The sky had darkened to an oppressive shade of dirty violet, which made the Blue more glaring. The whole scene was like an old photograph spoilt by splashes of heavy-handed colour added later, gaudy and artificial.

I knew we should leave but I had another question. 'When did they flood it here?'

'Ah, now, that's an easy one to remember,' said Agnes. She still looked younger, as though the act of recalling the past had erased some of the years from her face. 'It was just before she left. The governess I was talking about before. Miss Jenner.'

I'm not sure whether it was the altered light and cooling air, or the mention of my grandmother's name when I had been absorbed in Agnes's story and briefly forgotten her, but I began to feel dizzy and nauseous.

'Are you all right, miss?' Agnes said, her face looming close, right into mine. 'You look a bit queer.'

To distract myself, I took some deep breaths and rubbed at my arms, where gooseflesh had risen.

'Has someone walked over your grave?' Agnes pressed.

I didn't answer her because that sweet, cloying smoke had curled into my nose again. The Blue's bright waters had been utterly still and empty, like an eye filmed and blind, but suddenly I thought I saw a face in the depths. I gasped and stumbled into Agnes, who put her arms out to steady me. Heart hammering, I looked again and the face, if it had ever been there, had gone. It had been a flash, a fraction of a second's glimpse, and I couldn't summon it again. All I knew was that it had been male. I thought of the drowned boys Agnes had mentioned but that didn't ring true. Not old enough, I thought, with a certainty I didn't understand. Perhaps it was the man who'd fallen to his death.

A ripple radiating out on the far side of the Blue, close to the cliff face, made me gasp again. I suppose I was expecting something to rise to the surface. Then, in a different part of the water, I saw another ripple, and another. Looking up at the glowering sky, I saw that whatever was making them came from above, not below. Rain had started to fall.

'There you are. I knew we'd get caught,' said Agnes, triumphantly, her hands still gripping me comfortingly. 'Come on, let's get under them trees again. They'll keep off the worst of it.'

All my dizziness gone, I felt completely awake in that eerie place. The rain was intensifying but something held me, and I think if Agnes hadn't been there I'd have found it hard to tear myself away. It wasn't just the dazzling, hypnotic water or what I thought I'd seen: something had happened there and it wasn't the death of the quarryman. I was sure of it.

Twenty-seven

Harriet

The weather continued to disappoint in the week following the walk back from church in the rain. In hindsight it seemed quite appropriate, for it was at this point that the equable, dreamy mood of the household began to disintegrate and turn. Even when it wasn't pouring, an enervating damp seemed to permeate every corner of Fenix House. The children were irritable and tearful, and their normally peaceable father was unusually exasperated, shouting at Agnes when she dropped a loaded tea-tray on his desk. The mistress, for her part, turned sulky and withdrawn, as if the last weeks with her brother had proved a surfeit of pleasure and, like too much cake, had made her sick.

Only the captain remained in good humour, though even that seemed pulled now by an exhaustingly intense undertow. Apparently oblivious to everyone else's bad temper, he cajoled the Pembridges into parlour games each evening and jaunts into Cheltenham during the day. Harriet continued to avoid him as much as she could, though she found it difficult to forget about him and the danger he seemed to emit as she taught her charges in the morning room. When she wasn't worrying about him, she was endlessly going over the conversations she had had with Robert, obsessively interpreting and reinterpreting every word, every glance. Frustrated as she increasingly was, because she couldn't see him whenever she liked, she was full of a secret joy too. There was a sort of euphoria in the way he had planted himself in her heart, never mind if it was hopeless. Dear Robert, she found herself whispering to herself in the hall and on the stairs and in her bed at night.

Late one afternoon, when she had dismissed Helen and Victoria for an hour or two's respite before supper, she lingered at the window she normally kept at her back, mindful that if she allowed herself to stare out of it, she would lose herself in daydreams. The thick mass of clouds that had overrun the sky were lit spectacularly from behind by an invisible sun, turning them a deep indigo edged with celestial gold.

Hidden in a small leather purse tied inside her skirts was a miniature of her mother, a scrap of fabric from a brown velvet dress she had loved as a child and wept over when it was outgrown, and the little dagger. She couldn't recall why she had taken to carrying the last item in her skirts but she liked to feel its smooth solidity. It was a comfort, just as the nearby presence of Captain Dauncey had the opposite effect. The knowledge that its discovery on her person would see her immediately dismissed without a character made no difference. It was supposed to be hers now, and that was all there was to it.

She had been about to open the purse so she could get it out and feel again the curious warmth of the metal when there was a knock at the door. She turned, her heart lifting in case it was Robert, but it was Captain Dauncey who strode uninvited into the room. In the flesh, and in a room with no one else but her in it, he was somehow even larger than she remembered him. He glanced at her hand in her skirts and she had to fight the urge to back towards the wall, like a naughty child caught in some misdemeanour.

'I need you,' he said bluntly, his eyes bright in the light from the window.

When she could do nothing but stare, her hand fluttering first to her breast and then down again to her skirts where the blade was secreted, he relented and smiled. 'For croquet, Miss Jenner, before you swoon to the ground. We're an odd number.'

He was gone before she could object to his insolence or refuse to play, leaving her with little choice but to follow him outside. He was waiting for her at the French windows, and she realized, as she edged gingerly past him, that they were in the same place he had approached her before, when the rain had run off him in streams and she had been able to smell his skin above the heady scents of the steaming garden.

Helen ran forward when she saw Harriet. 'Did Uncle Jago persuade you to come and play with us?' she asked eagerly. 'You can be my partner, if you like.' She looked down at her feet and frowned. 'I'm not very good, though, so I won't mind if you'd rather not.'

'I thought she might like to partner my nephew,' said the captain, suddenly so close behind her that she could feel the heat of his breath on her neck. 'What do you say, Bertie? As you're such a staunch admirer of Miss Jenner.'

A scarlet stain crept rapidly up the boy's neck. Harriet

moved smartly away from the captain, who was trying not to laugh.

'What do you mean by that, Jago?' called the mistress, querulously, from the far side of the croquet lawn. In the distance, thunder rumbled.

'Oh, I couldn't possibly say,' he said, shaking his head in mock-seriousness.

'Bertie?' The mistress was annoyed, her hand tightening around her mallet. 'What nonsense is your uncle talking now?'

Always a truthful boy, Bertie flushed even darker. He tried to speak but nothing came out until he gulped and cleared his throat. 'I – I suppose Uncle Jago saw me delivering a note to Miss Jenner's room on Sunday last.' His face was sunk in misery.

'A *note*?' said the mistress, with distaste.

'A love letter, I'll be bound,' said the captain, gleefully. 'Come now, you must tell us what it said.'

'I'm afraid you're mistaken,' said Harriet, clearly. 'There was a note but its contents were quite innocent. I asked Bertie for his help with one of my lessons. He is so very good at the names of the plants, trees and creatures here in the garden that I asked him to write me a list of butterflies we might see.'

'We've not once had a lesson on butterflies,' objected Victoria.

'Not yet,' said Harriet, firmly. 'But we shall. I had planned it for tomorrow, in fact.' She gave the captain a stony look and had the pleasure of seeing a flicker of irritation cross his face. Bertie, she knew without looking, was glowing with gratitude.

If she'd thought spoiling Captain Dauncey's sport would lend her a sense of power, then she was mistaken. As the game of croquet progressed, she felt increasingly claustrophobic. It was a strange sensation, especially as she stood outside on the broad lawn, the whole of the valley spread out at her feet. The thunder, which had been content to remain in the background, now grew louder. It was drawing closer, close enough that it was possible to discern the echo it made as it reverberated off the lime-stone cliffs behind the house.

'Let's go up to the Devil's Chimney to hear it better,' cried Victoria, though with no real hope of the idea being taken up.

'Don't be absurd, Vicky,' said the mistress, with a frown at the sky. Her mouth had set in a petulant moue: she and her favourite child were losing. 'We shall have to abandon the game, before the lightning gets too close and the rain comes down. Goodness, what weather we're having!'

'We might go up there, Lulu,' said the captain. At his words, Victoria whooped and threw down her mallet. 'The rain is miles away yet. With the thunder clashing and echoing up there, it will be quite thrilling. Besides, if it starts to rain hard, we can shelter under the trees. We should all go, even the little governess.'

He looked at Harriet and, though she wouldn't meet his gaze, she could feel his eyes boring into her. She grim-aced as a sharp bolt of pain tore through her head. Shutting her eyes, she felt the more familiar clamp and squeeze follow it. Her legs prickled coldly.

'Are you ill, Miss Jenner?' said Helen. 'You've gone white.' She put a gentle hand on Harriet's arm.

'I – I'm afraid you will have to excuse me,' she said faintly. 'A sudden headache. I shall have to lie down.' This was not just a glimmer, though it was certainly connected to it. It was more than that – more even than when, as a little girl, she had known in her bones that there would be a fire. This was closer, somehow: a red mist curling through her mind signalling imminent danger.

She pushed her mallet towards Helen and turned to leave, her eyes half closed against the waves of pain still eddying through her head.

'Jago!' she heard the mistress call. 'Jago, what are you doing?'

As Harriet heard this, she felt him suddenly next to her. The rasp of his breath seemed horribly loud.

'I will escort Miss Jenner inside,' he called, to his sister. 'In case she falls.' He grasped her shoulder with one hand, the other pressed into the small of her back. She could smell his scent again, beneath the soap he had washed with that morning.

She didn't have the strength to shake him off so they proceeded slowly towards the house together. No one behind them spoke. She could only think dimly that the mistress was too furious to say anything more in front of the children. Harriet would pay for this, she knew, but for the moment she didn't care. All she could think of was how she might escape the captain's clutches.

In the relative gloom of the parlour, out of sight of the croquet lawn, he dropped his hand to curl it around her waist. Pushing past the pain in her head, she tried to shake him off but he held her effortlessly, a mouse in a hawk's talons.

'Oh, Miss Jenner, I'm only trying to help you,' he said, in a low, teasing voice. She felt as though she could hear his blood surging through his body, darker and thicker than hers. She closed her eyes against the pain in her temples.

Then, suddenly, another voice. It sounded to Harriet like balm.

'Let me take Miss Jenner to her room, Captain,' it said. 'You go back outside now.'

In her confusion, Harriet thought for a moment that it was Mrs Rakes – the polite but firm authority in the voice, perhaps: a voice that in its very courtesy brooked no easy rebuttal. The captain let go of her so abruptly that she swayed where she stood. When she was steady again, the pain in her head ebbing, she opened her eyes. To her surprise it was Agnes.

Twenty-eight

It wasn't long after the abandoned croquet game that Harriet found herself in Robert's company again and this time they were quite alone. The day almost gone, she had returned to the makeshift schoolroom to retrieve her opal ring, which she had been twisting around her finger and finally taken off during the last hour of lessons. It was precious to her, having belonged to her dead mother; her father hadn't had the heart to sell it, giving it to Harriet instead. As the afternoon had not long deepened into dusk, no one had yet been up to light the gas lamps in the hall and she was picking her way carefully so that she wouldn't walk into a plant stand or slip on the polished tiles.

As she approached the study door, she saw a narrow strip of warm light under it and knew he must be inside. She paused, wondering whether the heavens would fall in if she dared knock. No doubt they would not but, still, she didn't have the courage, not yet. She had just set off towards the morning room again when the study door opened.

'I – I didn't knock, did I?' she said, turning in surprise. She couldn't think how else he might have been summoned at that precise moment.

He smiled. She could just make out the gleam of it, though his face was in shadow. 'I do not believe so. Why – did you intend to?'

She blushed and wished she had her ring on so that she might have something to do with her hands. She was acutely aware that her own face was well lit by the room behind him.

'I simply had an urge to stretch my legs,' he continued, 'and here I find you, Miss Jenner. Harriet.'

She started at his use of her first name and glanced around the hallway. Below their feet, she could just make out the rattle of saucepans and the murmur of conversation between the servants, but everything above stairs was quiet.

'Would you like to come in?' he said, seeing her furtive look.

She was about to decline politely, saying she had only come to fetch her ring, when she thought of the empty evening stretching ahead. He watched her closely as she took a breath, then passed under his arm and into the study, just as she had the last time. She had only to duck a little: there was at least a foot in height between them.

Once inside, she gazed around the room with pleasure, finding it even more handsome on her second visit. He'd pushed the window open to its full extent and through it she could smell the scents of the garden, as well as the melancholy dampness that always crept in with the gloaming. The sun that had finally put in an appearance during the late afternoon had just slipped below the horizon, leaving the sky aflame with vivid streaks of pink and orange. Bathed in its warm light, the mahogany of the bookshelves shone, the gold leaf on the books' spines glinting and winking as she moved around.

Instead of returning to the desk, Robert remained standing close to her. The sky seemed to intensify even as they watched it in silence. Harriet knew that someone should speak, the yawning silence not awkward but too intimate, yet her mind felt empty of everything but physical sensation – all the witty and intelligent observations she rehearsed when she was alone vanished along with the sun.

'I so enjoyed our talk on the way back from church the other week,' he said finally, the words spoken so softly that she found herself turning her face up to his.

'Yes,' she breathed. She could smell him, cool and fresh as water, and something else that was oddly comforting. It was starch, she realized. Her father's collars had once given off the same aroma, but that was many years before, when Harriet was still a small girl. Before the fire. Before Louisa and her family had blighted their lives.

Robert cleared his throat. 'I hoped we might have a chance to continue it, perhaps this coming Sunday.'

'I would like that, although . . .'

'Although?'

'It is difficult for me, Mr Pembridge.'

'Robert, please. Surely, when we are alone, you can call me by my name?'

'Robert, then. Whatever you wish me to call you, it remains difficult. I would not want anyone to think that I . . .' She did not know how to put it and shook her head.

'A man is allowed to walk and converse in the open air with someone employed in his household, is he not?'

'Yes, of course, but what we are doing now would be looked upon much more dubiously.'

In the quiet that followed, she could hear his breathing. It was not quite steady, just as hers was not.

'But, you see, there were some things I wanted to say to you, before the others caught up with us,' he tried again.

Without being asked, she sat down in an easy chair close to the unlit fire. She felt she needed a little less proximity to hear what he had to say.

'I find myself drawn to you,' he continued. 'In truth, I have felt that connection since the first day we met. I shouldn't admit to such a thing, not even to myself, but I find I cannot help it. And I think after all that it's easier to say it here, in the shadows, than it would have been in broad daylight, on the way back from church.'

Harriet didn't know how to respond. Part of her wanted to rush to her room so she could play out the scene in safety. Another part wanted to stay in the hushed and comfortable study for ever. The whole thing felt as though it floated free from reality. He was right: there was daring to be found in the dark.

'I have finished the book you gave me,' she said suddenly. 'I wanted to thank you for that again. It was such a kind gift.'

'I'm glad you think so. I . . . Well, I only recalled the plot in its entirety after I'd given it to you, and I was anxious that you would reach the end and think me –' He stopped and flung himself into the chair opposite her. 'I remembered that it was about a governess, that was all. I would never presume to think that . . . Oh dear, I am not explaining myself very well.'

She couldn't help it: disappointment flooded through her. Of course he could not have intended to send such a bald message. He had only just met her. He was married. She looked away so he couldn't read her face.

'I have offended you.'

She shook her head.

He leaned forward in his seat and craned to see her expression. 'Did you ... did you think I gave it to you knowing . . .? Oh, I would now, believe me.'

At that, she turned to him and he shrugged half angrily.

'I have tried to deny this connection, or else dismiss it as nothing much, but I am unable to. I know it's wrong. I am a husband and a father. I love my children.'

'I know you do.' *And your wife?* she wanted to add. *Do you love her?*

'Sometimes, when I am on the train or if I can't sleep, I talk to you in my mind.'

She looked at him sharply.

'You too?' he said. 'Ah, now that will be a comfort to me, though knowing it will only make it harder to stop.'

They sat quietly for a while, though Harriet knew that their minds were busy – hers was certainly: she was trying to absorb all he had said, as well as appreciate that she was alone with him now when soon she wouldn't be. *This is what it would be like if we were married*, she thought. *We'd sit either side of the fire and sometimes we'd simply be quiet like this, with no need to fill the silence with silly chatter.*

'What are you thinking?' he asked.

She laughed. 'I shan't tell you.'

'But I want to know everything about you. I feel as if I know you to your core and yet I know almost nothing about you at all. Tell me a secret about yourself, just one – something that no one else knows.'

She wondered what he would think of her, whether he'd imagine she was teasing him or whether he would look at her with fear, as her father once had. The dark pressed around them, cushioning her and making her brave.

'Very well. I will tell you my secret and you must decide whether or not you believe me.'

He leaned forward, amused and intrigued. 'Yes?'

'Occasionally, I see pictures of the future.' Her heart was beating wildly in her chest, though she kept her voice steady.

He laughed and frowned at the same time, unsure how to respond. 'Like a fortune teller, you mean?'

Unsmiling, she held his gaze. 'I said it would be up to you whether you believed me. I have been like this since I was a little girl of about Helen's age. One night I had what my father dismissed as a bad dream, but I knew was something quite different. I was filled with dread because I knew for certain that there was going to be a fire. I could hear it and smell it as though the room around me was burning. The next morning my father went to the auction house he owned and found nothing left but charred timbers. He was not insured.'

Robert was serious now. 'And since then you have had more of these . . . premonitions?'

'I call them "glimmers" because they do not usually provide a clear picture. It is sensation more than anything. And, yes, I have had some since then. There is one that comes to me periodically – I can't make it out, though I try, in case one day I can send a warning. I was too late for my father.'

'No, you were not too late. But you were only a child and he didn't understand what you were telling him.'

She looked at him, the good man sitting opposite her, who seemed to understand her so well. She had always felt guilty about the fire but some of that lifted away now, smoke dispersed by a country breeze in summer.

'Thank you for telling me that,' he said. 'For trusting me with it.'

She smiled, suddenly embarrassed. 'I don't expect a rational man like you to believe it.'

'It is no more a leap of faith than what we are asked to believe in church.'

'But I don't think you do believe much of what we are told in church.'

He smiled wryly. 'Very astute of you, madam. I do, however, believe you. My instinct tells me to.'

He got to his feet and regarded her seriously. She swallowed, unsure what he was about to do, but certain that he would begin by taking her hands in his. She could already feel the warm solidity of them as she rose and moved towards him. They were almost touching when there was a knock at the door.

'J-just a moment,' he said loudly. He gestured for Harriet to sit in a hard chair by the desk and then, after smoothing down his jacket, strode to the door.

It was Mary. She was carrying a small tray with a glass of something amber-coloured on it.

'I've brought your usual, sir,' she said, her sharp eyes taking in Harriet's unexpected presence and the darkened room in a glance. 'And shall I light the lamps for you?'

'Oh, yes, Mary. If you would. Miss Jenner and I had just finished our discussion. How very dark it's grown since you came in to ask my advice, Miss Jenner.' His jovial

234

tones rang out falsely and Harriet looked at her feet out of shame for both of them. Their cocoon of intimacy had been pierced.

Once Mary was fully occupied in lighting the gas, Robert saw Harriet to the door, with a last, lingering look as he held it open for her. Taking a great risk, which made her cheeks burn afterwards, he reached for her hand as she passed him, their fingers briefly entangling. The touch lasted only a second, but it was enough to carry her upstairs in a daze, as if she was walking not on the mistress's prized Wilton runner but on the lightest of clouds.

Twenty-nine

As the days of Captain Dauncey's visit had turned into weeks, Harriet had come to view the relationship between him and his sister as unusually close. Indeed, privately she thought it unnatural. The pair not only spent every waking minute together but their physical intimacy seemed to go well beyond normal propriety, even in a private house. Harriet was an only child so perhaps knew nothing of sibling relations, and yet ... She had never seen Helen nuzzle Bertie's ear, and neither could she imagine it, even when they were older.

The mistress was like a woman in love, or at least a foolish woman in love: constantly on the verge of hysteria, face flushed, fingers – one of which now wore a gaudy ring of lurid yellow gold brought back from India – forever seeking her brother's hand or sleeve or lapel. She professed to sleep badly; she had lost her appetite for the cakes and sweetmeats she normally couldn't resist; she insisted the doctor was called out three times in four days because she couldn't breathe or sit still or be laced into her gowns without bursting into tears. The sad truth was that, despite her genuine adoration of her brother, Captain Dauncey's much-vaunted visit was making her unhappy. Harriet had come to realize that it was possible to love someone too well.

The situation was tidily illustrated for her when she

came upon them one day, in the short stretch of passage-way between their rooms. Fortunately they didn't see her and she was able to melt back into the shadows – though not before the mistress darted forward to kiss her brother in the hollow at the base of his neck, where his open shirt revealed a crop of the thick blond hair that also covered his forearms. Humiliatingly, the captain pushed her away, as if she had initiated an intimacy that was too extreme even for him and, though he did it playfully enough, the mistress went off in a storm of tears. Harriet caught the roll of the captain's eyes before he followed his sister into her room and shut the door.

Louisa's fractious over-sensitivity, which at times made not just her brother but the entire household feel as if they were walking a high wire in a stiff breeze, continued for another week or two. Harriet alone felt almost grateful to the mistress for keeping the captain so close. As he was almost never alone, he was unable to approach her. In fact, since the episode on the croquet lawn, he couldn't even risk a casual comment thrown in her direction without his sister's wrath coming down on his head for at least half a day.

As for his nocturnal liaisons with Agnes, Harriet had no idea if he continued to go to her under the cover of night, once the mistress was safely insensible after a generous slug of one of her sleeping tonics. Either way, and as tightly wound as the mistress was, it seemed inevitable that she would eventually find something to be justifiably jealous about. She had fished for it long enough.

It was the unfortunate Bertie who tied the noose with which his uncle would hang himself. It was inadvertent, of course, there not being a single conniving bone in the boy's body, but Harriet thought it rather fitting that the man who had so teased his poor nephew over an innocent note to the governess would be undone by his own dropped letter. The mistress had missed its delivery at breakfast because she hadn't risen in time, so if the captain hadn't carelessly lost it on the stairs on his way up to see her, the secret he was hiding in India might not have come to light.

As it was, Bertie had come back in from the garden to sharpen his pencil and spied the missive on the third step from the top, gleaming white paper against the gloom of the unlit staircase. He wasn't a nosy boy but he caught sight of the sender's name as he scooped it up and was still holding it when he was admitted to his mother's sitting room. Which was why, when the captain snatched the letter from him and his mother asked Bertie sharply who it was from, he answered, 'It says on the back that it's from a Mrs Dauncey in India, Mama.'

Bertie might have been fobbed off with tales of distant great-aunts in Calcutta or neglected second cousins in Bombay, but the mistress was nobody's fool. When the captain reluctantly admitted that he had been married four months earlier to a 'little thing like you, Lulu, though of course not so lovely', her exclamations of incoherent rage could be heard almost as far away as the ice-house. Some hours later, when Harriet went down to the kitchen to ask Mrs Rollright about the nursery supper, Agnes was still repeating the story, as if only she had overheard the scandalous episode, her eyes wide and her mouth twisting as she tried not to laugh.

In fact, every soul within Fenix House's walls knew that the mistress had launched the teapot at the captain's head before taking to her bed. Harriet, for her part, could not share Agnes's glee at such a dramatic turn of events. As the days passed and no rapprochement between the siblings was forthcoming, she grew increasingly concerned. She began to feel again the sensations she had come to dread. Her legs prickled and fidgeted ceaselessly, and on the fourth morning of the mistress's self-exile she woke with a crushing headache.

The dream that she'd woken from might have offered her some clue as to what lay ahead, but the clamping ache at her temples rendered her incapable of grasping its message. There was nothing left but the bright lights that spun and exploded behind her eyes when she closed them against the pain, reminding her of a kaleidoscope she'd had as a child.

That day she was hardly able to conduct lessons. Every time she tried to concentrate, she saw the jewel-bright colours flashing in her peripheral vision. Occasionally she thought she could smell something too, but that was nearly as elusive as the dream. Only once did she come close to identifying it: as something like the captain's overripe scent. That made her shiver, even in the rather stuffy morning room. More than a few times that day, she found her fingers reaching for the little dagger that was now always secreted in the folds of her skirts. Aside from thoughts of Robert, it was the only thing that provided even a modicum of comfort. For Harriet knew only too well that, as long as the mistress continued to sulk, leaving her brother to his own devices, she couldn't feel safe.

The mistress's foibles, demands and tantrums aside, the rest of the household seemed oblivious of what felt like imminent danger to Harriet. Mrs Rollright continued to grumble about the amount of food she was required to produce at all hours, while Agnes, though excitable, was only slightly more clumsy and work-shy. Mrs Rakes, as usual, glided serene and unruffled through the turbulent waters: when Mary tried to air the mistress's sour-smelling, overheated rooms, thus admitting dangerous airs from outside, Mrs Rakes emerged unperturbed from the hour-long reprimand, her arm around the tearful housemaid.

Only Robert seemed to share Harriet's discomfort, having had to spend far more time in the evenings with his brother-in-law since the latter's estrangement from Louisa. As Dauncey's host, he clearly felt he had no choice but to fill the large vacuum of time left by his inconsolable wife, but the two men had nothing in common and their forced companionship created quite a strain, especially when Robert asked how the captain had secured such a long period of leave. It had been an innocent question but the captain had grown so belligerent that everyone within earshot suspected that he had got himself into serious trouble with his regimental superiors.

Harriet believed this awkwardness was one of the reasons Robert had taken to calling into the morning room each day, ostensibly to see his daughters but also to see her. It was as if the uneasy hours he spent flailing around for topics of conversation with Captain Dauncey made him even keener to seek out the easy flow of his and Harriet's talks, which, since the episode in the study, had been frustratingly snatched: the captain appeared with uncanny regularity every time they contrived to speak to each other. Fortunately, he avoided the morning room when lessons were taking place; he'd been severely rebuked by the mistress early on in his visit for distracting his nieces, though everyone had known it was because she didn't want him to spend time with the governess. Thus, the morning room became the only place Robert and Harriet could reliably exchange a word or two without his overbearing presence.

He almost confessed this one day in an undertone that even Victoria's bat-like hearing couldn't catch: he was finding the rest of the house rather frenetic, he said, compared to the tranquillity of the schoolroom. Another day, a little more boldly, he said that leaving the house when he was required to for his railway work would be something of a relief, if only he could take her with him in the brougham to continue their discourse. As for his wife and brother-in-law's tangled relations, though he never said so explicitly, it was obvious he found them unseemly and also rather tedious.

Of course, he didn't have to say anything at all – Harriet understood him perfectly. Their affinity was undeniable and, while his compliments thrilled her, it wasn't what was said during their brief meetings that generally signified. It was the nuance and subtlety that hid between the lines they spoke. It was the way the air tightened and hummed and the sun outside the window intensified, making everything it lit seem richer and finer. It was the way Robert's dark eyes looked right into hers, only to glance away as if he had read something in them that scalded him.

One morning, he was brave enough to marvel at their mutual sympathy in front of his daughters, and Harriet suspected that Victoria heard him that time – or at least comprehended her governess's answering blush. It was the only thing that explained the impertinent outburst that followed.

Robert had hardly closed the door with his usual soft click when she piped up, 'You like my father, don't you, Miss Jenner?'

Harriet lifted her head too fast. Victoria was a study of innocence, wrapping one of her flaxen curls around her pencil, her eyes wide and strikingly blue in the sunny room. Helen, who had been immersed in drawing a map of the Americas, also looked up at the mention of her beloved parent.

'Of course I like him,' said Harriet, carefully. 'He's a good man, and a very good father to you, Victoria.' She rather rushed the words and licked her lips self-consciously.

'Do you think him handsome, though?' persisted the little girl.

Harriet felt herself colouring again. 'I think that you should get on with your sums.'

Victoria, knowing she had won, went back to her books without another word. Harriet returned to her own book, which was a heavy and extremely dry account of Richard the Lionheart's forays into the Holy Land. For all her grasp of it, she might as well have been reading Arabic.

Something was going to happen before long at Fenix House, she could sense it. Things were shifting under her feet, ripples of unrest that would soon strengthen into waves that would shake and realign everything. Her unease around Captain Dauncey had only briefly ebbed after the day of the croquet match. Now, in the wake of his prolonged banishment from the mistress's favour, it was advancing with renewed force.

It occurred to her that, were she still as bent on revenge as she had been, she could have used the circumstances to her advantage: exchanging coy smiles with the captain, lingering in parts of the house where they might happen upon each other, thinking up little flirtations that would excite him the next time they met – all the things, in fact, that she had begun to do for Robert's benefit. Any connection with the captain would be sure to injure the mistress far more than any growing intimacy with her husband. But even without the deep feeling she now had for Robert, she couldn't have borne to encourage the captain. It went against all her instincts. Any fascination he had inspired in her as a Dauncey had fled; his magnetism to most women was reversed in Harriet – he repelled her.

Unfortunately, her aversion seemed only to increase her value to him. Again and again as the days filed past, the weather settling into a prolonged heatwave, she shied away from his meaningful looks and ignored his heavy-handed compliments. Without his sister clamped to his side, he was becoming ever more daring, ever more insolent – anyone who cared to watch for half a minute could see that.

She had caught Agnes's eyes flash from his face to her own and back again more than a couple of times when she had passed them in the hallway. After the third such instance, Harriet felt she had to say something to the maid, especially because of Agnes's unexpected help after

243

the croquet match. She managed to catch her on the attic floor one morning before the girls were awake. Each day Agnes brought hot water up for Harriet and the senior servants – it seemed like a good opportunity to speak with her, before the rest of the household were fully alert. Harriet herself had woken at dawn and forced herself to stay awake so she didn't miss the chance.

'Agnes,' she called softly. The maid was stretching at the top of the stairs, her hand at her neck as though it was stiff from a fitful night on her hard pallet. 'Agnes, can you come here a minute?'

'Is the water not warm enough?' the maid began, when she reached Harriet. 'It was hot when I left the kitchen. I haven't got time to be going up and down.'

'No, no, I'm sure the water is fine. I just wanted to ask you something.' As she spoke, Harriet realized what a foolish idea it had been. It was too late to turn back, though, and she ushered Agnes into her room and closed the door.

'I've got to get on, miss. If you've a complaint, you'll have to see Mrs Rakes about it.' Behind her affronted expression, her eyes were wary.

'There's no complaint. I wanted to ask you about Captain Dauncey.' Her voice sounded much firmer than she felt.

Agnes folded her arms. 'What of him?'

'Well, first, I wanted to thank you for what you did the other week, when you helped me upstairs.'

'That were nothing. You're better off with a woman helping you than a clumsy great man, that's all.'

'Yes, you're right, of course.' She saw that Agnes was

looking not only confused but sceptical. She had made a mistake in asking the girl into her room. To Agnes, Harriet probably wasn't that much lower than the mistress, what with her books and cleverness and pretty fire-opal ring. She turned the latter nervously on her finger now.

'So, what did you want then, miss? I don't mean to give cheek, but I must get back to the kitchen soon or I'll be late starting on the fires and Mrs Rollright will give me what-for.' She backed towards the door.

'I just . . . it's just that I didn't want you to think anything untoward . . . anything not quite . . . well –'

'What – between you and the captain?' Agnes smirked and hid it ostentatiously behind a chapped hand. 'Why would I think that, miss? He's friendly to any woman with breath in her, as far as I can make out. I wouldn't take it personal, if I were you.'

Harriet cursed her complexion, which seemed so quick to heat these days. 'No. I mean, yes, and I'm sure that you're right. It's just that I –'

'You have to be firm with the likes of him, miss.' Agnes giggled, half bobbed, then went on her way. After she'd disappeared down the stairs, Harriet sank onto her bed, and thanked God that, in her flustered state, she hadn't also mentioned Robert.

Thirty

Grace

Agnes and I hurried across the remains of the gravel drive, the rain pelting us hard now we were free of the woods and its sheltering trees. Despite the solidity of the housekeeper, who was still supporting me on one side, my mind hadn't yct returned to the present. It was still on the shores of the Blue. I wished I'd felt the water now, dipped my fingers into that unreal liquid. I was already forgetting how odd the place had made me feel. In fact, I was wondering when I could possibly return there. I felt it like a living thing at my back, high up beyond the thick ranks of beeches, birches and firs: a living thing with a low, rhythmic pulse, calling me back.

It wasn't until we had almost reached the house that I remembered who was inside. Victoria. A picture of how I had always imagined her from my grandmother's descriptions lit in my mind and it was that that finally broke the mesmeric powers of the Blue. To me, Victoria was all light and shine: platinum curls and pale pinafore, tiny white teeth bared in a mocking smile or a howl of rage. In that moment, I wasn't sure I wanted to lose her, too – another piece of my grandmother's story altered almost beyond recognition. I'd already had to get used to Bertie and Agnes grown old, the sorry state of the house, and the Pembridge patriarch hidden in the attic. Even the ruins were gone. And now Victoria too? With luck, I would be able to creep upstairs unobserved.

If we had used the front door, I might have stood a chance. As it was, Agnes had naturally headed for the servants' entrance at the side of the house, where steps slimy with moss led down to a door into the scullery. I let her go ahead and was still pulling off my borrowed boots when I heard an unfamiliar voice in the kitchen. Its clipped vowels betrayed a privileged upbringing and its tone, bordering on strident, offered a clue to its owner's character. That, at least, didn't seem to have changed.

'Oh, there you are, Agnes!' I heard her exclaim in the next room. I stayed where I was in the scullery, out of sight. 'Thank *goodness*. The beef is in danger of being burned to a cinder and there's no sugar in the bowl. I've looked everywhere for more. I said to David, "She's probably packed her bags and left you, and serve you right, too." But here you are, half drowned but still with us.'

I swallowed nervously and stepped into the kitchen. There was no other way unless I darted back up the steps and went round to the front door, which seemed ludicrous. Besides, now that I had heard her, my curiosity was piqued. I wanted to see how she had turned out.

'Ah, you must be the new governess,' she cried, when she spotted me. She was half a head taller than Agnes and, though her face was in shadow from the window set high in the wall behind her, I could clearly see the outline of her hair. It was still as light as I had imagined it, but the ringlets had gone. Perfectly straight and smooth, apparently giving off its own pale light in the dingy room, it was parted low on one side and had been shingled to her ears.

While I stood dumbly staring, she strode forward and stuck out her hand. 'Victoria Pembridge. Well, I should say Granger, but I've never liked it much. Doesn't feel like me.'

'Grace Fairford.' I took her hand. 'How do you do?'

'You're from Bristol, aren't you?'

I nodded. She was a good-looking woman but the prettiness had gone, strengthened and hardened into handsomeness. I felt sure she had chased it off as feminine silliness, just as she had cut her hair. The eyes, though, were surely the same, and just as I had pictured. Round and bright, only a shade or two paler than the waters of the Blue.

'If Essie wasn't going to join the Ladies' College, I'd consider bringing her to you,' she said, those eyes appraising me coolly as she spoke. 'We're lucky to have such a decent school here for girls. In my opinion, the girls' school is rather better than its counterpart for the boys. God knows, Bertie didn't seem to learn much in his day. Everything he knows is what he taught himself in the garden and woods. I went to the Ladies' College myself. Always in trouble – I seem to attract it – but I enjoyed my time there enormously. Half my Freedom League members are old pals from those days.'

'And how old is your daughter?'

'Essie's twelve and she's missed such a lot of schooling while we've been on our travels, but what could be more educative than seeing the world? Twelve!' She shook her head. 'How the years have simply whizzed by – I can hardly believe it.'

Essie was younger than I'd thought; Victoria must have become a mother quite late. The girl was hardly older than Lucas and yet she was the same generation as his father.

I must have looked distracted because she fixed me again with those startling eyes. 'Are you quite well, Miss Fairford? You seem rather a dreamy sort for a governess. We had one back when I was very small who was as sharp as a tack. More than a match for my antics.'

I made the effort to smile. 'I'm all right, thank you. I just . . . well, you looked familiar for a moment. Déjà vu, I think they call it.'

She paused, and I hoped she hadn't entirely dismissed me as an idiot. 'Well, as I was saying, it would be no bad thing for Lucas to have a fellow scholar here but Essie has expressed a burning desire to go to school. I've rhapsodized about the Ladies' College so much that it's hardly surprising. It's the reason we're back now, to catch the beginning of the new school year. We've missed the first week after a spot of trouble securing funds for the boat-train – Granger was being even more parsimonious than usual, which left us stranded in a rather dismal *pension* at Deauville – but she will start tomorrow.'

'You two back for good, then?' asked Agnes, in surprise.

'The girl wants to put down roots and I can't blame her. She loved Antibes and Juan-les-Pins and her French was coming on in leaps and bounds while we were there – she did all the ordering for us because my accent is abysmal – but I'm the traveller and I've been awfully selfish about it. In truth, I was desperate to go to Egypt for the winter – I'm certain Carnarvon is about to make a

breakthrough and if I could be there when he does . . .'
She sighed with longing. 'But Essie has held me to my promise and rightly so.'

'So she'll board, I suppose?' I said. 'Agnes mentioned that your husband's house is out towards Tetbury. That's a reasonable distance, isn't it?'

'Oh, that would be a terrible bore and I can't bear for Essie to board, though I'm sure she would relish the idea. No, we'll be moving in here next week. We'll stay at the Queen's until things are arranged.'

'Moving in here?' Agnes was scandalized.

'I thought you'd be pleased, my dear. What with Essie and myself, as well as Miss Fairford, we women will be as numerous as the men. Besides, Fenix House is the worst I've seen it. You probably don't notice, here every day as you are, but I bet our new arrival would have something to say about the state of the place.' She glanced at me. 'It's positively mired in gloom, not to mention dirt. Thank goodness, quite frankly, that I came back when I did.'

'What's wrong with your Hampstead place? There mus' be plenty of schools in London for the young 'un.'

'It's been taken for another year. They're terribly nice people and they always pay on time so I couldn't possibly turn them out. Besides, Essie'll have plenty of time to enjoy London when I shuffle off this mortal coil and she inherits the house. The girl wants the Ladies' College and who am I to refuse her? I have never known a child so enthusiastic about the prospect of school.'

'But where will you sleep?'

'Don't be ridiculous, Agnes. There are plenty of rooms. We can take over Mama's old bedroom and parlour –

Essie is accustomed to sharing quarters with me so she'll be well pleased to have her own room, even if it is adjoining mine.'

'They haven't been cleared since the mistress died. I don't like going in there, if truth be told. There's a queer feeling in them rooms of hers.'

Victoria rolled her eyes. 'You're as bad as Bertie. If the rooms haven't been cleared, then it's high time they were. Good grief, what do you all do with your days?'

'I have plenty to keep me occupied, thank you very much,' the housekeeper huffed.

'Well, all right, no need to be offended. I'll enjoy a good spring clean anyway, and never mind if it's autumn.'

'Have you broke the news to His Nibs that you're going to bide here now?'

'Oh, yes,' said Victoria gleefully, and quite suddenly I could see the naughty child shining out of her. 'His face was something to behold. He'll get used to it, though, and it was my house long before it was his.'

'Well, I'm sure Lucas will be thrilled,' I broke in. 'He's mentioned Essie more than a few times.'

'She's up there with him now. I said she could tell him the good news. How are you finding him, by the way?'

'I believe there's been some improvement. He's sleeping less in the day for one thing.'

'Good for you. David has been ridiculously overprotective of that boy since Frannie's death. It does the child no good at all. Agnes agrees with me on this, at least.'

The older woman nodded sagely. 'If you ask me, no child of that age should be allowed to decide whether he comes down or stays abed all day.'

'Absolutely right,' nodded Victoria. 'Of course, I'd like to see him at the boys' college, but I accept he's too fragile for that. Essie's presence will definitely help – Lord knows she's the only person in the world he appears to like. She's dreadfully patient with him. Not many girls would deign to sit with a boy who's so much younger. I said to her, "I don't know what magic spell you weave but he's quite tamed when you're with him." Now, I really must take up this sugar or David will have even more to grumble about. Agnes, I've got time to go up and see Pa before you serve, haven't I?' She caught my look of surprise. 'Please tell me someone has explained about him to you.'

I shook my head. 'Though I'm afraid I have seen someone who must be your father – heard him too. The first time I had got up in the night because I couldn't sleep. I – I don't think he saw me.'

'Well, he wouldn't. He's as blind as a bat, these days, poor old darling. My brother is going the same way too, as I'm sure you've noticed. Luckily my eyes are as sharp as they ever were. I must get it from Mama – she was eagle-eyed enough for two. That's where the blue comes from, anyway.'

I took a breath. 'I wondered about the older Mr Pembridge, but, well, I didn't like to pry . . .'

'You should have been told, my dear. Not least because you're sleeping on the same floor as him. He must have given you quite a turn if you came upon him stumbling about on the landing. Please don't think we treat him cruelly by keeping him up there, Miss Fairford. It's just that he is no longer the Papa we grew up with. He prefers his own company and chooses to be in the attic. He would have been happy in Mrs Rakes's old room but we had the whole north end made into one enormous room for him some years back. He likes the house to stay as it was, and never mind that the place is gradually falling down around our ears.

'As time has gone by, he's become ever more reclusive – and don't think I haven't tried everything to tempt him out. But he only becomes distressed and confused, loses sight of the years, if you'll pardon the pun, so we've learned to leave him in there. He doesn't want to do anything but play with those trains of his anyway. It's as though the last few decades haven't happened, quite frankly. We adore him, of course, and so we do the kindest thing, which in his case is to let him be.'

'Trains, you say?' I thought about the strange, muffled noises I'd heard: the vibrations and, once, a whistle.

Victoria sighed fondly. 'Model trains. Pa used to work for the railways. Mainly for the GWR. God's Wonderful Railway, he told us it stood for when we were small. He was a great admirer of Brunel.'

A hot surging pain went through my head, dissolving as quickly as it had arrived. In its wake, I saw the Exchange clock in Bristol: the black hand and its shadowy red twin, ten crucial minutes behind.

'The GWR,' I repeated stupidly, blinking away the last of the pain.

'You'll have travelled on it yourself, being a Bristol girl. Pa loved his work and then . . . Well, I suppose he's never got over it. You should see that room of his – not that you usually can. He keeps it in the dark, these days. I've never understood why he insists on that. You'd suppose he'd want all the light he could get with his eyes being as weak as they are.'

She shook her sensible head in bafflement and fixed her gaze on me again. 'Now, Miss Fairford, I'm glad to make your acquaintance and I wish you well. Don't be afraid to stand your ground if my nephew tries to interfere in your methods with Lucas. He's all bark and no bite, David, so you mustn't be cowed. As for your new charge, well, he can be a little devil, I grant you. It's a sight more complicated with him. You'll probably have to improvise there, I'm afraid. Essie and I will help you once we're settled in.'

She turned to Agnes and accepted a newly filled bowl of sugar and a pair of silver tongs streaked with tarnish. She was about to leave when something occurred to her and she looked back at me. 'Oh, and do consider coming to a Freedom League meeting, won't you? The Cheltenham chapter has been limping along but I'm going to take the reins again now I'm back in the town permanently. We could do with some young blood – Cheltenham is overrun with majors' wives and old bossy-boots like me. I feel as though we've rather abandoned our sense of purpose since the war ended and the men came home. It's all tea and cake now. Not like the old days, when we were out banging the drum with our sashes and banners. Ah, well.'

Without waiting for a response she was gone, bustling purposefully down the dim passage towards the stairs. The kitchen without her felt rather forlorn. More than the shock of meeting Victoria, though, was that, contrary to everything my grandmother had told me about the naughty little girl she'd once been, I liked her very much indeed. I wondered what had happened to change her in the interim. Perhaps something had simply made her grow up.

Thirty-one

The following Monday dawned crisp and cold, the turning leaves like flames licking against the clear blue sky. It was another of those autumn days I had mentioned to Lucas – the kind that always reminded me of watching Clifton's schoolgirls hurrying to catch the morning bell, envious of their uniforms and satchels, and the alliances they were effortlessly forming. I was glad Victoria's Essie wasn't going to be kept at home as I had been.

I hadn't met her on Saturday in the end – only spying her from an upstairs window as she and Victoria left, apparently on foot. As entranced as I'd been by her mother in the kitchen, I found I couldn't take my eyes off the slight girl at her side, her long swirl of hair catching the last of the day's light. As if she felt my gaze on her, she glanced back as they went through the old gates, but I don't think she saw me standing there, with the darkness of the room behind me.

With Monday's lovely weather and the promise of Victoria and Essie's return, I felt more optimistic about my situation than I had since my arrival. Leaving Lucas with a book about the solar system, having hit on it as a topic of great fascination to him, I went off in search of Pembridge. By now, I had grown familiar with Fenix House's rhythms: what time Agnes could safely be approached for a cup of tea, when Bertie was likely to undertake his daily inspection of the garden, and where Pembridge was to be found during the day. As I'd already discovered, he preferred to use the table in the dining room rather than his grandfather's study for his work, whatever that was. It wouldn't have been my choice: it never got much light and always smelt of the previous night's supper.

I suspected it was partly to avoid the portrait of his late wife and partly to irritate Agnes, who always had to clear away his books and pens to set the table for the evening meal. Lunch at Fenix House was a scrappy affair: if you were hungry – and Bertie frequently forgot to eat at all – you went down and prised what you could out of Agnes. This was usually something tinned or powdered – Agnes kept great stocks of corned beef, pilchards and pears, and incorporated Bird's Custard into every dessert, presumably because none of it ever went off or required any fiddly preparation. When Lucas didn't insist I eat with him in his room, I had taken to eating a plateful of odds and ends from the pantry down there with her.

Sure enough, when I got to the dining room, Pembridge was already installed at the huge table, books and papers spread out, regardless of the mess left over from the previous night's supper. Agnes had obviously neglected to change the cloth again.

He looked up when I came in. 'Don't tell me,' he said wearily. 'After meeting Aunt V you've found yourself galvanized by sisterly zeal and have come to tear a strip off me.' He reluctantly marked his place in the book before him and shut it with a bang. Dust rose from the old pages in a cloud.

'Mrs Granger did say that I must stand my ground

with you, Mr Pembridge.' I smiled so he knew I was joking, feeling quite proud of my daring. 'She is the more intimidating of the two of you, so here I am, obeying her orders.'

He laughed: a dry, humourless bark that he looked as if he wanted to take back as soon as it was out. 'So, Miss Fairford, what can I do for you?'

'I'm happy to say that Lucas and I are getting on rather well. He's been reading a great deal and is really quite an expert on that wireless set of his. The thing is, I'm worried that he needs more stimulation than I can offer him alone.'

'Do you wish for me to hire him a circus?'

I looked down at my feet.

He sighed. 'Sarcasm comes too naturally to me. What have you in mind?'

'Nothing very exotic. Some more books, perhaps – he seems to have discovered an interest in the planets and stars – and your permission to take him outside sometimes.'

'He's too weak.'

'I don't mean that we should hike through the woods. Just a breath of air in the garden would put some colour in his cheeks, I'm sure. It'll be too cold soon but it's still quite mild at the moment. The weather's been lovely today.'

Pembridge frowned as though the state of the weather had never occurred to him. 'I'll have to think about it.'

'Thank you, that's all I ask.'

I turned to go when he spoke again. 'So you're getting on all right, then, the two of you?'

'Yes, very well. Did you not think so when you came up earlier?'

He flushed. 'How did you know I was there?'

I shook my head with a smile, realizing I didn't quite know how, just that I had seen him on the other side of the door as if it had been made of glass. 'I'm not sure. A lucky guess, perhaps.'

'I don't check because I mistrust you, Miss Fairford. I hope you know that. It's just that I have been, well, impressed by your progress so far and I like to hear the boy sounding so bright. I just didn't want to disturb you – or inhibit him – by barging in.'

'Well, you're very welcome to listen, sir.'

'Please, I would rather you called me David.'

'I'm afraid you've become "Pembridge" in my head already,' I said, with another smile.

'Indeed? Well, I shall have to call you Fairford, then, like we're all chaps together.' He smiled properly at me for the first time that day, and I marvelled again at how it transformed him, making him look at least a decade younger. 'So, Fairford, old boy, I'll let you know about this going-outside business. Why don't you come back tomorrow about the same time and I'll have an answer for you then? Get Agnes to bring us some tea up – and cake, perhaps.'

I smiled, then retreated, before he could change his mind.

Thirty-two

Later that week, having secured permission from Pembridge to take Lucas out soon, I received another letter from my grandmother. Lucas was having his afternoon nap when Agnes remembered to give it to me, and I decided to go to my room to read it in private. As I climbed the stairs, I was busy wondering what the new missive could possibly contain, which was why I didn't notice Robert Pembridge's door was ajar until I was passing it.

I crept to the threshold and put my eye to the crack. It was silent within and I couldn't make anything out: any light that might have spilled in from the landing was blocked by me standing there. I pushed the door open a few more inches, grateful that the reasonably new wood didn't creak.

It was still dark within but there was now just enough light to compensate for the deep gloom, illuminating hulks of furniture, an unmade bed to one side and something spread across the floor I couldn't make out immediately. A shuffling sound made me step back and drop my letter, which landed with a small thud.

'Is someone there? Vicky, is that you, my dear? Or is it dear Essie?'

The voice was less frail than it had been that night. Less confused, too. Summoning my courage – really, how frightening could an almost blind old man be? – I tapped on the door. 'Mr Pembridge? May I come in?'

I stepped inside without waiting for a reply. Though I still couldn't make out much, I could see that the old man in the wing chair next to the dying fire had turned to me. Using his hands for leverage, he tried to get up.

'Oh, no,' I said, rushing forwards. 'Please don't.' I helped him back into his seat.

'It's so dark in here,' he said, as if surprised. 'Why is it so dark? I can't see a thing.'

'I'll open the curtains,' I said, hurrying to the nearest window. There were three altogether – I supposed there had been one each for the rooms that had once housed Fenix House's housekeeper, cook and maids. The curtains were lined and heavy, pooling on the floor as if they had been made for larger windows downstairs. Perhaps they had, and had been brought up to the attic to block out as much light as possible, at Robert Pembridge's request. I pulled the first set open and started to move towards the next when something caught my eye that stopped me dead. Taking up perhaps two-thirds of the floor – it was a miracle I hadn't trampled right through it – was the train set I'd been told about.

The vague picture I'd had in my head was of a paltry thing compared to what Robert Pembridge had assembled. Not only were there yards of track laid out in perfect miniature, but bridges and hamlets, a tiny church with a golden weathercock atop its spire, cotton-wool sheep grazing in a green field, and even tiny people, some tending cottage gardens and others waiting in hats and coats on the station platform. One little girl in a blue dress was sitting on a fence waving a scrap of white handkerchief, while in a signal box next to the sheep field, a signalman leaned out of the window, head turned, his gaze for ever fixed on the line at the horizon, waiting for the next train to appear. There was just one engine, waiting in a siding, a magnificent piece of craftsmanship in black and red, pulling three carriages. The whole thing was, in its own way, quite exquisite. A picture of my parents briefly flickered in my mind, then guttered out.

'Has she been giving you trouble again?' the old man behind me said, with a low, rusty-sounding chuckle. 'Our own little devil, that one.'

I looked up in confusion, still slightly stunned by the Lilliputian world at my feet. 'Do you mean Lucas, Mr Pembridge? Actually, he's been very easy today. He's busy making models of the planets and they're awfully good.'

He frowned and rubbed his eyes. The skin on his hands was spotted with age and almost translucent. I could see every bone rippling underneath it. 'Lucas, you say? I'm not sure I know any Lucas. Do you mean Helen's boy? He came to stay only lately, looking very smartly turned-out in his school cap. Big grave eyes peeping out from underneath the brim. I don't know where he got those from. Helen's aren't so dark. She takes after me in colouring.'

I stepped carefully around the train set and dragged a battered old footstool close to the wing chair. Gently I took the old man's hands in mine. They were so light I was afraid I would crush them, the skin loose around the narrow bones. I searched his face for something familiar. He had the same brow as David, who in turn had passed it on to Lucas. And despite the difference in their colouring, there was something in the set of his eyes that had been replicated in Victoria.

He had been looking in the direction of his miniature railway but now he squinted at me. 'I still can't see much,' he said. 'But it's always been such a dark room. I shall have to talk to Dilger about cutting back those conifers again.'

I wondered which room he thought he was in, and how many decades ago. The thought of the past being so real to him that he was still in it was like walking into the frigid breath of a haunted room. For the moment, he truly believed that Dilger was somewhere in the garden, pruning and planting on a bright autumn day in the last century. He took for granted that the house still bustled with staff, that everything was polished and spruce and new. That his son was a little boy battling with his Latin verbs at school down the hill in Cheltenham. That his daughters were also at their lessons, in the morning room; and his wife was deciding which dress to wear. Perhaps that was no bad thing when the reality was so altered: everything changed, decayed or lost.

Though there was now plenty of light slanting in at us from the window I had uncovered, I thought it might help his eyes if I opened the other curtains, but when he felt me pull away he held on tight, his grip surprisingly strong.

'Don't leave, Harriet,' he said. 'Not so soon. Where have you been?'

I held my breath as he reached out tentatively and began to stroke my hair, his arm trembling with the strain of the movement. 'Like spun gold, it is,' he said. 'Even in a dark room like this one, I can see it. It's got a light of its own.'

We sat like that for some time. The sun streaming in through the window was warm and I began to feel sleepy. Robert Pembridge let his hand rest on the top of my head. Its slight weight was an immense comfort. I had almost drifted off when he began speaking, so softly I almost didn't catch the words.

'How could you just go like that, Harriet, without a word? You didn't even say goodbye to me.'

I lifted my head slowly so I didn't startle him but his eyes were closing, then began to flicker under bluish, paper-thin lids. I managed to get up without waking him and found a blanket to tuck around his legs. When I got to the door I saw the letter I had dropped and bent to retrieve it. As I walked back to my room after closing the door softly, it occurred to me that the letter was the closest that governess and employer had come to each other in nearly half a century. It now seemed obvious that their relationship had been more intimate than my grandmother had led me to believe. Bertie had hinted at it when we'd been inside the maze, but I had assumed his father had merely been inconvenienced by her departure.

I remembered the torsion clock she kept on the mantelpiece in her room in Clifton. With its intricate movement on display under a glass dome, I had thought it beautiful, coveting it so much that she had promised to leave it to me one day. It wasn't just its exposed delicacy that appealed: there was something peculiarly comforting about the way it kept time, its trio of suspended spheres twisting first one way, then the other. The reliability of each returning rotation seemed far preferable to the hour and minute hands of the face, which were always pushing forwards relentlessly, with no thought for the past they were leaving behind. It didn't keep time very well, but that hadn't mattered to me. It had been her wedding present from the Pembridges, I suddenly recalled. I had forgotten she'd told me that. Why she had received a costly wedding present, presumably paid for by the man she hadn't even said goodbye to, I simply couldn't fathom.

Back in 1910, my parents newly taken from me, I'd had my own shadows to contend with. But now, transported to Fenix House, I wondered not just about what she had told me but what she might have left out. It struck me for the first time that the hesitations that had sometimes punctuated her recollections might not always have been lapses in memory – especially when her powers of recall were generally excellent. But perhaps I was conferring too much significance on some old stories because I was in a place that was, disconcertingly, both strange and familiar.

Thirty-three

My grandmother's third letter began almost without pre-amble.

Dear Grace,

You remember I told you about the fire that was heralded by the first glimmer I ever had? And the girl with her ice-blue eyes – you must remember her? Well, it was not the fire that was my father's undoing, it was her. His business might have recovered if he had still been in possession of his savings. That he was not was entirely the fault of that girl and her father, Josiah.

The scheme had at first seemed so promising. Josiah Dauncey had come to our house one evening full of enthusiasm for a new invest-ment that was sure to make many times over any sum that was put in. He stayed for supper to discuss it further, drinking two bottles of my father's best claret and eating the lion's share of a haunch of beef. I was brought down to say goodnight and felt the spark of excitement and shared purpose between the two men as clearly as I could see the greasy shine on Josiah's lips in the lamplight.

As I said in my last letter, my father, Richard Jenner, made a comfortable living from his ownership of an auction house, which specialized in selling antiquarian books and maps and the like. Josiah Dauncey, less loftily but rather more lucratively, owned a successful and burgeoning hansom cab firm. Neither man, then, knew much about what constituted fashion. Josiah's daughter Louisa, however, took a great interest in its every vagary, whether for the person or the house. It was she who had convinced her father that a man could not possibly fail if he were to invest in wallpapers, particularly if the colour of those papers was an unusually bright, clear green.

What was even more attractive about the proposal was that while many of the green papers finding favour in the most fashionable houses at the time had a tendency to blacken, this paper, thanks to some quirk of manufacturing that was never fully explained, kept its emerald brilliance for far longer. Furthermore, it was not only wall hangings that could be made from the formulation an associate of Josiah's had stumbled upon. The same dyeing process could be used for any number of goods: from garments to toys to tall, tapered candles. Thus the investment, in essence and to my father's initial bemusement, was in a colour.

It was wallpapers, though, said Josiah, that would make them rich men. 'I have seen them with my own eyes,' he said, as he poured himself another glass of claret and swilled it down. 'I know nothing of what women like in their drawing rooms or boudoirs, and I couldn't tell you the difference between Scheele's green and Paris green if my life depended on it. But I do know this method produces the greenest green I have ever come across.' He laughed and slapped the table. 'Are you in, Jenner?'

It was only a week or two after my father had indeed invested a large sum in what he came to refer to later, with admirable wryness, as Dauncey green, that he read of a family in Limehouse whose three children had mysteriously perished, one after another. Their symptoms were like those of diphtheria but there was no other evidence of the disease. A doctor who was quoted in the article was convinced that the culprit was the arsenic present in the green wallpaper lately hung in their bedroom.

'Nonsense,' Josiah said, when my father had handed him the

newspaper. 'God knows how many miles of green wallpaper hang in houses up and down the land. Half the country would have dropped dead by now if it was poisonous.'

'Nevertheless, I could not live with myself if it turned out to be the case,' my father replied. He had given the matter much thought and had decided to withdraw his entire investment. It wasn't only his concern that such papers might be banned or fall out of favour, it was that he couldn't live with himself if there was a possibility – however slim and unproven – that he was contributing to anyone's suffering. He already viewed his money as tainted: the investment he had pictured as bright coins the colour of my hair was now clouded with noxious verdigris.

When Josiah saw that his friend would not be persuaded or talked around, he grew angry. It was as if he himself was the injured party. My father was a mild man who, perhaps naively, expected others to be as reasonable as he. When Josiah first refused to see him at his club, my father was wrong-footed. Instead of demanding his portion of the investment back, as Josiah would certainly have done in the reverse situation, he sent messages of apology, which eventually resorted to pleading. Josiah remained staunchly offended and our money was not returned. Fatally, my father held off. He had not wanted to invest in something that could harm people but, if the money had already been used, there was nothing to do but wait. As soon as it was made back, he decided he would take what was his and withdraw – and hang any profit.

At first there were delays in production, then a crucial ingredient of the process became difficult to procure. Then the mysterious associate who had told Josiah about the opportunity in the first place apparently went abroad and could not be traced. All of this Richard Jenner discovered through the odd letter Josiah periodically deigned to send. When these eventually dried up, still my dear father procrastinated. He did not feel as though he could involve the law: he had signed nothing and received no receipt for his money; Josiah's few letters were carefully vague. It had been a transaction between friends. There was no proof of anything.

Perhaps I might not have blamed the daughter for the father's treachery, had it not been for my father's last attempt at communication with the man who had once been his closest associate. He had decided to take me, his daughter of ten, with him – to impress upon Josiah Dauncey that financial loss does not only injure the man but his family too.

I had never before been to the Daunceys' house – and, in fact, my father hadn't been to this one, which had only recently been purchased. It was a good distance from their old one, and my father's, in the heart of London, where the noise of other people never really ceased. Instead, this new acquisition was to be found down one of Hampstead's tranquil, almost-rural streets. I suppose they had moved there, as other city-dwellers did, for the healthful air.

In many ways, the house was the idealized sort a child might draw, with a broad front door set in the middle of a square expanse of red bricks, with plenty of large windows arranged symmetrically around it. To reach it, you opened an iron gate and passed along a neat path bisecting a pretty garden of fruit trees. The chimney stacks at either extremity of the roof belched smoke, which spoke of warm, comfortably furnished rooms within.

I still remember it so clearly, though I went there only on that solitary occasion. That day, I stood outside and, once I'd absorbed it all, I began to shiver, the chill, country-smelling air seeping right into my bones.

The door was answered by a maid, who had admitted my

*father to the old house on numerous occasions but now looked
impassively back at him.*

*'Ah, Nell,' he said. 'Will you tell Mr Dauncey I have come to
see him? My daughter is with me, as you see.'*

'Who shall I say is calling, sir?'

*'But, Nell, you know who it is.' He sighed when she didn't
move. 'Tell him it is Mr Richard Jenner.'*

'Wait there,' she said, and closed the door smartly.

*He didn't say anything to me while we waited and I minded
painfully his silence, the father who always said he talked more
than an old woman. He had taken his hat off and was turning it
round and round in his hands. I saw that they were reddened by
the cold and not quite steady. Later, when I was older and came
upon the phrase 'to go cap in hand', this image of my father
haunted me, making me first cry, then seethe with anger for him.
By then he was dying, shrunken even from what he had been
reduced to on that bitter day in Hampstead.*

*After some minutes, Nell was back. 'He can't see anyone
today,' she said bluntly. 'He says to write to him.'*

*'But I have. I have written a dozen letters and he has replied to
none. I beg you, I would not come here were it not absolutely –'*

*The door was pulled further back to reveal a girl of seventeen
or so. She wore a cap-sleeved dress of pale blue taffeta edged with
lace. A score of tiny cream bows ran down the front of its skirt.
Her left cheek was flushed prettily from sitting too close to one of
the fires I had pictured; the right was as pale and smooth as wax.
While she regarded us, she twisted a lock of her pale hair into a
tight ringlet, which defiantly unfurled itself as soon as she dropped
it to begin on another. Her eyes were the same shade as her dress.*

*'My father will not see you, Mr Jenner. You had better leave.'
Her voice was both light and hard.*

'Dear Louisa, you are looking so well. I am glad to see you again. Might you not be able to persuade him to give me just a few minutes of his time?'

'I'm sure I might, but I will not. It is unfortunate what has happened but there is always some risk in business, Mr Jenner.' She was repeating what she had heard her father say, in justification; even then I understood that.

My father bowed his head sadly. 'You once played a hand of bezique with me, do you remember?'

'I'm afraid I don't,' she said, with a glacial smile, her eyes flicking down to me and making me flinch. I began to back slowly down the path, unable to stop myself. I wished desperately to be at home again, in the dirt and confusion of the city, where there were greater failures than the Jenners and where no one would be able to hear over the general racket the great ragged sobs trying to escape me.

In the short time we had spent in vain at the Daunceys' black and brass door, the day had stealthily withdrawn. The tips of the grass and the fallen leaves were stiffening with a creeping frost, and the trees had lost their colour and texture, darkening into flat silhouettes. I risked one backward glance before climbing into the cab that my father had rather imprudently told to wait. Two figures, their features lost in shadow, stood at a downstairs window. I knew the portly outline of Josiah so the person who had joined Louisa must have been Jago, the son, younger than his sister but already half a head taller. I was at least grateful the warm light behind them hid their expressions, because I was sure they would be full of contempt. I could only tear my eyes away when Louisa — her impatience somehow evident in the movement — reached out to close the window's shutters.

A single sentence reverberated around my head as we made the silent, defeated journey back to the city. It mirrored the rhythm of

the horse's hoofs as we clattered over cobbles and were jolted
through potholes and deep ruts. She enjoyed that. She
enjoyed that. She enjoyed that.

I never forgot her but I tried to put her out of my mind. In
truth, I didn't expect ever to see her again – or that brother of
hers. When I did, that day on the street a year or so later, I
realized I had assumed the Dauncey family would disappear from
my life, along with my father's money. That they hadn't – that they
were presumably still living in comfort in Hampstead, that Louisa
had been courted and was now in a smart carriage on her way to
marry in the church where I myself had been christened – came as
a bitter blow. If only I had known – if only the glimmers had
granted me a glimpse of the future – that the next time I would
see her I would no longer be a helpless child but a grown woman
able to take revenge.

And there the account ended, quite as abruptly as it had
begun. I had been so immersed in the story that I felt
quite disorientated in my little attic room. I went to the
window and stood on tiptoe so I could see the view. Heavy
white clouds were scudding fast over the valley floor, their
shadows like lumpen beasts blundering through the fields
and hedgerows. It felt odd to see so much open space
stretching away to the horizon when my mind had been
among the throng of London. I looked back at the bed,
where I'd left the letter, my grandmother's neat black
strokes now at an unreadable distance. *What has this to do
with anything?* I thought. *Why is she telling me now?*

Then something occurred to me. I went over and
picked up the pages, running my eye over the neat letters
again. Sure enough, one word jumped out at me. *Dauncey.*

Where had I heard it before? I closed my eyes, trying to recall if my grandmother had mentioned it when I was a child but, no, it was a name I'd heard much more recently. Suddenly I had it: Bertie talking over dinner on my first night. He'd said that Vicky had got all the Dauncey looks and then, on that tour of the garden, I was sure he'd told me that his strapping, mutiny-crushing uncle's name was Jago. Agnes, too, had mentioned a Hampstead place that had been let when I'd first met Victoria; perhaps it was the same house, still in the family.

Was I to take it that my grandmother had come to Fenix House to exact some sort of retribution? Had coincidence brought her there or had she sought out the hated Louisa, biding her time until she could take up a position in the woman's house? Remembering what Robert had just revealed to me, I wondered if he'd been embroiled in the enmity between his wife and governess, a pawn in my grandmother's plans for revenge. There was something about the idea that made me shudder.

The letter was also making me question anew my own purpose in retracing her steps. Yes, she had said it was meant to be, but perhaps that was only so I could finish what she had started almost half a century earlier. I quickly dismissed that: the notion seemed ridiculously melodramatic, even given my grandmother's fondness for a sensational story. This was real life, after all.

I was starting to wish I'd never read the letter. I had always felt comforted by the idea of the past, which to me had always been the time before bad things happened. Now even that was spoiled, and I suddenly wanted to slough off history's dead weight. My grandmother, Robert

Pembridge and Bertie were in total thrall to the years gone by. She hadn't answered any of my questions about home, or even made reference to it. I felt in that moment as if I was the only person who knew it was 1922. Even David Pembridge, who could only be in his thirties, seemed determined to deny the passage of time, his mind always straying back – or so I presumed, from the old news-papers, the banished portrait – to happier years before his wife died; before the war. And Agnes was no better, as stuck in the same narrow grooves as the rest of them.

Only Victoria – the thought of her like a lamp turned up high in a dark room – was truly living, pushing forward into the bright future, as I had decided I wanted to. She had brought with her to Fenix House some of the outside world's energy and vim; it had crackled around her as she bustled about the house, a trail of it scattering behind her, like phosphorescence lighting the sea at night, or a low, thrilling hum. Suddenly, I couldn't wait for her and Essie to move back in.

Thirty-four

Harriet

Afterwards, when she had left Fenix House, Harriet wondered if she could have avoided what happened if only she had been more like Agnes. Not exactly like Agnes, of course – she never forgot her shock at coming upon the maid and the captain in the kitchen that night – but a little more friendly, a little more free with her smiles. The captain had no doubt seen how she lit up in Robert's presence and contrasted it with his own, quite different, effect on her.

If she had been chilly and prim and spinster-like with all of the men in the house, he would soon have forgotten her. Her bright hair, large grey eyes and hand-span waist were diverting to a man initially, perhaps, but they were not so remarkable that they would have sustained his interest with a new bride, a worshipping sister and a maid who was free with her favours. No, it was the spark between her and Robert that had been the flame to Jago Dauncey's dark, blundering moth.

The next opportunity for Robert and Harriet to be alone came unexpectedly. They had not planned it but found themselves powerless to resist when Fate acted to part the ways for them. It was a Saturday afternoon, the morning's lessons and lunch long over. Helen was curled up in the parlour with a new book and Victoria had been put to bed, a summer cold having turned her feverish and uncharacteristically limp. The mistress was ensconced in her rooms and Harriet hadn't seen the captain all day. She presumed he'd grown bored and taken the brougham into Cheltenham.

She had not long returned to the morning room to write her monthly letter to the elderly cousins who had briefly taken her in when there was a knock at the door. She knew before he entered that it was Robert. The gentle tap might have been Mrs Rakes but it was not: in her mind she could clearly see him on the other side of the heavy door, hesitant and tentative, his ear to the oak to listen for her response.

'Come in,' she called, her easy tone belying the pounding of her heart.

When he came in, she saw that his face was more determined than she had yet seen it.

'Miss Jenner, I find myself here again.'

She smiled at him. 'Yes, though I'm afraid your daughters are elsewhere, Helen reading and Victoria —'

'I know where they are,' he interrupted. His habitual calm and measured demeanour had abandoned him. Distractedly, he picked up a small volume of poems, then a stick of chalk, which broke in half in his unusually clumsy grasp.

'Mr Pembridge, has something happened?' she enquired.

He looked up at her, then away, but in the moment he met her gaze directly, she was shocked at the depth of emotion she read there. 'No, nothing has happened,' he said harshly. 'At least, nothing outside my own mind.'

She didn't know what to say. In truth, and for the first time, she felt a little afraid of him – or, if not him, then his feelings. Usually they had to leave so much unsaid, even as they discussed Helen's love of geography or Victoria's latest escapade, but now she sensed that he was preparing himself for some declaration and was not convinced she was ready to hear it. Not because she didn't feel strongly for him – oh, she did – but because then it would be out, and that, she feared, would change everything between them.

In her heart of hearts, she had always known it was hopeless. Yet again, Louisa had what Harriet didn't, yet wanted so badly. Once it had been a secure footing in the world, now it was Robert. And so, even while she let herself entertain the prospect of romantic entanglement with a married man, she knew that one day it would have to cease. She simply hoped to avoid that time for as long as possible. What she had failed to anticipate was how vulnerable such a situation would make her, a paid employee whose future, if she needed to seek work at another house, depended on a good character.

'Miss Jenner, will you take a walk with me?'

Troubling thoughts still turning in her mind, she hesitated. If she went, she might find herself on the path to ruin. And yet, even as she considered it, she was rising to her feet. 'In the garden?'

'I thought perhaps a little further, if you are willing. It's so very warm today. I thought it would be cooler in the woods.'

A small tremor went through her and she couldn't for the life of her tell if it was excitement or fear. Perhaps it was both, entwined so tightly together as to be indistinguishable.

The heat, pervasive enough in the shade of the house, was oppressive in the garden. Droning bees veered haphazardly from one bloom to another, seemingly drunk on the syrupy air. Harriet's undergarments clung to her hot skin and her hair lay heavy on the back of her neck. She surreptitiously pressed her handkerchief to her forehead and felt it wilt and dampen.

'Louisa tells me we are to have a celebration next week,' he said, once they were well clear of the house. She glanced up sharply: he usually referred to her as his wife.

'Oh? And what is the occasion?'

'Jago's birthday.'

'I cannot think what Mrs Rollright will contrive to make that hasn't already been enjoyed by the captain,' she said lightly.

'Oh, fear not. Mrs Rakes is upstairs at this very moment, receiving instructions.'

'She is feeling better then, Mrs Pembridge?'

He shrugged. 'For now. Until a new ailment presents itself. Or a new obstacle to her wishes.'

Harriet was at a loss for what to say. He had only mentioned Louisa in passing before; now his tone was openly weary and cynical. Her breath felt short at their passage into uncharted waters. She was grateful they were walking: if they had been murmuring to each other in the morning room under Victoria's gimlet eye she was not sure how she would have managed to stay composed.

'Captain Dauncey is thoroughly approving of his sister's plans, needless to say,' Robert continued. 'I'm not sure how he has secured her forgiveness after confessing to the existence of a wife, but secured it he evidently has. I know not when. Only yesterday, he was her nemesis and now she wishes to throw him a party. One might almost admire him. He will relish the glare of the limelight; that is certain. A sense of entitlement must be a family trait.'

They wound their way slowly up the series of lawns, past Dilger's glorious eruptions of colour and scent. Robert seemed blind to the extravagant beauty around them, his eyes on his feet, his breathing harder now the incline had increased. Not that Harriet could concentrate on the garden: her mind was racing. For Robert, deliberate, delicately treading Robert, was now voicing hard opinions she had long held. She felt as though he had plucked them straight out of the most private recesses of her mind.

She took a breath. He had never yet disapproved of her being frank with him. 'What is it that has made you so bitter today?'

'I'm sorry. I did not mean to talk of them to you.'

'No, I mean what has changed? Why are you so angry today about two people you have known for years?'

'Well, I hope you don't think I am jealous of them – of either of them – particularly after our talk on the way back from church and our meeting in my study.' He attempted to smile but she could see how troubled he was.

'No, I don't think that. In the case of Jago . . . of the captain, why would you be jealous of a man like him?'

'Is his sort not dashing and heroic to women?'

'To Agnes, perhaps. And possibly to his sister. But not to me.'

'And why is that? He is an army man who serves the

Empire, who stands taller than most fully dressed men in his stockinged feet. He carries a sabre and a revolver when other men – men like me – sign papers and attend meetings.'

Harriet smiled at the words that echoed Agnes's weeks before.

'Why do you smile? Are you laughing at me?' His voice trembled slightly.

She turned to him in astonishment. 'Robert, you are not yourself today. Of course I'm not laughing at you. I hoped that, despite our positions, we were friends. I would never laugh at a friend.'

He coloured. 'Please forgive me. You're right, I am not myself. I am changed, and the new clothes of it do not yet sit comfortably on me.'

They walked on, deep in thought. Harriet put her hand to her breast. Beneath the scratchy stuff of her dress, she could feel her heart racing. Neither had really noticed where they were going so they had not left the garden and taken the path to the woods, after all. Instead they found themselves at the upper extent of the Pembridge land, close to where the ice-house was swaddled beneath its cloak of moss and earth, and where the narrow birch trees offered a little shade from the climbing sun. She wished they were in the dimly lit study again. She had felt braver there.

'Come a little further,' he said. He held out his hand and then, remembering himself before she could take it, put it in his trouser pocket. 'Now that we're here, there's somewhere pretty I'd like to show you.'

It was a small glade behind the ice-house, where a patch

of startlingly green grass had sown itself, carried on the breeze from the manicured lawns below. Clearly Dilger and Ned never ventured this far: the grass, woven with wildflowers, was long and luxuriant. In one corner there was a small, sturdy bench, the wood silvered by the elements. When Harriet sat down and noticed the view for the first time, she gasped. The valley and the distant hills, seen from so high up the garden, were made even more spectacular by their frame of curving birches. It was so clear that she could make out the River Severn in the distance, a twist of mirror glass in the sun. Much closer and immediately below them, the vivid green geometry of the maze was, by contrast, a marvel of man-made precision.

Robert was not looking at the view: he was looking at her. 'You approve, then?'

'Oh, yes,' she breathed. 'I did not even know this spot existed. Bertie didn't take me up so far when he showed me around.'

'I'm not sure he's even found it. I'm not sure any of them have. I'm afraid I'm rather possessive of it. I've even told Dilger to leave it be.'

Harriet felt the rhythm of her heart quicken again. He had brought her to his private place; another line crossed.

'Miss Jenner.'

She was too shy to turn to him. Instead she kept her eyes trained on the mercurial glint of the Severn.

'Harriet,' he tried again. 'I talked of change. It is you who has changed me.'

'I don't know how that can be,' she whispered. Even as something like joy began to seep warmly through her, she fought the urge to pick up her skirts and run. It was not coyness. She had never before felt so young compared to Robert, though there was only a decade between them and neither of them were children. She felt very much like a girl in that moment, though.

'I think you do know,' he said, reaching for her hand. It seemed very small in his, very small and very pale. 'Harriet, will you look at me?'

She forced herself to meet his eye. Her nervous swallow sounded loud in the quiet glade and she had the sense that the place was listening to them intently. She glanced around.

'I told you, no one knows this place,' he said soothingly. 'There's nobody here.'

A cold prickle, which felt even colder in the sultriness of the day, spread upwards from her ankles. She looked about again, less cursorily this time, peering deep between the ranks of pale birches. She thought she saw movement: a flutter of leaves, a flash of colour that wasn't dun or fern green, but then it was gone. 'I thought I saw –'

'If it was anything, it was a bird. Or, I don't know, perhaps it was a ghost.' He laughed. 'Or one of those – I can't think what they're called – those spirits in the trees.'

'A dryad.'

'Yes. Of course you would know. Ah, to speak to a woman who prefers books to gossip and fashion. I don't imagine you are even slightly interested in the latest style from Paris, or have any idea which poor bird's exotic feathers should adorn your hat this season.'

Harriet frowned, a little disappointed: it was the first time he'd misunderstood her. It even distracted her from her nerves. 'I'm not interested in such things to the exclusion of everything else, of course, but that doesn't mean I wouldn't like some pretty things to wear occasionally. It would be dishonest of me to say otherwise. The truth is, I don't have the money for them, and I don't have the occasion to wear them.' She sighed. 'My position in the world means I must dress modestly, invisibly – plain, high-necked gowns in grey or black. But when I see some of your wife's things I wish I might have them. Hah! We are back to envy again.'

She fell silent, wondering where that outburst had come from. It was not the reply Robert had hoped for. He had meant for her to agree with him, so that he might continue to romance her, all the while leading her gently towards the declaration she knew he was preparing to make. Perhaps he wouldn't now, though, and at the thought she felt frustrated again. It vied with the urge she still felt to run. She had never felt so contrary. She had longed for a moment like this; more than that, she had hardly dared to imagine such a scene. Now it was playing out, she couldn't do much more than worry.

'I fear we have gone off down the wrong path,' he said gently. 'I did not mean to be insensitive. Harriet. I said you have changed me since your arrival.'

'I do not know how you can –'

'Please, let me finish or I will never get this out. And I need to say it to you, or I think I will go mad.'

She made herself look at him. She desperately wanted him to embrace her and she desperately wanted to be back in the peace of the morning room, alone.

He pressed her hand between his. 'Since we spoke of our connection in the study, I have wrestled with my feelings. I have tried to contain them, not for my wife's sake, but for my children's. However, it seems they will not be contained. I believe I have fallen in love with you, Harriet. I do not know how I have gone on all these years without you. I look back and the past seems empty, hollow, colourless. I do not know what to do. I cannot think clearly. I lie awake at night and think of you on the floor above me in your little room and it hurts me like a physical pain to stay away.'

She saw how exhausted yet exhilarated he was. His eyes glittered in their bruised-looking sockets. This was no longer a diversion to him, if it had ever been. He truly loved her. For the first time, it occurred to her that she had stolen the heart of her enemy's husband, then felt sick for it. Her feelings for Robert had always been genuine: he was not a prize to be won. In fact, he couldn't be competed for at all.

'Robert. I am – so very flattered that you –'

He let out a noise that was almost a sob. 'You're flattered. Oh dear.' He shook his head. 'That is not what I hoped to inspire in you.'

'Wait, you misunderstand. I am overwhelmed. My thoughts are disordered.'

'But you have known something of how strongly I feel, surely.'

'Yes . . .' she took a breath '. . . and I return the feelings.'

'You do?'

'Of course I do.' Now she had admitted it, and nothing cataclysmic had happened, it was as if a stone had rolled off her chest. Allowing him to grasp both her hands in his, she finally forgot where they were, and that someone might come across them.

Robert closed his eyes in relief. 'I didn't know. I thought

then, when you said you were flattered, that I had made a fool of myself. And, worse than that, far worse, that you felt nothing much at all.'

She shook her head. 'I should not say so – it is so terribly forward – but I felt that connection between us from the very first moment we met. A true affinity.'

'For me, it was like finally being jolted awake.'

'But, Robert, it is hopeless, is it not? As you say, you have children. You also have a wife. All of this.' She gestured to the house and gardens below them. 'Such respectability.'

'I love my children, of course I do. But . . . well, I do not love my wife, and I find I am no longer ashamed to say so. I have sloughed off the guilt I have felt for years about it. I see now that she is impossible to love and that I never did love her.' He took a deep breath. 'She is everything I have come to despise.'

Harriet shivered and the glade came back into focus. What was that, over by the ice-house? 'Nevertheless,' she heard herself say, 'she remains your wife.'

'You sound so cold.' He dropped her hand and turned to look out over the valley.

She said, more gently, 'Robert, think for a moment. I have almost nothing in this world.'

'You have me.'

'No, I don't, not really. Not in any way that matters. All I truly have is my position as a governess and the respectability that confers. I have the good opinion of a handful of people, I hope, and I have some distant cousins in their seventies. I have my dear father's name, which I will not ruin, just as I will not ruin myself. That is all.'

'I am a foolish man. I thought you truly returned my

feelings,' he said piteously. It did not suit him and she rounded on him, suddenly furious.

'I do – oh, I do – and I have only just told you so, have I not? But I can't see how it can be any more than a hopeless fantasy. In that sense, nothing has changed. You know, of course you know, that nothing can possibly come of these meetings, and of these declarations.'

Instead of replying, perhaps sensing the futility of it all, he reached out for her. She tried to pull back but he held her fast, his mouth coming down on hers, his hand at the small of her back. For a moment, just a moment, she allowed herself to stop struggling. Her mind ground to a halt and all was sensation. But then, with a last gasp of self-preservation, she managed to extricate herself.

'We will go away from here, begin a new life somewhere else,' he muttered, reaching for her again.

She didn't trust herself not to succumb once more and got dizzily to her feet. Though she had never heard the words before, she somehow knew that they had been said many times over by men made desperate in the moment. She had no doubt he meant it now, but she also knew that he would never leave his children once this fit of passion had passed. More than anything, she wanted to sit down next to him again, but all she could see were lurid pictures of what happened to the women who gave in under similar circumstances. She had already gone so much further than was wise in her situation.

A raised voice, petulant in tone, coming from below, brought her smartly back to the little glade. Robert was gazing at her imploringly and seemed not to have heard. It came again: the mistress wanted her husband.

'Your wife is calling for you,' she said dully.

The alarm in his face told her that he had reached his limit of bravery for that day. She wished she could despise him for it, but she didn't: she only loved him. Her eyes stung with tears and she watched him get to his feet through their blur. He was peering anxiously towards the house and did not notice her distress.

'I must go, for now,' he said heavily. 'Will you ... It might be sensible if you remain here while I go ahead. She must not see us.'

'No, she must not.'

'Harriet, I –'

'Go now, Robert.'

When he'd gone, hurrying past the ice-house, like a boy certain he would be slippered by a fierce nanny, she sat back down on the bench and allowed herself to weep. She didn't hear the approach, the leather boots swishing through long, dry grass. He was standing almost at her feet before she noticed him.

'Captain Dauncey,' she said. There was nothing she could do about her appearance, or the quaver in her voice. She swiped at her eyes with the damp handkerchief and blew her nose.

He sat down next to her, in precisely the same spot Robert had occupied just minutes earlier. Before she could stop herself, she retreated a few inches from his bulk. He smelt of soap and sweat and spice again. She shifted her prickling legs.

'I wonder if I may call you Harriet too?' he began. He had heard everything. That much was clear. 'Although, wait,' he continued. 'Yes, I think on second thoughts, that

I actually prefer Miss Jenner. We had a governess at home, you know. Well, Louisa did. She had a string of them but it's the last one I remember. Miss Foster. A curate's daughter, of all things. She was younger than the others. She arrived when I was sixteen. Unlike you, she was one of those women who can't help but like me. Big brown eyes and soft brown hair, she had, and a crooked little tooth next to the front one that turned in on itself. Of course, Lulu sent her packing without a character when she realized what we were about. My sister never could stand to see me with anyone else.'

'What do you want, Captain?'

'Oh, come now. Can't you play nicely for once? I haven't asked you for anything yet.'

'But you will, so why don't we save ourselves the suspense?'

He chuckled, stretching his arms out along the back of the bench. 'Quite a view from up here, isn't it? No wonder my wife's esteemed husband kept it for himself – and now for his paramour.'

Harriet stood up but he caught her arm. 'Not so fast, little governess. Suffer me a moment longer.' He pulled her down beside him again, letting his fingers brush against her side as he let go of her arm. Her heart was thumping painfully in her chest. It was a different sensation from the nervous excitement of earlier, closer to real fear.

He laughed to himself again. 'My, how my sister already despises you. If she knew you had captured her husband's heart as well as my interest, she would tear you limb from limb.'

'And you will tell her, I suppose?'

'I haven't decided. Not yet, certainly.'

'They say there is no time like the present,' she said recklessly.

'Then they are wrong. The pleasure is in the anticipation. Perhaps I could demonstrate that to you.'

Harriet's head was starting to hurt and she put her fingers to her temples to massage them.

'Oh, you don't fool me with these feminine aches and pains,' said the captain, as he watched her. 'An attack of the vapours on the croquet lawn, I ask you. Well, there's no fiery-tempered Agnes here to guard you this time.'

'Please,' she whispered. Her head was pounding and she cursed it. How could she defend herself if this happened every time she was in danger? With some effort she opened her eyes. 'I must return to the house now or I will be missed. Please let me go.'

He considered her, then made a grab for her nearest hand. 'Goodness, how can anyone be cold on a day such as this? You need your blood warming.' He brought the delicate skin of her inner wrist up to his mouth. It felt a thousand times more intimate than a kiss on the back of her hand, and she knew he must be able to feel her speeding pulse under his lips. She could feel the warm, damp imprint of them lingering even after she had wrenched away her arm.

He regarded her with a blend of amusement and bald desire. 'Go, then, Miss Jenner. I won't stop you. But remember what I have heard and seen today. I would hate my sister to be hurt. The last weeks have been hard enough on her. It was a dreadful shock to find out her beloved brother has got himself a wife. God knows what she'd do if she found out that that wife was half native – a delicate, wide-eyed little piece who's pale enough to pass, if you don't know who her mother was. I can't tell you how restful she is compared to English wives, with all their prattling and pouting if they don't get their way.'

Harriet didn't need to be told twice. She was passing the ice-house when he called after her.

'My finding you so compromised today was meant to be, Miss Jenner. I think it will help bring us together, don't you?'

Thirty-five

Grace

Victoria and Essie were due to return the following Sunday. In the interim, I had been getting on quite well. In truth, I was rather proud of myself. Spurred on by the revelation that my existence needn't always be contained within the walls of a too-quiet house, I had kept the example of Victoria at the forefront of my mind all week.

Whenever I felt like letting Lucas sleep for another hour while I took an unnecessary nap myself, I went straight downstairs and read him a story or invented a new game for us to play. When I heard Pembridge's heavy tread in the hall, I didn't scuttle the other way in case we had one of our more awkward conversations. Instead I met him with a smile. I was unfailingly cheery with Agnes, who had stopped giving me suspicious, sidelong looks and had even started smiling back. One evening, I spent almost two hours looking at Bertie's butterfly books with him.

Of course, I couldn't shake off the past so easily. Questions echoed around my head, particularly at night, when the house had a way of groaning and creaking as it never seemed to in the day. Sometimes I thought I heard the servants' bells ringing, but Agnes never mentioned it so I assumed it was a trick played by a mind floating between dreaming and wakefulness. That faraway ringing came to represent to me what had gone before, the ghostly remnants of a time that did not want to be forgotten, however hard I might try.

As I bustled purposefully through my days, Lucas became ever brighter and more responsive, while his father seemed less bemused when I wished him a rousing 'Good morning!' The former's room was now spotlessly clean and tidy, earning me Pembridge's respect – he had been rendered speechless when we first called him in to look at it. I hoped it wouldn't be long before I was able to persuade him to accompany Lucas and me on an expedition around the garden.

I realized that, in trying to convince the others of my new-found zest for life, I had begun to convince myself. The only nagging concern I had was for my grandmother, and all the unanswered questions I had for her. Though I had written straight back to her last letter, I hadn't had a reply from her for a number of days.

Then again, as much as I wanted to know what had happened with the girl she blamed for her father's demise, what Robert Pembridge had been to her, and why her account of her departure from Fenix House in 1878 had now been contradicted by two people, I also felt reluctant to delve back into the past. I was trying to forge ahead, and knew that thinking of what had gone before would only pull me back. Perhaps I was actually a little relieved that she hadn't yet replied.

A week earlier I had hurried up into the woods to avoid meeting a grown-up Victoria. Now I anticipated her and Essie's return with a lift of the heart. I had already decided I would ask Victoria whether she had meant it when she said I should go to one of her Freedom League meetings. I was also hoping she would invite me to have lunch with the family. I had much to report to her on Lucas's progress, which was such that Pembridge had seen fit to compliment me on it three times now. The latest occasion had taken place in the parlour. I had gone in to retrieve a cardigan I'd left there the previous evening and come upon him squinting at his newspaper in the half-dark.

'I'll open the curtains for you,' I said, marvelling at how easy it was not to be cowed, once you'd started. 'You'll strain your eyes otherwise.'

He put the paper down and cleared his throat. 'I was meaning to say to you . . . I looked in on Lucas earlier.'

'Yes?'

'He reeled off a list of things you two had done together. Talked of nothing else, in fact.'

'Good, I'm glad. We've had a few altercations, of course. I don't think he's ever been allowed to lose a game before so he lost his temper when he did, but generally we're getting on rather well. I still want to take him out into the garden and you said I might soon, if the weather was good enough. It's not too cold yet.'

To my surprise, Pembridge simply nodded, saying that we could try whenever I thought best, his dark eyes watching for my reaction. I think he was pleased that I was suitably taken aback, just as *he* had been when he saw Lucas's pristine room. As for the excursion outside, perhaps Victoria and Essie's return would make the perfect occasion for it.

The next morning, I heard Victoria's voice before I saw her. I hurried downstairs to find that Pembridge and

Agnes had already gone outside. Bertie, however, was hovering on the front doorstep in his slippers.

'Oh, Miss Fairford, she's come early,' he exclaimed. 'I haven't smartened myself up yet so I can't let her catch sight of me.'

'Why is everyone outside? Have they got piles of luggage with them?'

He laughed, half disbelieving, half admiring. 'She's only bought a motor-car! I can't think what possessed her – she's such a one for walking. They're trying to get the gate open so she can drive in. I don't think it's been opened in a decade.'

I went down the steps and, just as Bertie had said, an upright little motor-car was visible behind the rusted old gates. Victoria and Agnes were crouching down and attempting to lift the side that had slipped off its hinges and wedged itself fast in the ground. Pembridge was watching them with his arms folded, his expression caught between amusement and satisfaction.

'Ah, here's Miss Fairford, come to lend a hand,' cried Victoria, when she caught sight of me. She gave me a broad smile and nodded towards Pembridge. 'Look at my nephew standing by while we women strain and struggle.'

He rolled his eyes. 'I thought you women were all for being treated as equals. If you can take our jobs, I'm sure you can manage a spot of lifting.'

'Oh, and I suppose if we hadn't stepped into your jobs while you went off to fight, then elves would have manned the armaments factories and worked the land?'

Agnes grunted agreement, a hand at her sore hip.

Pembridge turned to me and gestured at his aunt.

'Behold, our very own Lady Astor. Fenix House will be her House of Commons, and we her audience.'

I could tell the exchange between aunt and nephew was well worn, with no malice or real ill-feeling behind it; it was obvious they had a good deal of affection for each other, however opposing their views. And, besides, perhaps they weren't as opposed as they pretended.

'Let's see if Miss Fairford can't help us get it shifted,' Victoria was saying. 'She's not very big but she looks the determined type. And where is Essie? What the devil is she doing while all this is going on, the lazy baggage? Essie, we need you!'

I looked up at the motor-car again and saw a small figure still sitting inside. As I watched she got out, giving me a better look at her than I'd had from the window that first time. She hadn't inherited her mother's pink and white colouring; her skin was darker. Her hair was almost as pale as Victoria's but somehow richer in colour. She wore it loose and long over her shoulders, where it gleamed.

'Tie that mane of yours back before you strangle yourself with it!' cried Victoria. She turned to me. 'I've been trying to persuade her to bob it. It's lovely hair, of course, much nicer than mine ever was, but she would find short hair so much easier for school. I cut mine off years ago. I was only keeping it long for Mama and after she died, well . . . I didn't do it to be fashionable – I was well ahead of all that, in fact. But Essie won't part with hers. And, mind you, who am I to say otherwise? It's her hair.'

'It *is* mine,' the girl said, and something about her voice – some liquid, musical quality to it – made me study her more closely. 'And I like it long, so there.' She deftly plaited it into a long rope and slung it over her shoulder.

'Miss Fairford, this is Essie, my daughter,' said Victoria. 'I don't believe you met last time. She was ensconced upstairs with Lucas until we left. How is he, by the way? I hope,' she shot a stern glance in Pembridge's direction, 'that you have been able to continue your promising start.'

I was still gazing at Essie, who looked back at me shyly, through long dark lashes. She hadn't inherited her mother's blue eyes either. Mr Granger's side had clearly triumphed when it came to their daughter's looks.

'Oh, yes,' I said, realizing they were waiting for my reply. 'Lucas and I are getting along very well. He's even going to join us in the garden today, if he's up to it, and if the weather holds. I'm sure he'll be determined to do so now his cousin is here to see him manage it.' I smiled warmly at Essie, who blushed at such attention from a stranger.

'Well, that all sounds jolly good, if you ask me,' said Victoria. 'Well done! If you don't mind my saying so, you seem to have come out of your own shell, too. There's a spark in your eye that wasn't there in the kitchen last week. David, don't tell me you've shown the girl a little of your once-infamous charm?'

'Oh, for God's sake, is this what it's going to be like?' he muttered, refusing to meet my eye.

Victoria chuckled. 'Now, don't blow a gasket, I'm pulling your leg. Come on, all of you, let's get this blasted gate open and then we can go up and see the boy directly. I wonder . . . perhaps even Papa will be up to a turn in the garden today!'

'Please, Aunt V, one thing at a time,' said Pembridge. 'The old man hasn't set foot outside since . . . well, since Frannie last persuaded him. The war was still on then.'

'We'll see,' she replied, gesturing at the truculent gate.

He bent and, with all of us helping – though Essie did little but dance around us calling encouragement – it eventually shuddered out of its hole and swung free, with a piercing creak. Victoria hurried back to her new toy and donned a pair of enormous leather driving gauntlets.

'Good grief,' said Pembridge, as she roared on to the drive at unnecessary speed, screeching to a dramatic halt at the edge of an overgrown flowerbed. Cases and bags of various sizes, many of them covered with steamer and railway labels, were lashed to the back and piled to the ceiling inside.

'After that lot has been taken in and we've eaten, I insist that you go for a spin, David,' she called, as she climbed out and slammed the door. 'Apart from Essie, she's quite the best thing I've ever had. There's even something called a luncheon drawer at the back – we can use it for picnics.'

'I don't know how on earth you afforded it,' he replied. 'I thought you were in penury again.'

'Well, I've had some more rent from the London house. Besides, I've known Mr Evans at the garage for absolute aeons. We've come to a tidy arrangement. I pay a little off here and there, when I can. It is, as they say, on tick. Besides, old Granger still sends me a bit every month and both that and the rent will go a good deal further now we're not going to be paying bed and board to those thieves on the Riviera. The hotels there are simply ruinous. Besides, Essie and I don't need that much, do we, darling? We can be pretty frugal when we put our minds to it.' She put her arm round the girl and pulled her close.

'Oh, Mums, you're squashing me!'

Victoria released her and turned to me. 'If you ever have daughters, Miss Fairford, be sure to send them away to school before they're twelve. They're quite impossible at twelve. They give one such withering looks. Essie has turned into an entirely different person in the last six months.'

We watched as the girl ran up the steps and into the house. 'I'm going to see Lucas,' she called, over her shoulder.

'You wait till you see her work her magic with that boy,' said Victoria. 'It's quite something to behold. Although it sounds as though you've got on very well yourself this week.'

'Yes, he's a good boy, really. He doesn't think much of Patience and he tipped over the board when I beat him at Ludo, but he's coming on.'

'Miss Fairford is being rather modest, Aunt,' said Pembridge. He had come up behind us. 'I was right about Lucas needing some womanly affection and attention. It's what women are good for, you see.'

'That, and so many other things,' said Victoria, airily. 'I'll have you know that Mr Evans said I was extremely quick to get the knack of starting my little Morris. He said that in another life – and another body, presumably – I would have made quite the mechanic.'

The fine weather had held while we ate – warm when the sun peeped out from behind the clouds and no wind at all.

Essie had insisted on eating with Lucas in his bedroom — they shared a plate, like a pair of urchins. Though I had been proud of the progress I had made with him that week, I had to admit that Essie's effect on him was quite startling. His limbs seemed to loosen at the sight of her and the pinched look his face habitually wore quite melted away, making him seem younger and softer immediately. You could hear them giggling from the bottom of the stairs.

As I hoped, I'd been invited to join the Pembridges for lunch and it was a markedly less sober affair with Victoria at the table. She and her nephew argued about politics quite contentedly during most of it. Bertie didn't say a word but, for all his professed fear of his sister, looked very happy to have her there, just as Lucas derived comfort and stability from Essie's presence.

'Right, then,' said Victoria, after they had abandoned another of Agnes's woeful puddings. 'Miss Fairford and I will go upstairs and attempt to wrest two generations of Pembridge men from their beds. David, go and see if those chairs in the little potting shed have rotted through yet. We could put them next to the bench on the old croquet lawn. You go with him, Bertie.'

As she turned to the door, Pembridge gave her an insolent salute. Catching him, I smiled without thinking and he smiled warmly back, his face reminding me of his son's. Following Victoria out of the room, I found myself walking as gracefully as I could, certain that he was watching me go.

'We'll tackle Papa first,' said Victoria, as we went up the stairs. 'I take it you've been properly introduced to him by now?'

I put Pembridge firmly out of my thoughts. 'Not as such. I did go and see him myself, though.'

'And? How did you find him? He's a dear old thing, isn't he?'

'He is, but I fear he was rather confused about who I was.'

'Oh, I wouldn't worry about that. It doesn't surprise me at all. He has his lucid moments, when he is just as he ever was, but his mind wanders dreadfully, poor darling. Sometimes I think he can't store anything new in his memory, though he has no trouble remembering Essie. That girl could charm the birds out of the trees with a toss of her hair, and she can certainly do no wrong in Papa's eyes. But he still forgets who Lucas is, and even David sometimes, so you mustn't take it personally if he's the same with you.'

'Oh, I wouldn't,' I said quietly. I didn't know whether I should admit that he had already confused me with my grandmother, who, to Victoria, would have no connection to me, and simply be a long-departed governess. By the time I'd decided I should say something, it was too late: we had reached the attic and Victoria was tapping at the door.

Her hand was already on the handle when she turned back to me. 'I presume you've seen the train set?' she murmured.

'I thought it was quite astounding. The detail is –'

She sighed. 'It's how he wishes it was. You know, before that day. Did he tell you about it?'

I shook my head. I had no idea what she meant.

'Hmm. Perhaps that's as well. Come on, and mind you

299

don't trip over some rolling stock or a signal box before I pull the curtains.'

Just as she had during lunch, Victoria quite filled the room on entering it, opening curtains, collecting plates and cups while keeping up a ceaseless chatter that was oddly soothing.

'Goodness, I don't believe Agnes has set foot in here since I last came. That woman has an astonishing capacity for idleness. I almost admire it. I feel horribly guilty if I'm still for more than two minutes. Now, Papa, Miss Fairford and I are here to take you outside in the sunshine. What do you think of that?'

'Miss Fairford?' the old man repeated, and looked around. I was standing with my back to one of the windows, where the light had now been permitted to stream in. If he could see me at all, and I still wasn't sure how blind he actually was, I would be reduced to a silhouette.

'That's right, the governess. She says she's already met you and seen your trains. MISS FAIRFORD, her name is.'

'Governess?' he said faintly, his eyes still blinking in my direction. I fiddled awkwardly with the cuffs of my white blouse and tucked a loose strand of hair behind my ear.

'Is it her?' he said wonderingly. 'Has she come back to us?'

Victoria raised her eyebrows at me. 'No, Papa, you know Helen is lost to us. It's been more than a decade now.'

He shook his head but she missed it, plumping cushions. 'No, not Helen . . .' he began.

'Yes, I'm afraid so, darling thing. I know how you miss her.' She turned back to me and spoke under her breath.

'It was rotten luck that it should have been Helen. She was always the one Papa loved best. I minded it terribly when we were small – he bought her a locket one Christmas with an inscription about being the beloved middle child. Well, I could have curled up and died of envy, but I understand now – of course he loved her more. It was a perfectly understandable reaction. She was very like him, with her books and so forth, while I was a little horror.'

It came to me with absolute clarity: the gold locket my grandmother was never without, dented but polished and swinging forward on its long chain as she bent over her newspaper to read. The inscription, to 'H', had been something about being 'betwixt and between, but beloved of me'. How had she come by such a precious thing? She had said it was from my grandfather, the travelling salesman who had elevated her out of the governess's strange limbo. And perhaps it had been: another locket entirely.

Taking the old man outside was a protracted exercise. Pembridge was summoned to support him on the stairs while Victoria shouted out when he should step down. When we finally arrived, Lucas was already installed in an enormous wicker chair that had seen better days – better decades, perhaps.

Pembridge went quite still when he caught sight of him there, and I thought for a moment he had changed his mind and was angry. Then I realized he was simply overcome by seeing his son out in the fresh air after such a long absence.

'He managed the stairs very well,' said Essie, with a smile. 'He only leaned on Uncle Bertie and me a couple of times.' She twirled the end of her plait round her fingers.

Her other hand lay protectively on Lucas's thin forearm. He smiled up adoringly at her.

'Are you sure you feel well enough to be outside?' Pembridge asked him anxiously. 'You must say if you start feeling tired or dizzy and I'll carry you back up. Are you warm enough?'

'Oh, do stop fussing, David!' cried Victoria. 'Can't you see the colour in the boy's cheeks? How bright his eyes are? He's not looked so well in *years*. Well done, you two.' She smiled at her brother and Essie. Bertie glowed.

Lucas's colour was an improvement on his usual pallor, though I thought he also looked rather feverish, probably from excitement. I tucked his blanket round him more carefully than Essie had to deter any draughts.

When everyone was settled, Agnes brought out a lopsided sponge cake and cut it to reveal a neat layer of cherries at the bottom.

'Quite remarkable,' said Pembridge. 'Every last one has sunk.'

'I think it looks pretty,' said Essie, earning herself a civil nod from Agnes. 'And you can save the cherry bit for last.'

'Do you remember that party we had in the garden?' Robert Pembridge piped up. He had been silent until then and I'd half forgotten he was there. 'She was there for that. I remember her hiding in the shadows.' He smiled to himself.

Victoria, who had stationed herself beside him as nurse, took the old man's hand and began stroking it. 'He's full of Helen today,' she said quietly to the rest of us.

'Well, he can speak of her, if he likes,' said Pembridge, with a shrug. 'It's his house, V, and she was his daughter. Why should he forget her?'

I met his eye. I wondered if he was also talking about Frannie.

'Of course he shouldn't forget her,' tutted Victoria. 'I just don't want him to upset himself.'

'He's not upset, look at him.'

Robert was still smiling, though I thought it was a sad sort of smile. 'She kept darting away when I tried to talk to her and then ... Well, perhaps it was all too much. What a fool I was.'

Victoria sighed, then seemed to relent. 'Well, Papa, that sounds right enough. Poor Helen dreaded any sort of public occasion, didn't she? I remember going inside to fetch a glass of water – I'd got hot spinning round on the lawn, showing off shamelessly, no doubt – and found her curled up with one of her atlases behind the screen in the parlour. I extorted a ha'penny from her not to tell Mama where she was. I claimed it the next morning.'

'Golly, I wish I'd thought of hiding in the parlour,' said Bertie, shyly. 'Colonel Thoresby got hold of me, wanting to know which regiment I would join when I finished school. He was appalled when I said I hadn't thought about it. I didn't dare tell him I had no intention of joining up, if I could help it.'

'No, no, no,' interrupted Robert. Bertie coloured and looked down at his half-eaten slice of cake. 'Not Helen,' the old man went on. 'I never mentioned Helen. She was hardly outside in the garden at all.'

I froze, suddenly convinced that he was going to say something about my grandmother. I could still remember the tenderness with which he'd stroked my hair when he'd thought I was her. I must have gone pale or blushed because Pembridge was looking at me oddly and, in my flustered state, I leaped to my feet, mumbling something about fetching a hat for Lucas. It was one thing for Robert to confuse me with my grandmother when we were alone, the thought of him doing it in front of everyone else turned me cold for some reason, my legs restless and prickling.

'Don't worry, Miss Fairford,' said Essie, taking off her own beret. 'He can wear mine.' She pulled it down over his ears and made him laugh. Her long hair shone in the fading sunlight and I sat down, feeling limp and weak. My head began to thump nauseatingly.

Fortunately, the old man seemed to have lost the thread of his memory. 'Who the devil is that with Essie?' he muttered to Victoria. He sounded like a querulous old man again, and the two children exchanged a smirk.

'It's Lucas. David's son. You know this, dear.'

'Lovely voice, that girl of yours.' He nodded towards Essie. 'I've always said so. Like water.'

I was reminded of the thought I'd had out by the gates.

'Not like my parade-ground tones, I suppose,' said Victoria, wryly.

'And who's the boy, did you say?'

'Oh dear, Papa, it's *Lucas*. David and Frannie's boy. Helen's grandson, though they never got to meet before she died, more's the pity.'

Robert was suddenly indignant. 'It was the boy I always felt sorry for, David. A boy needs a father. It was the only thing dear Helen ever did to anger me. Why couldn't she have just got married like everyone else?'

Victoria exchanged a weary look with Pembridge,

whose countenance had immediately darkened, like a fast-turning sky. He glanced at Lucas but the boy's concentration was back on Essie, who was demonstrating how to make a cat's cradle, her narrow fingers flying. I rubbed my legs and shifted position so I didn't have to look at her hair, which was too bright in the lowering sun.

'Vicky, do you hear me?' continued Robert, irritably. 'Don't tell me she was married because I would never forget such a thing. I remember you and that Granger cove at the altar as if it were yesterday.'

Victoria glanced at me and I realized that even she was embarrassed. It didn't sit easily with her. 'All right, Papa, you win,' she said, with a sigh. 'Helen was never married.'

'Good God, this is turning into a farce,' said Pembridge. 'What other family secrets are you planning to reveal, Grandfather?' He sat back in his chair and tried to look as though he found the whole thing darkly amusing, but his face had reddened. In his agitation, he dropped his cake fork to the plate with a clatter, making Bertie jump.

'I told you,' continued the old man, apparently quite undaunted by Pembridge's expression. Probably he couldn't see it. 'I wouldn't forget my own daughter's wedding. It was that boy and her. She always admired him so, though Lord knows he hardly ever said a word.'

Essie looked up. Victoria shook her head minutely, and she went reluctantly back to her game.

'Boy?' I said, before I could stop myself. It was partly out of relief that Harriet Jenner had apparently been forgotten, but I was also fascinated. Family stories I knew very well – my grandmother had always told them, along

305

with all her other tales – but recently I had heard so many conflicting versions.

'Oh, he's long gone now. I had to dismiss him when we found out,' said Robert, sorrowfully.

'Actually, if we must rake up all this ancient history, I think it was Mama who got rid of him, and with great alacrity, too,' sniffed Victoria. 'Even from her bed she still ran this house.'

Pembridge stood. 'It's time Lucas went back inside,' he said.

'No!' cried Lucas. 'Please, Father. I feel so much better out here.'

'Oh, do let him stay a little longer,' wheedled Essie.

Pembridge paused. I had never seen him so indecisive, or so stricken, and wished I could somehow rescue him. Surrounded as he was by family who already knew, I wondered why he was so upset about an old scandal. Perhaps it was because of Lucas, who was presumably too young to know anything of his father's apparent illegitimacy, but the boy clearly hadn't heard anything – entranced as he was by Essie's game. The only outsider was me and I couldn't imagine why he would mind my hearing about it. I was only the governess, after all.

'As you wish, then,' he said, and strode off towards the house.

Victoria waited until the children had resumed talking among themselves, then leaned towards me. 'I may as well tell you,' she said quietly. 'You're practically one of us now. It's not such a terrible thing, really, though it seemed to be at the time. I must say, though, I do think it hastened Mama into her grave. That and her penchant for quacks' remedies.' She glanced back at her father but he seemed to have nodded off. 'It was the gardener's boy,' she mouthed. 'Dilger's Ned. Lord knows when it happened, or where. But happen it did.

'Of course, he wasn't a boy by then, and she was no longer a girl. Papa is always stuck in the 1870s. No, she was twenty-three he and had been promoted to under-gardener by then. I was twenty and rather vague about the . . . mechanics of the whole thing. It seemed so very unlike her that I simply couldn't imagine how it had happened. But there you are. People, even those closest to us, are impossible to know entirely. We only ever see a series of acceptable surfaces.'

She forked a piece of cake into her mouth and chewed it thoughtfully. 'I think it rather frightens some people when they discover that someone they thought they knew intimately is capable of something entirely unpredictable – and in Helen's case entirely shocking. I've always found it rather exciting. What about you, Miss Fairford?'

An image of my grandmother glowed in my mind, though we were talking about Helen. I pushed it away. 'I can't say I find it exciting,' I said hesitantly. 'I think it's frightening to realize that you might not have been shown the whole picture. That the whole picture has been kept from you.' I saw again the twisting mechanism of the clock that had supposedly been my grandmother's wedding present from the old man opposite me. The man who had looked for her afterwards, and had been talking so wistfully of her today.

Victoria was staring at me curiously. 'You sound as though your people kept their cards very close.'

'My grandmother. There was only my grandmother.

My parents died when I was young. And, yes, I'm beginning to see that she did. And that she didn't. She brought me up with stories about her past – so many stories, scores of them. Lately, though, I've been wondering whether she told me so much in order to hide the things that really mattered.'

'Needles hidden in a haystack, that sort of thing?'

'I suppose so. Drops of blood in a pool, perhaps.' Victoria snorted and I blushed, laughing. 'I don't know where that came from. I'm not usually so melodramatic.'

'It sounds like the title of a terribly gory sensationalist story. Like something Agnes would relish. Or Essie, perhaps.' She grimaced.

As there was no sign of the housekeeper, Victoria and I began to gather the cake plates and forks. Essie helped Lucas to his feet. Bertie, I realized, had wandered over to inspect a rosebush that would soon need cutting back for winter, if anyone thought to do it. Robert was still dozing.

We were almost at the stairs down to the servants' quarters when Victoria caught my arm with her free hand. 'Don't mention Helen's scandal again to David, will you?' she said quietly. 'You saw how he stormed inside. He's very torn up about all that. He can't help but be ashamed of the circumstances surrounding his birth. You can't blame him, can you? We're not in Bloomsbury.' She rolled her eyes and let go of my arm. 'He adored his mother underneath it all and, in some ways, he's very like her. Thankfully, though Ned was a gentle enough soul, there's barely a trace of him in David. Only his colouring testifies to the whole thing not being some sort of immaculate conception – those black eyes are Ned's. David took Helen's death very badly, not least because he was very hard on her as a boy – precisely because of where he came from, you see. He blames himself for what happened to her, though it wasn't his fault, of course. And then there was Frannie.' She nudged open the baize door with her hip. 'Poor David, sometimes I think he blames himself for her death, too. It's madness if he does, of course. How could he be responsible for Spanish flu? It wiped out half the world.'

Thirty-six

The Indian summer we had enjoyed didn't linger after that Sunday afternoon. Soon enough, I couldn't precisely recall how it felt to go outside wearing just a thin cardigan. While those in the town deep in the valley were eased into the colder weather, we on the hill were plunged straight into an early winter. Icy winds shook the sash windows during the night, and each morning the frost blanket was a little thicker, a little slower to melt. I took to wearing every warm garment I possessed all at once in the barely heated house.

On the mornings when the sun deigned to shine, the garden was startlingly beautiful: every overgrown bush and dead branch transformed into a white and sparkling wonderland, as though someone had dusted it overnight with finely ground diamonds. It reminded me of my grandmother's rendition of *The Twelve Dancing Princesses*, who had gone underground each night to dance among trees dripping with jewels, silver and gold. Lucas, with a boy's more prosaic tastes, said the frost looked like sugar.

Though it was by now well into October, I hadn't yet had another letter from my grandmother. Worry rubbed at me, like a stone in my shoe, but there was an element of liberation in it, too – as guilty as it made me feel to entertain such a thought. I couldn't help it, though: I'd been so long under her wing that I couldn't help but relish a little independence.

Sometimes, when I was busy in the present, the shadow of the past was easily dismissed. I told myself that she or I had recalled things wrongly or – more convincingly because my grandmother was nothing if not sharp – that she had turned the truth into a narrative suitable for her granddaughter, with pink carpets instead of bare boards and no hint of impropriety with her employer. But a passing conversation with Bertie brought to light yet more distortion – and I knew I was right to have misgivings. She had lied outright, not merely to protect me.

Bertie and I were in the garden again. It was one of those crystalline mornings that showed the frost off so perfectly: bitterly cold, of course, but worth it for the clarity of light. Agnes had given me an ancient fur tippet to keep my neck warm. It smelt of dust and the sickly remnants of an old-fashioned and heavy scent, like rotten flowers. I was fairly certain it had once belonged to the mistress. Thankfully, the cut-glass air of the garden soon freshened it.

Bertie was coming down the garden's winding path when I met him; judging by his red nose and watering eyes, he'd already been outside for some time.

'Oh, hello there!' he cried, when he finally spotted me. 'What a glorious day it is.'

I smiled. 'Isn't it?'

'How are you getting on with old Lucas, then? Still making progress?'

'I think so. He has his bad days, of course, and there was a nasty fit last week, but I hope he's a little more settled now than when I first met him.'

'Oh, undoubtedly. Of course, Essie has always done

him good so, what with you and her in the house, he'll be transformed – he's already quite changed for the better. I don't know if David has said so – he's not very effusive, my nephew – but he's very grateful to you. I've known him all his life, you see. I can tell when he's pleased. It's not always visible to the naked eye but I can sense it.'

To my annoyance, I found myself smiling broadly, and turned my face towards a nearby bush so he didn't notice. 'He's said a few things, actually, and he hasn't made any complaint, so I presume I'm giving satisfaction. He doesn't strike me as the type to hold back if he's *un*happy.'

'Ha, yes, quite. He certainly doesn't bite his tongue when I get on his nerves. Shall I walk with you a little, Miss Fairford? I won't be offended if you'd rather be alone, but I don't think I'm quite ready to go inside yet. Agnes is baying for my blood.'

I laughed. 'Please join me. I'd like that. What have you done to Agnes?'

'Left a pile of wet clothes in a heap on the floor. She blew up – said she'd been picking my clothes up for nearly fifty years and it was high time I learned to look after myself. She's quite right, of course. Poor girl, I never thought of it like that – you know, the tedium of it. I never really thought about tidying up at all.'

'I suppose if you had followed your uncle into the army you would have been trained to be tidy.'

I said it casually, the connection arriving in my head quite naturally, but it reminded me that I'd long wanted to ask him more about the mysterious Dauncey uncle, whom my grandmother had never mentioned, despite his presence as a house-guest during the single summer she'd been there.

'I would have made an appalling army officer,' Bertie said now, shaking his head at the unlikeliness of it. 'Of course, I was still a boy when I last saw my uncle, but we were already like chalk and cheese. Poor Mama. How she'd have loved a small replica of him. I think she loved him more than anyone, you know, perhaps even Victoria.'

'Did he not come back from India again, then?' I probed. 'I think you said he was here at the same time as that governess you liked so much.'

'Miss Jenner? Yes, that's right. Goodness, what a kerfuffle when he went! The house was in positive uproar – Mama wailing, Mary running up and down fetching tonics and smelling salts and, in the end, a bottle of brandy. Even Agnes was distraught, going about with a face as pale as milk. Mind you, I think she'd been rather sweet on the dashing Captain Dauncey. My uncle had that sort of effect on women,' he said, with a slight blush. 'Quite different from me, you see. I've always been invisible to the fairer sex.'

'Not to me,' I said, and took his arm. We had reached the upper garden, close to where the narrow ranks of silver birches lined up, and beyond which lay the ice-house. It was colder up there, without the shelter of the house, and I shivered. Our mingled breath was clearly visible.

'You said he disappeared,' I prompted. 'Presumably he went back to India.'

'Well, that's what we thought, but apparently he never returned to his garrison. Mama discovered that when she tried to find him, writing letters to everyone she could think of. He'd been in some trouble in the army, it transpired. Disciplined for drinking and violence. Naturally, Mama didn't say much to us but I had the impression he'd been thrown out, actually. He was here for an awfully long time that summer – I remember hearing my father asking Mama how he had been allowed so much leave, not that he got a civil reply. Her brother could do no wrong in her eyes.

'We weren't allowed to mention him after he left that summer, not in front of her, but I assume he went back to India to find his wife and then, no longer in the army, went native, so to speak. Another theory, and this may have been a grisly seed planted by Vicky, it seems unlikely enough, is that he got roaring drunk and tumbled overboard during the voyage back. I suppose we'll never know now. Either way, we never heard from him again. It was as if he'd simply vanished.'

I stared at the spectacular view laid out in front of us. The maze looked like some glorious confection of iced marzipan and, in the far distance, the twisting ribbon of the Severn glittering in the wintry sunlight. There was something I couldn't quite get hold of – something to do with this uncle. Nothing was accidental when it came to my grandmother. And then, like a gift, Bertie handed me the answer – or, at least, something that might lead me to it.

'I think Miss Jenner found my uncle's presence as difficult as I did that summer. I suspect things with Mama would have gone a little more smoothly if he hadn't been here.'

'Oh?'

'Poor Miss Jenner. She didn't mean to, I'm sure of it,

she wasn't like that. But she turned my uncle's head. Quite literally. He would watch for her, and when he found her, his eyes would follow her about. I think now, in hindsight, that her card was marked after that. Mama could never share her brother with any of us, let alone a pretty young thing like Miss Jenner.'

Thirty-seven

After Bertie's revelations about his uncle, I spent the next few days feeling distracted. So much so that Lucas eventually lost his temper and told me, quite imperiously, that I could go to my room if I was not going to listen to what he had to tell me. That made me laugh, and him all the more furious, but he grudgingly let me stay.

He wouldn't hear of doing the spelling test I had planned and suggested we listen in on his crystal set. In the end, because it would look a little more educational should Pembridge choose to drop in on us, as he now occasionally did, I said we might draw each other's portrait. Both of us were soon absorbed in the task, though another part of my mind was far away, even as my pencil sketched in my pupil's sharp little features.

I had always sensed that Fenix House was brimming over with secrets as well as sadness, but I had never expected to be told any of them by the Pembridges. In that, I had been wrong. Both Victoria and Bertie had given things away – or, rather, had trusted me with family stories I would never have expected to be privy to. 'You're one of us,' Victoria had said so offhandedly in the garden, little knowing how much it would mean to me.

I had always been envious of those who were part of a large family. Some of the books I had loved best as a child featured large, rambling clans, with brothers and sisters, aunts and cousins crowding into the narrative. Since my tenth birthday, I had only ever had my grandmother and, as much as I loved her, and as much as she loved me – enough for two or three people – I had always yearned for the noise and chaos two people could never muster between them.

The large household that Fenix House had been in the days of my grandmother's brief tenure was as idealized to me as the American Carr family in *What Katy Did*. Its disintegration by the time I had arrived was far sadder than the neglect of the house and garden. It never occurred to me as a little girl that, had I been a Pembridge, I would have lost the privacy and peace I took for granted as an only child, that a small sister like Victoria would probably have stamped on and torn my books, just as she had Helen's. All I had seen were the numbers, and the safety conferred by being among them.

With my new optimistic way of thinking, and now that Victoria and Essie had returned, I didn't think it would take much to bring the Pembridge family back to life. Perhaps they would once again be as happy as they had been in my grandmother's day. Not that I was so sure about that now – Bertie's stories of those days were much more nuanced in mood and tone than the versions I'd grown up with. Even with the whirlwind of Victoria on the scene, secrets were still creating rifts at Fenix House. Some were more recent – I still didn't know how Helen had died – and others, disturbingly, seemed to date back to the summer of 1878. Like 1910 to me, 1878 felt like a significant way-marker in Fenix House's history, the point at which its now-tangled roots had taken hold.

With some effort, I focused on the boy in front of me. He was frowning with concentration and didn't lift his dark eyes from his sketchpad for a full minute as I watched him.

'Lucas, don't forget to look at what you're drawing,' I said gently. 'You should look as much at your subject as you do your paper. Otherwise you'll draw what you think an eye or an ear should look like, and not how it actually is.'

'Oh, I'm not drawing you any more,' he said in surprise.

I laughed. 'What, then?'

'A comet crashing into the earth.'

'That sounds very dramatic.'

He nodded cheerfully. 'It's smashed into the sea and made an enormous tidal wave, which will drown everyone. Can I see yours?'

I held up my half-finished sketch of him. I was quite pleased with it. The nose was wrong but I'd captured something of the fierce expression in his eyes.

'That's rather good,' he conceded.

'Can you see how much you look like your father around the eyes?'

'I think I'm like my mother.'

I didn't know what to say to that and went back to sketching, though all I was really doing was going over the same lines I'd already drawn, adding more shadow and smudge.

'That's what people always used to say, anyway,' he continued, his tone carefully casual. He'd also returned to his drawing, pressing hard on the paper as he coloured in the flames of his comet. 'They think I can't remember. It wasn't so much my eyes and things. They said it was how

I looked when I spoke or laughed. That was when I looked like her.'

'You must miss her,' I said tentatively. I was terrified I would say the wrong thing, though I would have been glad to talk of my parents after they died. My grandmother had never encouraged it, thinking it would upset me too much, I suppose.

Lucas frowned. 'Of course I do.' He paused. 'The worst thing is when I can't remember her face. I get frightened that I won't ever again.'

'I suppose you could always go and look at her portrait if you were worried about that. It's a very good one.'

He frowned again, this time in confusion, and I realized he hadn't seen it, or had spent so long in his room that he'd forgotten such a thing existed. 'Yes, I could do that,' he said slowly, unwilling to admit to either.

I put my sketchbook down, wondering if I dared. I studied Lucas's small face, his expression so vulnerable, and decided. 'Shall we go and see it now?'

He shrugged without looking up, but he was gripping his pencil tightly and his cheeks were flushed.

'Come on, then.'

It was hard not to creep down the stairs, despite telling myself that I was doing nothing more than showing a child his mother's picture. I knew Pembridge must have shut her away for both of them, though, and didn't relish the possibility of meeting him in the hallway.

The study, when we got inside it, was colder even than the rest of the house. Our breath came out in short, sharp puffs; we were both nervous. It was dark in the corner where the portrait hung and I wished I'd brought the oil lamp – it must have dated from before my grandmother's time, and was essential still in augmenting the unreliable electricity supply.

Lucas had gone to the window and was poking his finger into a small patch of ice that had formed where the frame leaked. I could see his breath hanging in the frozen air. 'It's over here,' I called softly. 'You need to let your eyes adjust a bit.'

He sidled over and, seeing how apprehensive he was, I put my arm around his thin shoulders. To my surprise, he turned into me, burying his head in the thick wool of my warmest jersey.

'It's a lovely portrait of your mother,' I murmured. 'Nothing to be afraid of.'

He raised his head and turned to the painting. Going closer, he put his hand out and stroked the dark folds of her skirt, which was as high as he could reach. I wondered if he remembered how the fabric had felt, just as I remembered the texture of my mother's peacock-blue one.

He gazed at it for some minutes, then turned to me. 'I can come back, can't I?'

'Of course, but we must tell your father.'

'He won't want me to see it. He'll think it'll make me angry, like I used to get.'

I thought of the damage to the passageway upstairs, and the broken window from my first day – which Pembridge had finally had mended. It hadn't even occurred to me that Lucas might damage the portrait, or anything else in the shuttered little study – all the frustration seemed to have ebbed out of him these last weeks. He was much stronger physically, too.

On the way back upstairs, Lucas took my hand, which he had never done before. I tried not to show I was pleased in case it embarrassed him, but I was very touched. My grandmother had insisted I was meant to be at Fenix House; that was the first time I felt she was right.

We hadn't been back in Lucas's bedroom long when there was a light tap at the door. Pembridge poked his head around it, giving me an unexpected smile. I wasn't used to these unprompted bouts of friendliness yet, though they were undeniably getting more frequent.

'I don't want to interrupt. I just thought I'd see how you were getting on.'

'We were supposed to be drawing each other's portraits . . .' I began, but Lucas had begun speaking too.

'We were drawing and then we went to see Mother's portrait,' he said, the words tumbling out, half anxious, half triumphant.

I tried to catch Pembridge's eye but he wouldn't look at me, even as he came in and pretended to admire Lucas's apocalyptic picture. 'What a busy morning you've both had,' he said tightly. A little muscle flickered in his jaw. It was only as he left that he addressed me. 'A word with you, Miss Fairford, if I may. When you have finished your art lesson, of course.'

He spoke so coldly that I flinched. Lucas looked worriedly between us and went to say something but Pembridge had already left, closing the door smartly behind him.

'He's angry, isn't he?' he said dolefully, once his father's footsteps had retreated. 'I shouldn't have told him. He hates to talk of Mother. I don't know why I did now. It was stupid of me.'

'No, it wasn't. It was only the truth. Don't worry, I'll explain it all to him.'

'He's not going to make you go away, is he?'

'I sincerely hope not. Besides, I'm not afraid of your father's temper.' Despite my reassuring words, I *was* afraid of it, and I was even more afraid that Pembridge would hate me.

I felt sick as I went down to the dining room an hour or so later.

'You had no business taking him in there,' he said, before I'd even sat down. 'I don't like him being reminded of her. What's the good of talking about things you can't change, can't bring back?'

I suspected he was talking about himself as much as his son again. Either way, and though the words were harsh, his heart clearly wasn't in it. He seemed more weary than furious.

'I should have asked your permission to go and see the portrait, Mr Pembridge,' I said, feeling slightly braver, 'but it did him good to see it. You see, he was worried that he was forgetting what his mother –' I broke off, seeing Pembridge's face flood with guilt.

Sighing, he rubbed his face with his hands. 'No doubt you're right. I thought it would be easier for him if it was shut away. I didn't do it to be cruel.'

'Of course not. And perhaps it was easier for him at first. But now . . . well, he seemed quite relieved afterwards. I think his worrying about forgetting her has been a strain in itself.'

Pembridge nodded and sighed again. We sat in silence

for a while, him deep in thought while I remembered Lucas's face when I'd left him. He'd still been a little anxious in case I was told off but he also looked lighter at heart. He'd spent the last hour telling me stories about his mother, games they'd played, stories she'd told him, and the mythical world they'd invented for the woods and the Blue.

I came back to the present when Pembridge pushed a small cardboard box towards me. I leaned over and saw that it was full of dark chocolates. 'Peppermint creams,' he said, with a sheepish shrug of the shoulders. 'They're my weakness. Those, and an expensive bottle of Bordeaux.'

'Oh.' I couldn't think of anything to say to this surprise admission so I took a chocolate instead. The rich dark coating and fondant centre melted together in my mouth. 'Gosh,' I exclaimed, my mouth full. 'They're good ones.'

I received a small smile. 'They arrived this morning. Agnes must've put them in here while I was upstairs seeing you and Lucas. I think Aunt V's finally sorted out our grocery order and that woman forgets nothing, even the chocolates her irascible nephew likes. I came down ready to give you what-for but then I saw them. Frannie introduced me to them. She loved anything sweet but these were a particular favourite. It sounds absurd but seeing them felt like a gentle prod from her not to be such a bad-tempered fool.'

'It doesn't sound absurd at all.'

'So you think I'm a bad-tempered fool, then?'

I coloured and began to protest when I noticed the now-familiar twist to his mouth. 'Oh, I see.'

He fixed me with those black eyes of his. 'You're quite a different sort of woman from Frannie.'

Still embarrassed, but now also intrigued, I busied myself picking out another chocolate so I didn't have to look at him. 'Oh?'

'She was very serene. She glided through life, swan-like and dreamy. You are rather more . . . determined.'

'Well, I suppose it's the first time I've been out in the world. The first time I've been on my own.'

'You've had to learn to stick up for yourself? Especially when faced with a difficult employer?'

I smiled. 'Actually, I find I'm quite enjoying my independence, these days.'

'You don't hate it here, then?' He looked just as Lucas did when he was worried and it softened me towards him even more.

'Not at all. I feel almost settled now.'

'Almost? Perhaps another chocolate will help.'

I blushed, not quite sure whether he was being genuinely charming or making fun of me.

'Go on,' he said, pushing the box closer. 'I mean what I say. I want . . .' he frowned as he searched for the right words '. . . I want you to feel at home here. You don't have to tiptoe around.' He smiled again.

We sat quietly eating our chocolates until he spoke again, in a voice so quiet I found myself leaning towards him.

'It was Spanish flu.'

I was unsure whether to admit that I knew already.

'Frannie, I mean.' He sat back in his seat. 'She came to meet me in London, after I'd been demobbed. There were people everywhere, celebrating, shouting in the streets. She must have caught it from some stranger.'

'Oh. How awful.'

'It was the speed of it that was so terrifying. She was perfectly well at breakfast and then . . .' He trailed off.

'I read about it. It must have been . . . Well, I don't know how it must have been.'

'The poor boy can only remember having both of us for a single day.'

'Do you think it's your fault because she came to London to meet you?'

He looked up at me in shock. I felt as though I could see in his eyes every bit of the guilt and fury he carried around with him. I did my best to hold his gaze, quite astonished at my own daring.

Eventually he nodded. 'Perhaps.'

I took a deep breath. 'When my parents were killed I blamed lots of things. The signalman who had fallen asleep, his baby son, who had kept him up for nights on end because he was ill, even time itself. My father had told me about Railway Time and how Bristol Time had been ten minutes slower. It sounds silly, perhaps, but I believed that if the GWR hadn't insisted on everything being standardized, my parents might somehow have escaped. It isn't logical, I know, but it made perfect sense to me at the time.'

I stopped, wondering why I was telling him all this, but he nodded at me to go on.

'As I got older, I began to blame myself. When I first thought of it, I wondered how I'd managed to go for so long *not* thinking it was my fault. You see, they caught an earlier train because it was my birthday. They wouldn't have needed to get that train otherwise – or if I'd gone to London with them in the first place. I was supposed to, you see, but I had a slight chill – nothing, really. I probably caught it leaning out of my window as I'd been forbidden to. I had been promised a birthday present from Selfridges – it hadn't long opened then. I was hoping they would let me have a puppy.'

Pembridge had been listening intently while I spoke, a crease of concentration furrowing his brow. Suddenly it deepened. He leaned forward. 'Your parents were killed in a railway accident? I had no idea. When was this?'

I sighed. 'It was my tenth birthday, a cruel little quirk of Fate. To everyone else, it was the day after the King's funeral. May the twenty-first, 1910.'

He sat back in his seat and shook his head. 'But . . . what an extraordinary coincidence. My mother died on that train.'

I started. Helen, who had loved her atlases and the stars and the novels of Jules Verne, had been on the same doomed train as my parents. To my horror, I began to cry.

Pembridge rooted in his pocket and pulled out a creased handkerchief. 'It's clean,' he said. 'At least, I think it is.'

I let out a strangled laugh, which turned into a hiccup. 'I'm sorry. I'm not generally much of a weeper. Not in front of other people, anyway. I had no idea your mother was on that train.'

'Well, why would you have?'

'I – I don't know.'

'You shouldn't blame yourself. You were just a child. It had nothing to do with you.'

'That makes no difference at all. You blame yourself for Frannie's death, when you can hardly have been responsible for an epidemic.'

'Perhaps, though, the guilt stems as much from getting out of it myself. The train crash was another time I cheated death – I usually came back here when Mother did, but that time I was going to stay at a school friend's instead. Anyway, what with that, Ypres and Spanish flu, I have quite a talent for it. I wonder if that's exactly what it is, a cheat, and those closest to me have been the ones to pay off the debt. First my mother, then Sergeant Potter, who was a much better soldier than I, and finally my wife.' He shook his head in disgust.

'What had you to do with the train crash?'

'Actually, it was rather like you, though less blameless because I was older, and because I was trying to give trouble. Your parents might have taken a later train, if they hadn't been wanting to see you on your birthday. Likewise, my mother was supposed to get an earlier one. She was coming here for a visit, as I say – my grandfather was meeting her at Swindon because he liked to do that journey after his retirement, to remind him of the old days, I suppose. She had intended to set off first thing, she was always an early riser, but then I threw my spanner in the works.

'When she knew she was going to be late, she sent a telegram warning him, saying I had been ill that morning, though I wasn't anything of the sort. In fact, I had picked a horrible fight with her. I won't bore you with the petty details. Suffice to say I was always harbouring some grudge or other against her. I wanted to be like the other boys I

327

went to school with, who all had brothers and sisters and, most importantly, fathers. No one else lived alone with his mother. I was worried I would be thought odd and singled out for it.

'I never knew my father. I expect you put two and two together after hearing my grandfather's ramblings that day in the garden. I hated being different – I even lied at school, made her into a respectable widow. I was always terrified someone would notice that things didn't add up – that my maternal grandfather had the same surname as me. Of course, no one ever did. Anyway, all that subterfuge, that feeling different, made me full of resentment towards Mother. I often said cruel things to her. She never told me off for it, which made it worse.

'So, I had been due to go and stay in Suffolk while she came here. Bertie was going back with her, too – he'd been staying with us because there was an exhibition on butterflies he wanted to see at the Natural History Museum.'

'Bertie was on it too?'

He gave me a quizzical look. 'It was a rare visit to London for him. Anyway, I didn't really want to go to Suffolk because there'd been a measles outbreak and I'd rather have just stayed at home. I think she knew that, and was trying to make the best of it because it was too late to cancel the visit. She was making a fuss about what I would take and whether I'd be warm enough and . . .' he looked down, deeply ashamed '. . . I couldn't stand it, God knows why. In short, I was particularly loathsome that morning.

'The result of my tantrum was that we all missed our trains. In my case, I displeased Gerald Atherton's mother by making their driver wait for two hours at Southwold station. In my mother's case, it killed her, and broke my grandfather's heart into the bargain. He was never the same after that, Bertie not much better.'

I didn't say anything. It would have done no good to say it wasn't his fault. It wouldn't have changed his mind, as I well knew. In the silence he got up and added another couple of logs to the waning fire. They shifted and rasped as they settled, the bark blackening and sparking as I watched. I hadn't noticed how chilly the room had grown while we were talking. Chilly and dark. Outside, the light had almost drained away, though it wasn't yet four o'clock.

'You've seen the train set, I gather?'

It took me a moment to register what he'd said. I was still lost in his memories. I could see it all so clearly. The impotently furious schoolboy, the placating mother. And then, after the accident, the bad news brought to him in someone else's house, far away from home. Broken to him by Atherton's father, perhaps, with an awkward pat on the shoulder and 'Rotten luck, old chap.' At least I had always had my grandmother. I had never been alone like that. I hadn't felt homesick for a while but then it washed over me. I'd had another letter from her that morning but I'd been so busy with Lucas, I hadn't even opened it. Guilt mingled with a sudden longing for her.

'Miss Fairford?'

'Sorry, what did you say?'

'The train set. You can't have missed it.'

'Oh, no. It's quite remarkable. I hope you don't mind

but I've been calling in to see your grandfather quite regularly – your aunt said it was all right. Yesterday he even let me change the signals.'

Pembridge flashed me a brief smile. 'An honour indeed.'

'I'm not sure he always knows who I am, but I enjoy his company. There is something oddly soothing about the train going round and round.'

'Well, of course, that's the point.'

'What do you mean?'

'The predictability of it. Nothing changing. Everyone in their place. The little girl waving, the signalman alert at his post . . .'

'Oh, I see.'

'V disapproves, of course. She thinks it's rather morbid – she's of the school of thought that it's unhealthy not to accept and then forge ahead, make the best of things. And I agree with her to an extent – you heard me earlier. That's why I don't like Lucas dwelling too much. But my grandfather's an old man. Who could blame him for wanting to retreat into the time before that day? He loved his work for the GWR and he loved my mother. In a sense, he lost both that day.'

My mind was full of the past as I climbed the stairs to bed that night. My grandmother's letter lay unopened next to my hairbrush where I'd left it that morning and I picked it up with some trepidation. There were so many pasts hovering in the air, like spectres – my own, my grandmother's, the Pembridges'. That there was a connection between my history and Pembridge's, through the train crash that had killed our parents, had moved and thrown me. There was comfort in it, somehow, and I heard Victoria's words again: *You're one of us now*. And what had Pembridge himself said? *I want you to feel at home here.*

I brought the envelope up to my face and breathed in a remnant of my old home. I hadn't realized it had a smell until I'd left it. There was a hint of roses, too – the scent my grandmother had always worn. I closed my eyes. Usually the familiar fragments of memory didn't come so easily, unless I was asleep; I suppose I was always too eager for more, which made them slip away.

In the first, I was the same height as the ladder-back chair at the head of the table, so I was perhaps eight or nine. There was something heavy in my arms and I knew I mustn't drop it by slipping on the polished wood of the dining-room floor. There was a sound too, but that was out of reach, just beyond my grasp. In the next, I was sleepy, my eyes still closed as I felt myself lifted up out of warm blankets into the cool night air. 'Wake up, darling,' my father whispered. 'There's something we want you to see.' The speaking part was new, though his voice was as familiar as if I'd heard it yesterday. To listen to it again after so long filled me with joy even as it made me cry.

The last fragment was entirely fresh to me, a memory that must have lain dormant and pristine since I was ten years old. This was a rare gift – I had so little left of the years before the accident, my mind having apparently wiped the slate clean for my own protection, and my grandmother so quick to fill the space with her own recollections.

We were on the suspension bridge, my grandmother, my father and I. It wasn't quite dark so the crowds gathering to see the comet were still sparse. The lights that festooned the bridge were switched off so that we could see the comet better, and the twilight was magical: a shadowy thickening deep in the gorge that brightened into clear, rose-pink skies.

I was looking up when I heard my name called. I turned in the direction of the sound but that was all I could remember, the darkness descending again and the rest of it lost.

I wiped my eyes with my handkerchief and put my grandmother's letter under my pillow without opening it. I wanted the comfort of my own past that night, what little of it I had.

Thirty-eight

It was at the end of that week that Agnes told me about Victoria's plan. A consummate organizer and lover of occasion, she had decided that a joint birthday celebration was called for in a few weeks' time. Lucas was due to turn eight the day before his great-grandfather would be eighty-one. The afternoon in the garden had been judged a success. Now, with Lucas's spirits and strength still improving and Robert no more confused than usual, she thought it was the ideal time to throw a party.

'It's been a while since we celebrated anything here,' Agnes confided, over the scrubbed oak table in the kitchen. She was kneading dough for bread, alternately slapping it down on the wood and squashing it with the heel of her hand. I was scattering flour whenever she gave me the nod that more was needed. We were quite easy with each other now and I had grown fond of her, despite her rough ways and blunt talk. If she needed the odd tipple to brighten her isolated existence on the hill, that was her business.

'When was the last time there was any kind of party like this, then?' I said. Robert had said something about a particular occasion when we were all in the garden.

'Oh, now, I reckon it must have been back in the days of Mrs Rakes and Mrs Rollright. They were housekeeper and cook.'

I know, I wanted to confide, as I so often did. *I probably know as much about them as you do.* Then again, perhaps I didn't. Who knew what my grandmother had left out or embroidered, even in the case of the more minor characters?

'Of course, there were always smaller dos for the family then,' Agnes went on. 'Cakes for birthdays and so forth. The mistress loved all that. I heard her say once that it was "the little treats that break the monotony on this accursed hill".' She laughed at the memory and flung down the dough with extra force. 'I always remember that – "accursed hill". At the time, I felt like she was speaking for me, only a sight more elegant than I'd have managed. She were right, on that at least: you need something different to look forward to. We all of us do, even lowly servants.'

'Even if it makes more work?'

'I reckon so. That's when anything interesting happens, isn't it? When things aren't running along their normal course.'

'What do you mean?'

Agnes paused. 'I don't know that I can explain it. People act one way day after day because they're always doing the same thing. Have them do another thing and they're not themselves.'

'Or they are, but you see a different side to them.'

'That's it. Something – or someone – brings a different side out. And then all Hell breaks loose, let me tell you. It don't take much, either.'

Agnes had been at Fenix House for almost half a century. She could have been talking about anything; there might have been a hundred dramatic moments in that time, especially when the mistress was alive. The first Mrs Pembridge seemed to have invited drama, from what Bertie and even Pembridge had let slip. But I wondered . . . My grandmother was a spirited person, not easily cowed. And what was it Bertie had said in the garden – that 'her card was marked' after she had inspired the admiration of his uncle? Perhaps there had been some sort of clash or climax that I could coax out of Agnes.

'So when did Hell last break loose on the hill?' I said lightly.

Agnes laughed mirthlessly. 'Well, that's what I'm talking about, ain't it?' She hesitated and then leaned over the table towards me. Flour rose between us as a fine mist. 'There were a proper party, the last we had. Not a plain old birthday indoors, like what Mrs V wants next week. A proper do, with all the neighbours invited and others besides. Fireworks, even. There were fifty here that night – more, I should think. The lower lawn was packed with them, everyone dressed up to the nines. The mistress were in her element, of course. Victoria, too, showing off and tipsy on the dregs from people's glasses. She and her mother both loved an audience.'

'What was the occasion?' I said, drawn in to Agnes's memory already: the voices tumbling over each other in the garden, dazzling showers of light in the sky and the servants' quarters a hive of industry, scullery door pushed back to catch a breath of cool air. My grandmother had never mentioned such a night but I was now certain it was the one Robert had alluded to.

Agnes still hadn't answered when I turned back to her.

Half a dozen different emotions flitted across her face in succession.

'Agnes? Was it another birthday?'

'That were the excuse,' she said slowly. 'But I think she'd have had it even if it hadn't been his birthday. She were trying to win him back with it – that much were obvious, even to the likes of us down here.'

'The mistress, you mean?'

'Yes, her. I wasn't the only one to think they were too close. It turned my stomach to see the pair of them some-times. It's not how things should be between brother and sister, not in my book.'

There he was again. The army officer Bertie could never live up to. 'The children's uncle,' I said.

Agnes looked at me sharply. 'That's the one. Captain Dauncey. What do you know of him?'

'Oh, only what Bertie's told me,' I said hurriedly. 'That he was stationed out in India. I think he was a difficult act to follow.'

The housekeeper threw the dough, with unnecessary violence, into a bowl to prove. 'Ha! Mr Bertie was always worth twenty of *him*.' She brushed the flour off her hands, went over to a cupboard and pulled out a bottle of sherry. She glanced at the clock. 'Sun's well over the yard-arm, what there was of it today, and the dinner's on. It must be about time for my daily constitutional. Will you join me?'

I was about to decline when I changed my mind. It was cosy in the kitchen. As well as the bread, Agnes was mak-ing some sort of stew that smelt nicer than the usual fare, of rich meat, onions and sage, the fragrant steam cloud-ing the windows. The old-fashioned range was producing more heat than any of the open fires upstairs and that, combined with the low ceiling, meant I was warmer than I'd been all day. I kicked off my shoes and stretched my legs out under the table.

Agnes lowered herself back into her chair with a grunt.

'Is your hip giving you trouble?' I said sympathetically, in part because I didn't want her to change her mind about telling the story.

'It gives me nothing but.'

'Is it your age?'

She tutted. 'The cheek of her!'

I coloured. 'I'm sorry, Agnes. I didn't mean to be rude. I wasn't thinking.'

'I was as young and lithe as you once, madam. In fact, it hasn't come with age – I hurt it, being clumsy. It were never right after that and then it got the rheumatics in it. The stairs in this place don't help.'

I was only half listening, the sherry pooling warmly inside me. The little glass had emptied itself very quickly and Agnes poured me some more. She was halfway down her second glassful already. 'What did you do to it?' I asked, biding my time so I didn't offend her.

She stared at me intently, as if she was deciding something. Eventually, she spoke. 'Mr Bertie show you the top of the garden when he took you round?'

I nodded, remembering again the dream I'd had before I'd even arrived. A young Bertie leading me up the winding path.

'What about the ice-house?' she went on. 'Did he show you that?'

'No. He mentioned it, though. Said no one had gone

inside for years.' Of course it had been I who had mentioned it, not him, accidentally bringing up something I shouldn't have known about.

Agnes nodded, a strange look in her eyes. She pushed back a loose lock of faded frizz with the inside of her wrist and poured another tot of sherry for herself. I knew I should go and wake Lucas from his afternoon nap soon but I didn't want to leave the warm kitchen yet.

'Did he tell you why it got locked up?'

I shook my head.

'It were on my say-so. The mistress said I was to lock it up and throw away the key.' She pulled out from under her blouse the string I'd noticed on the first day, with the large, ornate key that dangled from it. 'I locked it, all right, but I didn't throw away the key. I've kept it on me all these years. Just in case.'

I frowned. 'In case of what? Why did the mistress want it locked up?'

'Have you ever seen inside an ice-house?'

'No.'

'I don't know if they're all the same, but the one here is like a brick dome built into the hill. Like one of them igloos Eskimo folk have in the North Pole. They're deep too. The floor falls away about six feet lower than the door. There's a ladder down the side to the pit where they store the ice.'

'So you fell getting some ice and that's how you hurt your hip?'

'Hold your horses. I fell, all right, but I weren't getting ice.' She paused and glanced behind her towards the open door. Her small eyes glittered and I realized she was tipsy from drinking the sherry so quickly. 'I were storing something, you see.'

'Yes,' I said, though I didn't really see at all. My brain felt slightly sluggish from the drink. 'What was it?'

'That don't matter now,' she said eventually. 'The point is, the mistress wouldn't have given two farthings if it had just been me falling down there, even if I'd broken my neck. It was Miss Victoria she was worried about, and rightly so. She were a little minx, that one, always wandering off and poking her nose into things that were none of her concern. There'd been a run of trouble with her that summer. First she'd gone missing on the night of the party, then she'd gone wandering up the ruins when they flooded them, asking to get herself drowned. And then there was the ice-house.

'That were the final straw. Mr Bertie had long been warned off going in there in case he got trapped but they'd never bothered locking the door – he were always a sensible enough boy. Now, Miss Vicky had no sense at all, but they thought the door was too heavy for her to open. It always had been before.

'The reason I fell were thanks to that little tearaway. She were always creeping around, not like Miss Helen, who was a good girl and always at her books. I'd propped the ice-house door open so it didn't close on me – there's no handle on the inside of that door, Miss Fairford, so you don't want to take your chances – and had just started clambering down when she appeared in the doorway. I were jumpy that day anyway, in truth, and she give me such a fright that I fell.'

A shudder ran through me. Agnes's words about the

handle had conjured up an unnerving image. I could almost hear the heavy door of the ice-house slamming shut, cutting off the light, and a childish voice crying out of the blackness in fright. I couldn't tell whether it was my imagination, or something like my grandmother's glimmers.

Not noticing anything amiss, Agnes went on, 'Even as I was lying there in agony, Miss Vicky was wanting to know what I was doing, like she were the Empress of India herself, tearing a strip off some politician. "What have you got there, Agnes?" she were demanding, as if it were any of her business. God in Heaven, I can hear her now.' She shook her head at the memory and threw back the rest of her sherry. 'So, that was bad enough, but later that day, she only went back on her own, didn't she? Miss Vicky were like a dog with a bone about things like that. I should've known she'd go back, but my mind were on other things. She were only stuck in there ten minutes but that were enough to put the wind up her.'

I took a gulp of my own sherry. The only glimmers of the past I'd ever had were jumbled memories of my own. None had ever been as clear as the one I'd just experienced. It had shaken me and the fire of the drink was comforting.

'It were Miss Jenner what got her out,' Agnes continued, nearly making me overturn my glass. 'God knows how she knew to look there – she didn't know about my fall – but she went straight up there and fished her out before the rest of us even knew she'd gone missing. Miss Vicky were hysterical, saying the air had run out. Of course it hadn't, not that fast, but she might have fallen like I did or frozen half to death if Miss Jenner hadn't got her out so quick. She were clinging to the ladder, apparently, too terrified to move, not even having got what she was after.'

Agnes picked at the sherry bottle label thoughtfully. 'It were that little adventure that changed Miss Vicky for the better. She didn't speak for three days after, if you can believe that possible. She were still cheeky afterwards, still had spirit like she has to this day, but the devil that had been in her was left behind in that ice-house. She were a nicer girl after and she didn't put herself in danger every other minute neither. You'd think the mistress would have been grateful but she didn't see it like that. Miss Jenner got her marching orders after that little escapade, never mind she probably saved the child's life.'

Everything whirled around my head in confusion. 'Wait a minute, her marching orders? She was dismissed?' Even before Agnes answered, my mind was racing through the possibilities, the trusting child in me trying to hammer my grandmother's version into some approximation of the truth.

Agnes nodded. 'If it hadn't been one thing, it'd have been another. The mistress wanted her gone. She were just looking for an excuse by then, that's what I reckon. Mrs Rakes saw it coming too – she liked Miss Jenner, we all did down here, though we tried to think her hoity-toity at first because she were clever. Well, Mrs Rakes come down here one day after there'd been some trouble with Miss Vicky getting ink all down her, and I heard her say to the cook, Mrs Rollright – and roll was the word, I tell you – "That poor Miss Jenner's managed to get herself on the

wrong side of *her* already. I fear she won't be here long."
Her being the mistress, o' course.' Agnes shook her head
as glumly as if it were still 1878.

'Her card had been marked,' I said softly, echoing Bertie's words.

'Exactly.'

Trying to put aside for the time being the momentous
news that my grandmother had not left her position vol-
untarily, I tried again to work out how everything fitted
together. There were threads connecting all of it: my
grandmother, the Daunceys, Robert Pembridge and perhaps even Agnes – but they were too tangled and
gossamer-thin for me to make sense of yet.

'A great deal seemed to happen that summer,' I said.
'Like knocking over a run of dominoes, one thing leading
to another.'

'You're as sharp as she was,' said Agnes.

I looked at her in surprise – I hadn't meant to think
aloud.

Her face was flushed, her body loose from the alcohol,
but her eyes were still keen. 'Harriet Jenner, I mean. Them
brains must run in the family, eh?'

I started at the word 'family'. 'Whatever do you mean?'

She chuckled. 'Just because Mr Bertie and the old master are half blind don't mean I am.'

I was unable to meet her eye. 'When did you realize?'

'Oh, not right away. But then I saw you that day in the
garden, when the master and everyone were outside and
Mrs Granger and her Essie was here. The sun was out and
your hair were bright, like hers used to be. Bit darker, but
close enough. After that, I couldn't see how I'd missed it.

It's the little things that remind me. Tucking your hair back behind your ears, even when it's neat. Twisting your ring round and round your finger, like you're doing now. She'd do the same with this opal she had. It's not uncanny, the likeness, but you could be a sister to what she used to be like. It's funny to think of her near half a century older, just like I am. She still alive, is she, your grandma? I'm guessing she's not your ma.'

I nodded. To my surprise, I felt quite relieved that someone finally knew of my connection to Fenix House's past. It was one less entanglement for me to worry about.

'Was it her idea for you to take the position?'

I couldn't see the point of denying anything else. 'Yes. To be honest, I still don't really understand why she wanted me to, though she's given various explanations.'

Agnes frowned. 'I've been trying to puzzle that out myself. I didn't think it could just be happenstance. Seems strange to me. I've been wanting to ask but I were trying to mind my business.' She gestured at the much-depleted sherry bottle. 'The drink's got a way of helping good intentions like that out the window.'

'I think . . .' I stopped. I wasn't about to mention the glimmers. 'Well, I wonder now that you've told me she didn't leave of her own accord. Perhaps there have always been loose ends she wanted to tie up here and sending me is a way of doing that.'

Agnes frowned. 'What did she say to you about her time here before she packed you off?'

'I suppose she told me what a little girl would be interested in – stories about the children, mainly, though I heard about you and Mrs Rollright, Mrs Rakes and the others as well. Everything here seemed very simple in her stories. Simple and happy. I thought I knew all there was to know about the place.'

She smiled grimly. 'So much for that, then. It's interesting she never told you she were dismissed.'

'In her version, the whole household was out on the drive to wave her and my grandfather off.'

'Your grandfather?'

'Yes, a man she met by chance, when he called at the house one day, selling encyclopaedias. She said he became her follower. An admirer, I suppose she meant. He was quite determined, though, my grandfather – he kept coming back to see her and in the end she agreed to marry him. Which is when she left and . . .' I faltered.

Agnes was completely nonplussed. 'All of us out on the drive, waving them off? And him, selling encyclopaedias at the door?' She shook her head, baffled. 'First I've heard of it.'

'So you don't remember him?' I said.

She paused, her fingers turning the sherry bottle. 'Well, I might be getting confused. Too many sherries, it must be.' She tried to laugh, glancing up at me and then away, her cheeks aflame. 'You see, the mistress always had a bee in her bonnet about followers – said we wasn't allowed them. I always thought it were because she didn't want anyone being admired except her. But perhaps it were different rules for a governess. I probably just missed your granddad calling, stuck down here scrubbing pans. Or else I've forgotten it.'

I knew to my bones she was lying – that she, like my grandmother, wasn't the type to forget anything. I could only think she was doing it because she felt guilty for telling me my grandmother had been dismissed. Or – and this seemed feasible – she was covering up that my grandmother had been dismissed in disgrace because my grandfather had been courting her, when it was forbidden.

I took a sip of my sherry, the wedding clock filling my mind, its movement twisting back and forth. I didn't bother asking Agnes if my grandmother had received it as a gift from the Pembridges. I felt certain now that she hadn't.

I must have looked upset because Agnes nudged my hand with her work-reddened one. 'Come on, drink up. And cheer up. What does it matter whether she met your granddad here or there? He must have existed, or you wouldn't be here, would you?' She attempted a chuckle. 'And don't you worry about me saying anything. Your little secret's safe with me, though Mr Bertie would be glad to know. He adored your grandma.'

'Please don't tell anyone.'

'I said I wouldn't now, didn't I?'

A bell rang. She puffed out her red cheeks and heaved herself out of her chair, leaving me alone in the kitchen with my whirring thoughts.

Thirty-nine

Harriet

Captain Dauncey took no notice of Harriet in the days following their altercation in the glade above the ice-house. Her initial relief at this quickly turned to discomfort. Their conversation, if it could be called that, took on the unreal air of a scene imagined in her head to terrify herself into sense. After the first few occasions they happened upon each other in the house and he ignored her, she found herself casting sidelong glances at him, almost as if she wished him to say something.

Her new and unexpected invisibility had been exactly what she had previously wished for, but now she had it, his customary leering seemed preferable, reassuring even. Such studied and, to her mind, satisfied silence after the threat he'd made seemed much more ominous than any teasing words he might have flung her way as they passed on the stairs.

Robert also kept his distance, and his counsel, though she knew to her marrow that he had experienced no change of heart. The burning looks he gave her when they had happened to coincide were enough to convince her of that a hundred times over. He was staying away for her sake, to protect her. It made her love him even more.

Each night, when the house had stilled, the last lamp had been turned down, and she was able to luxuriate in the only private minutes the waking day held, she allowed herself to think of him. Just as she had once denied herself any unrealistic daydreams, she now refused to admit their opposite. Any black thoughts were turned back from the door of her mind: not only the looming certainty of disgrace if things continued, but the paucity of any solutions to the situation if they were discovered.

For even if they did not mind the scandal, what could they do about the insurmountable problem of Mrs Pembridge? Unlike her brother, she would not conveniently board a ship back to India at the end of the summer, and disappear from their lives, however fervently they might wish her to. Besides, there were the children. Robert would never leave them, and Harriet would never wish him to.

Apparently ignorant of Harriet and Robert's inner turmoil, the weather continued fair and settled, as if in preparation for Saturday's celebration. The days went on hot and windless, while the evenings stretched out long and golden. Observing this, the mistress declared herself delighted. To Harriet's relief, she seemed to know nothing of what had taken place in the glade, though this was tempered by a nagging disquiet. The captain was surely only biding his time. He had said as much, had he not?

'I think we shall have fireworks on Saturday,' the mistress was heard to announce to Mrs Rakes. 'After dark, just before the guests begin to leave. Jago always loved them as a child. Dilger, John and Ned can set them off from the top lawn. It will round the evening off beautifully.'

Victoria was thrilled at the prospect; Bertie less so. 'It's just that I'm worried for the animals, Miss Jenner,' he confided, his small brow creased. 'Mama wants them set off quite near to where the woods begin and they are sure to frighten the birds and bats that roost there, not to mention all the other creatures on the ground. What of the squirrels, for example? They won't like it at all. Nor the badgers and hedgehogs. Did you get my note about squirrels, Miss Jenner? They are such extremely cautious animals. I wanted one as a pet once, but could I catch one? I could not.' He chewed gravely on his lower lip.

Helen was anxious for different reasons, and Harriet wondered if such a thing could be contagious; a sort of catching miasma in the very air. If so, it was herself who had infected the Pembridge children with it.

'What if a firework comes towards us, Miss Jenner,' Helen said anxiously, during lessons on Friday, 'instead of going up towards the sky? Would it hurt?'

'It will go right through you and make a great burning hole, like this,' said Victoria, forming a circle with her fingers and placing them against her pinafore.

'Nothing so ridiculously dramatic will happen,' said Harriet, firmly. 'We will be standing at a safe distance, far below where they'll be setting them off.'

She didn't feel soothed by her own reassuring tone. What she felt, almost overwhelmingly, was trapped. Not only by the looming threat of the captain but even a little by Robert. He had been so overwrought up there on the bench; overwrought yet full of purpose. She spent her days in perpetual fear that a scream would go up from the mistress, confirming that he had seen fit to confess his feelings for the governess. A small part of her wanted him to; most of her was terrified at the notion. If only they had a little more time, a little less to occupy them in the house, and that there were fewer onlookers who might guess what was going through their minds when they came upon each other unexpectedly.

Despite her feelings, which now ran very deep, to the extent that she could hardly bear the thought of a future without Robert in it, she also, conversely, toyed with the idea of simply leaving. She did this every few minutes, daring herself to pack her valise and simply flee on foot to the railway station, whence she would catch the first train that came in. Though it meant leaving Robert behind, there was a queer sort of relief in the idea of taking one train after another, heedless of its destination, hardly even caring if she doubled back on herself, as long as she kept moving.

She might go north and lose herself in the smoke-belching sprawl of Birmingham. Or further up the country still, until the grit of England's industrial heart was shaken off and the tumbling green hills of the Dales rose up to greet her. Perhaps it would be better to go south, though, to the coast where she had gone with her father. Or, better yet, east, where nothing would remind her of days past. As far east as it was possible to go before the land ran out, to the flat fens and huge skies of Norfolk. She traced her finger over Helen's well-thumbed atlas, up, down and across, until Victoria asked what she was doing.

The truth was that she was as afraid to go as she was to stay, so she did nothing, petrified by her dilemma. That she was paralysed by something she had helped to set in motion was an irony that had not escaped her.

Despite the long days of teaching, and the longer nights spent wondering if her employer was similarly sleepless and beset by turmoil, Saturday's celebration came around quickly enough. Invitations had been extended outside the house and the family's near neighbours were more numerous than Harriet had imagined, hidden as they were by the dense woods and the hills that dipped and wove, like a coastline pitted with secret coves, each obscured from the last. The guests began to arrive as the stifling, seemingly endless afternoon admitted the possibility of a cool evening. The shadows had lengthened and the light was softening, the hard white beam of the day's heat finally dissolving. In another couple of hours it would be dusk.

The neighbours, along with a handful of guests whose carriages had scaled the hill from Cheltenham, numbered a few dozen. As the festivities would continue into the evening, none had brought their children, and Victoria in particular was relishing the attention she was receiving as the baby of the gathering.

In a blue satin dress that perfectly matched her eyes, she raced from guest to guest, pulling on sleeves and begging prettily for sips of champagne. Harriet, who by now knew Victoria as well as either of her parents did, watched closely, partly as a distraction and partly out of a genuine concern. The little girl's high colour and glassy eyes were surely signs of an imminent tantrum from over-excitement.

Bertie, in contrast, was pale with concentration as he mingled dutifully with the guests. Standing as straight and stiff as a poker, his hands clutching each other behind his back, he was answering well-meant questions about his school and pastimes like a man who had been told he would otherwise be shot. Every so often he stole nervous, darting glances at Harriet, who smiled and nodded encouragingly. She wished she could make him laugh by telling him he looked just like one of his anxious squirrels but she feared such an observation would only injure his fragile pride. She hoped his admiration of her was nothing more than a childish phase. She wasn't sure she could juggle another man's expectations in that house.

Having accounted for Bertie and Victoria, she looked around for Helen, then remembered that she was behind the screen in the parlour, doubtless praying that no one would notice her absence and drag her out. It was a risky strategy: her new moss-green dress would be crushed, which would be sure to annoy her mother.

Harriet herself had made no extraordinary effort with her appearance. This should have been in wise deference to the mistress, but was actually because she had no choice in the matter, having nothing new to put on. She didn't dare spend any of her earnings on such things, sensing she should save every last penny for some future emergency, though what that would be she didn't know, the glimmers remaining stubbornly silent. That evening she would have to be content on the periphery, all but invisible in her dark grey dress. Though in other circumstances, both moral and fiscal, she might have enjoyed stirring the mistress's irritation with a different way of putting up her hair, or a new trimming in a bold colour, it currently suited her to disappear into the background.

Despite the drabness of her garb, she had caught Robert gazing at her a few times, a set expression on his face. She was thankful for her dark dress then, finding it easy to slip into the throng and out of his line of sight, unobtrusive as a fleeting shadow. Almost no one asked her who she was – she signified no more than a maid. Less, even: Agnes, charged with refilling people's glasses and being rather brazen about it, caught the eye of a few men until Mrs Rakes took her aside for a sharp word.

It was while she was watching this exchange that Robert approached her.

'Miss Jenner,' he breathed, next to her ear, making her startle. '*Harriet*. Please. I must talk to you.'

At such close quarters, he looked quite ill, the lines on his forehead more pronounced, the whites of his eyes scored with tiny broken veins. She glanced around to see if anyone had noticed the two of them and saw that, for the first time in days, Captain Dauncey was staring directly at her. He gave her one of the sly smiles that infuriated as much as frightened her, and she turned back to Robert.

'We cannot talk now,' she said urgently. 'Your wife is not ten feet away and her brother is watching us.'

'But these last days have been agony for me,' he pressed on, his face inching closer to hers, much too close. Her eyes darted about the assembled guests again and she was amazed to see that only the captain had noticed them. 'I have tried to stay away from you,' he continued, 'but it has only made it worse.' His eyes were fixed intently on hers, as if no one else in the world existed. Something close to irritation eddied through her that he could be so helpless and indiscreet. She hadn't expected that of him. She had thought he was made of stronger stuff.

'Robert, we cannot talk here,' she implored. 'Tomorrow, when all these people have gone and normal life has resumed, perhaps we can go for a walk with your daughters, as we did before. We will have all the time we could wish for then, but please, you must stop now.'

As though she hadn't spoken, he tried to take her hand. She shook him off as though he'd scalded her. She could smell brandy on his breath. 'I believe you must be in drink, sir,' she said coldly. 'I do not want to speak to you. I – I lied when I said I returned your feelings. I lied.'

Her words, cruel but necessary in that moment, penetrated. He stepped back in shock and then, without another word, turned and walked away. Instead of his usual, comfortable stride, he held himself as though he had been kicked. She wished she could follow him into the privacy of the darkening, virtually empty house and tell him she hadn't meant it, but there was something about the evening that required her to keep her wits about her, alert as a deer in the woods, a note of danger just discernible in the flower-scented air.

The yearning she had felt for Robert was being stifled by cold, crushing panic. It was she who had helped launch it, true, but its gathering momentum now terrified her. Half hidden in the darkest recesses of the lawn, within the crowd but apart from it, she found she could see things with terrible clarity. Her love for Robert was now hopelessly entangled with Captain Dauncey's threats. The situation was becoming more dangerous for her by the hour. If Captain Dauncey didn't speak to his sister about Harriet's conduct, Robert would give her away with his heedless behaviour.

The party played on, the light thinning and turning violet, though the air remained warm and still. Scents lingered for longer than usual without any breeze to disperse them and, though she couldn't see him for the moment, Harriet could detect the heady reek of Captain Dauncey's cheroots. Swirling just under it, subtler but just as pungent in its own way, was the mistress's new scent, of which she had applied too much. Jasmine and something almost rotten.

Forty

Harriet was distracted from thoughts of Robert and the captain when a shriek went up on the other side of the lawn. The mistress, who only minutes before had been calling for another toast, was now going from group to group, clutching first at one guest and then another. Her awareness of how she looked as she did so – bosom heaving, lily-white hands fluttering – warred with the anxiety that showed in her face. As if she had overheard Harriet's observation of this, she swivelled her head and unerringly picked her out of the shadows. Though she must have been upwards of forty feet away, Harriet flinched at the look the mistress fixed her with.

'You!' she cried. Every face turned to peer into the gloom towards her, and Harriet had to resist retreating further. 'Where is my daughter? I cannot see her. She is supposed to be in your charge. Where is she?'

Harriet, so long the silent watcher, could not gather herself quickly enough to speak. Instead she shook her head dumbly, which seemed to incense the mistress.

'What is wrong with you?' she spat. She was close now but, never one to neglect an audience, hadn't dropped her voice. Some of the guests were whispering among themselves; the scene was becoming embarrassing.

'Which daughter do you mean, Mrs Pembridge?' she managed to stammer. 'I believe Helen is –'

'Not Helen! I'm speaking of Victoria. Where is she?'

Harriet tried to remember when she had last seen the little girl in her blue dress. She had been entirely absorbed in her own thoughts. She remembered seeing her twirling on the grass, arms outstretched. She had spun until she collapsed in a heap that had earned her a round of applause. Harriet didn't know when that had been but felt sure it had been significantly lighter then.

'I – I haven't seen her. At least, not for twenty minutes, perhaps half an hour.'

The two women stood staring at each other. The ground sloped so that for once Harriet stood as tall as Louisa. Even so, she trembled under the mistress's hostile gaze.

'And what about my husband? Have you seen him?'

The whispering of the crowd swelled to a steady hiss.

'He went into the house some time ago. I haven't seen him since.'

'Well, if he does not wish to speak to our guests, he will make himself useful by finding our daughter.'

She was quite intoxicated, Harriet realized. Her fury had briefly sobered her, kept her gaze steady, but now, as she slipped into the familiar groove of irritation at her husband's shortcomings, Harriet could hear the slur in her voice.

'Oh, Jago!' she exclaimed, turning to her brother, who had followed her. She pressed her face into his chest. 'Where has she gone?'

'You're quite hysterical, woman,' he chided her. 'She was here a moment ago, charming your guests like a circus turn. She's probably in the house or further up the garden.' He gestured towards the upper lawns, which had lost all colour in the dying light. The woods beyond were already dark, a shadowy mass above them.

Harriet spoke without thinking: 'She couldn't have gone to the ruins, could she?'

The siblings turned to her as one, their eyes pale and unearthly in the diminished light. 'Why would you think that?' said the mistress.

Harriet glanced at the captain. For once, he wasn't smirking. 'She is quite fascinated by the place,' she said, 'and I . . . well, I heard her talking about it earlier with her uncle.'

It was true. Just as on the day they had played croquet, Victoria had been wheedling to go to the ruins that afternoon. She had said she wished they could take their guests there, that they would surely be impressed by such an exciting, mysterious place. But it was her uncle who had put the idea into her head. Harriet had overheard him. 'It would be quite a setting for our little firework display,' she had heard him say. 'Think of the noise as they went up, the sound booming and echoing off the rocks like cannon fire.'

Victoria had clapped her hands in excitement. 'Oh, yes, do let's have them there! Tell Dilger, Uncle Jago, please tell him. He won't listen to me.'

Now the captain scowled at Harriet and turned to his sister. 'She had some notion in her head about setting off the fireworks up there. As if we could have dragged all these old matrons and majors up there for any such thing.' He shrugged. 'But that was hours ago. She would've forgotten all about it.'

To Harriet's astonishment, the mistress regarded her brother with contempt. 'Do you not know your niece at all? Victoria has the memory of an elephant, and when she is determined to do something, she won't be put off. She bides her time. It was always the same with her. Bertie, Helen, well, it wouldn't occur to them to hatch some sort of mischief. Victoria thrives on such plots.'

The captain shook his head. 'It's black as pitch in those woods now. No young girl would go up there on her own and there's no other way to the ruins.' He beckoned Agnes to him and handed her his empty glass. 'Fill it up, will you? And be quick about it.'

He was nearly as drunk as his sister, though he hid it better. Harriet could see it by the way he had planted his feet too widely apart on the sloping lawn, and the exaggerated manner in which he had relinquished his tumbler.

'Never mind your drink,' said the mistress. 'Agnes, go and fetch my husband. Tell him Victoria is gone to the ruins and he must go after her.'

'I will go,' said Harriet. She wasn't yet convinced the silly girl had even left the garden but she herself would do anything to escape the mistress and her brother at that moment.

'You?' she said, turning back to peer at Harriet. 'Well, I suppose you might. After all, if you had been minding her, as you are paid to, she would not be missing at all.'

'She cannot go alone,' put in the captain. 'I will go with her.' He took up one of the lanterns that had been placed around the garden as the twilight deepened.

'You will not,' retorted the mistress. 'You will stay with me in case I should have one of my turns. I feel quite giddy already. Dilger can go with her now. He knows the land better than anyone. Where is he? He must be up the garden, in preparation for the display. Oh, you're here.'

As if he had materialized there by some sorcery, Dilger was suddenly at her shoulder. 'Excuse me, missus,' he said, his hand fumbling at his cap as if he wasn't sure whether to tip it or take it off altogether. 'I've counted 'em three times and so's Ned but it's not coming out right.'

'What are you talking about?' the mistress shrilled. 'What's not coming out right?'

'The fireworks,' the gardener said slowly. 'We're missing two of 'em. There's no accounting for it. We've twice checked the shed where they was being kept. No sign of 'em. I thought, well, you might know where they've gone.'

'I?' The mistress's voice rose again. 'What would I want with the fireworks?'

The gardener frowned and shuffled his feet.

'Victoria was looking at them with me this afternoon,' said the captain, wearily. 'She dragged me up there. She was telling me which did what and how much each had cost. She's been interrogating Ned about it for days, apparently.'

The mistress's eyes rolled back. Dilger and the captain both went to catch her, though she managed to stay upright. 'She's taken them with her!' she moaned. 'She means to have her own display. Oh, she will set fire to herself! She will be scarred and no man will have her!' She straightened and looked hard first at Harriet and then Dilger, whose steadying hand she had shaken off. 'Go, both of you! What are you waiting for? I will send Mr Pembridge after you. And tell Ned to search the outbuildings. And someone else search the maze. Lord, will no one fetch me a chair before I fall down and break my neck?'

Harriet hurried away, her relief at retreating from the mistress's fury still outweighing any real concern for Victoria's welfare. She had no sense whatsoever that the little girl was in any peril and turned to the gardener. 'Mr Dilger, I am perfectly capable of going on alone if you would help Ned search the outbuildings and the rest of the garden. I see no sense in us both looking in the same place. Besides, I'm sure any minute now we'll hear the cry go up that she's found.'

He gave it some thought, then nodded. 'Ned can see to the garden right enough. Us two'll take the path up until it forks. Then I'll go right and you go left to them ruins, if you're all right to go on without me. The way I'll take is the darker. There's more firs up that way and they don't let the light in so much. The way's harder, too – more likely to trip yer. It'll be bright enough at the ruins, where the trees open up.'

Indeed, the woods, when they were enveloped by them, were not as dark as they appeared from the well-lit garden. It was quite a clear night, with a full moon that had pulled itself free of any stray clouds. It was a strange sort of moon, more like those she had seen from her bedroom window in London, on the nights when there wasn't enough wind to scour the sky clean of chimney smoke. Large and dully orange, it looked as though it had been dipped in sepia.

They passed under a sizeable gap in the canopy of beech leaves and she stopped to inspect it properly. Every crater was visible that night; every ancient, long-dry sea etched into its surface. She hoped Helen wouldn't miss it, hiding inside.

Dilger, noticing the lack of footsteps behind him, stopped and looked back. Seeing the governess's upturned face, he followed her gaze. 'What a night for a blood moon,' he said. 'I'd rather look at that than any fireworks.'

'A blood moon,' she repeated wonderingly. 'I never heard of such a thing.'

'Didn't you, now? And you a governess?'

Harriet blushed. 'I know quite enough to teach. I could tell you the name of that old sea up there, I just hadn't –'

'Don't take it wrong, miss. P'rhaps it's one of them country things.'

'Why is it called that?'

'I don't rightly know. I think it's some sort of eclipse, but whether it's the sun going behind the moon or the earth or the other way about, I couldn't tell you.'

'Perhaps Helen will know. She does nothing but look at charts of the stars and the like.'

They went on for a while in silence, Harriet's mind still on the moon. She was still not convinced that Victoria would have come so far. Soon enough, Dilger stopped again.

'Well, miss, if you're happy to go on by yourself, this is where the path splits.'

She'd gone along the path to the right only once and it was as dark as Dilger had predicted.

'Will you be all right?' she asked. 'It looks utterly black down there.'

He chuckled, a low, comforting sound in the silent

woods. 'I'll be right enough, Miss Jenner. I could do it blind. Will you be all right, I should say?'

'Oh, of course you could. How foolish of me, and, yes, I shall be fine.' In fact, now that the moment to go on alone had arrived, she did feel nervous. Before Dilger saw it and thought her cowardly, she held out her hand for one of the two lanterns he'd been carrying. 'It's only another five minutes or so to the ruins and I expect Mr Pembridge will be along directly.'

'I expect he shall,' said Dilger, with another chuckle. 'The mistress will've made sure of that.'

He went off whistling and Harriet felt bereft when, after a couple of minutes, she could no longer hear him. She kept walking, her eyes on her feet so that she didn't trip on an errant tree root or loose rock. Around her, the blood moon's strange light glowed through gaps in the trees. It turned everything to a muddy umber, so that she couldn't easily summon the colours that the leaves and earth and sky should have been, and would be again the next day, when the sun was high.

There was no sound in the woods that was loud enough to contend with her boot heels coming down on the packed earth but she knew, if she stopped, that she would hear things. The rustle of creatures in the dry under-growth and up in the branches of the beeches. Was anything watching her? Suddenly fearful, she swung her lantern out in an arc and caught a flash of reflected light quite close by. A fox's eyes, perhaps. She hurried on, cross that something as commonplace as the descent of night could make a benign place seem frightening.

It didn't occur to her that she should be shouting

Victoria's name until she had almost reached the clearing. She came to a halt at the edge of the tree line. The moonlight glanced off the ruins in a peculiar way, illuminating the tumbledown walls so that they gave off a dull sheen. Where it couldn't reach, it created unnerving pools of deep shadow, big and black enough to hide a man. She wasn't sure whether her reluctance to leave the cover of the trees was for fear of what those shadows might contain, or how exposed she would feel under the moon's rusty beam. Sternly, she reminded herself that she was there to find someone, not hide from imaginary beasts and monsters.

'Victoria!' she called, not much louder than a stage whisper. 'Come out if you're here, or we shall miss the fireworks.'

She sounded entirely ridiculous, and not because of the words, though they were feeble enough. It was because the little girl was not there, had never been there. It seemed preposterous now that anyone had thought she would be. Inwardly, Harriet cursed herself for thinking aloud to the mistress. There was no one among the ruins and she didn't need any dubious gift to tell her that: her animal senses were enough. And, besides, though Victoria was certainly plucky, what child of her age would come to this eerie place alone as darkness fell? The captain had been right about that, at least.

Even so, she called once more, for the sake of thoroughness, and even dared herself to take half a dozen steps out into the clearing. It was at this moment that she heard something behind her, the shape and detail of the noise muffled by her own footsteps. She stopped where she was and held her breath. In the few seconds since she had left the safety of the trees, the quality of the air had altered. It felt thicker, heavier, more difficult to breathe; it was suddenly freighted with danger.

Her hand felt for the little dagger she kept tucked in her skirts but, even as she did, she saw it gleaming on the washstand where she had left it after opening another innocent missive from Bertie. Alone in the dark wood, she felt its loss keenly.

'Robert?' she called into the dark mass of trees, in a quavering voice. 'Robert, is that you?'

There was no answer, only a silence and stillness that now seemed unnatural, though she couldn't have said why. She held her lantern aloft but its unsteady halo of light only made the spaces between the trees more blackly impenetrable. She put it down on the ground, suddenly wanting both hands free of encumbrance, but did so clumsily. It rolled over with a dull clink.

She moaned and knelt to right it but the oil had already doused the flame. It wasn't that the moonlight wasn't enough to see by but the homely glow of the lantern had been a comfort, a connection, even, with the house and the civilizing influence of its guests. Now she was entirely on her own.

Except that, when she looked up from where she still crouched, she saw that her earlier instinct had been right. She was not alone.

Forty-one

Grace

It wasn't long before the presence of Victoria and Essie altered the atmosphere of the house for the better. All its fragmented parts seemed to come together in subtle ways, with everyone spending less time alone in their appointed places and more together, usually in the parlour. With the exception of Robert Pembridge, we were all there one evening when Essie declared that she'd seen a hat I should buy. She, Lucas and I were playing whist while the others read their books in different corners.

'It would suit you so well, Miss Fairford. I said so to Mums. Didn't I?' She raised her voice in the direction of her mother, who peered at us over half-moon reading spectacles.

'She did indeed. I don't give a fig for all that fashion nonsense but I'll admit that Essie has quite an eye.'

'It's a lovely dove colour with a darker-coloured flower above the ear on one side,' the girl said, her finger twirling a lock of her hair around her finger. 'Mums, can we take Miss Fairford into Cheltenham so she can try it on?'

'Well, I don't know, my love. She may not want to.'

'Oh, but you do, don't you, Miss Fairford? We could go to the Cadena Café for tea afterwards. They do such a good one and it's only half a minute from the milliner.'

She looked at me pleadingly and I found myself nodding, as charmed by her as everyone else was. Besides, I had hardly ventured into town; I was in danger of becoming as housebound as Agnes and Bertie.

In the end, Victoria cried off the outing, saying she had to drive out to see her husband. 'I need to thrash something out with him,' she said, when Essie asked why. 'You two carry on. I'll take you down the hill and you can get a bus back up. Or walk – it'll do you both good.'

I enjoyed my time with Essie immensely. I felt a sense of total ease with her that I didn't have with anyone else – even Lucas, with whom I spent so much of my time. The closest I could get to the sense of affinity I had with the child was my relationship with my grandmother, but it seemed freer, lighter than that, somehow.

First we went to the milliner's, where she insisted that I buy the neat felt cloche she had seen in the window. It swept fetchingly low over one eye and she clapped her hands when I tried it on. 'I knew it would suit you! It's like the ones Mums and I saw in France, and so much more sophisticated than the old-style ones.'

'Did you like France?'

'Oh, it was wonderful, especially the Riviera. Mums thought it rather silly and much too expensive, but it was awfully romantic. Each evening after dinner, we would walk along the front and the moon would be shining on the sea, and all the little boats that were moored up would be bobbing gently on the water. One night there was an enormous one all lit up with music playing and people dancing on the deck. Mums said they were bound to be Americans. Another night, an Italian wanted to draw my portrait and followed us for miles until Mums told him off.'

After I'd bought the hat, we went to Cavendish House and I was persuaded to buy a long, cornflower-blue scarf and a pair of silver strap shoes I had no practical use for. At the perfume counter, Essie asked if they had Chanel's No. 5 in yet, which earned her a blank look, and I thought how different she was from her mother, who had probably never thought about wearing scent in her life. Our last stop was Boots – I bought some vanishing cream and Essie borrowed the new Agatha Christie detective story from the circulating library. She had been planning to spend all her pocket money on a lipstick the colour of peonies but, fearing Victoria's wrath for both of us, I managed to distract her with a tiny pot of rose-pink rouge that was natural enough to go unnoticed.

Essie was the first person to ask me about my life before I'd arrived at Fenix House – well, except Pembridge, I had to concede. She was fascinated by my status as an orphan, and there was none of the embarrassed sympathy I would have expected from someone older. She also quizzed me about my grandmother, and I was sorely tempted to reveal the connection with Fenix House. I knew how much she would delight in the coincidence, though of course it was no such thing.

'Have you any photographs of her?' she said, as we waited on the Promenade for the bus that would heave us back up the hill. I said I would show her when we got back: there was no chance, after all, that she would recognize my grandmother, even if her mother might have done.

As the hill got steeper and the bus slowed, Essie grimacing melodramatically from the seat opposite at the engine's protestations, I realized I hadn't felt a pang of homesickness for a while. There, in the warm, slightly stale fug of the lower deck, Essie larking to make me laugh, I felt oddly right in the world. Once again, I understood my grandmother's staunch assertion that I was meant to be there.

That evening, as I went up to bed, I heard Robert Pembridge coughing behind his door. He sounded as though he couldn't get his breath so I went in without knocking. He was trying to sit up but the coughing fit had left him too weak to manage it. He was shockingly frail and light when I pulled him into a sitting position. At my feet, the model train was trundling along its tracks at a measured pace. I wondered how long it had been doing the same predictable loop.

'Thank you, my dear,' he said, when he was settled and I'd made him sip some water. 'I am not myself today but I'll be well enough for work tomorrow, you'll see.'

'Work?' For a foolish moment, I wondered if Victoria had roped him into preparations for the joint birthday party.

'I have some business in Swindon. It wouldn't do to miss it. The men need me.'

There seemed little point in contradicting him so I simply smoothed down the bedclothes and drew up a chair so I could sit with him. Ever since I'd talked to Agnes in the kitchen, and she'd given away the fact that my grandmother had been dismissed, I'd wanted to press her further. Had she really been sent away because of the incident involving Victoria and the ice-house, or was that the acceptable excuse for a much more grown-up and sensitive reason? Something to do with her closeness to Robert Pembridge, for instance. Agnes, however, had proved tight-lipped, changing the subject and even plying me with tinned treats for Lucas in an attempt to distract me. I wished I'd asked her more when she'd had the sherry bottle out.

Now that I was alone with Robert, I wondered if he could enlighten me. It was a risk: I didn't want to upset him or somehow trick him into believing I was my grandmother, especially when Victoria might come upon us, but I wanted to know the truth. As it was, Robert didn't make it very difficult.

I'd gone over to put some wood on the fire when he began to speak. I couldn't hear him at first – the wind was getting up and it always seemed much more violent in the attic than anywhere else in the house, tearing around the draughty eaves mercilessly. I went back over and asked him to repeat what he'd said, part of me – a selfish part I wasn't very proud of – hoping he thought I was her again.

In fact, he didn't. I don't know who he thought I was in that moment. Perhaps he just wanted someone to confide in who wasn't part of the family.

'I was saying, my dear, that I hope I don't frighten you away, too,' he said, with a sad smile. He patted my hand. 'You remind me of her in this light.'

'Miss Jenner, you mean?' I said. I went over to the door I'd left ajar and shut it softly.

He nodded. 'I scared her off, you see, and then she was

dismissed before I had time to make amends. I knew she'd gone when I came back and saw Bertie's face. He adored her too, though he was just a boy. I think part of me had expected it but it was still a shock when it happened, and especially that she went without a word. But perhaps it was all too much for her. Perhaps she thought it would make things worse to wait, do you see?'

I nodded, though I didn't.

'Of course I was terribly jealous, though it took me years to admit it to myself,' he continued. 'All that time I wasted, resenting her for it.'

'Jealous of whom?'

He shook his head ruefully. 'My own brother-in-law. He'd noticed her too, I could see that, I had eyes in my head – eyes that worked then. And he was the sort of man who knew what to say to women, knew how to . . . charm them. God knows I'd watched him with my wife for long enough.'

'But she was his sister.'

'Theirs was an odd relationship. For siblings it was extremely intense, especially on my wife's side. One got accustomed to seeing them together but occasionally I'd catch sight of them as a stranger would, and found it quite . . . distasteful. Excessive. Always entwined around each other. Louisa would feed him at the table sometimes, wanting him to try some new delicacy that Mrs Rollright had produced. I hardly knew where to look.

'So he had my wife wrapped around his little finger, but I had made my peace with that years before, even if it did make me uncomfortable. But that summer when she came . . .' I wondered where his thoughts had taken him.

The little train was just approaching the signal box. Its polished wheels gleamed in the firelight as it carried on towards the miniature station.

'I've always been rather weak, you see,' he said finally.

I covered his hand with mine. He didn't seem to notice.

'I was weak when I left him there with her at the party. And I was weak afterwards, when I decided she preferred him. Instead of asking her, I stayed away, licking my wounds, and then she'd gone. I didn't look for her, you know, not for years. If it hadn't been for Helen, I'm not sure I would ever have done so. I've never been one for risks.'

'Helen?' I said. 'But how . . .'

He blinked at me in confusion and I saw he'd slipped again, his bearings lost inside his own memories.

'Helen, you say? Is Helen coming?'

'No, I'm afraid Helen isn't coming.'

'That was weakness, too.' He sounded completely lucid again. 'The way I view it, I lost them both through my own weakness.'

Forty-two

There was no let-up in the cold weather during the first weeks of November. Outside, the ground was slippery, but one day, when Lucas was intent on his crystal set and I felt I'd been cooped up for too long, I decided on another walk in the woods. I went by myself this time – Agnes said she couldn't risk falling on her bad hip. Besides, I wanted time to myself to think. Busy as I'd been with Lucas, I didn't feel I'd had enough time to reflect properly on what Agnes and Robert had lately revealed to me of the past.

Of all the things Agnes had said in the kitchen, one phrase echoed over and over until I could hardly make sense of it any longer, the words turning into meaningless sounds. It was what she had said about my grandfather: *He must have existed, or you wouldn't be here, would you?* I heard the rising intonation of the question in her voice, and though she'd meant it to be reassuringly rhetorical, it was a question I now kept asking myself.

Obviously my mother had had a father – it was just that, since my talk with Robert, I was starting to wonder if he had been the man my grandmother, now I thought carefully about it, had only rarely mentioned. Not only were there no photographs of him that I'd ever seen, but I realized – somewhat to my shame – that I didn't even know his first name. I had never seen her wear a wedding band, though she wore half a dozen other rings that, as Agnes had noticed, she absentmindedly twisted when she was distracted. You don't pay much attention to these anomalies as a child, accepting what you have always known at home because you are distracted by the myriad questions the world at large throws up – but I was noticing them now.

As I climbed the path through the woods, the physical exertion somehow cleared my mind of the present's everyday preoccupations: how Lucas was getting on, whether Pembridge and I would soon have one of the little chats I now looked forward to, when Essie and I might go into town again – that sort of thing. I was left with a possibility that I had so far refused to admit, though it might have explained my paltry knowledge of my grandfather, as well as my grandmother's dismissal by the mistress. Potentially, it also explained why I'd been parcelled up and sent to Fenix House. In this version, it was not just because of some glimmer of my grandmother's, it was because I was one of them. A quarter Pembridge through my mother's father.

I stopped and looked back towards the house. I was already quite high in the woods; all I could see of the house were its chimneys, rising through trees that were now mostly bare of leaves. From four of them smoke issued, grey plumes almost indistinguishable from the dirty white sky. The one visible above the northern end of the house was surely coming from Robert's attic room.

I really had done my best to push the past to the back of my mind, especially when Victoria and Essie had first moved back into the house. It was hard, though. To me, the entire place was underpinned and undermined by the lost years, all paths leading inexorably backwards. Try as I might to look forward, with Victoria as my model, I was always lured back. The trouble, whether I liked it or not, was that my own place in the present was entirely informed by what had happened before. Whatever had happened to my grandmother – and especially what had happened between her and the man now grown old in front of that fire – had the power to change everything.

I think my mind had been skirting round the possibility that Robert could be my grandfather for a while, but it was only there, on the path leading into the woods, that I let myself articulate it. If it was true, then I wasn't just a bystander, a minor player who would soon be gone from the narrative, I was as much a part of Fenix House's story as Lucas or Essie.

Perhaps I should have felt exhilarated by this or even scandalized. In fact, the idea that I might be a Pembridge made me feel a bit sick. That didn't make sense – I had always wished for a larger family, and who better than the Pembridges I'd heard about since childhood? I feared that one of the reasons I didn't like it – and this was a second possibility I hadn't wanted to face until now – was my complicated feelings for my employer. I still didn't know exactly what I thought of him – sometimes he was kind, at others he was difficult; what I did know was that he occurred to me often. On the days that I made him smile or found his eyes lingering on me, I went to sleep happier. If he was my cousin, it cast a different light on why I was drawn to him: nothing more, perhaps, than some innate understanding on my body's part that we were related. I had had so little experience of the opposite sex – even my memories of my father could be counted on my fingers. Perhaps I was so green that I couldn't tell the difference between romantic and familial love.

Realizing that I was almost at the Blue, I came to an abrupt halt. My stomach churned and I put out my hand to the nearest tree for support until the pang of nausea eased. I was left with a sensation remarkably like fear, and I knew that couldn't be just from the notion – which was really all it was – that I might be a cousin of David Pembridge. I'd found it hard to leave the Blue last time I'd gone there, with Agnes; now I had a positive aversion to the place. I knew if I went on another few feet, I would catch my first glimpse of pale turquoise through the trees but the mere idea of it had me backing away. I hadn't thought about it, instinct taking over – which reminded me of my grandmother as a little girl, retreating down the path at the Daunceys' house, frost under her feet as it was now under mine, frozen twigs and leaves crunching and cracking, like warnings.

I knew the Blue was frozen over – Bertie had been full of it over dinner a few nights earlier – and I was suddenly convinced that if I was to carry on up there, I would see that face again, this time trapped under a sheet of ice. I hurried back the way I'd come, grateful that Pembridge wasn't there to see me giving in to such a hysterical idea.

Back in my room, the fear so entirely melted away that I felt rather silly, I saw that Agnes had been in to sweep – now quite a regular occurrence. My bed had been moved slightly and I could see something white against the skirting-board, right where my grandmother's initials had been carved. I reached for it and realized it was her last letter. I'd been reluctant to read it when it had arrived – assuming it to be another chapter in her life before Fenix House – then forgotten about it. I opened it without expectation that it would provide any of the answers I wanted.

When I saw that she hadn't even pretended it was a letter this time, I sighed. It launched straight into the continuation of her story, describing her father's decline – how he'd grown so weak that she had taken over running his reduced affairs, her skill at copying allowing her to sign cheques and letters in his hand. She then told me about the elderly cousins who'd briefly taken her in, and finally of her success in obtaining the position of governess at Fenix House. There the account broke off, half the page left blank. I turned over and discovered that it was a letter after all.

Dearest Grace,

I finish there because you know the rest, don't you? Or perhaps you would disagree, which brings me to the questions you asked in your last letter. I'm sorry I neglected to answer them but I had faith that a clever girl like you would work most of them out by herself, given time.

So, am I right? Have you by now put two and two together about the Daunceys? Can you imagine how I felt when I realized that Louisa Dauncey and the mistress were one and the same? That, orphaned and virtually penniless, I found myself practically a servant in the household of the girl I had hated for so long? I have to tell you now – as I couldn't when you were a child – that thoughts of revenge took root in my mind as I sat opposite that vain and spiteful creature in her fussy little sitting room.

But then something happened to me and, though I hated her still, any desire for retribution simply ebbed away. I suppose I fell in love — and not just with her husband but the rest of them, too, even that little devil Victoria! And they loved me back, or so I like to think. But something else happened to me, which meant I had to leave. Though I was only there for a single summer, that place changed me — for better, for worse and for ever.

When you understood who the mistress had been, did you wonder why I would send you to Fenix House — even more than you already had? You'll have found your feet there by now, so it's not too soon to explain more of why I asked you to follow in my footsteps. You see, it wasn't just that I saw you there — your hand on the gate instead of mine — it was that I sensed a happier outcome for you than I ever had. I saw and felt it so clearly that I knew it was that rare beast: a glimmer I could be sure of.

In that vision, the house had changed — you didn't tell me that, Grace; perhaps you didn't want to upset me — but I knew absolutely that there was great happiness and contentment waiting there for you. Not only that, I knew that you would bring Fenix House joy in turn — that your presence would help unlock it from its malaise, not only reversing its sad decline but rubbing out the worst wrongs of the past.

As for what's left of my story, I didn't know how much I should tell you before you left. My first instinct was to tell you everything, but then I wondered . . . I've grown so used to looking after you all these years that I sometimes forget you're not my little girl any more — a little girl who once needed me to fill her with my memories so she would forget her own. That's why I decided to let you work out the rest for yourself, if you felt you needed to.

Perhaps you'd rather look forwards now, away from your old grandmother's past and towards your own future, and who could blame you? It looks to be a bright one, my darling.

All my love, H

As with her previous letters, this one seemed to throw up as many questions as it answered. It confirmed what I had indeed guessed about the Daunceys, of course, and she had also admitted her love for Robert. This much I hadn't expected – he had made it sound rather more one-sided: something closer to an unrequited passion.

But what was this 'something else' that had happened to make her leave? (I noticed that she still hadn't quite admitted she'd been dismissed.) The incident with Victoria in the ice-house surely didn't warrant any secrecy after so long. My mind kept straying back to the other new arrival that summer. She had now made a couple of references to the Daunceys, plural, but only one throwaway mention of a grown-up Jago. Even so, I couldn't quite dismiss him as a member of the chorus. He was a Dauncey and, besides, I was beginning to learn that my grandmother omitted and excluded for a reason. It was only lately that Robert and Louisa Pembridge had featured, and look how important they had turned out to be to her – one capturing her heart and the other her sworn enemy. She'd even told me there was more to work out.

This overt hint that the shadow of the past continued to throw the present into shade made me consider what she'd said about me. I hoped I was making some difference to Lucas's previously cloistered existence but I wasn't so arrogant as to believe myself capable of transforming the fate of Fenix House single-handedly, a new bird rising out of the ashes solely on my account. There was obviously more to it than my skills as a governess.

I read it all again, trying to hear the words in her voice and guessing where she might have placed the emphasis, in case that yielded any more clues. Whichever way I tried it, I kept coming back to the notion I'd admitted on the hill. I had to be part Pembridge.

Forty-three

The morning of Lucas's birthday and Victoria's planned gathering dawned dull and cold, as if it could hardly be bothered to shake off the night. 'A true November day, when it never seems to get light at all,' said Bertie, ruefully, from the window. 'It's terribly lowering to one's spirits, I find, when it's so dreary. I feel quite morose and it's not yet ten.'

'Oh, jolly good,' said Pembridge, drily, though he didn't look much cheerier himself. He glanced at me and I found myself avoiding his eye. I'd done this a few times since I'd read my grandmother's last letter and wished I could stop it. She had suggested that I might like to forget the past but it was easy for her to say so. I couldn't move forwards until I knew what had happened to her, and therefore who I was. She seemed to have great faith that I would be able to work out every detail by myself but I couldn't see how. Everything so far was guesswork; the certainties were rare.

Bertie was still peering out of the window at the desultory weather. 'Perhaps it might improve, although I rather think it looks like snow. Gosh, it's simply ages since we had a proper party. It's positively nerve-racking. Do you know if Vicky invited any of the neighbours, or those women in her Freedom League? I'm such a dolt when it comes to social chat.'

'I sincerely hope not.' Pembridge scraped some marmalade over his cold toast. He'd been late to breakfast, his eyes ringed with shadows, and I wondered if he'd passed a bad night. Dreaming about the trenches, perhaps, or Frannie. I dismissed as ridiculous the idea that he minded my new coolness towards him. 'I'm quite as bad as you at talking to people I barely know,' he continued to Bertie. 'Worse. At least you're awkward but polite. I'm just awkward.'

'They're terrifying, those women,' Bertie said. He turned to me, his eyes large and owlish behind their spectacles. 'Have you braved a meeting yet?'

I shook my head, though I still intended to go. If I wasn't careful, my grandmother's history was going to drag my every optimistic intention out of me, piece by bright piece. I didn't want to sink back into the torpor of my first weeks. Victoria and Essie, a clean female wind, blowing away Fenix's stubborn cobwebs, had done much to save me from that. They, and my friendship of sorts with Pembridge, which I was on the way to spoiling.

Lucas was the brightest light in the gloom of my troubled thoughts. With the promise of his beloved Essie's presence in the evenings after she returned from school, he was making excellent progress. He took his medicine when he was supposed to and was sleeping far less in the day. He was a thoughtful, clever little boy who picked things up quickly; he'd already exhausted the study's books on astronomy, which had become an established passion to rival the wireless. In preparation for his birthday, I had sent for an illustrated book of the solar system, in which each planet had been wonderfully rendered in colour and to scale. It had cost me a fortune but I was already excited to see his face when he opened it. I hadn't expected to grow so fond of him, but caring for him barely felt like work.

He had come down for breakfast that morning, as he now occasionally did. Still easily tired, he usually returned to read quietly in his room after these forays, but that day he was too excited about the imminent celebrations to rest.

'You'll wear yourself out before it's even begun,' I warned him, as he wandered restlessly about, picking things up and putting them down again, then standing on tiptoe so he could see himself in the glass above the mantel. He crossed his eyes at his reflection.

'And I can see you doing that,' I said mildly.

'When will they be back from the bakery?' he asked.

I clasped my head in mock exasperation, making him laugh. 'For the fourth time, about eleven!'

'And what's going to happen when the party begins?'

This had become a familiar ritual over the last few days, and I didn't really mind repeating myself, just to see how far he'd come. 'Well, first we'll have a special lunch and then we'll have some cake and then, if you're extremely good, you might be allowed to open your presents. And after that, if the weather improves, we may go for a walk. Or we may stay indoors and play some games instead, if people prefer.'

To Lucas's delight, as he'd taken my guess at eleven o'clock quite literally, Victoria and Essie returned at a quarter to, an ebullient honking announcing the little Morris's arrival on the other side of the gates. Lucas rushed out to let them in, Pembridge following rather less enthusiastically. 'And so it begins,' he said laconically, as he went out. I thought it unlikely that anyone else would be coming – Robert was still not very well and Lucas cared only that Essie was there.

I hung back, suddenly unsure of my place, as I still occasionally was. I wondered if it had been easier in my grandmother's day, when the boundaries had been more clearly delineated. With no staff but Agnes, and Pembridge's aversion to what he referred to darkly as 'the old order', I didn't float between staff and family; sometimes I felt more like a distant cousin brought lately into the fold. I was now trying not to think too much about the possibility that this might be the truth. Part of me yearned for it, while another part didn't want to believe it, for all sorts of reasons.

Once Victoria had taken the large white cake box down to the kitchen, she went straight up to see her father. She was back again in a matter of minutes, saying reluctantly that, as he hadn't yet shaken off his chill, she thought it best he didn't come down for lunch. Everyone was a bit downcast by this until Essie had the novel idea of taking the celebration to his room, so he wasn't left out of the proceedings. When this plan was put to Agnes – who was already slightly offended that she hadn't been entrusted with baking the birthday cake – she sighed and huffed and said it would give awful trouble, but Victoria and I persuaded her between us. Robert's room was certainly big enough, even allowing for the train set, and Bertie remembered an old trestle table that could easily be carried upstairs and assembled there.

'Oh, well done, Bertie. With the cloth on it, no one will know the difference,' said Victoria. 'Papa can stay in bed and have a tray. Essie, you're a clever old stick. It's an inspired idea.'

Wearing an expression of acute long-suffering, Agnes transported cutlery and condiments up to the top of the house, while Pembridge and Bertie struggled up with the table. In fact, once the curtains had been opened and the best tablecloth had been spread on the scratched old boards, it looked surprisingly cheery in there. Robert, from his position on the bed, propped up by half a dozen pillows, seemed weak but glad of the company, and even allowed Lucas, whom he remembered without prompting, to play with the train set.

As well as a surprisingly tasty dinner of roast beef and Yorkshire pudding, Agnes had made a shape of an indeterminate colour, which she up-ended on to a scratched silver platter with a flourish. Not quite as set as it might have been, it wobbled perilously.

'Good Lord,' said Pembridge, when he clapped eyes on it. 'Ought I to poke it with a stick to check that it's really dead?'

Lucas and Essie found this hilarious but Robert didn't catch the words and Victoria was forced to repeat them loudly twice, by which time Agnes, red with indignation, had stalked out with as much dignity as her hip would allow.

'Did you hear that Lord Carnarvon has finally got somewhere with his endless digging?' said Victoria, once the children's hilarity had subsided and everyone was eating. 'They've found Tutankhamun's tomb now – the one they've been after. I was reading about it in the newspaper this week and thinking how excited Helen would have been. She loved those ancient Egyptians almost as much as all her star charts and planets and what-have-you. Apparently, when Howard Carter got the first peek inside, Carnarvon asked him if he could see anything, and he said, "Yes, wonderful things." I thought that entirely thrilling when I read it.'

'I'm not sure that I approve, quite honestly,' said Bertie. Unusually, he'd been drinking sherry steadily since we'd sat down. It had made him relatively outspoken.

Victoria rounded on him. 'What of? The Egyptians?'

'I just think they should leave the poor man be. This King Tut chap, I mean. I don't much like the thought of people poking around in my grave in thousands of years' time.'

'I think that's extremely unlikely,' put in Pembridge.

Bertie lowered his spoon. 'Well, I think it's a horribly uncivilized thing to do. I can't see the difference between Carter and any other common or garden grave-robber.'

'It certainly won't bring them any luck,' I said, the words somehow on my lips before I'd even thought them.

Victoria gave me a strange look. 'I'm sure the treasure will make up for any superstitious nonsense. And they're hardly grave-robbers, Bertie. They're proper archaeologists from proper museums. Carnarvon's spent a fortune of his own money on it.'

'Did you know we had three globes in the Hampstead house when I was a boy?' said Pembridge, unexpectedly. 'Not that Mother ever got further than Rheims.'

'Well, it was I who was the adventurer,' said Victoria.

'Helen was forever poring over maps and Lord knows what, but she preferred to stay at home. She read Papa's Jules Verne novels over and over again when we were children, you know.' She turned to Robert in his bed. 'Do you remember, darling, how Helen used to borrow your Jules Verne books?'

I remembered. My grandmother had told me it was one of the first things she and Helen had ever talked about.

Robert looked up from his bowl. 'What is this stuff?' he said, ignoring Victoria's question and poking at the shape with his spoon. 'It's a damned peculiar colour. Are we being fed scraps from the nursery?'

Agnes, coming back in, fortunately just missed this last comment. Still slightly offended, she had brought up a platter of cheese and biscuits, which she dumped in the middle of the table.

'What do you think of this Tutankhamun business?' Victoria said warmly to her, in silent apology for the criticism of the shape. 'Do you think it's right that a man should be dug up years after he's been buried?'

To my surprise, Agnes looked straight at me. Her already high colour had deepened. 'I think, if he's doing no harm where he is, then he should be left alone,' she said eventually. As she limped out, I saw her hand go to her breastbone, where I remembered that the key lay hidden. She stopped in the doorway.

'Everything all right, Agnes?' said Victoria. 'Take no notice of David. I think the shape is actually rather good.'

The housekeeper turned slowly. She pushed back her hair with the inside of her wrist. 'It's gone,' she said simply.

'What has, dear?'

'My key. The one I wear round my neck.'

'How mysterious. I've never noticed you with any key. What's it for?'

Pembridge and I both caught Lucas's movement in the same instant: an almost imperceptible nudge of an elbow into Essie's ribs.

'Lucas, do you know something of this key?' said Pembridge.

The boy shook his head. Essie was staring at her plate, a blush spreading up her neck.

Victoria digested this with astonishment. 'They're up to something!' she exclaimed. 'I'd know a guilty expression at ten paces. Goodness knows, I used to see enough of them, usually when we'd been caught after I'd talked Helen into some misdemeanour or other. Essie, don't ever turn to crime. Nor you, Lucas. Guilt is written all over you. Come on, hand it over.'

'It's only a key,' said Lucas, sullenly.

'It's my key,' said Agnes. Her voice shook. 'You had no business taking it, Master Lucas. I don't know how you did.'

'I didn't take it, I found it.' He looked petulant but was near tears, I could tell.

'Where did you find it?' said Pembridge.

'On the turn in the stairs. It was on a bit of old string.'

'What's all this about a key?' broke in Robert. 'A key to what?'

Lucas shrugged.

'He honestly doesn't know,' said Essie, pleadingly, to her mother. 'He would have told me otherwise.'

'Agnes?' said Pembridge. He was sitting back in his

chair, looking as though he'd decided to find the whole episode amusing. 'Don't tell me you've got some treasure hidden away, too. Should someone telegraph Carnarvon in the Valley of the Kings and tell him there's something better here?'

'It's nothing like that, sir.' Agnes seemed to sag, all her usual fire doused. 'Nothing important. If he gives it back, I'll say no more about it.'

When no one moved, Essie leaned over to whisper in Lucas's ear. Reluctantly, he undid the top button of his shirt and fished inside for the string, which he brought out sheepishly. At the end of it, the key turned slowly. It was even heavier than I remembered and I couldn't imagine carrying it comfortably round my neck for years on end. What had she been storing down there when she fell and hurt herself that required such vigilance? Just then she glanced at me and I realized she was frightened. I shook my head slightly at her, not understanding.

'I know that key,' said Bertie, tremulously, from the other end of the table.

'Bertie, you've been warned about going up to that ice-house a dozen times.' Everyone turned in astonishment to Robert, who went on poking obliviously at his portion of shape with his spoon. 'I've told you, stick to the woods if you want to explore. You'd run out of air in two days if you got trapped inside, and I don't want your sister getting one of her foolhardy ideas. Is this some sort of protest on Mrs Rollright's part, do you think?' He gestured at his bowl. 'Extraordinary stuff.'

We all stared at him, the penny dropping that he was somewhere back in the previous century. This always gave me gooseflesh, as though Robert was looking into a mirror on a past world that was as real as ours – we just hadn't learned how to see it.

'Agnes, you really are a dark horse,' exclaimed Victoria, after a pause. 'Why on earth have you been keeping the key to the ice-house round your neck? We haven't used the place for decades. Is David on to something? Have you got buried treasure in there?'

'It was locked up deliberately,' said Bertie. 'Don't you remember, V? It was because you got trapped inside. I suppose you were too small to remember. It was your fault, you know, causing such a hullabaloo all summer. If it hadn't been for you, Miss Jenner would never have been sent away.'

Victoria was stunned by this outburst into a rare silence.

'Miss Jenner?' said Robert, his spoon suspended shakily in the air. 'Did someone mention Miss Jenner?' He dropped it with a wincing clatter and managed to tip the contents of his bowl onto the bedclothes.

Agnes rushed forward and pulled a cloth from where it was tucked in the belt of her apron. She began dabbing at the spill, tutting. She seemed glad of the distraction from the key. Robert was clutching at the sheet anxiously while she fussed around him and I wondered what he might be about to reveal.

I was just thinking this when he raised a trembling arm in my direction. For a terrible moment I thought he would accuse me of being Miss Jenner and make some sort of declaration, but then he began to speak and I realized he was pointing to the window behind me.

'It's snowing,' he cried. 'I've never heard of snow in August!'

'August?' exclaimed Victoria. 'Papa, it's November and the snow has been threatening all day. Why do you think the fire is lit?'

I turned to look at the flakes, which were soft and large, the sort that settle. Transfixed by their silent, unhurried beauty, it was only when I turned back to the table that I noticed.

'Where are Lucas and Essie?' I said sharply.

Pembridge peered around as though they might be hiding in a corner. 'They were here just a moment ago.'

The key had gone from the table. 'The ice-house,' I said. 'They've gone anyway.'

Without another word, Pembridge and I ran out and down the stairs, an awkward Agnes on our heels. As we hurried up the lawn, a picture came into my mind, so vivid I thought it was a glimmer. In it, Lucas was choking, Agnes's old string around his neck and caught on a rusty old nail inside a dark chamber made of brick.

The door of the ice-house, when we got to it, was closed and my heart clutched painfully with fear, not just for Lucas but lovely Essie. An image of her lit up in my mind, like a star in a dark sky: her slim white fingers twirling her hair into long, loose ringlets, her legs crossing and uncrossing themselves as she tried to settle in the parlour after dinner, a flash of her small white teeth when she laughed. Not a still picture, like a photograph, but a blur of movement because Essie was perpetually restless.

I got there first and tried to wrench back the door. It didn't budge an inch but then I noticed the key, which had been discarded on the ground and was now dusted with snow. I grabbed it and jammed it into the lock.

'I can't turn it,' I said to Pembridge, desperately. 'It's stuck.'

He took over, twisting the key back and forth so vigorously that I was terrified it would snap off. Eventually the mechanism relented and Pembridge flung back the door.

'Lucas!' he shouted, his voice echoing in the dark void of the hollow chamber. 'Essie! Are you there?'

There was no answer.

'I'm going down to check. You can't even see the bottom, it's so dark down there. They might be . . . unable to answer.'

I shuddered as he swung himself on to the ladder.

'I wouldn't go down there if I were you,' said Agnes, who had just arrived, out of breath, yet as pale as I'd ever seen her. 'It'll be rusted through and you'll break your neck.'

He took no notice and began descending the rungs.

'Do be careful,' I half whispered.

I heard him land in what must have been old leaves or rubbish at the bottom, followed by more rustling as he searched the subterranean gloom for the children.

'If they even managed to get in here, which I doubt, they've gone now,' he called up, his voice light with relief. 'There's nothing down here but cobwebs and sawdust and some old bag.'

I looked at Agnes, who was still breathing heavily beside me, but she wouldn't meet my eye.

'So where have they got to, then?' said Pembridge, when he'd locked the ice-house firmly behind him. His relief short-lived, he ran nervous hands through his dark hair. 'For God's sake, he knows how much I worry.'

I looked around the monochrome garden, which in the waning light was all grey bark, dead leaves and gathering snow. I was searching for a warm flash of colour that might have been Essie's hair but what I saw instead were footprints. They were faint but there were two sets and they led up through the woods.

'They've gone to the Blue,' I said, pointing. 'They know it's frozen over and Lucas has been asking to go ice-skating in the Winter Gardens for a couple of weeks now. Essie said she would teach him, apparently, but I didn't think he was up to it yet. I was going to talk to you about it but then . . .' I'd not discussed it because my grandmother's last letter had arrived and made me so awkward around him.

'It won't hold them,' said Agnes. 'It's not been cold long enough for that.'

We hurried after Pembridge, who'd already set off towards the woods.

The route up to the Blue was never an easy one, even in good weather. With the slippery frost and settling snow, and the worry of what might have happened already to the children, it was the worst sort of endurance test. Though the snow wasn't yet thick, it still managed to hide loose rocks and errant tree roots and we all tripped more than once. Finally I saw the turning beyond which the trees cleared and the land fell away to form the bowl of that strangest of lakes.

I was somehow in the lead now, my breathing coming fast yet steady, but as I reached the turn, I smacked hard into someone else. Essie.

'You're here,' she half sobbed. 'Oh, you're here. Lucas

is in the water. He fell through. I said he mustn't, I said the ice was too thin, but he wouldn't listen.'

Pembridge ran on without a word, kicking off his shoes as he went.

'It's all my fault,' Essie cried, her voice rising. 'I said I'd teach him to ice-skate but I didn't mean here! I told him not to go out on it. I knew it was going to happen – even before it did, I could see him in the water. I tried to tell him but he wouldn't listen.'

'I know how strong-willed he can be, sweetheart. It's not your fault.' I took her hand and we raced after Pembridge.

There was no sign of Lucas when we got there, only a small ripple out towards the middle of the Blue, where the ice had apparently broken through, leaving a large, jagged hole that looked almost indigo against the surface. It was clearly thicker in some places than others and I could see why Lucas had taken the risk. Pembridge, too, was just about to stride out over it when I heard a faint tapping.

'David, wait,' I shouted out. 'Listen.'

It came again, more of a scrabble of noise this time.

'There,' cried Essie. She'd gone further round the shore of the Blue, closer to where the limestone cliff rose up to tower over the scene. She pointed down into the ice about three feet from the edge.

I ran round and leaned out to brush the loose snow from the surface, David joining me to help. As we cleared it, a small splayed hand pushed against the ice. Essie and I screamed. David thumped the ice next to it with his fist and though it vibrated it didn't crack. A little face appeared where the hand had been, cheeks drained of all colour, lips blue and dark eyes wild with panic. I fumbled for the miniature dagger in my pocket, thinking for an awful moment that I'd left it in my room, but then my fingers grasped it – the metal hilt that was always oddly warm to the touch.

'Here,' I said to David. 'Use this.' The blade wasn't large but it was sharp and it went right through. Careful not to touch Lucas who, to our horror, had begun to drift away, eyes closed, he hacked a rough circle into it and then pushed it through. Reaching down – the Blue not too deep at the edges – he was able to get hold of his son under the arms and pull him out.

He was so still that I thought we were too late. David turned him on his side and, after a terrible pause when I don't think any of us drew breath, he coughed and a gurgle of water came out from between his poor cold lips.

'Thank God,' David whispered, gathering him up in his arms. 'What possessed you to go out on that ice?'

He didn't mean Lucas to answer but the little boy was too exhausted anyway. Essie began to cry in earnest, relief flooding in to join the guilt. 'I'm so sorry. I'm the oldest, I shouldn't have let him go out at all. I thought we could just peep in the ice-house and then he'd forget about it, but when we couldn't get in, he said he wanted to try and skate on the Blue. I didn't know whether to go back to the house and tell someone or follow him.'

I put my arm round her. 'You did the right thing in staying with him.'

Essie looked at me with brimming eyes. 'He said it was his birthday and that I was being a misery-guts when I said we oughtn't to go.' She wiped her eyes on the sleeve of her jersey. 'I just knew he was going in. I saw it and then it really happened.'

I took out my handkerchief and gently wiped her face. 'Never mind, it's all over now. No one is hurt.' David was rocking Lucas gently back and forth, his jacket tucked around the boy's thin shoulders. I put my hand out to touch his arm gently, and when he looked at me, I made myself meet his eye. 'We should get him into a hot bath,' I said.

He nodded, and we began the slow descent to the house. The snow was falling more heavily now, huge gauzy flakes that were so light they blew around in different directions. Above us, the sky was as white as the ground, pregnant with drifts enough to last out the day and into the night. I took Essie's hand again. The snow was settling on her hair and long eyelashes and, for a moment, I felt dizzy, disorientated. I stopped and closed my eyes while I waited for it to pass, oddly comforted by her small hand in mine. With the other, I felt in my pocket for the little dagger that David had given back to me.

'I've seen that knife before,' Agnes muttered in my ear. 'Where'd you get it?'

I glanced at Essie but she hadn't heard. 'My grandmother gave it to me. Why?'

'It weren't hers to give, that's why. It were the mistress's, bought for her by *him*.' She was looking at me with a mixture of fear and suspicion.

'Who?' I whispered.

'Who do you think? Her brother. Captain Dauncey. It's some religious thing he picked up in India.'

I was so confused – and perturbed – by the revelation that I didn't think to ask her what was hidden in the old bag in the ice-house until we got inside. Letting Essie run up the stairs to her mother, I looked around for Agnes but she was nowhere to be seen.

Once Lucas had had his bath and a cup of hot Bovril, we all returned to the table to give him his presents and try the shop-bought sponge cake. We had tried to persuade him that he should go straight to bed but he'd looked so heartbroken that David had given in. At some point, up in the grounds above the house, he had simply ceased to be 'Pembridge' to me.

'Where is Agnes?' he said now, echoing my own thoughts.

'She's gone to lie down. Her hip was giving her terrible trouble,' said Victoria. 'I think the poor thing must feel responsible for what happened because it was her key. She looked terribly worried.'

'It should never have been taken and used,' said David, with a stern look in Lucas's direction. 'I've half a mind to give this present to some other, more deserving boy.'

Lucas looked horrified until he saw that his father was smiling. Not his usual lopsided smile either, but the rare kind that transformed his face. Feeling someone's eyes on me, I looked across the table to see Essie watching me. She had caught me staring at David and was grinning. Blushing, I stuck out my tongue at her.

'What is my present, Father?' Lucas was saying. He was wreathed in smiles now, his cheeks pink from the bath, though his eyes were hollow with exhaustion. He'd need to stay in bed the next day.

'You'll just have to open it and see.'

It was an oblong box, about three feet long. I had no idea what it was either; David had confided in no one. Lucas began tearing off the brown paper.

'It's a telescope!' he cried, face suffused with delight. 'A real one, too, not a toy.' He lifted it carefully out of the box to admire its black and brass casing.

'What a jolly fine piece,' said Bertie. 'Lucas, your grandmother Helen would have been thrilled with a present like that.'

'Apparently it's quite a good one,' said David, his face as pink with pleasure as his son's.

'And it will go perfectly with my present, Lucas,' I said, handing over the wrapped book. He was almost as pleased with it as he was with the telescope, and I received another rather dazzling smile from his father, which, to my annoyance, made me colour again. I didn't dare look at Essie to see if she'd noticed.

After all the presents had been opened – including a stout pair of boots from Victoria and Bertie and a subscription to *Wireless Today* from Essie – Victoria said she would go and make a pot of tea.

'Poor Agnes looks like she's seen a ghost,' she said, on her return. 'She's lying down with her face to the wall and will barely say a word. Do you think I should send for the doctor?'

'It's obviously to do with that key of hers. Perhaps she was hiding something down there,' said Bertie. His tie was askew and his cheeks were flushed. He must have been on his fifth sherry. 'Is that why you were ferreting about in there, V, when you got yourself trapped?'

Victoria frowned. 'It's odd but I can't remember that day at all and you know I've a memory like the proverbial elephant.'

'Probably the shock,' said David, thoughtfully. 'Your mind protected you from it by forgetting the whole episode. Anyway, I went down there and I'm afraid there's no treasure to report. Nothing but a rotten old bag.'

'A bag!' exclaimed Victoria, sounding like Lady Bracknell. 'Now, wait a minute . . . That might ring a bell.'

Just then, a real bell rang downstairs. Robert, who'd been asleep since we'd returned, stirred and muttered something unintelligible.

'What was that?' said Bertie, eyes blinking in disbelief. 'It wasn't one of the servants' bells.'

'Good Lord, it must have been the doorbell,' said Victoria in astonishment. 'That hasn't worked since Mrs Rakes retired.'

'Well, who the devil can it be?' said David. 'We're all here.'

Without knowing I was going to, I stood up, my chair scraping loudly on the floorboards. Everyone turned at the sound. 'I've got a feeling it's my grandmother,' I said rather wildly.

Forty-four

Harriet

High above the noise of the party, in the silence of the ruins, the extinguished lantern at her feet, Harriet watched as a shape, a shadow within the shadows, peeled itself away from the dark mass of the woods. She took a step backwards as it moved towards her. Retreating again, she heard something strike the lantern as it continued to advance on her. A boot against metal. She gasped as the shape was suddenly bathed in umber moonlight and became a man. She had known it could not be Robert, who would have spoken up by now to reassure her, but it was still a blow when she saw who it actually was.

'Little governess.'

'We can go back to the house now,' she said in a rush. 'Victoria is not here. I've already searched.'

'No, she cannot be here,' he said, quite kindly. 'I have just seen her in the garden. Ned discovered her with her pilfered fireworks in the Cucumber House or the Mushroom House, or whatever Lulu christened it to hide the fact that her husband is not as rich as she would like. Now she is found, they're about to begin the display.'

'Well, we should lose no time, then.' She smoothed her skirts and unthinkingly went to retrieve the lantern. Her breathing was too rapid – she would grow dizzy if she couldn't calm herself.

'Oh, let's not rush back. I need a few moments to recover after that climb. I've let myself grow indolent here, eating Mrs Rollright's endless puddings and cakes.' He was attempting to sound casual but Harriet could hear the excitement in his voice. There was little evidence now of his earlier inebriation. His pale eyes looked sober in the moonlight.

'I will go ahead then, Captain,' she said, as firmly as she could. 'I don't want to miss the fireworks and I would not want Mr Pembridge to come up here unnecessarily. He will be here any moment now. In fact, I'm surprised he isn't already.'

'No fear, Miss Jenner, I told him there was no need. I said that Victoria was found and that you had gone to your room with a headache.'

Her heart was fluttering, like a bird in a trap, but, making a huge effort, she looked at him steadily. 'I won't ask why you did that but I will go back now. You stay if you wish.'

She gripped the useless lantern tightly and walked quickly towards the trees. She should have run but, despite her prickling legs and thumping heart, she could not quite convince herself there was the need. She understood the necessity when, with just a few strides, Captain Dauncey had caught her up and grabbed her arm.

'This coyness of yours is tiresome,' he said, an edge creeping into his voice. 'I told you we were to stay here a little while, together.' He moved his hand down to grip her wrist and squeezed. The lantern fell to the ground with a clatter. 'What delicate little bones you have. They're hardly thicker than toothpicks. Not like my bonny Lulu.'

She tried to pull away but he held her effortlessly.

'Why don't we go back to where I can see you properly?' he continued, steering her back towards the ruins, where the blood moon's light could illuminate them again. 'I wish to see the prize I've caught myself.'

'I am no prize, sir,' she said. A detached part of her was astonished by how much stronger he was than her. She simply could not loosen his grip on her arm, despite her increasingly desperate movements.

'Oh, I don't know about that,' he said. 'My brother-in-law certainly seems to think so. Were you hoping it was him when I appeared out of the dark?'

'If I did, it was only because he is a gentleman who would never dream of manhandling me as you are.'

'I beg to differ, Miss Jenner. On the contrary, I am quite sure Robert thinks of little else these days but manhandling his comely governess. Have you seen him lately? He is a man in crisis, his collars askew, his beard in need of a trim, his eyes sunk with lack of sleep.'

'Well, I assure you that has nothing to do with me.'

'Why are you keeping up this pretence? You know I witnessed that touching little scene up above the icehouse. I saw the pair of you embrace – you just as willing as he, I might add. I saw you both tonight, too, with your heads together, never mind the neighbours looking on.' He got hold of her other wrist and pulled her closer. 'I can't help but wonder what you would be doing now, if I was Robert. Would you allow him another embrace?' He wrenched her closer again, though she was pushing back with all her might. 'And what then? This is a dramatic setting for a seduction, don't you think? Would you have let him seduce you, Miss Jenner? Would you have given yourself to him?'

'Captain, please!' She was truly frightened now. His expression in the weird light was both intent and wild.

'Please what? Are you so full of desire that you will have me instead? I know what girls like you wish for. You are all demureness and modesty when it suits, with your severe little costumes and tidy hair, but underneath you're no better than the whores who service our garrison. I told you about Miss Foster, the curate's daughter, didn't I?' He laughed without humour. 'She opened her legs even quicker than I could have hoped, and I don't think I was the first fellow she'd obliged, either.'

Harriet knew she had to escape now, or she was done for. She kicked him hard in the shin and in the instant he loosened his grip, she ran. Even if she could not hope to reach the garden before he caught up with her, then perhaps she might hide in the wood's dense undergrowth, where no moonlight penetrated. He would surely grow bored eventually, and return to the house. But even as she thought this, a loose rock tripped her and the ground came up to meet her, fast and hard. He was on her in half a second, his bulk pinning her to the ground.

'Would you have had Robert give chase?' he grated, as he roughly turned her on her back, got to his feet and began dragging her towards one of the tumbledown buildings. Struggling as she was pulled through the dirt, Harriet wanted to scream, not just out of terror but in bitter frustration: she knew she could have outrun him

402

had she not been so clumsy – he was already out of breath from chasing her that short distance. She didn't cry out because she had to conserve her energy. Besides, no one would hear her from the ruins.

It seemed horribly wrong that one person could over-power another so effortlessly if they chose to. Though she continued to resist him, twisting and writhing at first and then, when she truly understood that he was never going to relent, trying to bite him, she knew in her heart that she had foreseen the danger of him from the start. *I can't stop him*, she thought helplessly, desperately. *He's going to do what he wants with me and there's nothing I can do about it.*

It was then that something in her stretched and broke, like the tension finally snapping in a frayed rope. She gave up the fight, becoming limp and still, and only dimly hear-ing the clink of his belt buckle as he pulled it loose. As he reached down with his free hand to pull up her skirts, she looked away from his now-contorted face, and instead trained her eyes on the sky high above.

The roof of the quarry building had mostly gone and she had an unimpeded view of the blood moon. To her left, the upper part of the cliff face was also visible. The rock was the colour of calamine lotion, much more pitted and scarred than by day. Harriet thought it was like the surface of the moon and decided to imagine that that was where she was, gazing down on the earth rather than up at the moon, thousands of miles away from what was hap-pening in the quarry. It helped not only with the horror of what was being done to her person, but the physical pain of it, too.

As he finally grunted and rolled off her, the first firework went up from the garden below. The great tearing screech, as though it intended to rend open the sky, was precisely the noise Harriet would have made herself, had she been able to. In the moment it reached its zenith and exploded with a bang, scattering jewels of gold and red across the sky, she heard a different sound, one much nearer than the firework above. It was akin to rotten fruit hitting packed earth. She tried to sit up but grew so dizzy that she lay down again, her eyes closed.

A series of fireworks went up in swift succession, the screeching and exploding and cracking all merging. Reverberating off the cliff face, like gunshot, the mass of sound and echo grew so loud that she clamped her hands over her ears. Such was the confusion that she didn't at first notice another sound – a sound that seemed to be coming from under the earth itself. In truth, it was not so much a noise but a vibration. She was just wondering whether she was imagining it – whether it was some manifestation of her mind in response to Captain Dauncey's terrible assault – when she was gripped around the waist and pulled backwards until she fell against a stone wall.

The strange rumbling of the earth, which had been growing more pronounced, as if to compete with the ostentatious popping and shrieking of the fireworks, reached a crescendo just as a particularly large firework disgorged its load of a thousand green sparks with a huge boom. *Dauncey green*, thought Harriet, vaguely, just as something fell to earth nearby, with a powerful, bone-shaking thud. Dust from the ground whirled around her and she began to cough.

A hand was laid on her back and it gave her such a

fright that she finally pulled in a ragged breath to scream.

'It's not him, Miss Jenner,' a woman's voice said in her ear. 'It's me. Agnes.'

Though there was a ringing in her ears, she heard the words quite clearly.

'Where is he?' Harriet whispered. She clung to Agnes, who had pulled Harriet in close so that her face was squashed between the other woman's breast and her warm armpit. She smelt of carbolic and kitchen grease. So different from the captain's scent, it couldn't have been sweeter to Harriet in that moment.

'I've seen to him, don't you worry.'

Eventually Harriet gathered herself enough to sit up. The air was still thick with rock dust.

'What happened? I don't understand. All the noise . . .'

'The top of the Devil's Chimney's come down, hasn't it? It's been threatening to go for years, o' course, but I reckon it was all those fireworks echoing off the cliff that finally did the job. Funny thing is, it only had to wait another three weeks.'

Harriet shook her head dumbly, her head spinning from all that had happened. 'Three weeks?'

'They were going to bring it down and fill the whole place with water from one of the springs what rises up there.' She jabbed a thumb over her shoulder at the cliff face, which was just beginning to gleam through the murk. 'The master had a letter about it, though he's kept it quiet from Miss Vicky, being as she loves the place. They decided drowning it would be safest, and might look pretty too. Well, it looks like some of the hard work's been done for them.'

'But the captain . . .' Harriet asked faintly. Even the word made her hot with shame.

'I've knocked him clean out. I come up here, saw him next to you and picked up one of them loose stones that's all over the place. Look here, did he . . .?' She let the question hang in the dense air.

Harriet hung her head, silent as she tried to swallow the sobs that were filling her throat.

'You don't have to say it.' Agnes sighed. 'I know his sort.'

As ashamed as she was, she had never been so glad to see anyone as she was Agnes. She would have trusted the girl with her life then.

'But – but how did you know to come?' she said.

Still squashed together as they were, Harriet felt more than saw the shrug. 'I heard the mistress send you up here and then, after a while, I realized I hadn't seen *him* for a time. I used to be sweet on him, fool that I was, so it's become a habit of mine to watch him. Then, just as I was wondering where he'd got to, Master Bertie come up and asks was you back yet. Well, I put two and two together. I knew a little scrap like you couldn't fend off the likes of him so I come up. I only wish I'd been quicker about it. I know what men like him are like – what they do because they can. But you, you were brought up nice, anyone can see that.'

Harriet nodded, unable to thank the maid yet. Her body's numbness had almost worn off and there was a great deal of pain between her legs and in the pit of her stomach. Even though it hurt to do it, she raised her knees, wanting to put her arms around them – around herself – as tightly as she could. She felt Agnes's warm hand on her back and had to bite down on the inside of her cheek so she didn't cry.

'Look, miss, we'd best go now, before he comes round.'

'But what will we say when –'

'He won't say a word about you or me, don't you fear. Not after what he's done. He got hit by a falling rock, or fell down drunk, that's what he'll say. Let him stagger back on his own.'

With Agnes's arm clamped around her waist for support, the two of them stumbled out of the shadowy ruin and into the clearing. She hadn't even noticed where the captain lay. Outside, she could see that, though it was still standing, the Devil's Chimney was much reduced in stature without its topmost stone. That, plummeting from a height of sixty feet or more, had destroyed the entire back wall of one of the other ruined buildings. If the captain had dragged her in there, they might both be dead. She wondered if that would have been better.

The fireworks resumed as they started down the path through the wood. If those assembled on the lawn had heard or felt the Chimney stone fall – and it was quite conceivable they hadn't at that distance – it was unlikely the mistress would have allowed such an uncouth diversion to spoil her planned entertainment. At the gate to the garden, Agnes brushed Harriet down as if she were a child, repinning her dishevelled hair with surprising deftness. 'I'll go on now,' she said, when she was done. 'You wait a few minutes before you follow.'

Harriet nodded. It was almost exactly what Robert had said to her in the glade at the top of the garden. Before the captain . . . But she let that thought trail away.

Agnes smiled encouragingly and squeezed Harriet's fingers. 'Be brave, Miss Jenner.'

After Agnes had disappeared, Harriet moved slowly into the garden. She felt bruised all over, as much inside as out. Standing in the shadow of the monkey puzzle's limbs, she absorbed the scene in front of her. It was much as it had been before she had left it. The only difference was that the crowd's heads were now craned back to enjoy the display, faces lit by the flashing sky. She might have been away for mere seconds.

Someone tugged at her sleeve and she looked down to see Helen's eager face. 'I crept out when the fireworks started,' she said. 'No one noticed I'd been missing at all.'

'Or I,' said Harriet, softly. No, that's not true, she thought. Bertie had noticed. And Agnes.

'I think the fireworks very pretty, Miss Jenner, but I should like to see a real comet more. Like the one in Mr Verne's book.'

It was such a relief to think about something so entirely apart from the grubby earthbound horrors she had just endured that she managed a half-smile. 'Do you know what the word "comet" means?'

The little girl shook her head.

'It's from the Greek, *kometes*, for "hair". A comet is a long-haired star.'

Helen beamed as she tipped her head back to see the sky again, her small face lovely in the flickering light. 'A long-haired star. Oh, I like that! Miss Jenner, have you heard of Halley's Comet?'

She had but she shook her head. Helen would enjoy

telling her and, besides, she was dangerously close to tears again.

'It comes round every – every so often,' Helen hurried on. 'I think it's seventy or eighty years, so most people only see it once in their whole lives. The next time it's due is 1910. I will be forty-one years old then – can you imagine? I worked it out. I do so hope I see it. It will be such a special year.'

Harriet smiled down at her. 'I'm sure it will be.' Something eddied through her then, a glimmer so quick and bright that she couldn't grasp it. Like a firework of her own creation, it exploded and was gone. Her mind returned to dark, like the sky above her, with nothing remaining but wisps of smoke. The firework display had finished.

Forty-five

When she had woken that terrible morning after the fireworks party, there had been a brief moment of forgetful bliss. She had expected to pass a disturbed night of terrible dreams, reliving all that had happened, but her mind had protected itself and let her sore, exhausted body rest. As the events of the previous night inevitably flooded back, she felt her pulse quicken and her skin bead with sweat. Was he still up there in the clearing? Or was he back in the house somewhere, only a couple of doors separating them?

She felt vulnerable in bed and threw back the sheets so she could get up and dressed. There, beneath her, was a brownish smear. For a moment, she thought it was her courses, come a week early, but it wasn't. She had bled because he had torn her. She thought about her poor father, how distraught he would have been if such a thing had happened in his lifetime and, for the first time, was glad he was gone. She didn't believe that dead people watched over their loved ones. Then she remembered the partial collapse of the Devil's Chimney and . . . But no. If that had been some kind of divine retribution, it had come too late and fallen too short. It was Agnes – and, unwittingly, Bertie – who had come closest to rescuing her, who had been her guardian angels.

Feeling as though she might faint dead away, she sat on

the bed and began to shake, the events of the previous evening only now sinking in. She started violently at a soft tap on the door, but when she couldn't bring herself to answer it, the door opened to reveal Agnes. The maid slipped into the room and closed the door behind her silently. To Harriet's disturbed mind, it felt as though she had summoned her.

'Oh, Agnes, how strange,' she stammered. 'I was just thinking about you, and how I hadn't thanked you for your help . . .' She stopped, humiliated anew, then noticed that Agnes's face, so reassuring the previous night, was now stricken and pale. 'What is it? What's wrong?'

'It was Mary who first got me worried,' she began, in a low, strained voice. 'She said his door was ajar when she came down. She was laughing, thinking it were funny that he'd been too drunk to shut it properly whenever he'd dragged himself in, long after the mistress had given up on him.'

Harriet nodded for her to go on, cold fear sluicing through her stomach. She clasped her hands together tightly in an attempt to stop them shaking.

'So, as soon as I could get away – Mrs Rollright's in a foul temper today – I went up to see for myself. There was no sign of him. His bed hasn't been slept in.'

Harriet put a hand out to the bedpost to steady herself. 'So he's still up there. Well,' she said, casting about desperately for explanations, 'the nights have been warm enough.'

Agnes stared back at her wordlessly, eyes wide and fearful, face chalky against her rust-red hair.

'What is it, Agnes? What are you not telling me?'

'I went, miss. I went up there to the ruins. I didn't tell

them in the kitchen. They thought I was going up to the parlour but I just went straight out the front door so they wouldn't see me. I got a bad feeling about it when I saw that room of his. I had to go.'

'And? Did you see him?'

The girl nodded. 'I did. And, miss, I think he's dead.'

'Dead?' The blunt word came out strangled and she dropped her voice. 'Dead? He can't be dead. He's as strong as an ox. He was probably too dazed to walk back when he came round so he stayed where he was. He's still sleeping – that's what you saw.' The words were for her benefit as much as Agnes's but the girl shook her head stubbornly.

'I know the difference between a sleeping man and a dead one. I didn't see it in the dark last night but there's a great gash on his head. He's gone a funny colour and his eyes . . .' She stopped and looked as though she might be sick. She drew in a long, shaky breath. 'He's gone, miss, I know he has.'

Harriet's mind raced furiously. Where Agnes had been the strong one the night before, the maid's abject fear now made Harriet's own terror briefly recede. She pulled the trembling girl down next to her and they sat in silence while she thought.

'We could hang for this, Miss Jenner,' Agnes whispered. Her teeth were chattering.

'We will not,' said Harriet, as firmly as she was able.

'But they'll find him.'

'And they will assume that he was hit by the falling rock, just as you suggested yourself last night.'

Agnes shook her head. 'You didn't see him, miss.'

'What do you mean?'

'The cut to his head. It's at the back of it, behind his ear, but sort of underneath. It's sharp-looking, too, like someone took a blade to his scalp. Besides, he's nowhere near where the big rock fell. He's up against a wall and it's still standing.'

'Perhaps we could move him, to make it look as though it was the stone, not a direct blow but a glancing one.'

'I don't know,' said Agnes. 'Them Scotland Yard detectives I've heard about, they're not stupid. They see things normal folks wouldn't notice or think strange. And I'm telling you, miss, if we went up there and moved him close to that rock, it would look strange to anyone's eyes, never mind the police. That huge stone what come down wouldn't have left a little gash like that. You could try it a hundred times and each one would squash him to pulp.'

Harriet had to agree with that. 'And if he'd been standing when it fell – and why would he have been doing anything else if . . . if I hadn't been there, too? – then even a glancing blow couldn't have been to the underside of his head.'

Agnes nodded miserably. 'They'll know it's fishy right away.'

Then Harriet remembered something else Agnes had said the night before. 'How long did you say it was until they flood the ruins?'

'A few days shy of three weeks. But I'd go mad waiting and hoping no one goes up there between now and then.'

'You may have no choice. How well hidden is he in the ruin where he . . . where you found us?'

'Oh, you'd never see him unless you went looking for him. I –' She fell silent.

'What, Agnes? You must tell me everything. We can't make any mistakes now or they will haunt us later.'

'I couldn't leave him as he was. I covered him up a bit, that's all.'

'With what?'

'Loose stones and slate from the roof from where it fell in years ago. A few branches and a bit of old canvas I found. I tucked it around him. I thought it would help with . . . well, when it starts to smell.' She swallowed.

Harriet stood up, her brain turning over different scenarios. 'It might work . . .'

'What might, miss?'

She knelt in front of Agnes and took her hands in her own, just as the maid had done for her the night before. Just as hers had been damp with fear, Agnes's were ice-cold. 'We must act now, before the mistress wakes. So that there is no search, which could uncover the body, we must make it look as if the captain has left of his own accord.'

'Left?'

'Gone back to London – or straight to the coast to make his way to India.'

'What – without a word to anyone?'

'I could forge a note. I've a knack for copying. He could say he wanted to slip away after the celebration because he couldn't bear to say goodbye.'

Agnes looked doubtful. 'That don't sound much like him.'

'The mistress would believe it, though, wouldn't she, if it flattered her enough? If she was given an explanation that appealed to her sense of romance?'

'She isn't right in the head about him, miss, that's for sure.'

'There you are, then. Now, it's no good sitting up here plotting when we're running out of time. I will get dressed and then we must go straight to his room.'

She left off her stays, did not put up her hair and was ready in two minutes. No one had yet stirred on the floor below. Just as Agnes had said, the captain's door was ajar, the bed beyond it tidy. What she hadn't mentioned was that he had left the rest of the room in a fearful mess. Shirts and collars were strewn all over the floor and the dressing-table was littered with coins and papers.

Before her nerves could master her, Harriet went over and plucked a sheaf of papers out of the chaos, folding them and tucking them away in her bodice. Something among them would do to copy from. Then she and Agnes set to work in silence, horribly alert to every sound that came from the other bedrooms as they shoved the captain's possessions into his trunk and large kit bag.

'Where will we put them?' Agnes hissed when they had finished.

Fear clutched at Harriet: she hadn't thought of that. If they couldn't hide his things, the plan would quickly unspool. 'We can't leave them here, and we're bound to be caught moving that trunk. I'm not even sure we could lift it.'

'We'll hide the bag,' said Agnes. 'That'll be easy enough. But we should leave the trunk as it is.'

'What? How can we?'

'He could never get that thing down the hill on foot and the carriage hasn't moved since yesterday morning.

John would know if it had been taken, and who would have brought it back anyway? A ghost?' She blanched at the last word.

'Yes, you're right, of course,' said Harriet. 'If he'd left so suddenly he would only have taken his kit bag. I can say he wants his trunk sent on in the note.'

'But who'll collect it the other end?'

'No one, but it won't matter. Any number of things could be the reason for that. With the trunk on its way and the note left, who'll think to question if he ever left at all?'

They glanced around the room a final time, then Agnes hoisted the bag on to her shoulder. They were halfway up the stairs to the attic floor when the mistress's door opened.

'Mary, is that you?' she called querulously.

Agnes took the remaining stairs two at a time, Harriet hard on her heels, desperately trying to keep her footsteps in time with the maid's. When they reached the top, Agnes shoved the bag at Harriet and pointed to the furthest door from the governess's own. 'In there,' she mouthed, before calling down the stairs. 'It's me, madam. Agnes.'

'Oh, I don't want you,' came the reply. 'I shall ring for Mary.'

Her door slammed and Agnes and Harriet exchanged looks of relief. It was a matter of minutes to secrete the kit bag in the trunk room, stowing it at the bottom of an old tea chest, which they covered with a pair of discarded curtains. A minute more and Agnes was back in the kitchen. Three floors above her, Harriet had begun a goodbye note in the captain's spidery script, the urgency of the task thankfully keeping her hand from shaking too much.

She'd had her last night of sound sleep at Fenix House. That night, the knowledge that the captain was not on his way to London but still up there, among the ruins, under the watchful gaze of the limestone cliff, frightened her terribly. Every tiny noise – a creak on the stairs, a disturbance on the gravel outside – set her heart pounding, convinced that it was surely him, dragging his broken body towards her. And then, when she did manage to snatch some sleep through sheer exhaustion, she dreamed of him anyway: horrible, lurid dreams in which his weight lay heavily on her again, except this time he was already stone-dead, his face grey and set like marble, his head wound revealing a sickly gleam of bone beneath dark, clotted blood.

When she woke from one of these nightmares, she had the fleeting urge to go up to the ruins once it was light to check for herself that he was still there. She dismissed it once she was up and dressed for the day – not because she no longer needed the reassurance, but in case she was seen. For what if she unintentionally gave someone else the idea of going there to look? All she could do was struggle through each day until the ruins were flooded, and the evidence of what had happened there was covered up for ever.

Forty-six

'Eighteen days,' Harriet murmured to her reflection. Her face was as pale as milk in the glass above her washstand, her grey eyes huge and fearful. 'Eighteen days until the ruins are flooded and it's all over,' she repeated.

Perhaps what had happened up there was meant to be, even if the glimmers hadn't told her so. They were never very reliable, after all. She decided that that was what she would tell herself whenever she doubted, whenever she began to tremble again, as she was doing now. She had to believe that it was in some way fated, and anything repeated often enough eventually convinced, didn't it? She had to hope that it would, and simply to hold on to her sanity in the days ahead.

Unable to stay still for long, she picked up the little dagger she'd been without at the ruins. Could she have used it on him, deliberately taken his life to stop him doing what he had done? She thought that she could and would have, and wondered why the Fates had involved Agnes, and made it accidental. Taking hold of the bed, she pulled it away from the wall, the castors squealing as though in pain. Kneeling, she unsheathed the small blade and began to scratch her initials into the skirting-board. She took her time and did it neatly, the small, precise movements calming her. For those few minutes, she felt anchored in the house again, less likely to be carried off into the unknown.

The captain's absence wasn't noticed until half past ten. His sister had returned to bed, once Mary had brought her breakfast tray, and the captain was assumed by the rest of the servants to be sleeping off the effects of the previous night's revelries. The first sign of discovery that he had left in the night was a single, piercing scream.

It was Sunday and no one had bothered to go to morning service at the church, so Harriet was sitting huddled on her narrow bed, the blankets around her because she couldn't get warm, when the cry briefly made her heart thud. She went to the door and waited, her breathing against the wood fast and shallow, her body tense. The mistress must have found her brother's letter.

Darling Lulu

You know how much I hate saying farewell to my beloved sister so I am leaving now, with the first dawn light. It's high time I returned to my company and my new wife – in truth, I should have left already and will probably have my knuckles rapped for it.

I will treasure these past weeks in your company, dearest Lu, so I hope you will forgive me for creeping away. Send my love to the little ones and my special thanks to Mrs Rollright for fattening me up so well. Regards also to your husband. I remain,

Your adoring brother, Jago

Though the mistress was distraught, the captain's reference to his new wife tempered her grief, reigniting her fury. 'If he chooses to sneak out like a thief in the night to return to his child bride, then we must let him go!' she was heard to shout at Mrs Rakes from her brother's deserted room. 'He assumes I will give chase so that I might snatch one more day with him. Well, he will be sorely disappointed. Let him begin his voyage with no one to wave him off. With luck, a storm will blow in and sink his ship, and he'll end up at the bottom of the sea. And, when that happens, what do you suppose his last thought will be? If only he had said goodbye to his sister *properly*!'

With that, she began her own storm of weeping. Mrs Rakes helped her to bed and came out with instructions that no one should disturb her for the rest of the day.

Harriet, having heard all of this unfold from her doorway in the attic, closed her eyes in relief.

The days that Harriet had to endure before the quarry ruins were flooded proved a trial to test anyone's nerve. The relief that came with the captain's absence was short-lived once she understood the Herculean task of behaving towards everyone, especially her sharp-eyed charges, as though nothing was wrong. What she desperately wanted to do, and could not, was lock her door and take to her bed. How she envied the mistress her freedom to do just that, not stirring except to ring for Mary, who was kept running up and down the stairs with all manner of treats and titbits from the kitchen.

In contrast, Harriet had no choice but to return to the morning room early on Monday, and spend the day fielding endless questions from Helen and Victoria about the party and the subsequent disappearance of their uncle.

Robert she would have probably avoided, even if he had not entered such a busy period at his work that he was kept away for days on end. Though she longed to tell him that she hadn't meant what she'd said to him on the lawn, she simply couldn't risk it. She didn't trust herself not to confess everything, once he was looking at her with those soft brown eyes of his. People were unpredictable, she knew, even people you thought you could trust implicitly. What would happen if she were to tell him the truth and he were to turn against her? He was a good man but Harriet hadn't known him very long; she couldn't predict how his love for her would fare against the knowledge of what had happened among the ruins – that she herself had been ruined.

Besides, she found it impossible to think about much beyond the flooding. Every hour and minute counted down towards that crucial day. When she was tempted to look further ahead, superstition stopped her, filling her with terror that Fate would turn on her.

Occasionally, in the day, with a benign sun at the window and her charges' neat heads bent over their books, it was almost possible to convince herself of what the rest of them believed – that the captain had left early on that Sunday morning and was now in London, or perhaps already aboard a ship bound for India. It was in the shadow hours of deepest night that this tapestry of lies fell to rags for Harriet, lying sleepless on her bed, eyes wide in the dark, stomach clutching with terror.

Eventually, the Thursday she had been waiting for arrived. To Harriet's profound relief, the mistress, still confined mainly to her rooms, had expressed no interest in the flooding, and Robert was safely away in Swindon. She had feared the flooding would be turned into some sort of family occasion, the whole household going up there to watch. Truly, she could think of little worse than witnessing that bowl of earth fill slowly with water, the Pembridges grouped around her for the spectacle.

In the event, that momentous day would have gone entirely unmarked at Fenix House, had it not been for another demonstration of Victoria's irrepressible adventurousness.

'Where is your sister?' Harriet asked Helen, when the little girl returned to the morning room after the midday meal in the nursery. Harriet had left the pair of them there just ten minutes earlier, inventing a loose button so she could retire to her room for a moment alone before afternoon lessons. She had found herself doing this more and more often lately, desperate to shut the door on the world so that she didn't have to arrange her face into a mask of calm normality. The strain was exhausting.

The little girl shook her head. 'She went out after you, Miss Jenner. I thought she might have gone to see Mama, but then I saw Mary coming out of Mama's room and she said Mama was sick and didn't want to see a soul.'

'Oh dear,' said Harriet, battling to keep her voice steady. 'What a day for her to go on one of her wanderings.'

'Why, Miss Jenner?'

'It's the day of the flooding so I think we should know where she is. Stay here a moment. I'll just check the nursery, to see if she has gone back up there.'

Victoria was not in the nursery, just as Harriet had known she would not be. She took the stairs down to the servants' quarters in a rush. Mrs Rakes was in the sitting room having a cup of tea and looked up at the governess's abrupt entrance.

'I'm sorry to disturb you, Mrs Rakes,' Harriet began, rather breathlessly.

'Not at all, Miss Jenner. What can I do for you? Has something happened?' She smiled kindly and Harriet wished she would not, for fear she would burst into anxious tears.

'I can't find Victoria. Only Helen has come down for afternoon lessons. She is not in the nursery and I fear that she has gone off on one of her adventures. I'm worried someone has told her about the flooding and she has gone to look.'

What she didn't add was that the last adventure Victoria had undertaken had led to Harriet's lone visit to the ruins on the night of the party. If Mrs Rakes made reference to it, she was certain that she would lose what little composure she had left.

Fortunately Mrs Rakes merely shook her head. 'I haven't seen her all day, only heard her – but that was this morning.'

Just then Ann came in with an order from Mrs Rollright. Harriet had barely spoken to the girl, who resembled Mary but had none of the older sister's fresh prettiness. Her hands were raw from her work in the scullery. 'I seen her, Mrs Rakes,' she mumbled.

The housekeeper turned to her in surprise. 'Oh? Well, where was she then, child?'

Ann had gone as crimson as her hands. 'I were getting the onions from Ned about ten minute back. She were in the garden.'

'Was she on her own?' asked Mrs Rakes, sternly.

'I don't know, I didn't look that careful. I just saw her in the distance, near that big bush with the purple on it. I thought Miss Jenner or her sister mus' be with her.'

Harriet didn't wait but ran through the kitchen, into the scullery and up the slippery steps to the garden. She was breathing hard by the time she reached the steepest section of the path up into the wood, but she didn't stop.

She found Victoria on the edge of the clearing, close to the spot where she herself had stood on the night of the party. The reminder, coupled with her relief on finding the child before she had either drowned herself or stumbled upon her dead uncle, made her furious and she rushed forwards to grab her, smacking her hard on the back of the legs. Victoria, taken by surprise and unused to such treatment, let out a shocked howl, then began to sob.

'Oh, I'm sorry, I'm sorry,' Harriet said, pulling the little girl to her. 'I was just so frightened you might have hurt yourself.'

She looked over Victoria's heaving shoulder and saw that water was already trickling steadily into the hollow of earth. Where it was deepest, it was probably already at waist height.

Victoria mumbled something unintelligible into Harriet's shoulder between bouts of weeping.

'What are you saying, little one? I can't hear you. What did you say?'

'I said, I want to go. It smells horrid.'

Harriet felt fear clutch at her heart again. She was right, the air smelt heady – sweet and, yes, rotten. She looked back at the ruins and realized that a cloud of flies hovered over them. High above, she heard a sound and noticed for the first time a group of men at the top of the cliff. It was they who had diverted the stream and were now watching the quarry fill with water. Harriet wondered what they could see from their lofty perch. Could they smell the foetid air? Perhaps the breezes up there would blow away any noxious fumes. But the flies. She prayed they would assume there was a dead animal somewhere under the stones.

As she stared up at the men, reduced to silhouettes in the bright sunlight, one raised his cap to her. Fearful of not returning the greeting, of snubbing a man who might wonder why she was so unfriendly, she raised a trembling arm.

'Come now, Vicky,' she said, as calmly as she could. 'Let's go back to the house, shall we? See if we can beg a treat or two from Mrs Rollright.'

The little girl peered at her suspiciously, her face streaked with tears and grime. 'You've never called me Vicky before. Is it because you were nasty and smacked me?'

Harriet breathed slowly in and out, still aware of the men peering down at them, of the decaying body lying there in the shallows. 'I'm sorry I hit you. It was only because I was frightened.'

Victoria frowned as she considered this. Eventually she nodded her acceptance of the apology. 'I forgive you. I don't ever get frightened. I'm lucky to be so very brave, aren't I?'

Harriet led her back under the canopy of trees. 'Indeed you are, my love, very lucky indeed.'

Forty-seven

There was to be one last conversation with Robert before she was dismissed. It was quite the least satisfactory exchange of her life and, after it, she went to her room and wept bitterly over her copy of *Jane Eyre*. Even if there could never have been a 'Reader, I married him' for her, she had still wanted him to know without being told how wretched she was, how desperately frightened for the future. It wasn't entirely fair, she supposed later, when the acute hurt of it had lessened and dulled: he had not her talent for knowing things he ought not to know.

They met on the lawn directly below the ice-house with the glade higher still. He had apparently just emerged from the maze.

'Ah, Miss Jenner,' he said, heartily enough, though his cheeks were flushed with embarrassment. 'I did not expect to see you here.'

'I wanted a little fresh air,' she said, hearing herself adopt the same false tones as he had. 'It is such a lovely day, is it not? As the girls are having their tea with Agnes to see to them, I saw the chance to steal out for a moment.'

'Oh, you needn't explain. You need not ask my permission to take a turn in the garden.'

'No. I . . . Well, I didn't want you to think I had abandoned my charges.' She laughed weakly and inwardly thought how absurd it was to be talking as they were.

426

What she really wanted to do was go to him and lay her head against his broad chest.

He shook his head. 'I would never think that of you, Harri— Miss Jenner. Not at all. I simply had no idea of the time. I've been in the maze – it's rather tranquil inside – and I . . .' He tailed off and looked down at his feet. She saw his Adam's apple move in his throat as he swallowed.

'So, we are back to Miss Jenner and Mr Pembridge now,' she said quietly.

He looked flustered again. 'Not if you do not wish it to be so.'

'We have not seen much of each other since the night of the party.'

He didn't immediately reply but stood looking towards the house. 'I saw you,' he said eventually, his tone utterly flat.

'Saw me?' She stepped back and half stumbled off the path, her boot heel sinking into the soft grass. It had rained the previous night. What had he seen?

'I watched you from the window of my room.' He was still staring at the house and she followed his gaze to the window that was his. It was foolish: no window at Fenix House afforded a view of the ruins. They were much higher, and obscured by the surrounding woods. She struggled to compose herself.

'And what did you see from your look-out?'

'I saw you leave the garden.'

'To look for your daughter, sir.' She hadn't called him sir for many weeks but there was some coldness in his bearing that had turned her defensive. She wasn't old or wise enough to understand that it was wounded pride.

'My daughter was in the Cucumber House,' he said dismissively. 'I saw her go up there myself.'

Harriet went very still. 'And you did not tell anyone?' She suddenly saw a different outcome to that night and it was clearer than any glimmer. A shout from an upstairs window, before she and Dilger had even reached the gate. She shut her eyes, and when she opened them again the vision turned to ash. 'But why did you not say where she was?'

'I only wish I had,' he said, with a bitter laugh. 'Instead I stood by and did nothing. I let him go after you, up the hill for a tryst in the woods.'

'A tryst?' She was incredulous. 'Is this why you are so cold towards me now? Is this why you have not so much as looked in my direction since then?' She could feel fury heating her blood, pushing it faster through her veins. It was the first time since the party she hadn't felt afraid and there was a strange sort of liberation in that, at least.

'And did you wait to see me return?' she added. He would have been able to see the gate, where Agnes had brushed her down, where she had stood a moment alone and found her face wet with tears she didn't know she had shed.

'No, I didn't see your return,' he said. 'I didn't want to see the pair of you, your secret smiles, a last embrace where the azaleas shield the path from the garden. I went to bed.'

She stared at him and saw a fleeting likeness to Victoria. He looked just as she did when Helen had been given something she herself coveted. It wasn't an expression that flattered either of them.

'You think yourself disappointed in me, Mr Pembridge,' she said, anger, frustration and sorrow mingling to make her voice shake. 'But it is I who am so very disappointed in you.'

She left him there in the garden without a backward glance. That was the last time she would see him. He went away on business early the next morning, and by the time he returned late in the evening at the end of the week, she had already packed her belongings. The mistress thought it prudent not to tell him anything about the dismissal until she was certain the governess had left the premises.

The incident that had finally offered the mistress an excuse to dismiss Harriet arose just as Harriet was starting to believe that she and Agnes would not be found out. It was to be the last of Victoria's transgressions that summer and it was to the ice-house. She had gone out into the dusk in only her nightgown, her feet bare, which would certainly have hastened a chill if she had been trapped inside the chamber for any longer than she was. As it was, she'd been inside only a few minutes when Harriet experienced a glimmer that was vivid enough for her immediately to stand up and run.

The emergency over, the rescue party were trooping back to the house when the mistress's voice rang out across the garden. She was leaning out of her bedroom window. It was the first time Harriet had seen – as opposed to heard – her in days. She was pale and drawn, her eyes sunken and bloodshot.

'What is all this?' she demanded. 'I have asked for little while I have been laid low but some undisturbed rest, so why have I been roused by this – this *commotion*?'

Then she caught sight of the bedraggled Victoria in her grubby nightgown. Though the worst of her hysteria had gone, her breath was still coming in great shuddering gasps.

The mistress's face hardened. 'Miss Jenner, come and see me immediately. I warned you about something like this.'

'Mrs Pembridge, may I just say that if it had not been for Miss Jenner –' Mrs Rakes began.

'No, you may not,' said the mistress, and slammed down the sash with a rattle.

It is possible that, despite her threats, the mistress did not really intend to dismiss Harriet. She was certainly very angry that her favourite child had been allowed to go off alone again; that, indeed, the girl might have *suffocated* in the ice-house because of her governess's continued negligence. But the exchange might have concluded differently. If Robert had been at home and able to intervene, if Mrs Rakes had been allowed admittance to the mistress's room to speak up for Harriet, if Harriet herself had not eventually lost her temper, the situation might not have escalated in the way it did. But all these things conspired and, by the time the sun had slid below the western horizon, Harriet was packing her valise.

Something had occurred to her in the mistress's overheated sitting room, the air reeking as usual of stale perfume, burned hair and the sharpness of the ammonia she swallowed daily to rid herself of excess weight. Puffed up with self-righteousness, plump from inactivity and too many sweet things, she continued to list the governess's faults and shortcomings, while Harriet realized that her time at Fenix House was coming to an end sooner than she'd thought. She felt it as strongly as if she'd seen a glimmer.

In truth, an escape plan of sorts had been forming in her mind since the morning she had forged the note from the captain. There had been a piece of paper in the pile she had taken to copy from that might prove useful if she was clever enough. She had also begun to face the fact that she and Robert could never be, not while there was still breath in the mistress. Finally, she had felt some of her old fighting spirit return when she woke the day after the ruins had been submerged. The captain still haunted her dreams but his hold on her waking hours felt significantly looser now. Given all this, it was perhaps no surprise that she said what she did to the woman who had remained her enemy. Later, she reflected that she might have said a good deal more.

After being shouted at for some minutes, Harriet simply put up her hand against the mistress's tirade. Taken by surprise to be commanded in such a way, the woman opposite her shut her mouth.

'Enough,' said Harriet. 'You are beginning to repeat yourself, madam.'

'I – I beg your pardon?'

'You do, do you? Well, if that is the case, then I must say that it is long overdue.'

Frowning in confusion, the mistress opened her mouth to speak, then closed it for the second time.

'You don't remember me, do you?' said Harriet. 'There has never been even a hint of recognition in your eyes when you deign to look my way, or from your boor of a brother before he went. I remember you, though, Louisa.'

The mistress visibly jolted at the use of her Christian name, which spurred Harriet on.

'Oh, yes, I remember you very well. You were a spoiled, vain and remarkably silly girl then and the years have done nothing to improve you.'

Louisa's eyes narrowed. 'Who are you?'

'I am Richard Jenner's daughter. Our fathers were once great friends. Many was the time Josiah Dauncey came to our house in London and enjoyed my father's generosity – his meat, his wine, and a bed when he was too drunk to return to his own. In turn, my father went to your house a few times, too – first to the one near ours and later to a better-appointed dwelling in Hampstead. I went with him there once, when I was about Helen's age. I remember it was cold – there was frost on the grass.' She saw her father turn his hat over and over in his hands while they waited for the door to be answered. She saw how they trembled as if it was yesterday. 'Do you remember, Louisa?'

She saw a tiny splinter of comprehension in the mistress's china-blue eyes. 'Jenner,' she repeated to herself. 'There was someone of the name Jenner, though I don't remember him being of any consequence. I'm quite amazed I can remember him at all. He came to our door demanding money a few times, I believe. Was that him? Was that your father?' A tiny smile curled her mouth on one side.

'The money he demanded was his own, which your father had tricked him out of. There was a scheme he was persuaded to invest in, a scheme you yourself championed.'

'Oh, wait. I do remember something of this. Was it wallpaper, green wallpaper?'

Harriet nodded, unable for the moment to speak. The memory of her father, vivid as it was, threatened to undo her.

'Yes, it's all coming back to me now,' the mistress continued. She appeared to be enjoying herself again. 'The scheme came to nothing, as these things do sometimes, but your father wanted his portion back. He seemed not to have understood the risk. What happened to you, then? He went away in the end, I believe, gave it up as he should have done in the first place.'

Harriet couldn't bear to tell her about the fire that led to her father's ruin. 'We did well enough.'

'Though not so well that you haven't had to earn your living. Well, you won't earn it from me any longer. You will leave at dawn and you will not tell anyone you are going. I don't want you eliciting sympathy you don't deserve from my children and the servants. I will tell my husband when he returns tonight, but don't expect any fond farewells from him either. I don't know why you came here – whether it was bad luck and unhappy coincidence, or whether you're here by design. If it was the latter, and you hoped to exact some kind of revenge, then you have failed, Miss Jenner.'

The mistress's curls bobbed with indignation and Harriet noticed for the first time how unwell she looked. She had aged since her brother had left, all her comely creaminess spoiled in just a few weeks. The mantel shelf behind her was crammed with bottles and vials containing sinister preparations, variously promising a flawless complexion, shining eyes and lustrous hair. Perhaps she would bring about her own undoing with them: some looked more like poison – the daily dose of ammonia certainly was. Only a room papered in dangerous Dauncey green would have been a more poetic form of justice.

Harriet turned to go but paused at the door. 'In truth, Mrs Pembridge, you have done me a great service by dismissing me now. I have been wretched with indecision ever since Captain Dauncey left – not wishing to abandon my pupils, of whom I have grown so fond.'

'Indecision? What decision does someone like you have to make in the world? Which plain dress to put on in the morning? Or, more fittingly now, perhaps, which place to take yourself off to next – the poorhouse or the bawdy house?'

Harriet smiled. 'Oh, another path has been cleared for me, madam, and I think that I shall take it after all. Would you like me to send your regards when I join him in London?'

The mistress's hands gripped the arms of her chair. 'Who? Who will you join?'

'Oh, Jago, of course.'

Without waiting for an answer, she closed the door smartly behind her. As she ascended the stairs to her attic room, she could hear an urgent peal start up downstairs as the mistress rang for help, the sound echoing through the house, like Harriet's own victory bell.

Packing her belongings late that same evening, Harriet knew she had one more thing to do before she went, one more service to perform for the family she was leaving. It was only Louisa she despised, after all. There was a glimmer, a powerful one, and she could not in good conscience keep it to herself. A version of it had been with her since adolescence, sporadically creeping into her thoughts just as they began to lose their bindings and drift, jolting her unpleasantly into wakefulness. Only very lately, however, had she grasped that it might involve the Pembridges. Or one in particular.

That old glimmer, she now understood, was connected to the one she'd barely been able to catch in the garden, when she'd stood with Helen and talked about comets. Later that night in bed, desperate to think of anything but what Captain Dauncey had done, she had gone over that lightning-fast glimmer again and again, until she had slowed it sufficiently to make sense of it. To add it to what she had already known for years. The fierce heat and light of a great explosion. The twisted metal and smoke that followed it. And, out of the mire, the redemptive flash of pure white, the black-clad figure stooping to gather it up. Something miraculous found in the ashes – that, she had long sensed. What was new was its dark twin in the scene. Something lost. She felt fairly certain it would be Helen. As for the dark figure she could glimpse only from the back, could it be Robert? She thought it could.

She wrote a note to him that was carefully vague in case Mary or Agnes picked it up, but still conveyed something of what she believed would happen in 1910. She hoped he remembered what she had told him that day in the darkened study. If not, the message would be rendered meaningless.

When she had sealed it, she waited until the household

had quietened for the night and crept downstairs to Robert's study. He wasn't back yet, she knew, so there was no need to knock. She tucked the envelope so just the corner of it poked out from beneath his leather-edged blotter. Then she hurried up the stairs to her room, fleet-footed despite the extinguished gas lamps. Her mind on other things, she didn't notice Bertie, a small shadow absorbed into the larger darkness of the hall.

Forty-eight

Bertie

Bertie knew Miss Jenner's light tread, just as he knew everyone's in the house. He didn't hurtle straight into sleep, like his sisters seemed to, and so was habitually witness to the house retiring to bed, one by one, each making their own unique noises as they closed their doors, undressed and heaved themselves into bed. There was a warped, creaking floorboard in the hall outside his door that only Miss Jenner had not yet learned to avoid. When he heard it that night, he couldn't resist seeing why she was going downstairs so late. He wanted to make sure she wasn't leaving under the cover of darkness. He'd heard his mother's raised voice and her bell ringing earlier, and he'd overheard Mary tell John that Miss Jenner was leaving not long after. The grief of it hadn't sunk in yet. He thought there was still a chance that she could be reprieved, if only his father came back in time.

He waited in the darkest recess of the downstairs hallway until she passed him on her way back to the stairs, close enough to touch, close enough that he could hear her breathing and smell her light, clean scent, so different from Mama's. When her door in the attic two floors above had softly closed, he went into his father's study. At first, nothing seemed awry or missing. If the moon hadn't been so bright he might not have seen it at all, a sharp white corner of envelope that spoiled the right angles of the desk's neat surface, a shark's tooth gleaming through murky water. He pulled it out and saw that it was sealed but had no name written upon it. He sniffed the paper and caught a vestige of her still on it. He thought it might be roses.

He had written many notes to Miss Jenner, probably a dozen. She had never replied to any of them, though she had always thanked him and been kind, especially when his uncle Jago had tried to rag him during a game of croquet, saying he'd sent her a love letter when it hadn't been anything of the kind. But still, and despite the kindness, it would have been nice to receive a note that he could have kept in the mint humbug tin with his other treasures. He was surprised how much it hurt him that she had written to his father – or, rather, he was surprised that he felt the pain in his chest as a physical hurt, which defied anything he had managed to learn in anatomy at school.

Holding the thin paper up to the window, he could just make out the black strokes of her handwriting, which he had judged on other occasions to be not only elegant and neat but *certain*. Not like his own wavering tangle. He wondered what she could have to say to his father. His mother had made her feelings very clear; perhaps Miss Jenner was begging his father to reconsider.

He turned the envelope over in his hands, tearful with indecision. The last time he had picked up someone else's letter, there had been a great deal of trouble, with Mama brought so low that she was confined to bed for days, and his uncle Jago so angry with him that he hadn't spoken a word to Bertie since. Hadn't even glanced his way, in fact. When Bertie had found out he had gone after the fireworks party, he'd felt nothing but relief. Only Mama and Victoria had been really sorry about it.

He was cold, he realized. He was also beginning to feel frightened, the familiar study altered by the moon's chilly gaze and the deep shadows it couldn't reach. Part of him knew he should leave the note for his father, but another part – a part that felt stronger – wanted it for himself.

He had seen them once, his father and Miss Jenner. They hadn't seen him; people didn't, he found, unless he made quite a lot of deliberate noise. They were sitting on the little bench at the top of the garden, in the pretty glade his father thought no one else knew about. He had been watching a pair of beetles behind the ice-house when he heard his father's voice. It had sounded odd – strained and high – not like it did when he argued with Mama: then it became slow and infinitely patient. Bertie thought that only made her more furious.

He crept out from behind the ice-house to see who his father was with but when he realized it was Miss Jenner he felt hot and slightly sick. He retreated as silently as a wild creature, weaving through the shrubbery instead of taking a direct path across the exposed lawn, desperate to reach the sanctuary of his room, where he could think about what he had just seen. He was so distracted that he almost didn't notice his uncle emerge from the French windows of the parlour. He had just enough time to duck around the corner of the house to avoid him.

In the silent study, he turned the letter over again. Recalling the episode in the garden had decided him. Clutching it tightly, he ran noiselessly up the stairs to his room.

Forty-nine

Robert
21 May 1910

Robert squinted at the large station clock suspended above his head, then checked his pocket watch. It was a handsome little thing but it had never kept time well. It was now running almost ten minutes late. If it hadn't been a gift from his elder daughter, he would have replaced it by now.

He turned it over and ran his thumb over the engraving on the back: '*For dearest Papa, with love from your H*'. Pulling out the pin, he moved it forward to the correct time and stowed it back in his breast pocket, reflecting that if a lifetime spent working on the railways hadn't instilled such punctuality in him then he might have missed his train.

He could see it approaching now, the billow of dirty steam, the slowing clatter, the flat round face of the engine, which had always looked to him like a clock face missing its hands. *Bristol Time*, he suddenly remembered, the almost-forgotten nugget of railway trivia making him smile. He had been on Bristol Time all morning. Now he was back on Railway Time.

Taking a seat in first class, he breathed in the familiar scent of a carriage on a fine spring morning. They smelt different according to the weather and season. Warmed dust, shaving soap and a hint of varnish on dry days; mackintosh wax and damp wool on wet ones. Winter after a downpour was the least pleasant, stale smoke and sour breath turning the tightly closed windows opaque. Since his retirement from the GWR, he had missed all of it.

There had been a time, once – a single summer, really, no more than that – when he had dreaded leaving the house in the morning, suddenly resentful that he had to spend the day at work in Bristol or Swindon, or wherever else he was required to go. When that had ended, as it surely had to, the railways had been the saving of him, the boarding of his regular service like stepping over the threshold of a dear friend's home. It was no less of a salvation for being a prosaic, tidy one: the reliably plotted timetables that filled a volume of two hundred closely printed pages; the solidity of the iron that was everywhere, from the engines to the buffers to the legs of the station benches; and the tracks – the tracks that never took you anywhere unexpected and frightening.

The journey to Swindon was so well known to him that he didn't really see the villages and pastures and remnants of ancient forests, even as he gazed out of the window at them. His mind was elsewhere. That summer had got hold of him fiercely again, wrenching him back like a surprise undertow. Thirty-two years ago. The number was incredible. He didn't think, if put to it, he would be able to account for most of them. It was half a lifetime away, more or less.

A year to the day when they'd buried Louisa in the little churchyard at the bottom of the hill, he'd gone there by himself. He'd knelt dutifully at the grave, and laid some of the hothouse blooms she'd always preferred to English flowers, but his thoughts weren't on the woman who had been his wife. Instead, they had gone back to the summer of 1878, just as they did now, as the train rumbled onwards towards Swindon. That day at the graveside, he'd been remembering the Sunday service when Bertie had gone to sleep and fallen off the pew. He'd remembered how she had smiled about it when they had walked up the hill together afterwards, in the soaking rain. Not his wife. Harriet.

It was then he'd decided he must try to find the woman who had been Miss Harriet Jenner. He'd had the idea of placing a notice in the Cheltenham periodical they had always taken, and which he had occasionally seen her reading in the house during her short tenure there. There was a standing advertisement in it that he now always made a point of turning to. It was for the Governess Institution on Rodney Road that had brought her to him, years before. There would be a lovely kind of symmetry in reaching out to her in the same newspaper, he thought, a sense of romance. But then he remembered that, wherever she was, she wasn't in Cheltenham, so she would surely never see it.

He read over the words he'd drafted for the notice again: 'Pembridge family seeks former governess, Miss Harriet Jenner, in the expectation that she would like to hear happy news of her charges.'

What a coward he was, hiding behind his children when it was he who wanted her to return. He took up his pen and scratched out the words, writing instead: 'Mr Robert Pembridge urgently seeks Miss Harriet Jenner.

He wishes to tell her that his wife is dead and that he is free to marry again, if only she will forgive him for being such a fool.'

That was what he ought to put in it. Scandalous it might be, but it was also the truth. If he had any gumption, he'd send it to *The Times* too, so that everyone in the country might see it.

He closed his eyes. The ink hadn't even dried when he had thrown the paper on the fire.

As the train left Stonehouse, he checked the years off on his fingers. Ten years since he had written out that plea for her return, then burned it. Four years since Helen had mentioned her old governess in passing and he, loquacious after three large brandies, had confided the feelings he once harboured for Miss Jenner. Thirty-two years since he had seen her last.

She would be in her fifties now. Would they even recognize each other if they were to pass on a busy station platform? He had always looked for her when occasion had taken him to London. The capital had been her home; it was where she had lost her beloved father; it seemed natural that she would have returned there when she left Fenix House. Sometimes he thought he saw her, as people do when they want something badly enough, transforming stout old ladies into Harriet's lithe form, following any woman whose hair glowed warmly in the sun, only to see when he drew closer that she was much too tall or that her nose, when she turned, was much too pronounced. He couldn't imagine her rose-gold hair turned grey.

He had told Helen all of this and, instead of being angry for her mother's sake, she had understood perfectly the affinity that circumstance had thrown up between her father and her governess. She knew, better than most, that the person you wanted was not always the person other people thought you should have. Her soft hazel eyes alight, she'd made him promise that, now a widower, he would look for Harriet Jenner as he had never dared before. They had even drunk a toast to second chances in Fenix House's parlour, the only light in the room coming from the waning fire.

The next morning, the brandy's effects long dissipated, the fire now ash in the grate, he had changed his mind, fearing disappointment if she could not be traced – and also if she could, but was happily married. Not to Dauncey, of course. He'd long abandoned his foolish jealousy and had never believed the story she had told Louisa – who had deserved it and more. A woman like Harriet would never have fallen for Jago Dauncey's coarse charms.

Helen was uncharacteristically stubborn when he told her of this change of heart, and said she would continue to look for her old governess, with or without his help. He was torn about this: a secret gladness threaded through the anxiety. Every time he received a letter from Helen, or visited her and David in the Hampstead house Vicky had inherited from her mother but let her sister live in, he was rigid with tension in case there was news. Every time she shook her head, he smiled and said it didn't matter, but it did. It did. Strangely, it mattered more as each year passed.

Thirty-two years. Where had they gone?

He looked out of the carriage window to see that they were pulling into Swindon. The journey had passed so swiftly that he took out his pocket watch again, to check if they were early. Unless, perversely, the watch had now begun to gain time, they were in fact a minute late. Trying to rid himself of memories decades old, he lingered on the platform until it had cleared and wondered if he should go and have a pot of tea and a bun. He didn't much want them but thought the act of buying and consuming them might anchor him again in the present, in the mundane. Besides, the train he was meeting was not due for another twenty minutes.

He had almost reached the door of the station's refreshment room when he heard his name called. On registering it, he realized that whoever was trying to hail him had probably attempted it a couple of times already.

'It is Mr Pembridge, isn't it?' the voice came again, loud and vaguely rural. There was something pompous about it. Puffed up, Vicky would have said. But also oddly familiar. He squinted down the platform, hand raised against the spring sunlight, and made out a portly figure bustling purposefully towards him. 'Of course it is you,' he called, as he approached, 'and not changed a bit since we saw you last! We thought we'd missed you.'

For a horrible moment, Robert couldn't place the man, let alone remember his name. But then all of it slid obediently into his mind, like pulling open an oiled drawer. It was the station master's assistant, Clarence Gibson. He had grown more rotund since Robert had last seen him, his cheeks flushed the colour of claret, eyes almost lost in the folds of his shiny face.

'Mr Gibson, how are you?'

The man's cheeks further darkened with pleasure. 'I'm honoured that you would remember me, sir, after all these

445

years. I'm pleased to tell you that I'm station master now. It'll be two years this summer since I moved up.'

'I'm very glad for you, Mr Gibson. I'm sure you do the job very well.'

'I do my best, sir,' he demurred.

Robert had met Gibson only half a dozen times in the course of his work and had never really liked him. He couldn't quite recall why now. The man was indeed pompous, and a little obsequious certainly, but those weren't reasons enough, surely. Robert had always prided himself on his understanding and tolerance of the men beneath him at GWR, and liked to lead by example.

There was an awkward silence and Robert realized he had missed his cue to speak. 'Ah, did you . . . You said you were afraid you'd missed me. Had you been expecting me?'

'No, no, though when the message came through I was pleased to have the excuse to welcome you personally to the station. Please, will you follow me to the office? There's one or two of the old-timers who'd like to pay their respects, I'm sure. I see you were about to step into the buffet. Well, there's always a pot of tea brewing in the office.'

Robert glanced up at the station clock and saw that he still had fifteen minutes until Helen and Bertie arrived. What harm could it do? He even – yes, he could admit it: he felt a little pride at being treated as though he was someone of consequence again; someone other than an old man with no purpose and all the time in the world to indulge hopeless fantasies about the past. It would be a nice thing to tell Helen about over lunch, too.

They were going straight back to Cheltenham once he'd met the train, getting off at the small halt nearest home and taking a cab the rest of the way. It had become tradition whenever she visited from London that he would meet her where she changed at Swindon. He always claimed it was so she had some company if David wasn't with her. In fact, he enjoyed those little forays and reminders of his working life. He liked to be on the old line again.

Of course, Helen didn't need company on this journey – Bertie had been staying with her for the past week, which seemed odd to Robert, even if there was some exhibition or other his son wanted to attend. Bertie had always claimed to hate the chaos of the capital, not even soothed by the proximity of the house to the Heath. Anyway, Bertie or not, Robert had wanted to keep to the usual routine, this time meeting both of them at Swindon. Bertie would no doubt want to go for one of his solitary rambles in the woods as soon as they got home, but Helen and he could have John drive them back into town. To Montpellier Gardens, perhaps, where they could have a stroll before enjoying an early lunch at the Queen's, just the pair of them.

In the staff room, Robert was presented to the men there as though he was a visiting dignitary. How Helen will laugh about this when I tell her, he told himself firmly. Firmly because, to his shame, he found he was rather enjoying the fuss. After he'd shaken everyone's hand and the men had gone off to their work, he was ushered into Gibson's small office. Robert judged it would not now be rude to ask again about the message the man had mentioned.

'Mr Gibson, you said something came through . . .'

'Well, blow me, I'd almost forgotten what with the pleasure of seeing you again.' He pushed a folded piece of paper across the desk. 'A telegram. I suppose they thought we'd know you here, to pass it on.'

Robert felt a lurch of disappointment as he opened it. It must be from Helen, saying she couldn't come. He badly wanted to see her. Bertie too, of course, but Helen particularly. He missed her, living in London as she did, though he understood that it was easier for her to be without a husband there. The thought of seeing her today had lent shape to the entire week.

DARLING PA STOP MISSED TRAIN AS DAVID UNWELL STOP NOT SERIOUS STOP CATCHING 08.45 EXPRESS INSTEAD STOP MUCH LOVE H STOP

His heart swelled with relief and happiness. She was still coming. She had spent extra on the telegram just to send him her love. He wondered what David had come down with and, indeed, why he was even at home – surely it was the middle of the school term. He had always been such a demanding boy, David, and Robert sometimes worried he was too much for his gentle mother.

'My daughter Helen,' he said to Gibson, who was waiting with a look of expectation, though Robert was certain he would have already read it – the flap had not been sealed down. 'She and my son have been delayed. They've caught the quarter to nine express from Paddington instead.' He brought out the pocket watch. The sun was bright at the grimy office window and it sang off the letters of her inscription as he turned it over. 'I suppose they have not long set off.'

Gibson was already checking his timetable. 'That will get them in at twenty past ten so I'm afraid you'll have a bit of a wait, sir. I hope you will stay here, in the comfort of my office. Perhaps you would like something to eat.'

Robert had been about to shake his head but then realized that he was rather peckish now. 'Why not? We will be having a later lunch. Perhaps a teacake would be a good idea, thank you.'

'And we must get you that cup of tea, too,' said Gibson. He went out, apparently to see who in the staff room was unoccupied. Robert got up and followed him, half hoping there would be someone else he could reminisce with while he waited. He wasn't sure he wanted to pass the time alone with only the station master for company.

Just then, a slight man rushed in, banging the door in his haste. When he saw Mr Gibson he straightened and whipped off his GWR cap.

Gibson pulled himself up to his full height, his expression sour. 'Reed! What do you mean by coming in here like a bull in a china shop? And aren't you supposed to start in less than thirty minutes? You should be on your way to the signal box by now.'

With some effort, Reed raised his head and met Gibson's eye. 'Sir, I'm very sorry to do it but I was hoping that you'd let me off today's shift. I would never ask but it's my youngest, you see. He's been bad with the scarlet fever for a –'

'Not work his shift!' exclaimed Gibson, turning to Robert with a look of mock incredulity. 'And him asking with just twenty-five minutes to spare till he's supposed to begin it! I call that some cheek. This is not the sort of carry-on the GWR tolerates,' he continued. 'Have you not a wife who takes care of your children, Reed?'

'It's not so much that, sir. It's that I've had no sleep these last three nights. The baby's been fretting that much, none of us has had a wink. I'm dead on my feet.'

Gibson waved his hand dismissively. 'And this coming on top of being late last month. I forget nothing, Mr Reed. You'd do well to remember that.' He tapped his nose and checked that his audience was still there. Robert was wishing he'd stayed in the office. He remembered only too well now why he'd never warmed to the man.

'Now, it happens that we have an important guest with us here today,' Gibson continued. 'Mr Pembridge was principal assistant over at the works before he retired. I'm sure he's as appalled as I am by your presumption.'

Robert wanted to say that, no, he was not in fact appalled. Further, that the man, Reed, looked bone-tired. His child was probably very ill, and no doubt there was little money, if any, for the doctor. He felt rather sick at the knowledge that the wretched man was probably only getting such a dressing-down because he himself was present. Gibson was putting on a show in his honour. Robert opened his mouth to speak but another man, previously unnoticed in the corner, where he was quietly reading a newspaper, spoke up first.

'I've just come off shift, Mr Gibson. I'll work Reed's if he's not able for it. It makes no odds to me and I'm not on tomorrow.' He and Reed exchanged looks. They were obviously allies and this seemed to infuriate Gibson further. His face had gone an alarming shade of purple.

'If you have finished for the day, Johnson, then I suggest you be on your way. You will not work another man's shift for him when that man is standing right here, perfectly fit for his duties, as far as I can see.' He checked the clock above the door. 'Reed, you have twenty-one minutes to relieve Potts at the signal box. You're more than welcome to go home to your bed, but don't show your face here again if you do.'

Reed looked as though he would protest, but merely pressed his lips together, nodded at Johnson and Robert and went back out of the door. Robert was glad that he let it crash shut.

'Men of that sort have to be ruled with a rod of iron,' Gibson said confidingly, once Johnson had also left. 'I'm sorry you had to see that, Mr Pembridge, but let me assure you, he won't be doing anything like that again in a hurry. Not if he wants to keep the house given to him by the GWR, he won't. Now, shall I get you that teacake if there's no one else to fetch it? Please take a seat in my office again, won't you, sir?'

I should have stuck up for the man, Robert thought, as he sat down. What was wrong with him? He remembered telling Harriet once – they had been walking, the sun warm on his back – how he always sought to understand the men who worked under him; how he tried to see them as people with the same preoccupations, desires and fears as him, regardless of the difference in position. But what good were such principles if you couldn't use them to defend a man poorly treated? He picked up the telegram from Helen again. If only they had caught the earlier train.

Later, he remembered that thought. *If only they had*

caught the earlier train. If only they had. And if only he had been less afraid to speak up for a man who was not fit to do his job. But he had always been afraid to do what would anger people, or shock them, even if it was right.

Fifty

Grace

Having announced to the room that it was my grandmother at the door, though I had no idea where my conviction had come from, a spell of dizziness overtook me and I sat down again.

'Your grandmother?' said Victoria, in astonishment. 'Did you invite her to the party? What a good idea! We are rather lacking in guests. I thought it best to put off my ladies and some of the neighbours, what with Papa not being at his best. But we would love to see your grandmother. Goodness, has she come all the way from Bristol for the afternoon? Well, she must stay tonight; she can't possibly go back in all this snow.'

David raised his eyebrows at me as I looked around anxiously. 'Are you all right, Gra— Miss Fairford? You've gone alarmingly pale.'

I had just managed an unconvincing nod when the bell rang again. Realizing it would be better if I got to her first, I tried to stand but my head spun.

'Oh, do go and let the poor woman in, David,' said Victoria. 'She'll be frozen to the step. Agnes is obviously out for the count.'

As he left, he gave me another searching look – not that I understood myself. I couldn't for the life of me work out what my grandmother might be doing at Fenix House – she'd said nothing about it in her recent letter. Hearing two sets of footsteps on the stairs a moment later, I felt nauseous at the thought of what she might be saying to David – not to mention what she might be about to say to Victoria and the others shortly. And of what they might say when they knew she was the governess who had been dismissed for what reason I still didn't know but suspected was to do with their father. I glanced at the sleeping old man, who would surely wake at the interruption, and took a shaky breath.

Of course, in fearing a scene of terrible awkwardness, I'd forgotten the power of my grandmother's innate charm and good manners. When she came into the room, David behind her, she was beaming and he was laughing appreciatively at something she'd obviously just said. On catching sight of me, she came forward and took me in her arms.

'Oh, my lovely girl,' she breathed into my ear, as we embraced. 'I have missed you so very much.'

The relief of being in the same room as her again almost overwhelmed me. My anxiety dissolved as quickly as it had gathered. I couldn't believe in that moment that I'd resented her, or how I'd survived without her. Even those instances of her not telling the truth, or at least withholding it, suddenly didn't seem to matter, not in the face of her being there, next to me. It was all so long ago, after all.

When the sob I was so determined not to let out in front of everyone had finally been swallowed, I looked nervously at the others. Robert, at least, remained asleep, his chin lowered to his chest. To my surprise – or perhaps not, given what the new arrival had been to him – it was the myopic Bertie who was peering hard at my grandmother. Victoria was smiling politely with no sign of recognition, waiting for the moment when she could dart forward and, as Fenix House's chatelaine, begin the introductions.

My grandmother, seeing Bertie stare, smiled expectantly at him. She seemed entirely undaunted to be back.

'Is it – you?' he began wonderingly. 'No, it can't be. But . . . Miss Jenner?' His eyes filled with tears.

My grandmother went forward and clasped his hands warmly. 'Bertie. Of course you've grown up. Goodness, I can hardly believe it's been so long.' When Bertie had recovered himself, a look of wonder replacing the tears that had threatened, she turned to Victoria. 'And what about you, little Miss Vicky? Don't you remember your old governess?'

For the second time that afternoon, Victoria was rendered temporarily speechless. After the initial shock, she rushed forward to embrace the woman who had once taught her her sums. When the exclamations of delight and surprise had died down, she turned to me. 'Why on earth didn't you tell us you were related to Miss Jenner?'

'I – I wanted to but . . .' I was unsure how to put it.

'Grace wanted to stand on her own two feet here. She'd been under my wing for so long and it was time she struck out alone. And, don't forget, dear Vicky, your mother asked me to leave. I'm afraid I didn't tell Grace when she applied for the position – I didn't want that particular cloud hanging over her. After all, what happened so long ago has nothing to do with her.'

She gave Victoria and Bertie another of her winning smiles, then caught sight of Robert.

'Oh, of course,' said Victoria, following her arrested gaze. 'You know my father, too. Papa, are you awake? We have a very special guest here to see you.'

As the old man's eyelids fluttered open, I wondered what was going through my grandmother's mind. She had once cared deeply for him, but he was now so old and faded, so reduced from the person she must have seen last. But perhaps he wasn't, not to her. As I watched her approach the bed, she looked as if someone had lit her up from inside. It made her young again – closer, no doubt, to how she had been then. For the first time, I saw how much my mother had resembled her; how I did, too.

She sat on the edge of the bed and gently took his hand. 'Robert, it is I, Harriet Jenner. Do you remember me?'

He started and, blinking rapidly, grasped her hand with both of his, as if to stop her slipping away again. 'Can it be you? Am I dreaming or have you come back to me?'

Victoria and Bertie exchanged anxious looks.

'Papa, dear, it's not Helen,' said Victoria. 'It's Miss Jenner, our governess in . . . in . . . When would it have been?'

'Eighteen seventy-eight,' Bertie said quietly.

'I know it's not Helen,' Robert said, as he tried to push himself up into a sitting position. 'You all think me an imbecile. My dearest Helen is gone. I know who this is. It's Harriet. They look nothing alike. Helen, in fact, was helping me to look for her before . . .'

My grandmother stared at him as he began to cough from his exertions, his poor chest heaving and rattling. I thought he had probably worsened over the course of the day, his face gaunt and his hands trembling. When he had recovered himself, he lay back against his pillows, eyes closed. A single tear rolled down his cheek. 'You have come back to me,' he whispered. 'I prayed that you would, oh, for so many years. And now you have.'

I looked at the people who were still his children. Victoria was half moved and half bemused, while Bertie seemed caught between happiness and dejection. I suddenly remembered David, who would surely think the scene rather ridiculous, and glanced back at him. He was looking not at his grandfather but at me. I almost flinched, his stare was so intense. He was my employer just as Robert had been Harriet's. For the first time, I could truly imagine how something might have sprung up between them, even in those very different times.

Fifty-one

Harriet

When she left Fenix House some three weeks after the captain's birthday celebration, she was convinced it would be for the last time. Summer had slunk away at some point between the party and the day of her departure. On that last morning, as she stepped outside, there was a distinct edge to the breeze that blew a strand of hair across her face. It was still early, not yet six, and no one in the house had risen. Still, she thought Robert might have heard her, or even sensed that she was about to leave, and come down the stairs after her. It was why she was moving so slowly, of course. She was hoping he would still catch her, beg her not to go, tell her that he would overrule anything his wife had said.

He had got in late from his work on the railways; it had been almost midnight when she had heard the click of the front door two floors down, but she presumed he would see the note she'd left him. Failing that, she assumed the mistress would be unable to resist telling him how she had dismissed the governess. But perhaps the tonics Mary had been taking her all day had rendered her unconscious, and perhaps Robert had been too tired to go to his study.

Harriet was halfway across the gravel when at last she heard footsteps on the stone steps. In hindsight, they were far too light to be his, but she still let her valise drop to the ground. It wasn't Robert, of course: it was Helen, her face stricken.

'Oh, Miss Jenner, are you really going? I might have missed you if I hadn't woken so early and heard you moving about. Weren't you even going to say goodbye to us?'

Her face crumpled and Harriet reached out to her. 'Helen, little love. You're right, I should have said goodbye. It wasn't because I didn't care, you mustn't think that. It was only because I thought it would be too upsetting.'

They clung to each other for a while, Harriet biting the inside of her cheek so that she didn't weep. She could feel rather than hear Helen's sobs, her chest shuddering through the thin stuff of her nightgown. Reluctantly, Harriet extricated herself from the embrace. 'You must go in, darling. You'll catch a chill.'

'I brought you this.' The little girl held up something that dangled and spun from a narrow chain.

'What is it?'

'It's my locket. Papa gave it to me but now I want you to have it, so you remember me. Look, it's even got your initial on it. Ours are the same.' She turned the oval locket and pointed out the 'H'. There was more to the inscription but the dawn light was too weak to read the tiny letters.

'I can't take this, Helen.'

She looked as though she would burst into tears again. 'Please, Miss Jenner. Then we will always have a . . . a connection.'

Harriet glanced up at the windows of the house. She thought she saw an upstairs curtain twitch. She must leave now, or it wouldn't be Robert who came down but his wife. She didn't feel equal to another scene with the mistress, not today.

'Well, Helen, if I am to take your beautiful locket, then you must have something of mine in exchange. Then we will each have something to remind us of the other.' She twisted off the fire-opal ring that she had worn for so long. 'Take care of it, won't you? It's not worth very much, but it belonged to my mother.'

Helen's eyes shone as she took it and slid it on to her thumb, which it fitted perfectly. 'As I get bigger, I will move it on to the other fingers,' she said. 'I will treasure it always.'

'And I your locket.' Harriet reached up, fastened it round her neck, then tucked it inside her dress. The metal was cold against her bare skin, but it warmed quickly.

She didn't take it off to read the rest of the inscription until she was safely on a train bound for London. *Betwixt and between you may be, but beloved of me*. A message for a middle child who had the distinction of being neither the first-born nor the baby. It could have applied to a governess such as herself just as well: neither family nor servant, trapped on the turn of the stairs. She stroked the H. It could so easily have been a gift from him to her. Perhaps, in her mind at least, this could be his farewell, as well as Helen's. His parting gift.

Her decision to flee to London was not simply a homing instinct, though there was reassurance in the anonymity the capital's crowds would offer. She had a plan: another kind of revenge against the Dauceys who, as far as she was still concerned, so roundly deserved it. She had only remembered the solicitors' names because they were worthy of one of Mr Dickens's tales: Juggins and Wraith. She could still hear the way Captain Dauncey had enunciated the names to his sister in the parlour one evening, his voice hoarse from too many of his filthy cheroots.

As with all the other occasions she had found herself eavesdropping, it wasn't that she'd meant to: it was simply that she always seemed to be walking past when something potentially useful was being said. It wasn't her fault that the captain's voice carried so – one might have argued that he *meant* others to hear what he said, whether it was about his popularity at the garrison, his unrivalled capacity for drink, or his financial affairs.

In order for her plan to be successful, she decided that her appearance must take precedence over the quality of her accommodation. She took a cheap room in a grubby street near Liverpool Street station and, as soon as the landlady had left her alone, sat down and wrote a short letter in handwriting that was not her own. She then caught an omnibus to Piccadilly, where she entered a shop that was smart but not frighteningly grand and spent almost all her remaining money on a warm cloak, stylish hat, beaded reticule, and a length of moss green velvet that she ordered to be made up into a fashionable gown, paying extra so that it would be ready within the week.

There was another place she wished to visit while she was so far west. She hoped it would steady her nerves for what she was planning to do once her dress was ready. She was expecting all signs of it to be gone, eradicated as if it never was – she knew that the fire had destroyed everything inside her father's auction house the night she'd smelt smoke on the air.

London wasn't a sentimental place – not the London she had known – and she was sure the charred hole in the street had long been plugged, that another dozen businesses would have passed through the replacement building since. What stunned her, and made her weep where she stood, even as barrows, hansom cabs and hawkers threatened to knock her off her feet, was that a wall of the original building had survived. On it, in letters faint but still visible, especially to someone who had known their shape even before she could read, was her own name – her father's name – a ghostly 'Jenner' marking the bricks, like a tomb to the man who had lost his livelihood on this very spot.

She had been there a long time when she realized she was shivering. Drying her eyes, she walked away without so much as a glance over her shoulder. If she had gone there to be galvanized, she couldn't have wished for more. The cold had made her clear-headed and resolute – and that feeling hadn't dimmed by the time her dress was delivered.

After hooking herself with some difficulty into the new gown, which was intended for a woman who did not have to dress herself, she placed the room's solitary rickety chair in the middle of the floor. Clambering up on to it, she peered at her reflection in the foxed mirror above the washstand. It was the only way she could view herself from head to toe. She was too far away to be able to see herself in any great detail but, still, she couldn't help but smile, so well did she look. Her natural antipathy towards the colour green had made her hesitate in the shop, but she was glad she had taken the woman's advice now.

'That one suits you best of all,' she had said, and she had been right. She had also remarked that the green brought out the warmth of Harriet's hair, and on that point she had also been correct – which made it rather a shame that by the time she put on the gown to pay a visit to Juggins and Wraith, every trace of gold and bronze had been eradicated, her hair dyed a startling jet black. To her surprise, it was just as the packet had promised – she had been worried that the noxious powder would turn it the colour of pond-weed. Combing it out over her shoulders to dry, she kept catching her eye in the glass.

Even allowing for the clouded glass, she looked like a completely different person: her skin more luminous against the newly dark tresses, her eyes even more enormous – especially once she had mixed a little glycerine with lampblack and dabbed it on her lashes. She had changed her hair to convince the solicitors of her story; only now did she realize that her transformation would also convince herself that, at least temporarily, she was someone else.

To her satisfaction, the solicitors' premises were only a few streets from where she had lived her previous life with her father. The captain had said that his own father had used them before him so their practice must have been there all the while, going about its business even as she grew up a quarter of a mile away. She felt as though in some strange way it had been waiting for her, and perhaps – from the moment Juggins and Wraith had taken on the dubious affairs of Josiah Dauncey – it had.

Earlier that morning, she had dressed herself with painstaking care, brushing the velvet nap of the new gown and arranging her hat so that her newly raven tresses were easily visible beneath. The cloak fastened only at the neck, which meant it billowed out when she walked, offering flashes of the rich green of the dress. She had no doubt that the finished ensemble was striking: heads turned from the moment she stepped into the street – and not furtively either, but as if she was something so exotic and apart from the everyday that their owners were permitted to stare quite openly.

Juggins and Wraith's small establishment was down one of the narrow medieval lanes that had survived in the old City, where the upper storeys of the ancient buildings lurched drunkenly towards those opposite, their proximity such that most of the available daylight was eliminated, giving the impression to those passing beneath that they were no longer outside. The premises, when she reached them, did not look entirely respectable, the bottle-glass windows filmed with soot and, above them, in flaking gold letters, the name of the firm, the 'J' of Juggins lying prostrate on its back. This, however, was of no consequence to Harriet, who had come too far to turn back; who, indeed, now had little choice but to continue forging ahead.

A bell rang as she pushed open the door, announcing her arrival. A young clerk with stringy, colourless hair glanced up, then straight back down to his ledger, with all the practice of someone who took care to make every visitor feel dismissed. That he couldn't help but look immediately back up, his eyes catching fast this time on the slight but arresting figure in the doorway, further confirmed the success of Harriet's altered appearance. The knowledge filled her with a novel and potent kind of power. As it flooded through her, she felt her spine straighten and her chin lift.

'I have come to see Mr Wraith,' she said clearly. 'My husband, Captain Jago Dauncey, wrote to make an appointment for ten o'clock this morning. Unfortunately he has been detained in the country, his beloved sister suddenly taken gravely ill, so I have come in his stead.'

The clerk consulted the ledger in front of him, running his finger up and down a scrawled list of what were presumably that day's appointments. 'I'm sorry, Mrs Dauncey, but I can't see anything in that name.'

'Please check again,' she heard herself say imperiously. She was prepared for this answer. Naturally there was no appointment: there had been no letter from Captain Dauncey. 'Perhaps you have entered the appointment on the wrong day.'

He checked again, turning pages in the ledger and studying those too. 'I'm afraid it is simply not there, madam. There has been no mistake.'

She had hoped he would be a little more apologetic. She changed tack, raising her hand to her breast and letting it flutter there. 'Oh dear. Then I am at a loss as to what to do. My husband said the letter was posted three days ago, from Cheltenham. He assured me there would be no difficulty in seeing Mr Wraith, with whom he recently left something of significant value. What a shame when he considers Mr Wraith to be such a great friend.'

The clerk held up his hand. 'Fortunately, madam, Mr Wraith is in this morning. If you will take a seat, I will go and see if he is available. If he is not, I'm afraid you will have to return another day.'

'But I do not have another day. Tomorrow I travel to Southampton where I am due to meet my husband. We are sailing back to India. Please make sure you impress this urgency upon Mr Wraith. I shall not take up more than ten minutes of his time. It is quite a simple matter.'

She gave the clerk a smile both dazzling and tremulous and watched him visibly relent. 'Just a moment, Mrs Dauncey. I will do my best.'

Once he had disappeared, she removed her cloak and checked her elaborate hairstyle still held. The shape of it felt odd under her hands – she was used to the simple knot she habitually wore at the nape of her neck. Satisfied that everything was in order, she opened her reticule to check the envelope was still safely stowed inside. She was convinced that if she could only get in to see Wraith and show him the contents of that packet, she would be successful.

The clerk was back within a minute, his demeanour subtly more obsequious. 'Mr Wraith will be very glad to see you, Mrs Dauncey, if you'd like to follow me.'

He led her down a dim, narrow passage panelled in wood, with the same dark boards creaking underfoot. At the end of it was a stout door, which opened into a large but low-ceilinged room. A well-built fire had made it airless, an impression heightened when Harriet noticed there was no window. Sitting behind a great slab of mahogany desk was an enormously fat man, who rose to greet her with some effort.

She recalled what she had overheard the captain once

say, during an elaborate meal of lobster, salmon in cucumber sauce, stuffed bullock hearts and Mrs Rollright's infamous pepper relish: 'You'll never meet anyone so unsuitably named as Henry Wraith. He's as big as an outhouse, while Juggins can't walk past the operating theatre at St Thomas's without fearing he'll be taken as a fresh cadaver. The pair of them ought to swap names, and I said as much to Wraith, to his great amusement.'

'Mrs Dauncey!' exclaimed Wraith now. 'What an unexpected pleasure. Thank goodness you were not entirely put off by Higgins here.' He waved the clerk away, then began the process of wedging himself back into his chair, mopping his forehead once he had accomplished the manoeuvre. This done, he looked Harriet over thoroughly. She felt her armpits prickle with sweat and was glad she had removed her cloak. She could already see why the captain had formed such a rapport with the man.

'Good Lord,' he said admiringly, 'Dauncey didn't exaggerate when he told me his new bride was a beauty. What he failed to mention was that she had joined him on his voyage from India. In fact, I was under the impression that –'

'Mr Wraith,' she began, in a low, confiding tone, her eyes demurely lowered, allowing her to look up at him prettily every so often through darkened lashes. 'You know my husband. He is a passionate man. A possessive man. If you must know the truth, he has kept me quite hidden away these weeks we have been in England.'

Wraith chuckled. 'Who could blame the man for keeping such a treasure to himself?'

She dropped her eyes again. 'I know he confided in you

467

about our marriage, of course – he knew you to be a man of the world – but he also knew his family would prove rather more . . . difficult, that his sister Louisa – Lulu, as he so fondly calls her – in particular might object to me as his wife. I'm sure you understand my meaning. So, after some weeks with me, he went ahead to Cheltenham alone, while I stayed on here. He was due to return yesterday and see you himself but Louisa has been taken ill. Perhaps he has told you how fragile her health is. We are due to sail from Southampton tomorrow evening so, rather than come all the way to London, he is intending to go straight to the port from his sister's house.'

'The two of you are returning to India, I presume?'

Harriet nodded, giving in to her urge to peel off her gloves. It was so very hot in the room. She laced her fingers together so that she wouldn't be tempted to put them to her damp forehead. Though she had rinsed her hair carefully, she was afraid the black dye might have loosened and stained her skin in the excessive heat of the room. She didn't know how such a well-upholstered man as Wraith could stand such an extreme temperature.

'I should take a boat out there myself,' he said, as if reading her mind. 'Find an exotic bloom of my own. As you can tell, I can't bear the English climate. The endless damp, the chilly air. I believe the blazing heat of India would suit me very well.'

'You would be very welcome to stay with us, should you ever decide to come,' she said, with a smile. 'Now, I apologize for returning to business but my time before departure is short and I have some errands yet to run today.'

468

Wraith leaned forward as much as his stomach would allow. 'Go on, Mrs Dauncey. What is it I can do for you? I am all ears.'

'Well, as you know, my husband entrusted you with something of value when he saw you last.'

'Yes?'

'A quantity of gemstones.' She swallowed. If the captain had invented the haul to impress his sister, she was undone. But, after a pause, Wraith nodded. Something in his expression had sharpened, though. His obvious admiration of her looks, her supposedly exotic blood, would only get her so far.

She rooted in her bag and brought out the envelope. 'Here is the receipt for them, which your clerk wrote out some six weeks ago.'

She pushed it across the desk. He picked it up and put on his spectacles.

'It seems a shame that Captain Dauncey did not see fit to put a ring on his new bride's finger,' he said, quite casually.

Harriet looked up quickly. He was no fool, Wraith. How had she forgotten to wear a wedding band when she had taken such care with everything else? She had meant to move her mother's ring to her left hand but then she had given it to Helen.

She licked her dry lips. 'Why do you think he wishes to have the stones returned, sir, if not to set a few in a ring for me? Unfortunately there was no time to have it made before we left India.'

Wraith folded the receipt and sat back in his chair, crossing his arms over his stomach. 'Mrs Dauncey, forgive

469

me, but I would feel more comfortable if I had a letter from the captain, giving me express permission to release these items to you. The receipt . . . well, it could have been picked up by anyone.'

'Oh, but I have that. How foolish of me not to bring it out in the first place. Jago – my husband – sent this to me a few days ago. He said he had posted the request for an appointment with you at the same time, which is why I was surprised it had gone astray. What a relief he was clever enough to send both.'

'Indeed. Sounds remarkably prudent for Captain Dauncey, if you don't mind me saying so.'

She pushed a second piece of paper across the desk. She had hoped she wouldn't need it, though she was confident she had made an excellent job of the forgery, the second of the captain's handwriting she had now made.

She had always been skilled at copying, amusing her father as a child by learning to replicate his signature so accurately that he hadn't been able to tell which were his own marks and which hers. Towards the end of his life, when he had grown too weak to sit at his desk, she had entirely taken over his correspondence, and no one had been any the wiser. She wondered if her father had ever written to Mr Wraith, over the matter of the money unreturned by the Daunceys. The thought made something deep inside her harden a little more.

After what seemed an age in the stifling room, Wraith reached into a drawer and pulled out a bunch of keys. Before he got to his feet, he beamed at Harriet, all suspicion apparently melted away. 'Well, Mrs Dauncey, everything appears to be in order. Let's find your wedding jewels for you. How well the rubies will look with your dark hair.'

She forced herself to smile back. *Almost there*, she told herself. *Just a few minutes more of holding my nerve.*

Not ten minutes later, Harriet was back on the street, a small but weighty parcel stowed right at the bottom of her reticule. Gripping it tightly, she nodded through the glass at the clerk, who still stared, and clipped quickly away. She was far too agitated to wait for, then sit in an omnibus so she decided to walk the twenty minutes it would take to reach the jewel merchants of Hatton Garden. The cool autumn air, even with the city's requisite tang of ordure and smoke, was delicious to Harriet. She filled her lungs with it.

Fifty-two

Grace

Once the detritus on the trestle table had been cleared away, the Pembridges disappeared to different parts of the house, as if sensing that my grandmother and I needed to be alone. Robert had gone back to sleep, his breathing more laboured than it had been since the previous night. If it made him happy, I hoped he was dreaming of a young Harriet Jenner.

We were the last to leave him in peace and I paused at the top of the stairs that led down from the attic. 'They've put me in your old room, you know.' I pointed to the door at the other end of the passage. The door that led to the humble little room my grandmother had so exaggerated. For the first time in my memory she looked a little sheepish.

'Ah,' she said wistfully. 'So you didn't get the rose-pink carpet and vast feather bed you were hoping for?'

'It seems they never existed. Why did you lie to me about something like that? It doesn't matter if you didn't have a great big room.'

'Of course it does. I created for you the room I would have liked, the sort of room I should have had.'

'And might very well have had, had things turned out differently?'

'Something like that. What harm did it do, to embroider a little? It was my past, my story.'

She had always won arguments, not that we'd had many. I had generally agreed with everything she said. Now, however, I felt some of my previous resentment rise to the surface. 'It wasn't just your story, though, was it?' I said. 'You sent me back here. You put me in it, and when I got here, some of it was wrong. It made me feel like the ground was shifting under me. I'd left home behind and then I felt as though I'd lost Fenix House, too. Or at least the Fenix House I'd always known.'

'I told you what you wanted to hear as a little girl, what I thought would interest you, amuse you.'

'Is that why you also omitted so much?'

She looked sharply at me. 'Shall we go somewhere to talk about this more privately?'

We went downstairs in silence and, guessing it the least likely room to be occupied by anyone else, I led her to the old study. She paused on the threshold, her hand on the wooden jamb and her eyes far away. Then, seeing my curious look, she passed by me into the room.

It was as dusty as last time I'd been inside but my grandmother didn't seem to notice. She went to the desk and lifted a corner of the dust-sheet away, running her hand over the tooled surface. With her thumb, she lifted one side of the blotter in the middle, then let it drop, sending up a flurry of dust almost as thick as the snow that was swirling outside the window.

'It was summer when I was here last,' she said softly.

'I know,' I said, frustration creeping into my voice. 'You told me that much.'

473

She didn't reply, her eyes coming to rest on the portrait of Frannie, as mine had. I was fleetingly glad for a solitary detail that had unquestionably altered since her days at Fenix House.

'Who's that?'

'David's – Mr Pembridge's late wife. Lucas's mother.'

'Yes, of course. And how do you like your employer?' she said, with an odd smile.

'I don't know. He's easier to talk to now than he was. We get along well enough. Why? Are you going to tell me he's got something to do with what you were saying in your letter? About me being so happy here?' I sounded defensive and knew I was flushed with embarrassment.

'Oh, darling, don't be cross. I have such a good feeling about you.'

Her smile, when I knew so little, was infuriating and I was just about to say so when she drew closer to the portrait and pointed. 'She's wearing my ring,' she said delightedly. 'Do you see the fire opal on her right hand? She's got it on her little finger but it fitted me on my ring finger. That was my mother's ring once, but I gave it to Helen when I left. She gave me her locket in return. She must have passed the ring to her daughter-in-law. I take it David Pembridge's mother *is* Helen. Where is she today?'

I stared at her. 'Don't you know? I thought you would somehow. She died in 1910.'

Her hand went up to her mouth and her eyes filled with tears. 'So he didn't get my note,' she said, half to herself. 'Or, if he did, he didn't understand it. Poor Helen.'

'What note?' I said. And then realization – or some clouded approximation of it – dawned.

'She was killed in the same train crash as Mother and Father. But you probably knew that, didn't you?'

Her face paled as I watched it. She went to the chair behind the desk and sat down heavily. 'The train crash?' she repeated. 'Helen? Oh, dear God, no. No, I didn't know anything of that. Grace, you know how the glimmers are. They are never a complete picture. You know I didn't see what would happen to your parents until it almost had, but with Helen it was different – the glimmer was so much vaguer, a flash of blinding light and then, clearer, a year, 1910. I had a bad feeling about her when I had it, but so much had happened that night and so much happened after it. I never had a glimmer about her again and I suppose the power of it faded. I did try to warn them when I left this place. Really, what more could I do, banished as I was? Oh, poor dear Helen.'

I went and perched on the window-seat, which wasn't deep enough to be very comfortable, and looked at my grandmother behind the desk. It dwarfed her tiny frame.

'You asked about my employer just now,' I said. 'What about yours?'

She was making a pattern in the desk's layer of dust with her fingertip. It was such a girlish gesture that I could momentarily see her again as she would have been. It was easy enough in that room, with the light from the snow outside making her hair glow in the gloom. In the shadows, her lithe form might have belonged to a woman half her age; younger, even.

'I keep thinking about that clock,' I continued when she didn't reply. 'The one you said the Pembridges gave you and Grandfather as a wedding present. How could they have done, when you were dismissed? Never mind about the pink bedroom that never existed, what about that? How could you have left that out? I understand why you might have done when I was young, but not now. Didn't you think I should know that minor detail before I left home to come here?'

'I'm afraid I bought the clock myself, when I got to Bristol. It was something solid – something that helped make the rooms I'd taken feel more permanent, more like the home I never thought I would have again. As for my dismissal, I didn't think you would agree to come here if I told you.'

I sighed. She was right. Of course I wouldn't. The glimmer's prophecy alone wouldn't have been enough against that. Something else occurred to me.

'That's why you thought it best I didn't tell them about my connection to you, isn't it? It wasn't because you wanted me to "strike out on my own", was it? It was because you were worried they'd throw me out if they knew. Well, Agnes worked it out. She saw the resemblance the other week. It was she who told me you'd been dismissed, though not intentionally. She thinks it very strange that you encouraged me to come here.'

'Does she?' My grandmother looked thoughtful. 'Yes, I suppose she must.'

I was just about to ask her about that mysterious dismissal when she stood, went over to the hearth and, before I could stop her, turned the handle that would ring the bell in Agnes's domain.

'What are you doing? I can go down and get us some tea, if that's what you want. Agnes isn't well and, besides, it isn't our place to ring the bells.'

She looked archly at me. 'Are we not good enough, then?'

I held up my hands in exasperation. 'Grandmother, it's not our house.'

'Do you not count as one of them, too?'

I stared at her, my breath held. Was she about to admit that Robert Pembridge was my grandfather?

'Robert said to me once that even the servants were part of the family. Not that his wife agreed, of course.'

I sighed again, still no closer to getting a straight answer out of her.

'I gather *she's* dead,' my grandmother continued.

Slightly unnerved by the vehemence in her voice, I nodded. 'Years ago, apparently.'

'I'm not surprised – the potions and miracle cures she used to pour down her throat. She wouldn't let any fresh air into her rooms, you know. She even had John paint the windows shut. She was convinced that harmful vapours and emanations would steal in and make her ill. The last time I saw her she looked dreadful – I could see how things would be for her, how she'd barely leave those stuffy rooms, how she'd be struck down by one malady after another. She had been pretty, if you like that sort of thing – ringlets and plump flesh and round blue eyes – but it was fast fading by the time I left.'

The door opened, making me jump. It was Agnes.

She didn't notice my grandmother, sitting as she was in the shadows, only me, illuminated in the window by the very dregs of the day's light.

She put an unsteady hand to her breast. 'Oh, it's only you, Grace. I thought . . . I thought . . . You see, no one comes in here now so when that bell started up it gave me quite a turn. I didn't know what to think.'

'You didn't think it was a ghost, did you, Agnes?' My grandmother rose to her feet. The light caught the side of her, her hair still streaked with rosy gold. 'Well, perhaps it was a ghost, of a kind.' She smiled.

Fifty-three

Agnes gasped and took a step back when my grandmother began to speak. I suppose she did look rather spectral standing there, the last trickle of daylight illuminating her queerly. Even in the gloom, I could see that the house-keeper's face had turned the colour of chalk again.

'Good God, you've taken a decade off me,' she managed to say. I could see her large bosom heaving with the shock of it. 'I never thought to see you again, even when I knew who she was.' She gestured towards me. 'You're here to pay her a little visit, I take it?' Her voice sounded oddly desperate.

'Of course she is, Agnes, what else?' I said, but then I wondered. I looked at her. 'Why are you here, Grandmother? You didn't say anything about it in your letter. Is it just to see me, or have you come for another reason?'

Agnes slumped into an upright chair without removing its dust-sheet.

'Oh, please don't worry, Agnes,' my grandmother said, going to her. She crouched stiffly at the housekeeper's feet and took her hands. 'It's not *that* I'm here about so I'm sorry if I startled you. It has nothing to do with you.'

'No?'

'I promise.'

Agnes considered this and eventually let out a shaky laugh. 'You won't be able to get up again, not if you stay down there much longer. We're neither of us as young as we once was.' She stood up, with a wince, herself. 'I'm glad to see you, I must say, and I never thought I'd say that after . . . Well, you know. Now, seeing as you rang, can I get you anything? I'm feeling a bit more myself, all in all.'

I looked at her in astonishment. She never offered anything that involved her going up and down the stairs.

'Oh, thank you, Agnes,' said my grandmother. 'A pot of tea would be lovely, if you're sure you don't mind.'

When she'd gone, I rounded on my grandmother. 'What was all that about? Agnes looked like she was about to expire. Is it something to do with whatever she's got hidden in the ice-house? David said there was nothing down there but a rotten old bag. Did you catch her stealing something all that time ago and she was afraid you'd come back to tell? She told me she'd stored something there back then – it was how she hurt her hip and why you ended up getting dismissed, supposedly. She told me all this one afternoon when she'd had too much sherry. After what happened at the Blue today, I wanted to ask her what this mysterious hoard was, but she went off before I had the chance. I feel it must all be connected somehow, but I haven't been able to fit the pieces together, despite your faith that I would.'

'The Blue?' repeated my grandmother, ignoring my sarcasm. 'What's the Blue?'

I waved my hand dismissively. 'It's where the quarry ruins used to be. Still are, I suppose, under the water. Lucas named it that – the limestone has made it this incredible opaque turquoise colour over the years.'

480

'I was there the day that place was flooded. The water was clearer then, of course.'

'It's a strange place. Beautiful, I suppose, but I don't like it.'

She looked at me sharply. 'No, I didn't either.'

I remembered something else. 'Agnes said today that the little dagger you gave me was the mistress's – that her brother gave it to her. Grandmother, I know it wasn't just Robert who . . . noticed you. You turned Jago Dauncey's head too, didn't you? Was that the real reason the mistress dismissed you? Because first her husband fell in love with you and then her brother found himself moonstruck too?' I could just make out her face and it looked as if I'd slapped it. 'What?' I faltered. 'What have I said?'

'Moonstruck,' she said, after a pause. 'What a strange word to think of.'

'But, Grandmother, am I right? Was that why she really wanted you gone from here?'

'Perhaps, but I couldn't have stayed much longer anyway.'

I leaned back against the cold window, my arms folded. 'This is all riddles to me. I'm trying to ask you about my grandfather.' My voice broke. 'There was no travelling salesman, was there? Agnes said as much, though she tried to cover it. It's Robert, isn't it? My mother was a Pembridge and I am too.' I went to her and knelt as she had done in front of Agnes. 'Please tell me the truth. I need to know if they are my family.'

She didn't say anything for a long time. Suddenly exhausted, I rested my head against her knee and she began stroking my hair. It had always soothed me as a child and it did then, in the dark and dust-sheeted study.

'I wish I could tell you that he's your grandfather,' she said eventually. I raised my head. 'I wish with all my heart that he was.'

I waited for what she would say next. I couldn't read her face – the day had finally surrendered to night. The snow must have just stopped because the newly waxing moon was now visible, just a narrow curve of bone-white.

I put my hand to my pocket and felt the slight weight of the dagger swing against my hip. Agnes had said it was his – the other one. Jago. I brought it out and held it up in the weak light. My grandmother started.

'It's not Robert because it was him, wasn't it?' I said softly. 'It was Jago Dauncey who seduced you.'

'He did not seduce me!' Her voice rang out in the room, shaking with anger and something I'd never known in my grandmother. It was fear.

'Did he . . . force you?' I swallowed. Was that why she had given me the little dagger? To protect myself as she had been unable to?

Her breathing was jagged and I suddenly felt awful for making her dredge everything up. I still needed to know, though, and felt that if I let her go now, she would skitter away from my questions for ever.

I removed the dagger's scabbard and laid the blade on the desk to the side of us. It glinted dimly in the moonlight, a darker twin to that bright paring in the sky outside. I remembered what I'd sensed and seen up at the Blue: the tobacco smoke that had curled through the air, the vibration of menace, and the face in the water – a face with ice-blue eyes. Dauncey eyes. I hung my head, the blood thrumming in my ears. His blood, partly. If I wasn't a Pembridge, I had to be a Dauncey.

My grandmother squeezed my hand. 'I'm so sorry, Grace,' she said softly. 'I should have told you I was dismissed, that I wasn't waved off on the drive and given a gilt clock. But I didn't invent all of it, not at all. Your grandfather was a travelling salesman – it's just that I met him after I'd got to Bristol. I didn't love him like I loved Robert – and I did love Robert a great deal – but he was a good man. He died when your mother was very young and I was terribly sad, of course, but I knew the two of us would get along well enough without a man in the house. Just as you and I did, all those years later.'

I tried one last time. 'Are you sure, Grandmother?' I said. 'Is that really what happened? There are no photographs or . . .'

'No,' she said. 'They were expensive, you know, and we didn't have much to spare. I was only comfortable later, when your father came along and fell in love with your mother. In terms of position – if nothing else, of course – your father married beneath him. Not that he thought about that for a second. He was entranced by her.' She sounded quite different now, all the fear and anger smoothed away.

As a child I had heard many versions of this story of my parents, and it was as soothing as her small hand stroking my hair. I knew I would never have the heart to speak to her of Jago Dauncey now. What good would it do anyway? The man I was reasonably certain had been my grandfather was long gone – lost to India or the depths years before.

'That brother of hers had nothing to do with it,' my grandmother went on, with a brittle little laugh. 'Of course he didn't. You're even more inventive than I to think of such a thing.'

I paused, then nodded slowly. Leaning into her, I closed my eyes and waited for her hands to reach out to my hair again.

Fifty-four

Harriet

So disturbed and distracted was Harriet's state of mind in the weeks after the night of the fireworks party that she didn't notice a particular date come and go. When she finally realized, her courses were already many days late. That had never happened before. Since her thirteenth year, she had been blessed with a highly regular visitor, which paid its call every twenty-eight days, as reliable as the new moon. By the sixteenth day, with no sign of it, she was so desperate for reassurance that she almost confided in Agnes.

What stopped her was the understanding that, once she had spoken aloud the terrible suspicion, she could no longer deny it to herself. She would see Agnes's expression of horror and pity and know that there would be consequences for her that no amount of diverted spring water could ever cover and drown.

Of course, while his seed continued to grow inside her, she knew she would have to leave. The only question was when, though she would have liked more time than she was ultimately given. She had only just begun to outline a plan that might save her from the poorhouse when Victoria decided to investigate what Agnes had hidden in the ice-house.

485

Fortunately, her plan – to raise some funds by first procuring, then selling the captain's gemstones in London – worked. The sum had not been excessively large – the rubies were small and far from flawless – but it had been enough for Harriet to start again, enough to reinvent herself as a widow in a new place.

She didn't look backwards when she boarded the train at Paddington, the packet of money tucked for safety inside her bodice. She felt herself to be done with London. However kind it had been to her during the previous week, the city would always be the scene of her father's ruin. Her head told her, as it had once before in the morning room, that she should go east or north, where there were no connections to her past. But her heart, which was still full of Robert, drew her back to his Great Western Railway. She could not return to Cheltenham; that went without saying. But Bristol was surely far enough away and large enough to hide in.

There, decked out in her half-mourning of lavender and grey, she began to prepare for the daughter who was coming. She knew it would be a daughter. As she had briefly turned herself into Mrs Dauncey, she now became Mrs Richards in her father's honour – a respectable widow whose husband had died bravely in the Kurram Valley of Afghanistan, during the battle of Peiwar Kotal. It seemed fitting that she use one of the British Army's endless conflicts abroad to hide the shameful truth.

It wasn't only her enduring feelings for Robert that made her want to stay in the West Country. She had discovered that she wasn't quite finished with the Pembridges after all. The glimmers had told her so. One night, seven

months after she had rented a couple of small but pleasant rooms just off Whiteladies Road, she dreamed of a
return to Fenix House by someone who resembled but
was not her. She saw this young woman's gloved hand on
the gate to the house that had so quickly become familiar.
The glimmer, she knew, was many years away. Something
told her that it wasn't her daughter she glimpsed, the
daughter who was now large in her belly. It was another
girl. A girl who would come later, who would be loved in
that house and would not be banished as she had been.

Harriet often wondered what she would do if she saw
Robert again. Whenever circumstances had taken her
close to the GWR station at Temple Meads, she had found
herself looking out for him. And then, two years after she
had left Fenix House, she had seen a man with Robert's
broad shoulders crossing Queen Square. Walking with a
measured, surprisingly graceful stride, he was some way
ahead of her but, still, she was almost positive it was him.
She followed him at a distance, growing ever more convinced. She was close enough that, had he turned, he
might easily have spied the bright hair that showed under
her hat, the thought making her stomach lurch with fear
and longing.

When he reached the corner of the square and started
down Queen Charlotte Street, she made herself stop, letting the gap between them yawn until he was just another
figure in a dark coat and hat. It was so very hard to do it
but she had no choice. Not only was it her future granddaughter's destiny to go there and this time make a success
of it, but she was also afraid. What if they had found him?
What if they had discovered her and Agnes's terrible

secret? There had been nothing about it in the Cheltenham paper she now took – and of which she scoured every column inch – but who knew what the next issue would bring?

One thing she wished she could ask him about was the note. Had he received it? And, if so, had he understood it? It was now late 1880: the year of reckoning she had seen when she had stood on the lawn of Fenix House with Helen was still thirty years off. It seemed impossibly distant; she told herself that there was reams of time to write another note if she was still worried the first hadn't got through. Besides, what if she was wrong? The night she had felt it she had been so disturbed after what that man had done to her.

Nineteen ten: the year of the comet's return and so much else they couldn't yet know. She sat down on a bench in the square and tried to lure the glimmer in again, hoping it might finally relent and allow her to see it clearly, but the memory remained stubbornly amorphous and slippery. Something lost and something found: that was all it would give up to her.

Fifty-five

Grace

After my grandmother and I had been in the study for what felt like hours, Agnes having been and gone and the tea drunk, there was another tap at the door. This time it was Victoria.

'I'm so sorry to disturb you but it's Papa,' she said. Her face was drawn in the light shining in from the hallway. She was apparently too distracted to wonder why we were sitting there in the dark. 'Miss Jenner – I mean . . . oh dear, I don't know what to call you now – he's asking for you. I – I . . .' Her voice cracked. 'I think he's fading.'

'Yes,' said my grandmother, simply. She went over to Victoria and put a steadying hand on her back. They looked odd there, the little girl grown up to be a good head taller than her old governess.

'I've been up to the Atkinsons' to ring the doctor but he'd just left to go out on another call,' she said. 'His wife told me he'll be hours yet and, of course, the snow won't help with getting up here. The first thing I'm going to do on Monday is have a telephone installed. It's high time. This house has slumbered in the past for long enough.'

'You're absolutely right,' my grandmother said, with a gentle smile. 'I'll go to him now, shall I?'

Even though I knew Robert wasn't my grandfather

now, I wanted to see him too. I had grown very fond of him. I don't think I wanted to let my grandmother out of my sight, either. My initial feelings had returned and I felt winded anew by how much I had missed her. I caught up with her as she reached the turn in the stairs. It wasn't quite as dim as usual up there – Victoria must have turned up all the old gas lamps as high as they would go.

'Can I come too, or would you rather be alone with him?'

She turned and smiled at me, then reached out to brush my cheek. I could smell her scent: clean with a hint of roses. 'Come on, then,' she said.

'Grandmother, why did you come now, if it wasn't for me? You still haven't said.'

Turning to me again, she sighed deeply. 'No, I suppose it was a more selfish reason.' She started up the stairs again.

I hurried after her. 'What?'

She pointed up to the attic floor. 'Robert, of course.'

'But he's been here all these years and you didn't come.'

She smiled sadly. 'I wanted to say goodbye. I realized I wanted to do that more than I was afraid to come and face my past. The thought of seeing you too made it irresistible.'

'Do you mean that Robert is going to . . .?' I stopped and swallowed, so I didn't burst into tears.

'He's very old, Grace. He doesn't mind going now, I think.'

'You saw that he would?'

She nodded. 'And I came.'

'Sometimes, when I've been in to see him, he's thought I was you.'

'Well, it doesn't matter now. You've been kind to him and he knows that he's loved, that's the main thing. He'll die safe in his own bed at home.'

I hesitated, afraid of seeing someone so close to the end of their life. I thought of being old one day myself, and of Lucas and Essie growing up, and David being even older than me. It made me desperate not to waste any more time.

'You'll be fine, Grace,' she said. 'There's plenty of time for you.'

I drew back, suddenly afraid of her strange powers, but she laughed softly.

'I can't see half as much as you think I can. You forget I know you best in all the world, that I can read your face better than anyone. That's not the glimmers, that's being your only parent for the last twelve years.' She reached for my hand and we went up the remaining stairs together.

A single light burned in Robert's room, next to the bed. Fittingly, the scene resembled an Old Master, the sleeping man in his old-fashioned cambric nightgown lit by the lamp's gentle glow, the rest of the room fading into deep shadow. The train set had been turned off, the engine and its carriages still and quiet, as though out of respect. Robert looked peaceful but ancient, his face sunken and deeply scored, his withered body a gaunt outline under the bedclothes. He seemed to have aged ten years in the last week.

The scrape of the chair I had brought over to the bed woke him and he blinked anxiously at us until my grandmother took his hands as she had earlier.

'Robert, it's Harriet. And Grace is here too. Grace, my granddaughter. Miss Fairford, as you know her. Lucas's governess.'

He didn't take his eyes from hers. 'Is it really you, Harriet? Vicky says I imagine things.'

'Yes, I'm here.'

'Will you stay with me? It won't be long.'

'Of course I will. That's why I came back. How could I let you go without saying goodbye?'

He smiled and closed his eyes. 'We did try, Helen and I. But you were nowhere to be found. I even thought of putting a notice in the local paper but then I realized you wouldn't see it, wherever you were.'

My grandmother bowed her head. I thought of her in her corner of the parlour, her finger moving down the columns of the paper she'd always read so thoroughly. 'Well, I'm here now,' she said eventually. 'And I'm sorry I only said goodbye last time in a note.'

'What note?'

'I left you a note, a goodbye of sorts but also . . .'

The old man sighed. 'I never had it. Perhaps Louisa saw it first. What did it say?'

'It doesn't matter now.'

'Did it say something about Hel—,' I began.

My grandmother shot me a warning look just as Robert seemed to notice me for the first time.

'Who's there?'

'It's Grace, my granddaughter. She lives here now, as governess to Lucas.'

He shook his head as though it was too much to absorb. 'Can't see her properly,' he mumbled.

My grandmother motioned for me to go closer, so that my face would catch the light.

'Pretty girl,' he said. 'Like Esther.'

'He adores Victoria's daughter, Essie,' I whispered to my grandmother. 'He never forgets her, even when he can't remember who Lucas and David are.'

'Esther,' she repeated. Next to me, her normally erect carriage stiffened even more.

'She was the saving of me,' Robert continued, a smile briefly smoothing his face. 'If it hadn't been for her . . .' He shook his head. 'My lovely Helen.' I could hear his poor throat trying to swallow a sob. 'I couldn't give her back after that, do you see? She was ours, then. She had nobody else.'

Both of us were leaning in to catch the words, which were almost a murmur and running into each other in a blur. He was growing agitated, two spots of livid colour appearing on his cheeks, his hands pushing away my grandmother's to pluck at the sheets.

'Hush, now,' said my grandmother soothingly, though I could see that she was trembling slightly. 'Do you know what he's talking about?' she whispered urgently to me. 'What does he mean by "give her back"?'

I shook my head. 'I have no idea.'

'I told them she was ours,' the old man said, reaching again for my grandmother's hands. 'She had no one else, so where was the harm? We've treated her like she was one of our own. Like a Pembridge. Ah, but she was such a perfect little thing.'

'It's all right, Robert. Everything's all right. Calm down now.' My grandmother stroked his forehead.

I went over the words again, trying to make sense of them. Something cold touched my temple and, distracted, I looked up, even thinking the ceiling had sprung a leak and a drip of ice-cold water had fallen from the rafters. Of course, there was nothing.

Essie. I thought of her, with her cloak of pale hair and the musical voice that had so struck me the day I'd met her, out on the carriage turn. I could hear the same voice singing and I had never heard Essie sing. One of my long-treasured memories eddied through me: I was in my father's arms and we had reached my parents' bedroom door, behind which I knew something momentous was waiting with my mother. And then another memory came, a different one. This time I was in my childhood bed and my grandmother was reading me *Jane Eyre*, the words barely registering because I was trying so hard not to cry about everyone but her being lost to me, my fingers rubbing at the smooth satin edge of a muslin square.

My grandmother stood up to reach a glass of water on the table next to Robert and jolted me back to the present. As she leaned over, her old locket swung forward and caught the lamplight. Inside it, I knew, there were three tiny locks of hair. Hers, my mother's and – clipped from my infant head, to account for its wispy lightness, fluff blown from a dandelion – mine. Or so I'd always thought. Surely my hair had never been so pale, even as a baby.

'Esther,' I said, and the name's two syllables were strange in my mouth. Strange and entirely familiar, like a song you think you've forgotten until you hear it again, and find you know all the words. I reached out for my grandmother's sleeve.

She turned to look at me. There was something in her grey eyes I couldn't read, something huge, though I was certain this time that it wasn't a lie she was hiding.

'Yes?' she said shakily. 'Why is he so upset about her?'

We stared at each other, and I knew she was going over Robert's words again, just as I had. She frowned as her gaze fell on the train set that snaked around the room at our feet.

'I lost Helen that day,' Robert said from the bed, a little louder, a little more lucid, 'and that was the most terrible thing I could imagine. But then there she was, a gift in the midst of all that . . . destruction. Such a perfect little thing, quite undamaged. It was Bertie who found her, wrapped her up in his coat to keep her warm. She was meant for us, you see. For me and for Bertie, and especially for my tough little Vicky, who couldn't have a child and so wanted one.'

Exhausted by his confession, his head fell back against the pillow and his eyes closed. I turned to my grandmother. 'I don't understand. Is he saying that Essie is adopted? Why do you look like that?'

'I don't believe it,' she murmured. 'I was told they were gone. All of them were gone. I asked and they said the fire must have . . .'

I began to cry, great ugly sobs. Even as they flooded out of me, I didn't know why. The sound of them roused my grandmother from her thoughts.

'Oh, darling,' she said, pulling me to her. 'What have you remembered?'

'Nothing . . .' But then I did remember. I suddenly knew what had been behind my parents' door. I knew what I had carried so carefully across the shining, slippery dining-room floor. I knew whose muslin square I couldn't sleep without after the accident. My little sister's. Esther.

'But why didn't you . . .?' I couldn't even finish the question.

My grandmother was ashen. 'I didn't know. I swear to you I didn't know. I thought she'd died with your parents. They said she had but they must have assumed it because they couldn't find her. You see, there . . . well, there was so little left.'

'But why didn't I know she even existed until now? Why didn't you ever speak about her? Why was she kept a secret?'

She took my hand and squeezed it. 'Oh, Grace. My poor Grace. You became so forgetful after the accident. I didn't notice it at first, I was so weighed down by my own grief and . . . well, I suppose I didn't know you as well then as I came to. Eventually I noticed there were holes in your memory – places you simply would not go, just like you wouldn't in the cemetery where they were all buried, do you remember?'

I shook my head.

'We only went there once, a few weeks after the funeral. Arnos Vale Cemetery. It was such a humid day – I remember feeling faint with it. It reeked of leaf mould but you seemed quite interested at first, particularly in the grander memorials, the table tombs with their columns and draped urns, the broken pillars I told you represented lives cut short. But when we turned up the path to their graves, you just stopped walking. I don't know how you knew they were up there – you were too young to go to the funeral, of course. I tried to coax you but you stood as silent and still as the stones around us, your face completely blank.'

She looked down, her face drawn with the old grief.

'We didn't go again. I told myself that it wouldn't help to force you. In truth, it was easier for me not to go, too, to think of them not in the ground but as you liked to imagine them, somewhere high and clear and safe, up among the stars. I decided it would be cruel to contradict you, to keep reminding you of all you'd lost – either by dragging you back to the cemetery each May, or by continually plugging the gaps in your memory. I thought forgetting was your mind's best hope of defence against such an awful, pointless tragedy.

'Sometimes, you seemed on the verge of remembering something – a song or a toy or a scent seemed to chime inside you and you'd get this look of longing on your face that broke my heart. But then, if I kept quiet, you'd set your little jaw and the light in your eyes would stutter and go out. Eventually, even that stopped. After that, it was just you and me. I'm sorry, Grace, if I did wrong. Truly I am.'

I tried to take everything in, my head whirling. I wasn't angry with her, I realized. There was something she had often said to me when I was growing up: 'All I ever do is for you, Grace.' And it was true, she had done it for me, to protect me. Just as she had tried to protect me from who my real grandfather was.

A light tap at the door made us both look up. It didn't wake Robert, whose face seemed younger now that he had unburdened himself.

It was her, a narrow figure and a swirl of pale gold hair that gleamed in the candlelight as she came in. Neither my grandmother nor I could speak. We could only stare at her intently, the girl we had lost twelve years before, the girl who had been there all along. Victoria's daughter. My sister. She blushed under our scrutiny, her fingers twirling her hair, her feet shifting under her. My mother had never been able to keep still either.

'I was playing cards with Lucas and I suddenly wanted to come,' she said, with an embarrassed shrug. 'I wanted to come and be with you.'

Epilogue

The whistle had blown and they were about to leave Paddington when the door to Helen and Bertie's carriage was flung back. A woman clutching a baby clambered in, helped up by her husband, who followed with two suitcases.

He was smiling broadly, pleased they had made it. 'Half a minute later and we'd have had to wait another hour,' he said rather breathlessly. 'We thought we had more time than we did. My watch had fallen behind by ten minutes. I suppose we were on Bristol Time without knowing it.' He laughed and got out a handkerchief to mop his brow. 'Fortunately the clock in the hotel lobby put us right.'

'We missed an earlier train ourselves,' said Helen, with a nod and a smile at the woman, who looked less certain, her face pale. 'We're going to be late to meet our poor father, who's waiting at Swindon.'

'My wife thought we should catch the next one,' said the man, as he took a seat next to the window and shook out his paper, 'but we have a birthday lunch to get back to.'

'They wouldn't have minded another hour,' said the woman, quietly. She had an unusual quality to her voice, thought Bertie. It was rich, almost like liquid.

'What a lovely baby,' said Helen. Bertie was always amazed by how good she and Victoria had turned out to

499

be at this sort of small-talk. He never knew what to say to strangers.

'Yes, lovely,' he echoed softly, though he could not even see the child from where he was sitting, buried as it was in its swaddling of pristine blanket. The mother's fingers were worrying at it, minutely adjusting the folds.

'My wife is rather anxious today,' said the man, gently, as he put a steadying hand on her tense shoulder.

'Oh, it's nothing, just a dream I can't shake off,' she said quickly, a tight little smile briefly lighting her face. 'I just want to get home, really. We have another little girl there, waiting for us.'

Soon, London began to fall away, deep, soot-stained cuttings of brick, and postage-stamp yards strung with dingy washing, giving way to larger gardens and spacious parks. Eventually, the sky came down on both sides to meet gently undulating fields and Bertie felt his body respond to them, his muscles softening, his breathing slowing. He couldn't stand the city, had only gone so he could spend some time with Helen, though he'd told her he wanted to attend an exhibition. He felt it was important to keep an eye on her this year, though he mocked himself for being so superstitious.

He must have dozed for a time, his book forgotten on his lap, because he woke briefly when the baby began to fuss. As the woman sang softly to it, he drifted off again. The sound became woven into a dream about the woods at home, a lilting, rather sad melody he couldn't recall afterwards, though he tried.

When he came to properly, they weren't far from Swindon.

'I hope Papa got the telegram,' said Helen, seeing he was awake. 'Poor David, he didn't mean to make us miss our train.'

Bertie elected to remain silent, believing that David had absolutely intended it, or at the least a good deal of fuss and inconvenience.

'I'll go and get a cup of tea,' he said. He needed to stretch his legs or he'd go to sleep again. He buttoned up the dark grey overcoat that Helen had insisted he bought in an over-whelmingly enormous new shop called Selfridges. He didn't know when he'd wear it at home but he was proud of it all the same. Helen said he looked like his father in it.

Suddenly remembering his manners, he cleared his throat. 'Can I – well, can I bring anything back for anyone?'

Helen smiled at him encouragingly.

'Oh, no, thank you,' said the woman, looking up with a smile, a proper one this time. She was pretty beneath her hat, and behind the anxiety that still pinched her face. She had a look of someone else, but Bertie couldn't think who. 'My husband and I don't need anything, and Esther had her milk while you were asleep.'

'Esther. What a pretty name,' said Helen, as Bertie stood and patted his coat to check that his wallet was where it should be. 'It means "star", doesn't it? Did you happen to see Halley's Comet last month? I've waited to see that since I was a little girl. Comet means "star" too, you know. "Long-haired star", from the Greek. Someone told me that once – a governess we had, long ago.'

'How charming. It sounds like the sort of thing my mother would say,' said the woman. 'She was a governess once upon a time, before I was born.'

'Oh, what was her name?' Helen was saying eagerly, as Bertie pushed open the door. Dear Helen; she was forever asking people if they had heard of a Harriet Jenner. He wondered if his father knew she did it.

As he let the door of the compartment swing shut, he thought about the strange little note that had not been meant for him. It was still hidden at the back of his wallet, a small wedge of paper folded four times. He resisted the urge to get it out and read it. He knew it by heart anyway. Didn't understand most of it, but he knew it all right. Patting his pocket one last time, he began to make his way to the luncheon car at the back of the train.

Acknowledgements

I could probably thank everyone I know for helping and encouraging me in some small way but to keep this to a reasonable length, I've narrowed it down to those who have been particularly invaluable.

First of all, my family. To my parents (steps and otherwise), sister Sarah, brother John and everyone else – thank you for being so supportive and pleased and proud. I am extremely grateful to my lovely husband, who is endlessly patient when I am guilt-ridden for wasting time, climbing the walls because I haven't gone outside for days, or cracking open the Prosecco for finishing a chapter. Thank you, thank you. Big love also goes out to my little Staffie, Morris: a more steadfast companion for a lonely writer I can't imagine.

Next, I must thank the outstanding team at Michael Joseph and Penguin at large – chiefly the brilliant Maxine Hitchcock, who is always so perceptive and kind, and Kimberley Atkins, who couldn't be nicer or more positive if she tried. Huge thanks to Clare Bowron, whose editing expertise made this book so much better. Thank you for helping me sort out a structure that was beginning to make my brain hurt, and for rightly pointing out that my servants were much too chippy with their employers. Working with copyeditor Hazel Orme for the second time was just as good as the first – thank you again for your eagle-eyes. Thanks also to talented art director Lee Motley, who is responsible for my gorgeous, evocative cover, and even drew the maze by hand to make it perfect.

Thank you to my fantastic agents, Kate Burke and Diane Banks – lately I've been lucky enough to have not just one but both of you in my corner and you've both been brilliant. What would I do without you? I dread to think . . .

My good friend Hayley Hoskins must get a special mention, not only for being one of the nicest people I know (with one of the best laughs), but for being my first reader – thank you so much for taking time out of your Greek holiday to dip into the past. My other writing friends and colleagues have also been brilliant cheerleaders. Thank you, Helen Maslin, Amanda Reynolds, Lucy Robinson, Kate Thompson, Dani Atkins and Sasha Wagstaff.

All my non-novel-writing friends have been fantastic but a few have been particularly generous since I've been published: recommending my books to other people, nominating them for their book groups, and – that old classic – moving them to more prominent positions on supermarket and bookshop shelves. Much love and many thanks to Louise White, Helen Hockenhull, Dwy and Rod Owen (my non-godparents), Chris Spellman, Nigel Keohane, Charlotte Sherborn-Hoare, Jade Smith, David Wood, Claire McLaughlin-Symon, Alyson Sheppard and Des Yankson.

I read lots of books but some were particularly helpful. Shire Library's pithy titles offer accessible snapshots of times past. *The Victorian Home* by Kathryn Ferry; *The Victorian Garden* by Caroline Ikin; and 1920s Britain by Janet Sheppard and John Shepherd, among others in the series, were a great source of period detail and colour. My nonfictional research into the lives of governesses came courtesy of Ruth Brandon's excellent *Other People's Daughters* and *The Victorian Governess* by Kathryn Hughes. Jennifer Davies's fascinating *The Victorian Kitchen* was another book that transported me. Thank you also to Cheltenham Library for its helpful staff and collection of a local periodical called *The Looker-On*, whose back issues are a mine of vivid insights into Cheltenham life during the 19th and early 20th century.

I also owe a debt of gratitude to assistant curator Elaine Arthurs, who answered my questions about historic railway practices and terminology after I'd paid a visit to STEAM, Swindon's fantastic museum of the Great Western Railway. I apologize to railway buffs if I've still got things wrong and, indeed, any lingering mistakes are my own – whether about signal boxes or anything else.

The Shadow Hour is a work of fiction but the setting is based on a part of Cheltenham that I often explore with my dog. Locals will certainly recognize elements of Leckhampton Hill, not least the glorious views, the Devil's Chimney and the remains of buildings once used by Victorian quarrymen. I altered the geography to suit the book's needs (there is no Blue), but there are steep, shady paths through the woods and a particular private house I'd better not name that were always at the front of my mind when I was writing – to the degree that I half-expect to bump into Harriet, Grace and the rest of them whenever I go back.

Lastly, I would like to thank all the readers who have tweeted or emailed me via my website to say they enjoyed *The Girl in the Photograph* or *Birdcage Walk*. You really do make my day. I hope you like this story too.

Two women.
Separated by decades.
Entwined by fate.

KATE RIORDAN

'Rich and atmospheric, like *Rebecca* this
novel casts an enduring spell' RACHEL HORE

The Girl
IN THE
Photograph

The real ghosts are the
ones who take up residence
in your mind . . .

Read an extract from Kate Riordan's
haunting first novel now . . .

Prologue: Alice

Fiercombe is a place of secrets. They fret among the uppermost branches of the beech trees and brood at the cold bottom of the stream that cleaves the valley in two. The past has seeped into the soil here, like spilt blood. If you listen closely enough you can almost hear what's gone before, particularly on the stillest days. Sometimes the very air seems to hum with anticipation. At other times it's as though a collective breath has been drawn in and held. It waits, or so it seems to me.

The word 'combe' means valley in some of England's south-westerly counties but the roots of 'fier' are more obscure. At first I thought it was a reference to a past inferno, or perhaps a hint of one to come. It seemed just the sort of place that would dramatically burn to the ground one night; I could imagine too easily the glow of it from the escarpment high above, smoke staining the air, the spit and pop of ancient, husk-dry timbers as the flames licked faster. But I was quite wrong: in Old English it means 'wooded hill', aptly describing the dense and disorderly ranks of hanging beech that leer and loom as you descend steeply towards the old manor house.

Things you would never accept in everyday life – strange happenings, presences and atmospheres, inexplicable lurches of time – are commonplace at Fiercombe. They have become commonplace to me. I have never grown accustomed to the darkness of night here, though. The blackness is total, like a suffocating blanket that steals over you the instant the light is turned out. When open eyes have nothing to focus on, no bar of light under the door, no chink of moonshine through heavy curtains, they strain to catch sight of something, anything. During those early nights here, my eyes would flick from where I knew the windows were to the door and back, until exhaustion turned the walls to a liquid that rose up me in oily waves.

Like a blind person, my other senses grew quickly acute for the lack of visual distraction. Even in the dead of night, when the house finally slept, I was convinced I could hear it breathe, somewhere at the very edges of my hearing, beneath the whisperings and scratchings I thought I could discern. Even in the day, when nothing looked out of the ordinary, I would still find my skin prickling with the vibrations of the place, something instinctive and animal in me knowing that things had been knocked out of balance, that something had gone awry.

I have been here a little over three years now, since the late spring of 1933. When I arrived from London I was not quite six months' pregnant by a man I wasn't married to. A man married to someone else. If it hadn't been for him and my own foolishness, and the subsequent horror and shame of my parents, then I would never have come to Fiercombe at all. What a strange thought that is now, after all that has happened.

When I think back to the time before I came here, it feels like someone else's life, read in a book. It's difficult for me to recapture how I truly felt about things then; how I went about my normal routine of working, the evening meal with my parents, going to the lido or the pictures with my friend Dora, and daydreaming about the man I thought I was in love with. I see now that I wasn't very grown-up.

I came just as spring was softening and deepening into languid summer. It was a beautiful summer – more beautiful than any I've known before or since – though I was still glad to put it behind me when autumn finally arrived. Too glad, perhaps. There were rifts in the valley that remained unhealed as the leaves began to turn but I was too busy forging my own new beginning to acknowledge them. The signs and clues were there; I simply chose not to heed them. I have let three years of contented life in the present chase away the unresolved past, just as the morning sun does the nightmare. Today's confession has changed all that and I can no longer turn away. They deserve better. They always did.

Alice

Four years earlier

In the summer of 1932 I had never heard of a place called Fiercombe. I was still living an ordinary sort of life then. A life that someone else, looking in, would probably have thought rather dull. That was certainly how I viewed it, though I was reluctant to admit that at the time, even to myself. After all, admitting it also meant facing the likelihood that nothing more interesting awaited me on the horizon.

It wasn't until after I left school that I began to feel a creeping sort of restlessness. I had got a full scholarship to the local grammar and I had liked it there – not just for the solace of its rituals and order but for its pervading sense of purposeful preparation. Preparation for what was to come after: the tantalizing, unknowable future. What shape that would take I had no idea. Much of its allure lay in its very amorphousness, the vague sense of expectation that edges closest on those perfect summer evenings of which England never seems to have enough. Evenings gilded with twilight, the perfumed air brimming with promise. Yet the mornings after those evenings always seemed to go on in the normal way – the world shrunk to a familiar room again, consoling but uninspiring, the walls near enough to touch.

Quite suddenly, or so it felt, school was long behind

me and I was a woman of twenty-two. Still nothing of any note had happened to me. I remained at home with my parents, I had a job that I could have done perfectly adequately in my sleep, and there was no sense that whatever I had blithely expected to lift me clear of the mundane was any nearer. If anything, it seemed to have retreated.

My mother was no less frustrated by my lack of progress – though for rather different reasons. I was a good-looking girl, she told me somewhat grudgingly, so why did I never mention any gentlemen friends? Why was I not engaged, or even courting? After the milestone of my twenty-second birthday had passed, she aired those anxieties with ever-increasing frequency, her expression at once baleful and triumphant.

Triumphant, I suppose, because she had never really wanted me to go to the grammar school, believing that girls with too many brains were fatally unattractive to prospective husbands. Though the shortage of men after the Great War had been the crisis of an older generation, there lingered a sense of urgency for unmarried girls, at least in my mother's mind. She also professed not to see the point of school beyond the legal leaving age of fourteen. Anything after that was for boys, and girls with plain faces, she said. After all, no woman could keep her job after her wedding anyway.

For the time being, my own job – one I knew I was fortunate to have when so many had no work – contributed to the household budget, an aspect of it that even my mother couldn't criticize. Each morning I took a bus south to Finsbury Park, where I caught the Piccadilly line to Russell Square. Just off the square was the office where

I was the junior of two typists to a Mr Marshall, a minor publisher of weighty academic books. I had a smart suit I had saved to buy rather than make, and two handbags between which I transferred the gold-plated compact my aunt had bought me one Christmas.

On my first day I had felt rather sophisticated as I walked to the bus stop, the pinch of my new court shoes a grown-up and therefore pleasurable kind of discomfort. A few years on from that hopeful morning and I still occasionally felt a vestige of that early pride – it was just that sometimes, particularly during the afternoons, which were so quiet I could hear the ponderous tick of the clock mounted on the wall, I couldn't help wondering when my life – my real life – would begin.

I had never had any sort of serious attachment to a man. Perhaps the closest I'd come was a boy at school, whom I'd let kiss me a few times. At the grammar, some of the lessons were mixed and David had been in my French class. He'd thought he was in love with me during the last summer we spent there and, during those drowsy afternoons, when the high windows were opened and the smell of cut grass made us long for the bell, he would stare at me across the room. His gaze made my skin tingle warmly, and left me conscious of how I sat, how my hair was arranged, and what facial expression I wore. But the truth of it was not love, or probably even lust. What I liked was the way he felt about me, and I'm sure he was more in love with the sudden intensity of his feelings than he was with the girl in the next row.

Now many of my friends – David Gardiner too, in all probability – were married or engaged, or at the very least courting, yet I had failed to meet anyone. Dora, who was forever trying to persuade me out to meet a friend of whichever man she was currently interested in, teased me gently for being so fussy. My mother, being my mother, was rather more direct.

'You'll be left on the shelf if you don't get a move on,' she said one Saturday, when I had been made to accompany her shopping on our local high street in a north London suburb. 'I've said it before and no doubt I'll say it again, but if you spent less time reading and more time out and about in the fresh air or going to dances, you'd give yourself a better chance.'

I remember we were in the chemist's shop, which was hushed except for my mother's voice and the bell that trilled whenever the door opened. The air smelt of floral talc and carbolic soap, and faintly bitter from the medicines and tonics that were measured and weighed out of sight.

We had an argument then – about lipstick of all the ridiculous things: she wanted me to buy a brighter shade than I could imagine myself wearing. That led to other topics of discord and by the time we were walking home, past the new cafe that had just opened opposite Woolworths, we had returned to the subject of my job and her conviction that I would never meet anyone if I remained in it.

'Why don't you try for work in there?' she said, nodding towards a girl behind the cafe's plate glass, pert in her smart uniform with its starched white collar.

Shifting the bags I was carrying to my other hand, I couldn't rouse myself to reply.

'I know you're a typist in an office in town, and that's all very fancy,' my mother continued, 'but May Butler's daughter Lillian met her husband when she was waitressing and look at her now, with a house in Finchley and a little one on the way.'

Lillian had left school at fourteen and eventually got a job as a Nippy in a Lyons Corner House on the Strand. According to my mother, Lillian had been admired half a dozen times a day by her male customers, solitary men in suits who'd come in for a plate of chops or some tea and toast. Eventually, apparently without much ado, she had married one of them.

'I don't want to be a waitress,' I said wearily.

'You shouldn't turn your nose up at it – you don't earn much more than the ones in the nice places do.'

'Yes, but I –'

'Oh, I know you think you're meant for better things but it hasn't happened yet, has it? And it won't while you're stuck up there with old Mr Marshall.'

What she could not possibly have known was that only a week after that desultory wander around the shops I would at last meet a man I actually desired, someone who would bring the world to life for me, at least for a time. In fact, the circumstances that would throw us together were already in train: an appointment made, a crucial hour already approaching. For it was in Mr Marshall's office – the obscure, dusty office my mother believed had already sealed my spinsterhood – that everything was about to change for me.

As if to further dramatize this episode, to darken the line that marked before and after, he arrived towards the end of a particularly silent, stultifying day. I remember that he was a little out of breath after climbing the stairs to our small office. A late summer shower was flooding the pavements outside and he brought with him the smell of damp wool and cologne as he came noisily through the door. Mr Marshall heard it crash back on its hinges and came rushing out of his tiny room to greet the new arrival, whom he had obviously been expecting. They made a curious pair: Mr Marshall, an inch shorter than me and probably half a stone lighter, only came up to his visitor's chest.

'Who was that?' I said to Miss Cunningham, after they had gone out to lunch, Mr Marshall not having thought to introduce us. Miss Cunningham was the senior typist and didn't like me very much, perhaps because she knew I didn't aspire to her job.

'Mr Elton? He's too old and too married for you to concern yourself with,' she replied crisply.

After I had made her a cup of tea she relented, unable to resist demonstrating that she knew more than I did.

'He's the new accountant, if you must know. The old one's retired and now we've got him. Bit too sure of himself, if you ask me.' She sniffed and went back to her work.

They didn't return from lunch for two hours, and when they did, Mr Marshall was uncharacteristically flushed, eyes glazed behind his spectacles. Miss Cunningham got up and pointedly opened a window, though I couldn't smell any alcohol on them; only the rain and the new accountant's cologne.

While she was at the window he crossed the room towards me and I saw that his eyes were the same shade of deep brown as his hair. He didn't have a single feature that stood out as exceptional but they combined in such a way as to make him handsome.

'Pleased to meet you,' he said, his voice low and unhurried. 'I'm James Elton.' He shook my hand. His was warm and dry. 'I've met the lovely Miss Cunningham, of course, but you are?'

'Alice,' I said, more bluntly than I'd meant to because I was thinking about my hand being cold. I was forever cold in that office, regardless of the season. 'Alice Eveleigh.'

When I left work a couple of hours later he was waiting for me in the cafe that I had to pass to reach the Underground. I spotted him before he saw me: sitting up at the window on a stool that looked silly and feminine beneath him. If he hadn't glanced up from his paper at that moment, and raised his hand with a smile, I would certainly have walked on. It would never have occurred to me to tap on the window.

Of course, I didn't know then that he'd been waiting for me; he didn't tell me that until later. Instead, he smiled his easy smile and, when I hesitated, gestured for me to come in and join him. We had some tea and he tried to persuade me to order a slice of sponge cake. We talked about this and that: London, the weather, of course, and what I thought of my job in Mr Marshall's quiet office. I said, rather primly, that I was very grateful to have it and he grimaced, which made us both laugh.

That was the beginning. Shared pots of tea became habitual until one fog-bound autumn evening he appeared out of the shadows as I left the office for the day and suggested that we had dinner together. It was too filthy a night for a paltry cup of tea, he said. Perhaps we might try this little restaurant he had discovered down a nearby back-street.

Afterwards, on the way to the Underground, he stopped and pulled me towards him. I would like to say I resisted but I simply couldn't. In truth, my face was already tilted up towards him before his lips touched mine. You find that once something like that has happened, it's very hard to go back to how it was before.

He was almost fifteen years older than me. When I was eight or nine, a schoolgirl with pale brown hair cut to the jaw, he was a newly minted accountant. Each morning he took the Metropolitan line into the City, his briefcase unscuffed, his newness such that he had not yet earned a regular seat on the carriage he always boarded.

His wife, when she came along, was a suitable, pretty girl called Marjorie. His domineering mother apparently approved; she and Marjorie's mother played bridge together, I think. He once mentioned in passing that Marjorie was an excellent tennis player, which I found both intimidating and fascinating.

When I met him he was thirty-six, already eleven unimaginable years into his unhappy union. He once said that you would imagine time spent like that would crawl by – the inverse of it flying when you are enjoying yourself. But in fact those years, packed tight with obligation – the tennis doubles and dinner parties and whist drives – had been compressed.

Once, when I think he must have been rather drunk, he confided that Marjorie didn't like the physical side of marriage much. He was desperately unhappy, he told me, time and time again. They had made a terrible mistake when they got married; they had never really loved each other; the whole thing had been engineered by their mothers.

After that first kiss, I went around in a fug of guilt and excitement. I didn't confide in anyone, not even Dora. I knew that, despite all her casually knowledgeable talk of men, she had never gone beyond a certain point and would never dream of doing so with a married man. You simply didn't, and the boys we had grown up with knew it as well as we did.

When I wasn't with him I thought about him constantly, indulging myself in the delicious agony of it all and mooning about, like a girl in a sentimental song. Precisely like that, in fact: it was around that time that Dora bought a gramophone record of Noël Coward's new song, 'Mad About The Boy', and played it endlessly. Every day I felt queasy as I walked past the cafe on my way home from work – in case he was there, waiting, and in case he never was again.

He didn't appear for three weeks after the kiss and I felt eaten away by misery. When I finally saw him in the cafe one evening, head bent over his newspaper, it was as though the whole world – the sour breath of London's air, the hollow clip of women's heels and the rumble of the Piccadilly line's trains far below – ceased to be. I knew that nothing would have persuaded me to keep walking. I had been a nice, bookish sort of girl, and now I was someone different. I felt as though my life was out of my hands. It was like an attack of vertigo.